Mereford Tapestry

Books by Charles MacKinnon

CASTLEMORE

MEREFORD TAPESTRY

Mereford Tapestry

Charles MacKinnon

DELACORTE PRESS / NEW YORK

Manufactured in the United States of America

First printing

Library of Congress Cataloging in Publication Data

MacKinnon, Charles Roy.
Mereford tapestry.
I. Title.
PZ4.M1583Me3   [PR6063.A246]   823'.9'14   73-19618

ISBN: 0-440-05589-X

for

Susan MacDonald

SKATE ... SKATE ... SKATE

Mereford

Roger Vernon

Sir George Vernon, MP
m. 1837 Alexandra
Estcourt

Hester Vernon

Gen. Sir Godfrey Vernon, KCB, KCMG, ADC
m. 1861 Adeline Fownhope
(daughter of Sir Foley Fownhope, Bt)

Capt. Henry Vernon, VC
m. 1888 Alice Mason

Col. James Vernon, CB
m. 1889

Edward Vernon, DSO, MC
m. 1916 Edwina Fownhope

Lt. Col.

Jocelyn Vernon, DSO, MC
m. 1944

Flying Officer David Vernon, AFC, RAF
m. 1972

Pilot

Tapestry

Philip Lancaster

Mary Lancaster
*unmarried alliance
with Timothy Hilton
(brother of Christopher Hilton, MP)*

Joanna Lancaster
m. 1885 Christopher Hilton, MP

John Vernon
m. 1919 Lucy Waterton

Timothy Hilton
m. 1922 Lady Elizabeth Paveley

Robert Vernon
m. 1939 Sally Brown

Anne Hilton

Officer Roger Vernon, RAF

Valerie Vernon (Vivvy)

BOOK I

The House at Mereford
1888–1901

Chapter 1

HOLDER the butler wore a serious expression as he hurried along the carpeted corridor. This in itself was unusual, for the servants at 121 St. James's Place lived tranquil lives. Disorders and upsets were as rare as snow in summer. Life belowstairs and life abovestairs was an orderly, dignified progression from one day to the next, tinged with a special solemnity because the master, General Sir Godfrey Vernon, K.C.B., K.C.M.G., was an aide-de-camp to the Queen.

Holder tapped lightly on the drawing room door and went inside. Lady Vernon, a voracious reader, was bent over a book and Sir Godfrey was peering over her shoulder. They looked up and Adeline Vernon smiled gently.

"Yes, Holder?"

"I'm sorry to disturb you, my lady, but I'm rather worried about Alice. It's her afternoon off and she hasn't returned. She should have been back by six and it's now almost eight."

"Oh, dear, so it is. Has she done this before, Holder?"

"No, my lady. She's very punctual as a rule. I'm afraid there may have been an accident, my lady."

"Thank you for telling me, Holder. Wait till after din-

3

ner, and if Alice hasn't returned you must go to the police station and make a report."

"Yes, my lady. Thank you, my lady."

Holder gave a courtly half bow and withdrew, closing the doors behind him. He returned to the servants' hall where the other servants looked up expectantly, but it was left to Mrs. Warden, the cook, to ask questions.

"Well, Mr. Holder, and what did her ladyship have to say?"

Holder sat down, carefully adjusting the tails of his black coat. He was something of a dandy as well as an inveterate snob.

"She advised me to wait till after dinner, and if the wretched girl hasn't returned by then, to report the matter to the police."

"Oo, the police," exclaimed Susy Wright, the chambermaid.

Holder shot her a disapproving look. She was twenty and the youngest of the servants, and he looked upon her as a mere child.

"Yes, Susy, the police. It's their job to find missing persons."

"That's right," chipped in the irrepressible footman, John Rudkin, "when you run off with that young feller from Number Thirty-seven I seen you with in the park last month, we'll get the police to you, Susy."

"That will be quite enough from you, Rudkin," Mr. Holder reproved. "What's this about a man from Number Thirty-seven, Susy?"

"I'm sure I don't know what Rudkin is talking about, Mr. Holder," she complained. "It's true I have met Mr. Long from Number Thirty-seven, but only to say hullo to. Really that's all."

"Mr. Long?"

"The footman, Mr. Holder."

"Long the footman," Holder corrected. Footmen were

not called "Mr." "I don't think I have had the pleasure. However, Susy, I would not advise you to become too friendly with anyone at Number Thirty-seven. They're a rackety lot there. The master is a Liberal Member of Parliament."

"Isn't Mr. Gladstone a Liberal, Mr. Holder?" Susy asked, genuinely puzzled. She was innocent and had much to learn about the mysterious world in which she moved.

"He is, Susy, and you will oblige us all by not mentioning his name here," Holder answered. "As you know, he was responsible for the death of General Gordon in Khartoum three years ago, and the master has not mentioned Mr. Gladstone's name since. Take my advice, girl, have nothing to do with the servants at Number Thirty-seven."

"That's right," Mrs. Warden confirmed from the comfortable depths of her own rocking chair. "Remember your position, Susy."

Strange though it would seem to a later generation, the servants at 121 St. James's Place most definitely had a position among their own kind. There were many subtle reasons for this. The house was one of the most desirable in exclusive St. James's Place, but there were more important considerations than that. General Sir Godfrey Vernon, K.C.B., K.C.M.G., A.D.C., was the son of Sir George Vernon, onetime lord mayor of London and until his recent death a Tory Member of Parliament, a man of some considerable wealth whose widow still lived in Cleveland Row facing York House and St. James's Place. Then again, Sir Godfrey had had the good sense to marry the youngest daughter of Sir Francis Fownhope, possessor of the second oldest baronetcy in the country, who had been both high sheriff and lord lieutenant in his day. In short the general and his lady had excellent family connections, were absolutely sound in their politics insofar as they had anything to do with politics, and lived at the correct address. Sir Godfrey, twice knighted, had been an

A.D.C. to Queen Victoria since 1877, and here again subtle distinctions intruded, for he was something of a favorite with Her Majesty and possessed more influence than
one might suppose.

Sir Godfrey's career had been quite brilliant. He had
been born in 1837, the year of the Queen's accession to
the throne. His commission in the 1st (Prince Rupert's
Loyal) Lancers had been purchased while he was only
sixteen. At the age of seventeen he found himself in the
Crimea, receiving a bloody introduction to soldiering. He
was at Inkerman on November 5, 1854, a Sunday on
which he received his first, minor wound. Later he was at
Sebastopol. He had been awarded the Crimea Medal, with
clasps for both engagements, and he had also received the
Sultan's Turkish Crimean Medal. At the age of twenty the
general next found himself involved in the Indian Mutiny,
and he received the medal for that campaign, with clasps
for Delhi and Lucknow. Here he was wounded again. His
wounds were only minor ones, but it did a soldier no harm
to have suffered in the service of his queen and country,
and Godfrey Vernon had contrived to do so with the minimum of inconvenience and discomfort to himself. At
twenty-three he was a captain of Lancers, and went off to
the war in China where he was awarded the Second China
War Medal with clasps for Taku Forts 1860 and Pekin
1860.

His active campaigning ended here and he felt free to
embrace a staff career, suitably adorned with small scars
and shiny medals. At twenty-four, when he married, he
became a major; at thirty he was a colonel; at thirty-five
he had scaled the heights to major general. He was an
absolutely brilliant staff officer, possessed of a pleasing
personality, who contrived to move in all the right circles
without ever offending anyone—in itself no mean feat.
The following year, 1873, the thirty-six-year-old general
was knighted with the Order of St. Michael and St.

George. At forty, Sir Godfrey became an A.D.C., at forty-two he was promoted to lieutenant general and finally received the Order of the Bath, and at forty-seven he reached his limit, full general.

He liked to call himself a simple soldier, and it was not a misleading description. There was nothing devious about his character. As a young officer he had campaigned actively and received his wounds, and then he had settled down in the War Office to pursue his career in a less hectic fashion. He was proud of his rank and his knighthoods—legitimately proud and not the least bit conceited—but most of all he cherished his position as A.D.C. to the Queen. Second only to his wife he loved the frumpy old lady. It would be difficult to say what would have happened had he ever been forced to choose between these two women in his life. Luckily such a choice was beyond imagination.

Now a tall, upright, good-looking fifty-one, Sir Godfrey Vernon gloried in a lady who was beautiful in that way reserved for fine-bred, upper-class English girls—none of the Royal Family ever achieved this subtle blending of delicacy, haughtiness, and attractiveness—and two sons whose feet were firmly set on the right path. Henry was already a captain in Prince Rupert's, and the younger son, James, was waiting for a captain's vacancy for which he was due. Sir Godfrey's was a success story in every detail, and if he was neither smug nor conceited, it was because of an innate fineness of character.

Holder, who had entered the service of the late Sir George Vernon as a boy, and who had been transferred to Sir Godfrey's household on the occasion of his marriage in 1861, would have found it almost impossible to put into words all the small but significant facts which gave him his own status among butlers. He was the same age as the general and had adopted many of his master's mannerisms, which was natural. He *knew*, with a sure instinct, that he stood high among his peers, that he had "position." He was forever telling young Rudkin how fortunate he was to serve in the household at 121 and what a gulf separated him from those who served at 119 next door.

Now he glanced at his gold half hunter, frowned when he saw the time, and said sharply, "Almost dinnertime. Rudkin."

"Yes, Mr. Holder."

Reluctantly Rudkin got up from his chair. He liked the comfort and warmth of the big servants' hall, the company of the other servants, and the stories he heard occasionally from those veterans Mr. Holder and Mrs. Warden. Sometimes his duties seemed an interruption in what was for him quite a pleasant life—certainly far more pleasant than anything he had ever known at home.

Mrs. Warden beckoned to Holder who obligingly came over to her side.

"What do you think can have happened, Mr. Holder? It isn't like Alice, and I'm sure there is no young man."

"Quite sure, Mrs. Warden?"

"Well, as sure as one can be nowadays with these young people. Still, she's twenty-three, Mr. Holder. She's no child. She has always been so quiet and no trouble at all, I declare. I do hope there hasn't been an accident."

"We can do nothing but wait, Mrs. Warden," Holder said, and the cook nodded. Wait they would, because Alice Mason did not return that night. Instead, the doorbell rang unexpectedly, and when Holder answered it, because Rudkin was busy elsewhere, he was astonished to see Captain Henry on the doorstep.

"Good evening, Holder," Henry said, stepping inside and handing his hat and cane to the butler. "Father and Mother at home?"

"In the drawing room, Captain Henry."

"Good."

"Will you be staying for dinner, sir?" Holder asked, remembering the hour.

"I don't think so, Holder. I don't think so."

Holder said nothing as he led the way upstairs, but he was thinking that it was uncommonly inconsiderate of Captain Henry to arrive just before dinner if he did not intend to stay and dine. A few moments later he announced the elder son of the house and discreetly withdrew to warn the others that more than likely dinner would be late tonight.

Lady Vernon exclaimed with pleasure at the sight of her elder boy, taller than either his father or brother. He was a full six feet, slim and active, with thick wavy dark brown hair and expressive dark gray eyes. He had the family features—"the Vernon stamp" as he himself had named it, a jutting nose and jaw and strong eyebrows—but his mouth continuously curled up with good humor as though he found life a constant source of amusement.

He kissed his mother with real affection and bade his father a dutiful, "Good evening, sir."

"Well, Henry," Sir Godfrey said before his wife could speak, "how is the regiment?"

"Fine, Papa, fine."

The general nodded, satisfied. If it was a ritual, this asking about the regiment every time he met one of his sons, it was a ritual with a meaning. He liked to know what was going on and to be assured that all was well within what he personally regarded as the finest regiment in the entire British Army, and which was generally conceded to be second only to the Household Cavalry. Sir Godfrey did not think overmuch of the Household Cavalry. In his opinion the 1st had a better fighting tradition.

"You'll stay to dinner, Henry?" Lady Vernon asked, putting away her book.

"No, Mama. I've already told Holder I can't. Indeed I'm

not sure you'll want me to stay," he added as he sat down beside a round table, thus startling them.

"Why the devil shouldn't we want you to?" Sir Godfrey demanded, using unusually strong language.

"You'd better wait till you've heard me out, sir."

There was something so serious in his tone that his mother and father exchanged a look of alarm, and Sir Godfrey sat down abruptly near the settee where Lady Vernon was seated.

"What's wrong, Henry?" his mother asked gently.

Captain Henry Vernon possessed a great deal of his father's direct simplicity. He understood words such as "duty" and "right and wrong" with beautiful clarity. Also he loved his parents deeply. He did not relish the task which had brought him to St. James's Place this evening, but it had to be seen through. For one brief instant, like a moment of fear before a battle, he knew panic and the desire to run away to safety. It passed so quickly that he was scarcely aware of it. He began awkwardly.

"I wonder if you've heard that Alice is missing."

Lady Vernon seemed puzzled. "Alice, my parlor maid?"

"Yes, Mama."

"Holder did tell us that she had not returned from her afternoon off. Do you know something about it?"

"Yes I do. She's been with me, you see, and she isn't coming back. I decided it would be better if she didn't."

His parents exchanged mystified glances again. What on earth was Henry talking about?

"What has happened to the girl?" Adeline Vernon demanded. Godfrey remained silent. If it was to do with servants, it was better to allow the mistress of the household to do the talking.

"Nothing really," Henry laughed nervously. "It's just that . . . well, you see . . . I don't quite know how to tell you. I've been seeing Alice for a long time, Mama, on her afternoons off. She, er, comes to my rooms."

"She does *what!*" This time it was Sir Godfrey, jerked out of his silence.

"Comes to my rooms, sir. The thing is that we're in love with each other."

"In love? With a parlor maid?" Sir Godfrey's astonishment was genuine. He could not conceive such a thing. How could any man possibly love a parlor maid?

"Please, Godfrey," his wife said with a small gesture. "That isn't why you've suddenly come here, Henry. What has happened?"

"Alice is having a baby. We're quite sure."

His mother turned white and his father uttered a hushed "Good God." There was an awkward pause.

"This is different," Sir Godfrey said at last. "I'll talk to you about your own behavior later, but meantime we must discuss what we are to do about the wretched girl. We'll have to look after her, you know. We have a duty toward her."

Henry's eyes flashed and he came as near to displaying temper as he ever would.

"I know that, Papa. I don't have to be told. I'll marry her, of course."

"Oh, Henry." His mother put a hand to her mouth.

"You'll do no such thing," Sir Godfrey said. "Don't be stupid, boy. We'll do everything we can for her and the child, but you certainly don't have to marry her."

"You're wrong." Henry was fully in control of himself now. "I do and I'm going to. I told you, we love each other."

"My dear boy, you're talking about your mother's parlor maid."

"I know that, sir. It isn't her fault she's a parlor maid. She comes from a decent home. Her father owned his own little business in Richmond. Unluckily her parents both died and did not provide for her, so she had to go into service."

"I know about that," his mother said. "I interviewed the girl and I recall exactly. Her father was a haberdasher."

"He owned his own little shop and they had a nice house," Henry interrupted.

"Perhaps so. I agree that she is a trifle above the usual run of servants, although we have always had the very best here, but that hardly puts her on your social level, my dear."

Sir Godfrey, who had been trying to grapple with the facts and who felt that he was living through a nightmare, finally decided to restore some sanity to the situation.

"My dear boy, you're out of your mind. The regiment would never stand for it."

Which was the end of that, of course. They would hush it up decently, look after the unfortunate girl, Henry would get the dressing down of his life which he would never forget, and they would go on, shaken but unde-feated. Officers in the 1st (Prince Rupert's Loyal) Lancers did not talk about marrying parlor maids.

"Of course not." Henry smiled in reply to his father. "Certainly they wouldn't. I shall send in my papers tomor-row morning."

"Send in your papers?" Sir Godfrey rose from his chair, turning scarlet.

"Godfrey," his wife said, alarmed. "Please."

"Did you hear the young scoundrel talking about send-ing in his papers? What the devil do you think you are talking about, boy?"

His voice had risen to a roar, which was indeed unusual for a man who was urbane, imperturbable, and always in command of himself and of the situation. He had begun to lose control as the world around him began to disintegrate. Captain Henry Vernon, promising young officer in a fine regiment, son of a general, grandson of a lord mayor and also grandson of a most distinguished baronet, talking of sending in his papers in order to marry one of his own mother's servants!

"Mama," Henry said, appealing to her. "You know what I mean, don't you? You must understand. We love each other and I'm not going to desert Alice now."

"Do you realize the disgrace and dishonor you will bring on the family?" Sir Godfrey shouted before his wife could get a word in. "Have you no sense of shame, you young cub? Are you determined to destroy us? I can see what's happened all right. This damned slut has put some sort of spell on you . . ."

His wife began to protest but he silenced her.

"Yes, slut. She's got a hold over you. You've lost your wits. Well, let me remind you of something. If you send in your papers to marry a servant girl, what will happen to your brother, your decent, honorable brother who is serving in the regiment? And what about me, damn you? How can I possibly continue to serve Her Majesty, a man whose son has run off with someone from belowstairs? You'll ruin us all."

"Please, Godfrey," his wife commanded, and her husband wilted before her look. "Keep your voice down, my dear. Henry, your father is right. We are not suggesting that you abandon Alice or treat her badly. She and the child will be provided for handsomely, but you must see that the family comes first."

She spoke with a slight smile on her lovely lips, a look of gentle understanding in her fine eyes. Henry, watching her, recognized her quality. She was a great lady indeed. The product of her class, she was perhaps its finest flower. How wonderful it would be to agree with her, to win her approval. She was that sort of woman—automatically you sought her approval. His mouth drooped. He had hoped for her support, but he could see that it was going to be impossibly difficult.

"I'm sorry, Mama. This family has wealth and position and it can stand a few misfortunes if it has to. Alice has nothing—except me. I don't see how either of you can expect any man of honor to abandon the woman he loves."

"Honor?" Sir Godfrey spoke in a low, sarcastic tone. "Do you talk of honor?"

"Yes I do, Papa." Henry took a deep breath. "I thought you, of all people, the gallant soldier, the perfect knight, the friend of a queen, the man who taught Jimmy and me about chivalry from the cradle, would be the first to understand. Just because she's poor and defenseless, are we to treat her as an outcast? Wasn't it the special duty of knights to succor widows and defenseless, fatherless children? Didn't you used to teach us that when we were young?"

"Fatherless children indeed! The girl has seduced and bewitched you."

"If you were anyone else I would hit you for that," Henry replied calmly.

There was another silence. The world, in truth, had turned upside down this mild bright evening of Tuesday, June 5, 1888.

"What are your plans?" his mother asked, playing for time. Sir Godfrey stroked his moustache and glared.

"I'll have to resign of course—from the army, from my clubs. I'll give up my rooms and we'll leave London. If you're worried about Jimmy's career or the Queen's sense of outraged propriety, you needn't. Nobody will know anything. We've kept our secret well."

"How can you possibly go on keeping it?" his father demanded. "People will want to know why you've resigned. What do we tell them?"

"Tell them I've gone abroad, run away."

"What will you live on?" his mother asked, thinking of the practical issues.

"Yes," Sir Godfrey sneered. "What? I swear, Henry, that I will cut you off without a penny if you persist in associating with this woman."

"Papa, let's get one thing clear between us. I am not *associating* with anyone. I am going to marry the girl I love and who is carrying my child. By all means cut me off, if you wish. I've got two thousand of my own, Great-Aunt Hester's money. I'll get a job and we'll find lodgings."

Job! Lodgings! His mother's eyes showed her agony. Had he any idea what sort of life he would lead from now on, cut off from his family and friends? He had been born here in St. James's Place, into a moneyed family. There had been nannies and tutors, carriages and horses, shooting in Scotland, the Queen of England knew him, sometimes spoke of him. Money, position, everything would go . . . and for what? Adeline Vernon was a realist. She had nothing whatever against Alice Mason, and certainly she did not do her former maid the injustice of imagining that she had seduced Henry. They were two young people in love, they would have talked it all over, and were fully aware of the terrific obstacles in their way. In some respects it was as difficult for Alice as for Henry.

But where would it end, when the first romantic flush had worn off? Would their love sustain them in a tiny house or in furnished lodgings? How would Henry feel a year from now, perhaps walking to work in the rain to some menial job? He had no training for any career or profession, he was a soldier. They might laugh at the gulf which separated them, now when their love was strong; but later, when they began to quarrel a little and to feel the inevitable strains that marriage imposes, that gulf would grow and grow.

"Henry, please consider this rash act a little further," she said.

"I have, Mama, but really there is nothing to think

about, is there? Even if I didn't love Alice, I would do what I am doing. I am responsible for her. I just don't happen to believe that if you are born rich and powerful you can behave dishonorably toward a woman from a lower social class. I know what other people do—they make 'arrangements' to get rid of the girl—and I call that despicable."

Adeline exchanged a hopeless glance with her husband who had now grown thoughtful. Sir Godfrey was in an impossible position. He loved his eldest son and loved him dearly, but he had his own conceptions of honor, duty, and responsibility. To him the Family was second only to the Queen—and both demanded that Henry remain part of the family.

"Dammit," Sir Godfrey said, "you're losing sight of the fact that you've behaved abominably. You talk of duty and honor when you are little better than an animal."

Henry said, "I'm sorry, Papa, but I must do what I think is right."

Sir Godfrey's disgust happened to be perfectly genuine. Unlike most other men in his position, he had never had an affair of any sort, but had suppressed his feelings until he met the beautiful girl with whom he had fallen madly in love. His was an exemplary life, as well as a very well blessed one, but it made it difficult for him to forgive frailty in others.

"You're entitled to your opinion," he said. "I must say I expected different ideas from my own son. However that's your affair. Nevertheless I mean it, Henry. If you persist in this ridiculous line of behavior I shall cut you off and forbid you this house. You will be no son of mine, do you hear?"

"I hear, Papa," Henry replied, miserably.

"I advise you to sleep on it. Come back and see us tomorrow. You can apologize to your mother and then we can call in our solicitor and discuss the affair calmly and sensibly. I don't think I have to point out to you how completely revolting and ungentlemanly your behavior has been. If you'd behaved like a gentleman in the first instance, this would never have happened."

Henry got to his feet, pale faced.

"I am sorry, Mama," he said quietly. "I won't wait till tomorrow to say it. I'm sorry I've spoiled everything here, but I'm not sorry I love Alice, and I'm not sorry I'm going to stand by her and marry her. If I'm ashamed it's because I've been underhand. I'd be far more ashamed to behave as other men in my position do."

He bent over and kissed her cheek and then tore himself away.

"I'll go now. I shan't return. I'll be at my lodgings for the next day or two and then Alice and I will be leaving London. If you change your mind, come to see us. If not . . . it's good-bye, isn't it?"

Adeline stifled a gasp of agony and her eyes pleaded, but Henry's gaze was steady. He gave her a little smile and made a tiny gesture with one hand, and then turned and strode from the room.

"My God, I'm dreaming," Sir Godfrey exclaimed.

"Poor child," Adeline murmured. "He thinks the world's well lost for love."

Her husband came and knelt before her.

"Have I done wrong?" he asked plaintively.

"No." She stroked his thick, strong hair. "I wouldn't have you any different, Godfrey."

"Then where have we gone wrong? How can he turn his back on everything he was brought up to believe in?"

"He's in love, that's all. If you'd had to choose between me and the regiment, Godfrey, or between me and your family, which would you have chosen?"

"But you're different," he cried in an agony of bewilderment.

"Yes," she smiled down at him. "That's the point, isn't it? I'm not a parlor maid."

"I don't understand," he sighed, and looking at that bowed head she knew he never would, and loved him a little the more for it. But she also loved her son, and she had to blink away the tears. The incredible had happened that day at St. James's Place, and none of them had been prepared for it.

Chapter 2

I N addition to his niggardly Army pay, Captain Henry Vernon had an allowance of a thousand pounds a year from his father. This was a princely sum for those times, although it was not regarded as anything special in the regiment, where the latest young cornet had an income of over eighty thousand a year. In Henry's case it did him well, for he did not gamble. The regimental barracks were in Featherstone Street, in the City, just off Bunhill Row and close by Bunhill Fields and the Artillery Ground, facing the headquarters of the Honourable Artillery Company. He kept two rooms in Jermyn Street which he used when he was not forced to spend the night in the barracks, and for the past two years Henry and Alice had contrived to meet almost every Tuesday afternoon when, from one till six, Alice had her afternoon off.

It had been a strange association, begun in defiance of every rigid convention of the day. It was even more of a danger for Alice than himself, because a girl in her position had virtually nothing except her good name. If they were discovered, she would be turned out without a reference, jobless, left to sink into London's mire, while the elder son of the house would be reproved perhaps and told to find some suitable actress. Yet they had both taken the risk, and as the months passed, each with its meager share of stolen hours together, their mutual attraction grew into love, and the love grew stronger. By the time Alice realized she was going to have a baby, she had ceased to worry about the future. She knew that Henry would never let her down. Even so, as she waited for him this evening, she was apprehensive. The future was uncertain. All that was certain was that there would no longer be rooms in Jermyn Street. It would be something less fashionable.

She heard Henry let himself in, and ran to the door. He took her in his arms and kissed her.

"That's what I call a welcome," he laughed, hugging her tightly. "Come on, let me get inside, my dear."

"What happened, Henry? Were they furious?"

He chuckled as he put down his hat, stick, and gloves.

"They were rather. I think I could do with a brandy to recover. One for you?"

"No." She was no drinker and shook her head firmly. "Tell me about it."

He poured his drink and told her as much as he could remember. There was a certain amount of confusion about it all, for so much had been said.

"There," he concluded with another laugh. "We'd better go out and eat."

Alice said in a quiet voice, "I'm frightened."

He raised his eyebrows inquiringly, but his eyes remained tender. She was a fine-looking girl, some six inches shorter than he, with simply wonderful thick, dark, lustrous hair, dark eyes, rather heavy brows, an oval face with good features and a full, generous mouth, good figure, and very fine hands. One would never have taken her for someone in domestic service.

"Why are you frightened, my darling?"

"Because you are having to give up so much. Am I worth it, Henry?"

"You know you are."

"You know what they say. You can't make a silk purse out of a sow's ear."

"If you're talking about fine ladies and gentlemen, my dear, you're talking nonsense. If you go back far enough in history, at one time we were all miserable peasants, or cavemen, or something. Some people rose and some didn't. What's more, the rising and falling process goes on all the time. The point being, my darling, that basically we are all sows' ears, so obviously you can make silk purses. And let's have no more such talk. You are the woman I love, we are going to get married. Now let's go and eat. Dinero's tonight because we must celebrate. Tomorrow I'll send in my papers. I don't think we'll have any callers from St. James's Place, you know."

"No," she said. "Not after all that, Henry." She came and sat on his knee and kissed him. "Oh, but, darling, I wish it didn't have to be like this. You love her ladyship . . ."

She stopped and they both laughed. "I can't help it," Alice said. "I've always called her 'your ladyship' and I can't get out of the habit."

"Never mind. I think Mama understood, but she can't do anything about it. She's as powerless as we are. It's the system you see, Alice. It's the system. The funny thing—and it *is* funny—is that they tried so hard to make a gentleman out of me, and they succeeded. I won't abandon you."

"You're the finest gentleman in England." She punctuated each word with a kiss.

"Most of my friends would think I'm the biggest fool, and that's what I find so confusing. Never mind, we have our own future to think about. We'll go to Reading, book in at a hotel and I'll try to get that job I told you about while we look for lodgings. Money is going to be a little tight. I don't suppose that worries you, does it?"

"Not in the least," she assured him. "Not in the very least. I've never had any, you see."

"Well, I've got plenty of clothes so I shan't have to spend anything on those for a long time. A job and lodgings, that's our first quest. Tonight I am still a gallant captain in the 1st Lancers, so tonight we celebrate. It may be a long time till we do so again. We'll have champagne."

"Just one glass for me."

"Of course, darling. I want all the rest myself. There will be no more bubbly till I've become rich and famous, which may be never."

"I don't believe it." She hugged him fiercely. "You'll succeed, Henry Vernon."

"I'll try anyway," he said. "No harm in trying."

Next morning he had to go out after breakfast, and left her to tidy the rooms. He had lost his manservant over six months previously and had decided against replacing him. It was safer without one. As she dusted and tidied, Alice felt a sudden warm glow. In future the housework she did would be her own, her own and her husband's. It wouldn't be work at all, it would be sheer pleasure. Mrs. Vernon— the name sounded wonderful in her ears. She knew how lucky she was that Henry insisted on marrying her. It could so easily have been different. She promised herself that she would make him the best wife that man ever had.

She was startled out of her reverie when the bell jangled. She went to the door, wondering who it could be. She opened it and recoiled. On the landing stood Mr. Holder.

"Good morning, Alice."

"Good morning, Mr. Holder. Won't you come in?"

"Thank you."

He came inside, took off his hat and put it on the hall stand. He followed her into the sitting room and accepted her invitation to sit down.

"If you're looking for Captain Henry, he's out," Alice said.

"I'm not. I came to see you."

"How did you know?" she asked.

For the first time she saw Mr. Holder appear awkward and ill at ease.

"The master told me."

"Sir Godfrey? Told you about Henry and me?"

"Yes. In confidence of course."

"Well, see that you keep it to yourself."

"I don't need you to point out my duty, Alice."

"Then get to the point, please." She was upset and in no mood to fence with him.

"Alice, what can I say to you? You've no idea what you're doing, girl. Captain Henry isn't for the likes of you. You know that. You've always been a good steady girl, sensible. Can't you imagine how this affects the family?"

"I think I know more about it than you do, Mr. Holder."

"That's no way to talk. Be reasonable, Alice. You're one of us, not one of them. I never thought you'd be a person to get your head turned. I really thought better of you, I did really."

"Thank you very much, Mr. Holder. I'd rather not talk about it."

"Now consider it, Alice, consider. Captain Henry has turned your head. The master tells me he is in love with you. You're a pretty young girl, so that's natural and young men fall in love, especially young army officers. But *you* ought to have more sense than to fall for that sort of thing. You know you couldn't take the place of her ladyship at St. James's Place, don't you? So how can you be a wife to her ladyship's son? It's not possible."

"What do you suggest?" Alice asked, dangerously meek.

"Come away from here. Come back with me."

"To be a parlor maid again?"

"Not at St. James's Place," Holder said quickly. Was the girl mad? Did she expect to be reinstated after such ungrateful behavior? If he had his way he would whip her, but Sir Godfrey had told him to treat her gently. "You will be given a place with Mrs. Collins. Same money too."

"Mrs. Collins? You think I'd go to work there? I'd rather starve."

"Mrs. Collins is a friend of the family."

"Yes, and wouldn't they like to get rid of her!"

"Now listen, my girl," Holder told her a little more sharply, "it isn't going to be easy to find a place for a girl in your condition. You can go to Mrs. Collins and when your time comes we'll send you away to the country to have the baby and arrange for it to be adopted—and Mrs. Collins will have you back. You're a very lucky girl indeed."

"Oh *am* I! My baby torn away from me and you call that lucky, do you?"

"You're not married." Holder looked furious now.

"I shall be, Mr. Holder. I shall be. I'm surprised that Sir Godfrey was so stupid as to tell you all about this and to send you round on such an errand. He must be very upset."

Holder said nothing, for the truth was that he felt the same. It had been most embarrassing to be admitted to such shattering family secrets and used as an ambassador. Secretly he felt that it was unfitting and wished heartily that it hadn't happened. Nevertheless there was nothing he wouldn't do for the general.

"You just go back and tell Sir Godfrey that the answer is no, and I will not tell Captain Henry of your visit—not this time, anyway."

Holder compressed his lips.

"Is that your last word?"

"My very last."

"You realize what you're doing? They're being generous, but after this they won't be. You may find yourself friendless and penniless, my girl."

"Would you like me to send Captain Henry round to see you when he returns, Mr. Holder?" Alice asked coolly. "Perhaps you'd like to talk to him?"

Holder stood up, red-faced. "On your own head be it. I always felt it was a mistake to employ you. You had ideas above your station, all because your father had a shop—or so you say! You know what your trouble is, don't you, Alice? You got a job right away with a good family. You should have worked first for some doctor or lawyer with only a cook general and yourself. You'd have known then just how fortunate you were to be in service at St. James's Place. It was a bad day for us all when you came into the house."

"Do you really believe that, Mr. Holder?" she asked, standing. "Captain Henry is going to marry me and that's what all the fuss is about. He's a decent man, you see."

"You're no decent woman," Holder snapped, his temper frayed. The smooth orderly progression of life had been woefully disrupted and he did not really mean what he said. He was really very unhappy about everything.

"You'd better go. If you stay I can't promise not to tell Captain Henry you've been here, Mr. Holder. Go now."

He turned and walked out, slamming the doors behind him, and Alice sat down on a chair, trembling a little. It was serious if the general had told Holder everything and sent him round to the rooms. She wondered how they had known that Henry would be out. The answer, although she did not know it, was simple. Holder hadn't known. If Henry had been in, there was a letter from Sir Godfrey to deliver, after which Holder would have hung about in the street, hoping for Henry to emerge and leave Alice alone. But the general had guessed correctly that Henry might have several things to attend to this morning.

She said nothing to Henry when he returned. Instead they talked about Michael Everard, a friend of Henry's in the regiment. Michael's father, Stanley Everard, owned a number of newspapers, among them the *Berkshire Herald*, with offices in Reading. Michael, who knew that Henry was going to send in his papers without realizing why, had obtained a letter of introduction from his father to the editor of the newspaper, a Mr. Robert Turner, and it was this letter Henry had been collecting from Michael that morning.

"Will you get a job, do you think?" Alice asked.

"Yes, I think so. After all, Stanley Everard owns the paper. Mind you, there's no saying what sort of job it will be, but it will keep body and soul together while I look around and make plans for the future. We'll manage all right, Alice."

"I know we will."

"Any messages for me while I was out?"

"No." She shook her head.

"I wasn't expecting any, really. I just thought . . ." His voice wandered off and she had an urge to comfort him, but she had no words of comfort to give.

Instead she kissed him and he smiled at her and held her hands, and she wished so much that she could solve all his problems.

It was the following morning, while they were packing, that James Vernon called at the flat. Henry answered the door and invited him in. James was very much a carbon copy of his brother, but two inches shorter and not quite so frank and open looking. He was fourteen months younger, and had always rather resented Henry's greater height, greater ability, and greater charm, and the fact that Henry had got his captaincy quickly while he, James, looked as though he'd have to wait . . . until now. Now there was going to be a vacancy, and as fate would have it,

Henry's resignation would probably give James his promotion. Far from pleasing him, this made James resentful. He did not want his brother's leavings.

James was a dandy. His hat sat at a carefully calculated angle, his boots gleamed, his suit fitted him like a glove. He removed his hat and put it down with his cane and gloves, tugged at his waistcoat, and then stroked his moustache. When he sat down facing them, he crossed his right leg carefully over his left, preserving the smooth fit of his trousers. Henry suppressed a smile.

"Hullo, Mason," James said, remembering to greet Alice.

Alice flushed at the added insult of his using her surname. Henry took her hand before speaking. "Alice, I'd like to present my brother, Lieutenant James Vernon. Jimmy, this is my fiancée, Miss Alice Mason."

James flushed and his glance dropped to Alice's left hand where he saw a diamond engagement ring. Henry was making a fool of him.

"You'll be putting it in the *Times*, I daresay," he said.

"Don't be silly, Jimmy. Nobody knows, and nobody need know. Neither Alice nor I want to make life difficult for the rest of you. I saw the adjutant yesterday morning and told him I'd just sent in my papers. When he asked why, I said I was fed up with life and wanted to go abroad. That's what everyone will believe, if you let them. It's up to you."

"I see. You've actually sent in your papers?"

"Oh, yes. There was no point in delaying. As soon as Alice told me the news, I knew I'd have to. The truth is that I'll be glad to stop all this hole and corner business. Do you realize that we've only been able to meet on Tuesday afternoons? That's all the time off one of our lucky servants gets, Jimmy—one afternoon a week, from one to six."

"Are you suggesting we treat the servants badly?" James demanded.

"No. I merely wondered if you'd had the same opportunity as I have of observing their conditions of service. However I'm sure you came for some other purpose."

"I heard the news and I came round to see if we can't dissuade you."

"Our parents tried to do that on Tuesday night."

"I know, but you've had time to sleep on it now. So have they. They aren't angry, you know."

"That's damned decent of them."

"Are you being funny?" James demanded.

"Not at all. Merely sarcastic." Henry looked blandly at his brother.

"I don't think that's amusing. Mama and Papa are both very understanding about it all. They're willing to be reasonable if you are."

"What's reasonable?"

"You could transfer out of the regiment. Papa can get you a place in the Indian Army. You wouldn't have to give up soldiering."

"How very jolly."

"You're making fun of me."

"Impossible, I assure you. Carry on, James."

James flushed under this bantering, not realizing how close to anger Henry was. He felt that his father could have come in person instead of sending Jimmy as a messenger.

"We'd see that Mason—Alice, that is," he corrected hurriedly, "we'd see that she had a decent job for life."

"Where?" Alice asked.

James, who was ignorant of Holder's abortive visit, for Sir Godfrey would never admit to a soul that he had confided in his butler, answered in all seriousness. "Mrs. Collins will have you."

"I don't think I'd have Mrs. Collins," Alice replied.

"You haven't much choice, have you?" James asked, raising his eyebrows and staring at her coldly. She *was* giving herself airs, he thought.

"Let me get it clearly fixed in my mind," Henry said. "You're willing to fix me up with a place in an Indian regiment—cavalry, I trust—and Alice with a place at Mrs. Collins's, and look after the baby . . ."

"Yes, of course."

"And all will be well?"

"Yes."

"What do we have to do in return for this magnificent bounty?"

James fidgeted. "Promise never to see one another again or to communicate with each other. The child will be brought up under its mother's name, and I regret it will not be possible for . . . er, Alice . . . to see the child after its birth."

"They're damned decent, aren't they?" Henry said, turning to Alice and grinning at her. "It's a pity we can't oblige."

"You refuse?" James asked. Personally he thought it was a very generous offer. Henry had blotted his copybook with a vengeance, and all that was going to happen was a transfer to India. It wasn't the same, of course, but there were some very decent cavalry regiments there, some good sport, a very pleasant life. Probably he'd get more promotion and come home a general, like their father. As for the girl, not many could be sure of a place for life. She was actually *gaining* as a result of her promiscuous behavior!

"I think you'd better go, Jimmy," Henry said gently. "Of course, you'll be getting your captaincy now, won't you? Well, you deserve it. I don't suppose we'll meet again. Take care of yourself."

"Is that all you've got to say?" James demanded.

"Yes." Although he maintained an insouciant front, Henry was sufficiently distressed to want to get rid of his brother. He hated saying good-bye and—although he wouldn't have admitted it even under torture—he was giving up a very great deal for love. He didn't mind, but he did not want to be reminded of it just at the moment.

"What am I to tell them at home?"

"Just say thank you, but the answer is no. And tell them not to worry—there will be no scandal unless they start it themselves. We'll disappear quietly."

"Papa's at Windsor next week. What's he to tell H.M.?"

"Tell her I've gone abroad, of course, what else? I've gone to South America."

"Why South America?"

"Because they'll make me a general. Bound to."

"You think that's funny?"

"Not at all. I'm deadly serious."

James got up and collected hat, stick, and gloves. His mouth was hard.

"If you want to know what I think, you're a rotter."

"You would. But give credit where it's due, Jimmy. You'll have no elder brother now. All the money will be yours, the house, the promotions. I shan't be spoiling everything by being fourteen months senior to you. When you're lieutenant colonel commanding, remember that. If I'd stayed in the regiment, you'd *never* have got it."

James flushed and turned his back. Henry followed him to the door and closed it behind him and leaned up against it. He let out a little sigh. For a long time now he had been living under the strain of a divided loyalty. The tragedy of it all was that he truly loved the regiment, that his great ambition had been to command it. All that was over now. It would never happen, because another love had come into his life. Some men, such as his father, could fall in love and it merely made all their prospects infinitely better; others, such as himself, were faced with sacrifice. It was something one had to learn to accept. He heard a sound and saw Alice in the doorway of the sitting room.

"Are you all right, Henry?"

"Yes, darling, just getting my breath back. It was a pretty contemptible effort, I thought. They shouldn't have sent Jimmy. That was a mistake. He's the world's worst ambassador. I'm going to have a drink."

He moved toward her, took her in his arms, and kissed her. She clung to him tightly. She would be glad when it was all over, when they were finally left in peace to make what they could of their lives.

They went into the sitting room and Henry poured his drink.

"Cheers. Here's to tomorrow," he said. "To all our tomorrows."

She smiled back at him. "I'll be glad to get out of London."

"So shall I, which is funny because I've always loved it. I remember how I used to hate the country when we went to visit Grandfather Fownhope. There was nowhere to go, nothing to do. He had a very fine country house indeed in Wiltshire, a lovely estate, but for a child it had nothing to offer. I used to long to get back to Town, to the walks in the park, which were far more exciting than being in the country. Funny, isn't it? I used to love watching the guards at St. James's and the Horseguards, but I never saw anything inspiring in pigs or geese. Of course we're only going to Reading, not to Outer Mongolia. It isn't far."

"A new start in a new place. I wonder how we'll like it."

"We'll have to. We have to get married, find a home of some sort, and find a job. That ought to keep us busy for a bit, don't you think? You won't have time to brood once we're there."

"Oh, I'm not broody," she laughed. "Not a bit. I'm the one who's looking forward to the future. Did James upset you much?"

"A little. Not too much."

"You're very kind, Henry," she said intuitively and he chuckled.

"What a funny thing to say," he replied, and she kissed him again.

Next morning they left. There was nothing to detain them and the sooner they went the better. Henry had no qualms about going without seeing his colonel—he knew that his father would smooth that over. The general was nothing if not resourceful. All his old life lay behind him now and it was better to forget it, to cut it off cleanly. There could be no looking back.

Fortunately it was a nice day, and that made a difference, for, no matter what people may say, bright weather brightens the spirit. They made a lot of silly jokes during the journey till they arrived at Comber's Commercial Hotel near the railway station.

They were shown to their room, a very modest, plainly furnished one. As Henry had told her, there would be no Ritz Hotel for them. They unpacked and then went out to walk around the town. They stood and held hands on a bridge over the Thames and walked along the river's bank. They also found the offices of the newspaper in King's Road. Henry would go to see the editor, Robert Turner, the following morning. They returned to their hotel to eat, and were pleased to find that the food was palatable if plain. It would suit very well until they were settled. That evening they sat in the small lounge and Alice had a rare sherry while Henry indulged in a whiskey.

"It isn't much, I know," he said, taking her hand. He gave her a smile filled with love. "You must be worried, Alice, wondering what is going to happen. It will be all right, I promise. One day we'll have our own fine big house outside town, our carriage, servants to do the work for you. You'll see."

"I don't want servants," she answered with a quick smile.

"You shall have them, just the same. No man likes to see his wife slaving over a sink or a stove. I'm sorry I can't offer you more now, but all there is between us and starvation is a bit over two thousand pounds . . . till I find work."

"It's a lot of money," she laughed.

"Until you spend it. I have a feeling that that two thousand of my great-aunt's will come in very handy one day."

"You stop worrying," she said. "Everything will turn out splendidly, I'm certain."

"How does it feel, pretending to be Mrs. Vernon?" he asked.

"I loved it when you signed the hotel register."

"Soon you really will be Mrs. Vernon. All this excitement isn't too much for you, is it?" he added, suddenly remembering that she was supposed to be in a "delicate" condition.

"Of course not. I'm fine."

She looked it too, the picture of health.

"You must see a doctor soon."

"My dear, there is no hurry. There's another six months to go before Henry junior appears."

"That's something to think about, isn't it? Names for the little beggar. Well, later will do."

He got up and went to the window and looked outside at the roofs and chimneys.

"So this is Reading. I've got a feeling that it's going to get to know the Vernons pretty well before we've finished with it." He turned and grinned broadly at her. "Little does it know what lies in store."

With that another couple came into the lounge and they had to talk in low voices. Even so they giggled rather a lot, for he was only twenty-five and she twenty-three, and they had taken the biggest step they would ever take in their lives, one which cut right across all the rules of the society n which they had been brought up.

Chapter 3

R OBERT TURNER, editor of the *Berkshire Herald*, was not
a man who was impressed easily. Both by nature and
by virtue of his job he had a persistent cynical streak. He
was not overwhelmed by a note from his owner recom-
mending this clean-shaven, military-looking young man
before him. Turner was in his late forties, with thick wavy
hair and a heavy beard and moustache. He dressed like a
bank manager and ran his newspaper with an iron hand.

"So you want a job. What can you do?"

"Nothing."

Turner waited but Henry did not elaborate, and Turner
liked that.

"No experience, eh? That might not be such a handicap.
You've had a good education?"

"I had several tutors. I was in the army."

"The point is, can you spell?"

"Yes, I think so."

"Do you read much?"

"Quite a lot. My mother had a mania for it."

"I've got a vacancy for a proofreader. I could give you a
trial. It's careful, painstaking work. You have to check
everything before it is finally printed. If you pass a mis-

take, we print a mistake and I don't like mistakes on this newspaper. I don't like them whether they're spelling mistakes, punctuation mistakes, or mistakes of fact. One's as bad as another. Think you could read proofs for me?"

"I think so."

"You'll get two pounds a week, but there are prospects."

"Thank you."

"Where are you living?"

"Comber's Commercial while we look around. We're both from London."

"I see. You should have tried the Temperance. The food's better and the rooms are cheaper. However I can give you a note to a woman I know who has lodgings not too far away from here, within easy walking distance of work. Nothing fancy—clean, decent, furnished lodgings. You could do a lot worse."

"I'm very grateful, Mr. Turner."

Turner nodded. He liked the way this young man did not argue, the way he accepted help readily. He had a feeling he would get along well with him. One day he would like to know the story behind it, why the young army officer—for plainly he was an ex-officer—had come to Reading to look for work, work as lowly as that of a proofreader earning two pounds a week. Robert Turner was willing to bet that Vernon had obtained his letter of introduction through social connections and that the Vernons, whoever they might be, had money. This one was an outcast, for some reason or another.

The interview was short, for Turner was busy and they had settled it all quickly. Henry went to fetch Alice from the hotel so that they could visit the lodgings Turner had recommended. She was both pleased and surprised when he said he was starting work on Monday morning. They saw the rooms—one bedroom, a living room, and sharing a bathroom. Cooking was done on a range in the living room and the place was lit by gas. The furniture was plentiful and sound, though far from beautiful. They arranged to have their two trunks sent up from the station and to move in that afternoon.

So began their life in Reading. Once they had settled into their lodgings in Wokingham Road, they quickly made themselves at home and comfortable. They were married a month after their arrival though neither the owner of the lodgings nor Robert Turner had known they were unmarried at first. Henry settled down to his new job and proved competent. The main quality required was one of painstaking care, which was something he had never had to show before, but he found that he had a flair for it. The number of mistakes in the newspaper went down, much to Robert Turner's satisfaction. The editor had a positive hatred of errors of any sort and took his job with deadly seriousness. Very soon he began to like his latest recruit.

By Christmas Alice was heavy and easily out of breath, as the time for her confinement drew near. It was something they both looked forward to eagerly, the birth of this first child, just, indeed, as they looked forward to their first Christmas together. Henry bought special delicacies for her and decorated the living room. The spirit of Christmas took hold and there was much laughter in the house. It was marvelous what a small tree, a little tinsel, and a few paper streamers could do to their lodgings. Henry shopped for a turkey and by waiting till the last minute got a large one at a bargain price because on Monday evening, Christmas Eve, the shopkeepers were eager to clear their stocks, and prices almost halved. Alice and Henry were delighted by his acumen, and with the shillings he had saved he bought some cheap sherry and some stone ginger wine.

Alice had some money of her own, a few pounds she had saved during eight years as a servant, and she bought Henry a gold tiepin with an attractive purple stone. She

had to part with two gold sovereigns, more than she had
ever spent on a single item in her life. It came in a small
box, which she wrapped in fancy paper and hid in a
drawer. Henry had cheated—that is he had drawn some
money from the bank, a small part of his capital, and
bought her a gold watch. It was not a question of "afford-
ing" it, he reckoned. With all the money he had in the
bank, his wife should have a decent watch just as she had
a decent engagement ring and wedding ring. Christmas
was an appropriate time to see to it.

Alice woke early on Christmas morning. She sat up
carefully in the big double bed with the brass knobs, and
glanced down at Henry's tousled head on the pillow. She
smiled gently as she eased herself out and put on a warm
dressing gown. She was self-conscious about her figure,
and did not like him to see her swollen body in daylight.
She took out the little box and a card from her drawer and
tiptoed through to the living room to prop them against
the green box in which stood the small Christmas tree.
Somehow he had beaten her to it, perhaps during the
night. There were three parcels and an envelope with her
name on them. She raked the fire, put on fresh coal, and
boiled a kettle for tea. Christmas Day and Boxing Day
were holidays for Henry. The paper only stopped publication for one day, but he had asked Robert Turner for an
extra day off. He related the conversation to Alice.

"An extra day? If I gave all the staff an extra day how
would the paper get published? What do you want an
extra day for?"

"It's my first Christmas with my wife, and the baby's
due next month."

"Oh, yes, and you'll be wanting more time off when the
baby comes," Turner snorted. "Your request is refused. I
can't allow you to establish precedents like that. However," he said, peering at Henry, "you're looking off-color.
You'd better take a day off. I suggest Wednesday."

"Thank you." Henry grinned.

"Don't thank me. You're a sick man. A day off on Wednesday will cure you."

Henry had to turn away before he laughed aloud. He had grown to like Turner enormously during the few months he had been working on the *Herald*. So now, Alice thought happily as she warmed herself before the kitchen range, waiting for the kettle to boil, they had two whole days to themselves. She was delighted with her lot in life. She had what she had always dreamed of, a place of her own. The rooms shone like a new pin, everything was neat and tidy and at the same time comfortable. She had washed everything—blankets, curtains, bedspread; even the rugs had been scrubbed. She had a home and a husband, in both of whom she could take pride, and soon there would be a baby. They were secure on Henry's two pounds a week, and there was money in the bank if ever things went wrong. The transition from parlor maid to housewife was a considerable one, and she felt herself to be among the most fortunate of women. Her only worry was Henry. It was because she had worked at St. James's Place for eight years that she realized so fully how much he had given up for her. She was still afraid that one day he would regret the step he had taken.

She made the tea and took it in to him, and shook him. He turned, blinked, and smiled.

"Hullo, darling. Merry Christmas."

"Merry Christmas," she answered, and kissed him. His arm went around her.

"I've brought your tea, Henry."

"You shouldn't, Alice. I've told you before, I can get up and make the tea in the mornings, and make breakfast. You should be taking things gently."

"Oh, rubbish. I'm as strong as a horse."

"But much prettier," he joked, stroking her thick hair. He got out of bed and sat down with her at the table in the corner. They looked out through the lace curtains at the street below as they drank their tea. It was a fine dry morning, not too cold. What a morning for a ride in the park, Henry thought, and then pushed away the thought guiltily.

"Is something wrong, dear?" Alice asked, noticing the fleeting frown.

"No, nothing at all. Shall we go and see what Santa Claus has brought us?"

She smiled as he took her hand to lead her into the next room. She felt a sudden upsurge of pleasure as his eyebrows shot up. He picked up the small box.

"You bought me something? You shouldn't have done that, Alice."

"Of course I should."

While she was opening her own three parcels, he undid the wrapping of his gift, opened the box, and stared at the gold pin. He certainly needed a tiepin, for the gold one his father had given him some years previously had been lost. How clever of her to have thought of it, for he had never mentioned the subject to her.

Then she was in his arms. "Oh, Henry, you shouldn't. It's wonderful. It's beautiful."

He chuckled as he hugged her to him while she stared at the gold watch in her left hand.

"Wind and set it for me, please," she said, handing it to him. She opened her other parcels. A box of candied fruits, of which she was extremely fond, and one of white, embroidered handkerchiefs. There was also a card from him. *To my own love. Henry,* he had written on it.

"You darling." She hugged him again. "We've burst the budget this month, haven't we?"

"It's Christmas. Anyway, what about you? It's a lovely tiepin, Alice. How did you know I wanted one?"

"I guessed you might. Is it really all right, Henry? I don't know how to buy things for men."

"It's perfect. I mean it. Where on earth did you get the money? You can't have saved that out of housekeeping."

"I have a little of my own. I've never told you about it. I saved a bit while I was working."

"By jove, a wife with private means and I never knew." He kissed her. "More tea? Where's your cup?"

They stayed in the living room by the warmth of the fire.

"Henry," she began nervously.

"Yes, my dear?"

"Do you miss home very much? I know you never say anything, but at times like this . . . well, I spent seven Christmases at St. James's Place myself, so I know what it was like."

"What *are* you babbling about, you little goose?" he asked. "Do you think I'd give up any of this to go back there? Is that what you think of me?"

"No, but . . ." She floundered, at a loss for words.

Henry put down his cup and saucer and picked up her hands. He stood over her, smiling down.

"Listen to me, for once and for all time, Alice Vernon. If I could go back, I would do it all over again. I have no regrets, not one. You've made me the happiest man in the world, do you understand?"

"Yes, it's just . . . well, when you got up this morning, something made you frown."

"You miss nothing, do you? I'll tell you what it was. I thought that it was a splendid morning for a ride in the park, that's all. Now, I can't go riding in the park, so I can do one of two things. Either I can forget about it, or else I can earn some money and go riding in a park here in Reading. It's very simple, and it doesn't mean that I have regrets over anything."

"I'm sorry. I worry so much . . ."

"I know you do, and I'm glad you've brought it up. You must stop worrying, Alice. I'm a very happy person now, happier than I have ever been in my life. Now, please, darling, no more worrying about me. Do you understand?"

"I think so." She squeezed his hands and tears welled up into her eyes.

"There." He bent and kissed her and they remained like that for several long moments, clinging to each other, supremely happy together.

On New Year's Day 1889 their son was born. It happened very suddenly in the middle of the morning. The baby wasn't due for another three weeks, and it took them by surprise. Henry hurried out to fetch the doctor, but by the time they got back they were too late. The baby had been born prematurely. It was stillborn.

Henry was far more concerned about Alice who looked waxy and white, and it was only after the doctor had reassured him that she was perfectly all right that he thought to ask about the baby.

"It wouldn't have mattered if I'd been here earlier. It would still have been born dead. But so far as I can see, Mr. Vernon, your wife is perfectly able to have other children. I'll see her again, naturally, but I don't think you need trouble yourself on that score."

"Yes, of course, thank you."

"She's quite all right. She'll be up and about in no time. There's nothing special you have to get, no special foods or anything of that sort. I know it must be a big disappointment to you, but there is nothing to be alarmed about. It's just something that happens sometimes."

"I see. Thank you, doctor."

Alice was almost heartbroken at first, for she was firmly convinced that Henry had set his heart on having a son and that he must have suffered a severe blow. In fact Henry was far less concerned about the child than he admitted. Somehow the prospect of fatherhood had not captured his imagination. That Alice was well after her ordeal was infinitely more important to him than the child born dead.

There was a sad little ceremony two days later, when a tiny coffin was buried in the churchyard. They had given the child a name, George. Just before the box was covered, Robert Turner turned up. It was all over in seconds as the tiny grave was filled in.

"I'd better get back to work," Henry remarked. "It was good of you to come."

"You'll do no such thing," Robert Turner said. "Go home to your wife, man. Don't you come near the office today."

"But who's going to take my place? Mr. Flack is off sick."

"I can proofread my own paper, can't I?" Turner demanded. "It may have a few more mistakes than usual, but we'll survive. Go home when you're told." Turner raised his hat and strode off.

He's an incredible man, Henry thought, the soul of kindness and terrified someone will find out.

The death of the child cast a momentary gloom over them but it did not last for long. In February Henry began to redecorate the living room in the evenings, and by Easter he had finished all the improvements Alice had suggested and to which the landlady had agreed. Their lodgings looked really attractive now. With the coming of the milder weather they began to go out walking together. The winter was over, and the world was stirring once again.

Henry liked to read the *Times*, and one morning he was surprised to see in its social columns a report of the wedding of his brother. Somehow or other he had missed the notice of the engagement. James, now a captain, had married a Mary Lancaster at St. Margaret's, Westminster. She was the daughter of Philip Lancaster, chairman of the Empire Bank. Henry knew very little about finance, but he had heard of the Empire Bank, a private company in the City which invested its funds in schemes to develop the vast British Empire. It was said to be extremely successful.

Henry could picture his brother in the full dress uniform of the regiment, the black and gold helmet with its scarlet plume and gold chin strap, the hussar-type tunic, scarlet with gold buttons and frogging, the gold aiguillettes and gold body lines, the ornamental cords attaching the helmet to the tunic, the horizon blue tights with the heavy gold stripe, the gleaming boots and spurs and the cavalry saber. He would be a wonderful sight. The 1st was one of the smartest regiments in the entire Army. There would be a guard of honor, of course, and his father would be resplendent in scarlet tunic and blue trousers, his chest covered with medals and stars. The general had always been an awe-inspiring figure in his dress uniform.

He sat for several minutes wrapped in thought. He could picture his mother, radiant and elegant. She would outshine the bride, of that he was certain. And what a fuss there would be belowstairs too. The servants would love every moment of it. Under other circumstances Alice might have been one of them. Come to think of it, under other circumstances it might have been his wedding in St. Margaret's, not James's.

How funny life was, he thought. He, the elder son, had had to marry in secret, partly because his wife was poor and had had to go into service, and partly because she was pregnant at the time of the marriage; yet James, the younger son—and in England nothing was less important than a younger son, not even daughters—James would receive a gift from the Queen of England, for, after all, he was the son of her favorite and longest serving aide-de-camp. That was unfair. James was no longer the younger son. James was *the* son. There was no Henry, not anymore!

Robert Turner found him sitting at his bench, and stopped.

"You look thoughtful, Henry."

"Oh, hullo, sir. I was just reading the *Times*. A society wedding. Do you know, I believe I'm a radical at heart."

"Are you? A radical?"

"I must be. I never realized it before."

Turner looked at him thoughtfully. "Can I see the paper if you've finished with it?" he asked.

"Of course. I ought to be getting on with some work anyway."

Henry pulled forward a set of galley proofs and his employer walked back to his office with the *Times*. There he opened it up and looked through the reports of weddings. He found what he was looking for almost at once. Captain James Vernon of the 1st Lancers, son of General Sir Godfrey Vernon, marrying at St. Margaret's, too. So, that was the Vernon family, was it? He got up and went to his bookshelves and pulled down his Burke's Peerage, Knightage and Companionage. His guess was confirmed. Sir Godfrey Vernon had *two* sons, and the eldest was Captain Henry Vernon of the 1st Lancers.

He put the book away and stared out of the window. What on earth had brought Captain Henry Vernon to him? Something to do with Mrs. Vernon, he suspected. What, he did not know, but the most likely explanation was that the marriage was socially unacceptable. She was a charming woman, but it was impossible to guess her antecedents. They might be anything from the highest to the lowest. She could not be easily typed.

Robert Turner's liking for his newest proofreader turned to admiration. It was not easy to step down from the sort of life Henry Vernon must have known, to drop from high society to a job at two pounds a week on a newspaper, yet Vernon had done it cheerfully and without resentment. He was popular with the rest of the staff. Everyone knew he was a gentleman, of course, it showed only too plainly, but he was affable, willing to learn, deferential to his seniors, and a hard worker. Apparently he had brought no resentments with him from that other world he had once graced.

Then Robert Turner snapped out of his reverie. It was none of his business. Vernon was an employee and that was all. It made no difference where he had come from.

Later on Henry retrieved the paper from Turner's little office and took it home that evening and handed it to Alice after supper.

"Have a look at the latest news. Jimmy's married."

Alice found the report and read it.

"Your mother and father will be pleased," she remarked.

"Yes. There would be quite a fuss belowstairs, wouldn't there?"

"I can picture it," she laughed. "Holder at his most pompous and Mrs. Warden talking about other society weddings she's seen."

"What is Holder really like?" Henry asked. "I've often wondered. He was pretty decent to me when I was a boy. He was good to both of us. Jimmy and I thought the world of him in those days. But I wonder what he was like, through your eyes say, darling."

"You could laugh at Holder very easily," Alice said. "He's a born servant, you know. He *likes* being a butler, especially at St. James's Place. He's an awful snob."

"Good for Holder."

"It would be wrong to laugh at him, Henry. Looking back, he took pride in his work, he did his job to the very best of his ability, he was devoted to the family and your going away must have hit him almost as badly as it did your mother and father."

"I wondered. It's a funny business, Alice, but you can live with servants for years, and you get to know them very well up to a point, but there's always a great gulf between you so that you never really get to know them properly, only as much of them as they let you know. I've often suspected that you knew us all much better than we knew any of you—except for you and me, of course."

"That's true," she agreed. "You'd be surprised just how much we did know belowstairs. Not much escaped our notice."

"What a sobering thought. It makes me feel slightly uncomfortable."

"It needn't, darling," she assured him. "We all thought the world of you."

He wondered what they thought of James, of his father, of his mother. "We'd better get off this subject," he laughed. "It's too tempting. Anyway, you have a sister-in-law whose father owns a bank. Think he'd lend us a tenner occasionally?"

Alice shook her head and smiled. "I doubt it. I shouldn't bother asking, if I were you."

"Somehow I don't think I shall." He stopped and a strange look crossed his features.

"What is it?" she asked sharply.

"Sorry, someone walking on my grave perhaps. It's just . . . one day things are going to be different. I don't know how, but one day they'll be glad to know us. Don't ask me how I know, it's just a foolish feeling."

He laughed suddenly. "It must be something I ate. Come on, it's a fine night. Let's go for a walk."

Chapter 4

AT the beginning of 1890, some eighteen months after they were married, Alice told Henry that she was pregnant again. This time he was genuinely delighted, for now he very much wanted a child. He did not know why, because he was happy enough with Alice, but the desire to perpetuate himself had become strong. He insisted that she see the doctor regularly in the hopes of preventing another mishap. Her pregnancy progressed in a most normal manner, and the months were spent in happy expectation.

One day early in the summer, Henry went to Robert Turner and asked if he could talk to him. Turner told him to close the office door and sit down.

"What is it Henry? Something wrong?"

"No, Mr. Turner. I'd like to ask for a day off, and I want to tell you why."

"You make it sound very portentous."

"There's a sign up in Everett's. The business is for sale."

"The grocer, here in King's Road?"

"That's right, Mr. Turner. I think I'll buy it."

"Oh." Turner blinked. "You want to set up in business, do you?"

"I do. I've always wanted to make some sort of start on my own, but I've been waiting till I knew the town better. I hope you don't mind. You've been very decent to me and I've enjoyed working here."

"Why should I mind, Henry? I admire ambition. Why Everett's?"

"It's in a good postion. I think it could make more money if the shop were more attractive and if he sold a wider range. I've talked to Alice about it and we have ideas."

"Have you got enough money?"

"I've a little over two thousand—it was a legacy," he explained.

"Will that be enough?"

"No, but I think I can get more from the bank. Would you be a guarantor if necessary, Mr. Turner?"

"I would, gladly. What is the price?"

"I don't know. I want to go and talk to them and then go to see the bank manager."

"Let me know before you settle anything. I may be able to help a little. I can find out exactly what the business is worth—not what they *say* it's worth, but what it really is worth. Tom Bassett will tell me, but he wouldn't tell you."

Bassett was the biggest grocer in Reading, highly successful. His opinion would be invaluable.

"That's very kind of you, Mr. Turner."

"Oh, rubbish. You go and see what you can find out and I'll drop round to speak to Tom Bassett. I tell you what—you've got a week's holiday due, haven't you? Why not take it now?"

"I could do that. The only thing is that this may not come off and I don't want to waste my holiday."

"Have the courage of your own convictions. I'll give you a day off today anyway, and if you still want to buy Everett's, you can take your holiday starting tomorrow."

"Thank you."

Edwin Everett's solicitors asked for two thousand, five hundred pounds plus stock at valuation, and Tom Bassett advised that the business was worth about one thousand, eight hundred plus stock. The lease had only twenty years to go before it came up for renewal and the place needed redecorating.

Henry had a meeting with the bank manager, and then saw the solicitors again. Two days later both parties were agreed—he would pay two thousand plus the value of the stock. When he told Robert Turner, the editor seemed genuinely pleased.

"I'll be your first customer," he said. "I'm glad you're setting up, Henry. I'll miss you here, but you're capable of better things. Maybe one day you'll be able to match your brother's wife's family, penny for penny."

"My . . . What do you know about my brother?"

"Captain James Vernon, 1st Lancers."

"How did you find out?"

Turner told him and Henry laughed. "I'm not very good at hiding things, am I? You must have wondered about me, why I came here."

"It was none of my business."

"I oughtn't to tell you, because it isn't entirely my secret, but somehow I want to. I wonder why that should be?"

"If it's in confidence I'll respect it, but don't say anything if you would rather not."

"Oh, it's nothing awful; it's just that Alice worked for us. She was a maid."

"I'd never have guessed."

"Thank you. You can imagine the uproar that caused. My father is an A.D.C. to the Queen, among other things."

"Don't spell it out. I can see it all and I'll never tell a soul."

"Now you see why I'm ambitious. I've nothing to do

with the family. They don't know where I am, so it's not showing off or anything, but I want to succeed on my own. I was cut off. That money I have was a legacy from a great-aunt."

"Things may work out better this way. Suppose they'd accepted you grudgingly, as a sort of second-class son, you wouldn't have liked that, would you?"

"No, but it would never have happened. You see they couldn't accept the situation. I realize that. I'm not sorry, or angry, or resentful. I miss the family, of course, but I wouldn't change things."

"I hope that now you're leaving the *Herald* you'll be a friend. I haven't had nearly as much to do with you as I'd have liked, because of the rest of the staff. I can't play favorites. Now that you're going to be on your own, I'd like you to visit me at home, to have supper with my wife and me. We've often talked about you and Alice."

"That's very kind of you."

"Not in the least. And talking of Alice, how is she?"

"Blossoming. Having a baby seems to agree with her. She looks healthier than ever."

"Give her my greetings, won't you? Getting back to business, I can let you have some advertising space at a special price—to oblige a friend."

"Now that *is* kind."

"Not at all. It's an investment in the future. You may become one of my biggest customers one day."

Henry had to close the shop for a fortnight while it was decorated and new fittings were installed. By the standards of seventy-five years later, Henry's shop was primitive. Bacon, cheese, and fresh food were kept behind the counter, fruit and vegetables were displayed in the middle of the floor, and the tinned and packaged goods were all round the walls. There were seven assistants, and the shop gave the appearance of being large and airy as well as attractively laid out.

Alice was pleased with the result and made one or two important suggestions. She was not going out very much now because the baby was due. On Thursday, July 24, 1890, a son was born in the Wokingham Road lodgings of Mr. and Mrs. Henry Vernon. He weighed seven pounds, five ounces, cried lustily, and was promptly named Edward Vernon.

Henry's joy knew no bounds. In two years he had acquired a wife, a son, and a business, and some good friends in Reading. He had traveled a very long way from the 1st Lancers—much further than he himself realized. He was now absorbed completely in his home and his work. There was only one minor drawback. The doctor felt that it would be better if Alice had no more children. Henry was astonished, for she was in excellent health, but the doctor was quite firm. Henry was so delighted by the advent of young Edward that the ill tidings did not give him much concern. They troubled Alice more, for she was opposed to the idea of only children. However she had to accept the situation when the doctor emphasized that it was not so much a question of her own life as that of any future child.

The baby and the business both thrived, Alice regained her slim and lovely figure, and Henry was among the happiest of men. They and the Turners visited each other regularly, and Henry began to make business friends in the town.

One morning in August he went out as usual for a cup of tea in a nearby tearoom, purchased his *Times* and sat studying it. This time he did not miss the notice, prefaced by the word VERNON. *To Captain and Mrs. James Vernon of Cleveland Row, a son, John.* So, Henry mused, they were living in his grandmother's house. It was a sensible arrangement—it was far too big for the old lady and she flatly refused to move. It would do James very nicely till in due course he took over St. James's Place, as no doubt he would—a long time from now.

It amused him that he, by buying the *Times*, could keep abreast of developments in his own family, but they had no way of finding out anything about him. At one time he had seriously considered changing his name, for he wanted to make the break complete, but something had restrained him. Now he was glad, because he was proud of his father and grandfather, and his own son and his son's sons might one day be interested in their ancestry. Of course it included Hubert Mason, haberdasher, of Richmond—and they would have to accept that too!

Early in 1891 the *Times* again brought him tidings. Adeline, wife of General Sir Godfrey Vernon, had died suddenly at her home, 121 St. James's Place, S.W.1. She was only fifty-one.

"What will you do?" Alice asked anxiously, for she was well aware of how dearly Henry loved his mother despite their few years' estrangement.

"I ought to go, you know. It won't be pleasant, but I owe it to her. Don't you think so, my dear?"

"Yes, I do. Where will you stay?"

"Hotel, of course. I shouldn't think I'll be away long. They won't welcome me, you know."

"I'm not so sure."

"I hope you're right. It doesn't say when the funeral is. I'd better get up to Town right away. Do you mind, Alice?"

"Of course not, why should I mind? You must go, and go at once. I'll help you to pack."

He gave her a grateful smile and together they packed a case and he set off. He took a room at the York, a quiet place in Bury Street, off Jermyn Street, quite close to home. He waited till after dinner before strolling round to St. James's Place. Holder, who answered his ring at the doorbell, stood gaping, the first time Henry had ever seen him completely at a loss.

"It's . . . it's Captain Henry."

"Mr. Henry now, Holder. Is my father in?"

"He's upstairs, Mr. Henry, with Captain James. Mrs. James and Lady Vernon are there too."

"Lady . . . you mean my grandmother is here?"

"Yes, Mr. Henry."

Holder led the way upstairs, knocked on the door and opened it, and said with monumental calm, "Mr. Henry, sir."

There was a silence while Holder withdrew. His father stood transfixed, James glowered a little, Mary stared with open interest, and his grandmother peered at him. It was the old lady who spoke first.

"Well, come inside Henry and let me look at you properly. I haven't seen you for a long time, you know. Come over here, boy."

He stood in front of her, his chin raised a little defiantly.

"Ha," she snorted, "you haven't changed a bit. How's that girl you married?"

"My wife is very well, thank you, Grandmama."

"Any children?"

"I have a son."

"Then why wasn't I told? I'm still your grandmother, aren't I? I didn't like the way you sneaked off without a word."

"I thought it would be less embarrassing . . ."

"Embarrassing, fiddlesticks. Once you reach seventy-five, nothing embarrasses you. Godfrey, aren't you going to say good evening to your son?"

"I was waiting for you, Mother. Hullo, Henry."

"Hullo, Papa."

"We'd no idea you would come. We couldn't let you know about your mother." His voice grew gruff as he spoke. "She so wanted to see you. We didn't know where you were."

"I know. That's my fault."

"Where are you staying?"

"The York, just a few yards away."

"You should be here. I'll send Holder . . ."

"No thanks, Papa. It's better this way."

"Much," James agreed, speaking for the first time.

Henry turned his glance on his younger brother and saw the sullen outthrust lip and the lowered brow. Oh, well, it was to be expected. He looked at the girl, pretty, a real beauty in fact. She had a boyish figure and fine features, wonderful fair hair, and an impish smile. She was smiling at him now.

"They haven't introduced us," Henry said mildly. "I'm Henry. They may have told you about me."

"That's not funny, Henry," James snapped.

"It wasn't meant to be, Jimmy."

"I wish you'd stop calling me Jimmy. My name is James."

"Oh, don't be such a pompous ass."

Mary laughed and James looked furious.

"You two can stop your bickering at once," Lady Vernon said crossly. "Godfrey, take Henry to see his mother."

Henry looked at her gratefully and followed his father to the room where his mother lay. The room was in darkness except for two tall candles. As he looked at her he felt tears welling up into his eyes. So beautiful, so young-looking—and he missed her so much that it hurt physically. This had been his mother.

"What happened?" he asked hoarsely.

"Her heart. It was bad."

"I had no idea."

"We only found out after you'd gone. This was the second attack. It was all over quickly."

"I'm glad." He put his hand to his eyes as the hot tears

rolled down his cheeks. He turned his back on his father. The older man stood awkwardly, seeing his son's shoulders heave a little, wanting to help but unable to do so. After a few minutes Henry pulled himself together. He bent over the lifeless body and kissed the cold lips.

"I hope you didn't mind my coming," he said when he had straightened up.

"No, I wanted you. I wanted you more than anything in the world."

Henry heard the naked emotion in his father's voice and turned, wide-eyed.

"You did, Papa?"

"Of course I did, you young fool. You're my son."

"I see. I'm sorry."

There was a silence.

"How's . . . how's your wife?" the general asked.

"She's very well indeed."

"And the baby? How old is he now?"

"He was born on the twenty-fourth of July last year, so he's about six months."

"What's his name?"

"Edward."

"Well, yes, it's fashionable, I suppose. After the Prince of Wales?" Sir Godfrey suggested.

"That's right. We called the first one George, after Grandpapa."

"I wondered about that. This is your second son, then?"

"The first was stillborn, two years ago."

"I'm sorry about that."

"We got over it, Papa. I read about James's marriage and their baby—the *Times*, you know."

"Quite. I suppose that's how you found out about your mother?"

"Yes. I felt I had to come, despite everything."

"Quite right," the general agreed. "Quite right. How's everything with you?"

"Oh, very well, thank you."

"You manage for money, do you?"

"Excellently."

His father blinked, wondering how on earth this could be. "What . . . er . . . what are you doing?"

"I'm a grocer."

"A grocer!"

"Yes. The choice of careers for ex-officers of cavalry is a bit limited. I worked on a newspaper for a time, proof-reading. Now I have my own shop. Business is good."

Sir Godfrey took a deep breath. Business is good! He never thought to hear such words from one of his own sons. Yet, he had to admit, they weren't nearly so bad now that it had happened. He had a son in trade. What of it?

"Are you still an A.D.C.?" Henry asked.

"Yes, yes."

"Did my going away make things awkward at all?"

"The Queen heard you'd left the regiment. I'm afraid I did as you suggested. I said you'd gone to South America looking for adventure and excitement."

"So it was all right?"

"Oh, yes, she commiserated with me."

"I'm glad everything has worked out well. Obviously the regiment didn't take it out on Jimmy as they gave him my captaincy. His wife seems a nice sort."

"Charming girl. Charming family. I'm afraid you'll find your brother a little . . . unbending."

"You don't have to explain. I know Jimmy well enough."

"We'd better go in. You'll stay for the funeral?"

"Of course, but then I must get back."

"Where is back?" his father asked. "I don't know where you live, you know."

"I live in Reading. I'd rather you didn't tell Jimmy."

"All right, if that's what you want. What sort of place is Reading?"

"Nice. I like it. Lovely countryside round about."

"A grocer in Reading." Sir Godfrey shook his head unbelievingly. "And you're happy?"

"So happy I can't even begin to describe it."

They stood silently, and then Henry walked back to his mother's body, kissed her again, and left the room, followed by his father. As they entered the next room, James stood up.

"Mary and I must go now, Papa. I'll call in the morning."

"Oh, must we, James? I wanted to talk to Henry," Mary said.

"Yes, we must," James answered stiffly.

"I'm staying till the funeral," Henry said. "We'll meet again."

"I'm glad to hear that," a smiling Mary replied.

When James and his wife had gone, Henry settled down with a brandy and told his father and grandmother all they wanted to know about himself and his family in Reading. They sat talking till quite late.

"Can I escort you, Grandmama?" Henry asked, looking at the time. "Or is your own carriage here?"

"I'm staying here till after the funeral."

"Of course, how stupid of me, otherwise you'd have gone with Jimmy. I'd forgotten he's living at Cleveland Row."

"I shall come to visit you," his grandmother said firmly. "It will be better than your coming up to Town. You might bump into some of your old friends and that would be awkward. You seem to have got along very well without the family."

"I've been lucky, but you needn't think I haven't missed home."

"Of course you did, but it was worth it, wasn't it?" the old lady demanded.

"Oh yes. I'd do it again if I had to. You must realize that I'm very happily married."

"Then your father and I are contented. She must be a remarkable woman, your wife."

"She is," Henry agreed, thinking of his shop, "in many ways."

"And she worked here as a servant. What a strange world it is. I'm going to bed now. You two can sit and talk."

"No, I must get back to my hotel too," Henry said, rising. "Thank you both for making me so welcome. I was rather uncertain what things would be like."

There was an awkward pause and then he kissed his grandmother good-bye. His father walked downstairs with him to the front door. He promised to return next morning before the funeral.

By agreement with his father he traveled to the funeral by himself next day. He was popularly believed to be abroad and there were a few mourners who would have been very curious to see him again, and very full of questions. Although it was a mild morning he wore a coat with an upturned collar and pulled his hat down over his eyes. He did not join the crowd at the graveside but watched from a distance and stayed behind till they had all gone. Nobody paid any particular attention to him, except Mary whose eyes were on him most of the time.

He lunched with the family, a sad sort of meal made sadder by James's sullen silence. Henry thought it strange that his brother should resent him so much. After all James had benefited by all that had happened, and he had done nothing whatever to harm James.

After lunch he returned to his hotel. That same evening, about an hour before he was due to return to St. James's Place to dine, he had a caller. It was his sister-in-law. He went down to the lounge and greeted her. She was very smart, very fashionable, he thought. They shook hands.

"This is a surprise," he said. "Where's James?"

"He had to go to the barracks. He's on duty tonight."

"Is he, by jove? Poor Jimmy. You shouldn't have come here, Mary. He wouldn't like that at all."

"I don't care what he'd like," she said. "It's all very well his saying you're a thoroughly bad hat, but I don't know you."

"Is that what he says?"

"That and worse. What did you do to hurt him?"

"Nothing at all. Nothing that you haven't heard a score of times, I daresay. Sometimes I've wondered why he should be quite so bitter."

"Oh, well, that's James." She shrugged as if it were of no consequence. "Tell me about yourself."

"Why? Vulgar curiosity? Do you want to know how I feel having sold my birthright for a mess of belowstairs pottage? Because, if so, you'll be disappointed."

"You *are* rude, aren't you? Do I seem vulgarly curious?"

He smiled suddenly and she smiled back. "I'm sorry. I'm on the defensive where Jimmy is concerned, and you're his wife. It was unfair of me."

"Oh, that's all right; I understand. I am curious about one thing, though—was it worth it?"

"Yes."

"I'm glad. I've always felt that the woman usually gets the worst of it in this life. My sister will be interested."

"Your sister?" he asked blankly.

"Yes, Joanna. She's older than I am. She's married to Christopher Hilton, the M.P. When I first heard about you from James, before we were engaged even, I told Joanna and she was fascinated. Not vulgarly," she added with a quick smile. "She said she was sure you'd be very happy, but I wasn't so certain. It seemed so much to give up, and men are selfish beasts."

"Is that what you think of us?"

"Most men," she answered calmly and he thought what an extraordinary person she was.

"You tempt me too much. I must ask if that applies to Jimmy?"

"Your brother is a model of rectitude as a husband. It was an eminently suitable match, he is very good looking, and I adore the Lancers' uniform. He is also a thoroughly selfish, arrogant, and spoiled person, which is precisely what he ought to be, considering everything."

He stared and hooted with laughter. He beckoned a waiter and ordered drinks.

"You're a strange one to be married to someone as predictable as Jimmy," he told her.

"My sister and I have always been unconventional at heart, but we try to conceal it."

"Not before me apparently."

"No, you're different. I'm glad I met you."

"I really can't think why," Henry protested. "I'm the most ordinary of people."

"I don't agree. One day they're all going to be terribly proud of you."

"Don't you believe it," he grinned. "They may forgive me eventually—time is a great healer—but one is never *proud* of a grocer."

"You're quite wrong. You'll see. Now tell me all about your wife."

To his surprise he found himself obliging her.

Chapter 5

Alice was as interested in family news as he had been. She listened avidly to his account of his trip to London and asked many questions.

"I like Mary," she said. "I like her very much. Her sister sounds interesting too. But James! Holder sometimes used to call him 'Sir James,' you know."

"Did he?"

"I shouldn't tell you things like that, should I? It's only belowstairs nonsense, but Holder always said James was full of his own importance."

"I suppose he is," Henry admitted. "He's got plenty to be proud of."

"Not his own brother apparently. I'm glad I shan't ever have to meet James."

"No, it's not very likely," Henry agreed, "but my grandmother has threatened to visit us and my father has said he will write occasionally."

"Are you pleased?"

"Yes, I am. Of course I am. It's nice to know my father seems to have forgiven me." He shook his head and smiled. "I'm really very lucky. I've got you and Edward, and now the breach with my family has been partly patched over. I wonder what I did to deserve it all."

"Is that what you think? That you're lucky?"

"No man was ever more fortunate, believe me."

She thought of their two furnished rooms, and wondered at her husband. That reminded her of a subject close to her heart.

"Henry, how is business?"

"It's fine. We're all right now."

"Can we afford something better than this? Soon, in a year or two, we shan't want the baby in our bedroom."

"I haven't forgotten. The truth is, darling, that we could move out into better lodgings tomorrow, but when I leave here I want it to be to a house of our own. We could move into the rooms over the shop, but I'd rather leave the tenants there and hang on here for a bit longer till I'm really firmly established. I have plans."

"What plans?"

"Wait and see," he told her playfully. "One day I'm going to surprise you. Edward will have his own room, but for the next year at least, I want to save as much as I can."

"Very well, I'll trust you," she said, "but it does seem silly living here when we're making so much money."

"By the summer I'll have paid back to the bank most of what I owe them, and we'll have enough to live on comfortably."

"So soon?"

"I think so. I'm using every penny to pay back the bank as fast as I can."

"Why the hurry?"

"Because I'll be wanting more money from them one day, and I want them to think of me as a man who pays back and does it quickly. I want them to have confidence in me."

"Ah, now I see."

"Don't worry, when the time comes you'll be just as deeply involved as you have been in this shop of ours. I never told you what Tom Bassett said about you."

"And what was that?" Alice demanded.

"He said you were worth a thousand a year."

"Poof, is that all?" she asked airily. "I expect more than that, Mr. Vernon."

"You shall have it, Mrs. Vernon. You shall have it. You shall have two footmen, I promise—one for each foot."

"Fool," she giggled, pushing him. He fell back on the settee with her on top of him. His arms went round her and his lips found hers. He kissed her passionately.

"My goodness, after all this time," she protested, flushing furiously as she met his glance after the kiss. "Anyone would think we were courting."

"So we are. We always will be." He stroked imaginary moustaches. "Ar, give me another kiss, me proud beauty." He began to kiss her again and this time she did not struggle.

A few months after Henry's mother's death, Lady Vernon came to Reading. She stayed at a nearby hotel for one night. The visit was a huge success because the old lady had no nonsense about her. She was intrigued by her small great-grandson, delighted with Alice, and made no bones about either fact.

Before she left she took Henry on one side and spoke quietly.

"You should be living somewhere better. I'd like to help you."

"I don't need help, Grandmama."

"Now don't be silly, boy. I can see, can't I?"

"No, you can't. I could move from here tomorrow, but I'm waiting a little. I mean it, Grandmama; I don't need money. My plans are working out and I'm going to succeed . . . on my own. Next time you come, perhaps, we'll be somewhere else."

"You must need money."

"I don't," he repeated stubbornly.

"You're in my will, you know that, don't you?"

He smiled at her. "That's kind of you."

"Rubbish. I'll make provision for Edward now."

"Grandmama."

"Yes?"

"Could you have a word with Papa? It's about money. He disinherited me and now he may want to change that. I think all his money should go to Jimmy since Jimmy is the one in society. He'll have to maintain St. James's Place and there's the regiment and everything. I'm the one who went away, and I really don't need money."

"You can say that? Living like this? Do you want to be a grocer all your life?" she demanded.

"There are worse things. Anyway, the whole point is that I shan't always be living like this. I'd rather you spoke to Papa. I don't want to seem ungrateful, but honestly, I'm the one who caused all the trouble. Jimmy's the one who stayed at home and did his duty."

"You don't mean that," she told him. "You did your duty by Alice."

"Yes, but not by the family. I just can't explain it, but I don't want the money."

"You'll have some of mine and like it."

"Yours is different."

She gave him a searching look. "I suppose it is. I think I begin to understand you, my boy. Leave it to me, but do please write to me, Henry."

"I promise," he agreed.

His father wrote to him about once every three months. The letters they exchanged were short and not very informative. This did not mean that they were unsatisfactory. The purpose of the letters was to maintain a contact and to reassure one another. This they could do in very few words indeed. In the late spring of 1892, however, Sir Godfrey's letter was longer than usual.

"I must tell you, in confidence because I am sure I am not supposed to tell you, that Mary has left James. She is living with her father in Belgrave Place. I don't know the details of what went wrong and why they split up, but James is inclined to be stuffy and not very good company for a spirited young girl who is only just twenty-two. I believe she may go to live with her sister and her husband in their house in Oxfordshire, somewhere on the Thames. Mary has taken the baby and James is furious about this. He has left Cleveland Row and moved back into his old room here. I don't see him much. He seems to be fully occupied with the regiment and his club, which is really all to the good as I can't give him much comfort in his troubles.

"I can't honestly say I am worried about either of them, as they are both very positive characters who know what they want from life and both are very comfortably situated. The main reason why I am writing to you at such length is that Mary asked me to, though I have no idea what lies behind this extraordinary request. I thought you hardly knew one another. Anyway, she seemed to think I should tell you."

The rest of the letter was filled with purely routine news and comment. Henry, like his father, wondered why Mary should think of him at such a time of crisis. What was it she had said? They'd all be proud of him one day? Something like that. She was an extraordinary person. Soon, however, he forgot about James and Mary and their matrimonial problems as his own plans began to come to fruition.

At the end of June he went to see his bank manager. The main business went remarkably smoothly. Henry wanted to borrow money to purchase a larger, double-fronted shop a hundred yards away from his present premises. The shop was a haberdashers, but Henry planned to turn it into a dual-purpose shop, adding children's clothing. He was able to point out that he had repaid the loan on his present place at almost twice the agreed rate, and that the loan had almost been liquidated. He produced audited accounts showing a remarkable increase in the volume of business and in both gross and net profits. The bank manager was impressed. He was certainly willing to venture three thousand pounds, using the existing premises as security for the loan. Henry was pleased by the ease with which it went, for his next request would require more arguing.

"There's one other thing. I would like another two thousand pounds."

"Yes," the unsuspecting bank manager said, nodding happily. "What for, Mr. Vernon?"

"To buy a house."

"To buy a house?"

"That's right."

"I don't understand, Mr. Vernon. Why do you want to buy a house?"

"To live in, of course."

"In other words, you wouldn't be using our money to earn more money?"

"No, but if I choose a good house, that in itself would be a security for the bank until the loan was repaid, say in ten years."

"I can't give a loan for that purpose, Mr. Vernon."

"Why not?" Henry demanded. "I'm going to be running two shops here in the town, one of them a double shop so that it is virtually three businesses. You've seen for yourself what I've done with Everett's. Surely I'm good for a further loan?"

"If it were a business venture it would be different, but it's only for a house. We don't lend money for houses."

"You ought to," Henry said. "A man in my position should have a decent address, after all. Don't you agree?"

"Certainly," said the bank manager who knew Henry's very modest lodgings.

"I'm plowing back every penny I can into the business, to repay loans, to make improvements, to pay my staff decently, and I take out only what I need. You know that."

"I do indeed," the bank manager concurred. Henry was a model borrower.

"Yet you won't lend me two thousand? One thousand then?"

"I'm sorry, I don't think I can agree to that. Look at your position, Mr. Vernon. You've proved your ability, and there's no argument about that, but now your existing business is going to be mortgaged to the hilt to pay for expansion. Your financial position is bound to be risky until you're firmly established in your new premises. If you succeed in putting up the turnover in the new establishment as you did in Everett's, that's a different matter. Frankly, Mr. Vernon, I'm not in the market to buy houses. If you were to fail now, I'd be stuck with a property I'd have to sell, possibly on a falling market. It would be a different matter if you could secure the loan in some other way."

"Would it?"

"Yes."

"You'd agree then?"

"Subject to the house being worth the money," the bank manager said cautiously. "I'm not giving you a blank agreement now on something you may come back on in the future."

"I'll be back, don't worry. I understand. You've made your position clear, but I'll be back."

When he left the bank he had no real sense of triumph, although today was just as big a day as the one on which he finalized the details of the purchase of Everett's. Then he had made the big step forward and set up in business of his own. It had been a small, if prosperous concern, but now he was expanding, he was going into big business.

When he told Alice about the new loan, she sensed that something was wrong. They discussed plans for the new shops for over an hour and then she faced him squarely.

"What's upsetting you, Henry? Something is."

"I wanted money for a house." He told her about it and she began to smile. When he had finished she held his hand and kissed him.

"You wanted to surprise me, didn't you? It doesn't matter, my dear. It's just as much fun if we do things together. We'll clear off the bank loan as quickly as we can, and when we can offer them some of the firm as security, we'll go back to them, and meantime we can look at houses. You hadn't even chosen one, had you?"

"No," he agreed. "I wanted to get the loan and then come to you and ask you to choose your own home."

"You're much too nice." She kissed him again.

"We'd better get out of here, though. We're going to have to wait a year or two longer, so I suppose we must move. I'll make inquiries about better lodgings, shall I?"

"You do that . . . and, Henry, stop looking so miserable. You've just got yourself another shop."

They moved at the end of the summer to a large, airy flat on Bath Road. It had two bedrooms, a living room and a separate kitchen, a fair-sized bathroom and pleasant hall. It was a ground floor flat and had a bit of garden, the first time Henry had ever had anything to do with a garden.

The move meant new furniture, so for a few months they spent at a greater rate than ever before. Henry left the flat to Alice and devoted himself to the matter of revitalizing his new shop. Again Alice was to prove invaluable. The old-fashioned haberdashers had the time-honored system of hundreds of little drawers banked up behind the counters, each one with a brass card holder and a white card neatly lettered with the contents. In short, ninety percent of the stock was hidden from sight. On top of the glass-topped counter, boxes were spread, their lids off. Even Henry could see that shopping was difficult. Far too much time was wasted in talking, in asking assistants about things. If people could see the stock, they could choose what they wanted and it would save time; or, to put it another way, it would create more time to serve more customers.

The inside of the shop was transformed. Some things simply had to remain hidden, but Henry's aim was to get as much as possible on view and to use the drawers for backup stocks. The children's shop was planned in the same way, and a separate entrance was put in so that one large shop became two small ones.

For a week or two things hung fire, and Henry and Alice held their breath. At last, after the summer, business picked up, and when it did it almost ran away with them. People flocked to the shops. The *Herald* wrote an editorial praising Henry Vernon's attempts to brighten shopping for the Reading community, and held him up as a model for others to follow. Others were slow to do so. Change costs money, and established businesses were reluctant to close down for alterations when they could make money by staying open. For this reason Henry found himself "stealing" more and more of other people's customers. About the only person who shared the joke with him was Tom Bassett. By Christmas 1892 Henry had turned the corner and was coining money in all three shops. People didn't have to ask where Vernon's was—the entire town knew only too well. Vernon's three shops quickly became familiar landmarks.

By the end of 1894 Henry knew he was in a position to dictate to the bank. He and Alice had been married for over six years and little Edward was a sturdy four-year-old, curly-haired and merry-eyed, very much his father's pride. Henry grew roses, for they were Alice's favorite flowers; and between his work, his small rose garden, and his family, he was happily occupied. There was a tranquillity about their lives in those days which gave them a tremendous sense of security, although Henry knew that he had not yet reached the goal he had set himself. There was a long way still to go.

He continued to write to his father about four times a year. James still occupied his room at St. James's Place, but Henry could imagine how lonely his father was now that his mother was gone. The general was spending more and more time at Court, for now he had nothing to distract him. He was still a vigorous, upright figure, the soul of probity, respected by a queen who was not a noted respecter of persons. None of these minor successes could fill the void in his life. James, it seemed, was obstinately unbending where Mary was concerned, demanding nothing less than unconditional surrender. Henry knew that Mary was far too spirited to submit to this, and she continued to stay with her sister. Young John, the same age as his cousin Edward, lived with his mother. It seemed James visited them very infrequently, yet, according to Sir Godfrey, James wanted them to return to London to live with him again. Henry wondered how it would all work out. None of it was good for the child he was certain.

Lady Vernon had not returned to Reading. She wrote more frequently than his father, and her letters were highly entertaining, but she was suffering from a severe stiffness in the joints of her legs and traveling was not pleasant, so she remained in London and recently had begun to suggest that they should visit her. It had been so long since Henry had sent in his papers and resigned from his clubs that everyone had forgotten all about him.

One day Robert Turner arrived at the flat at teatime. Henry had just come home and all three of them sat down together.

"I didn't come just to drink Alice's excellent tea," Robert began. "I've got something that will interest you both."

"What's that?" they asked.

"You told me that you were looking for a house out of town, a good property. Well, one's coming on to the market. I know because the advertisement is going into the *Herald* on Saturday. It's very cheap."

"What is it? Where is it?" Alice asked eagerly.

"It's called Mereford House and it's at Spencer's Wood. Do you know it at all?"

"That's out on the road to Basingstoke, about four miles from town, isn't it?" Henry asked. "You remember it, Alice? Nice countryside."

"That's right," Robert confirmed. "It's quite a big place, Henry, and it may be too large for what you want. It's got four large rooms downstairs and six bedrooms with two dressing rooms upstairs, as well as a small wing at the rear to provide for the servants. There's a decent coach house, but the kitchen is not very nice and there are no bathrooms. It's going cheaply."

"How cheaply?" Henry asked.

"I don't know what you'd *get* it for, but they're only asking eighteen hundred. There's about six acres of good ground, but like the house the grounds need attention. It's owned by an old man called Cambray who's lived there alone for years. He's going to live with his married daughter now. Not many people want a house that size and it needs a minimum of a few hundreds spending on it straight away. Quite frankly Cambray isn't interested in driving a keen bargain. He only wants to get a fair price and move out."

"How do you know all this?" Henry asked with a smile.

"I made a few inquiries before coming to see you. The house might have been no use."

"A few inquiries indeed," Alice scoffed. "I'll wager you've been to see it."

"Well, I did have a quick look," Robert admitted. "You see, it really could be a very fine property and it's a very reasonable price too. I know how much you've wanted a house of your own. What I really came about . . ." He hesitated and looked awkward. "I know how disappointed you were about the bank loan. I could lend you the money myself."

"My dear Robert." Henry stared at his friend. "That's the nicest offer I've ever known. As it happens I think I can go to the bank now and get it from them. We've been doing very well and I've repaid a lot of their money."

"I'm glad to hear it. Nevertheless you may want a bit more than they can offer you. I imagine you'll want to do a lot to the house. Another thing, the furniture is for sale. Some of it is rather uninspiring, but he has some very good pieces, and I know he'll let it all go for a song. The old chap just can't be bothered. I . . . er . . . I made an appointment for you both to go out there tomorrow morning at ten. Do you mind?"

They burst out laughing.

"What would we do without you, Robert?" Alice asked.

The following morning they set off in good time. It was a dry bright day with a cold nip in the air and the horse's hooves rang against the hard surface of the road. Alice's cheeks were flushed and her eyes sparkled. Even more than Henry she had dreamed of owning their own house, ever since he had told her he had gone to the bank to demand a two-thousand-pound loan. Her dreams were far from grandiose. What she craved was the ultimate security of a home that belonged to them, that was not rented, and one that they could alter to suit their tastes.

Just before they reached the village called Spencer's Wood they turned off to the right, following a signpost which bore the single word "Mereford." About a quarter of a mile along a winding lane they came to the entrance to the property, a sagging wrought-iron gate supported by two carved stone pillars with heraldic beasts on top. The drive needed weeding, the hedges were untrimmed, and there was a dilapidated air about the place, yet despite all that their pulses quickened. It would take so little to put it right, and one could easily picture it in summer when it had been tidied up. The house was partially concealed by the branches of leafless trees, and then as they rounded the final curve of the drive they saw it clearly, a tall, square, stone house with a handsome pillared portico, tall windows, and tall chimneys.

"Oh, Henry," Alice said in a hushed voice. "How nice it is."

It was too, although it was really rather a plain building. Henry puzzled over it for a long time, and it was only after he had lived in it for a year that he came to the conclusion that it must be due to the fact that the proportions were exactly right.

Richard Cambray was looked after by an equally aged and infirm manservant who admitted them. It was far nicer inside than Alice had anticipated. Certainly they would want to redecorate, but it could be lived in and some of the furniture was really good. She let Henry do the talking while she sat silently calculating how much curtain material would be needed here, how much carpeting there, what should be decorated now and what could be left till money was more plentiful.

The old man, who had been born in the year that Napoleon escaped from Elba and who had celebrated his twenty-first birthday in the year that Texas became independent of Mexico, was courteous and not terribly interested. To Henry's hesitant offer of two thousand for the house and its contents, he agreed without a murmur. It would save him all the trouble of offering it on the market. This way he could get his money and go away to Dorset to his fifty-year-old daughter who would care for him in his declining years. He was, after all, almost eighty.

It was arranged that Henry would meet Mr. Cambray's solicitor that same afternoon. When they left the house, less than an hour after entering it, before they got into the carriage they stopped in the drive to look at its expressionless front.

"Well, that's going to be our home, it seems," Henry remarked lightly.

"It's so big. Are we being foolish, Henry?"

"I don't think so. It's a bargain. We can't lose by buying this. Dash it all, I could buy it and sell it and make money," he exclaimed, sublimely unaware that his grandson would live in an age when men would buy and sell property for a livelihood, and a highly profitable one too. Had he been thinking less of his other businesses and more of the house, he might just possibly have got in on the very ground floor of the property racket. As it was he was content in the knowledge that money spent on Mereford would be spent wisely.

"It's going to take a lot of looking after."

"We'll have servants," he said in a matter-of-fact way. "Not many perhaps, but—say—two or three in the house, and a gardener. We'll need a gardener who can double as groom and coachman."

"Servants?" She giggled. "Imagine that, Henry."

He turned and exchanged a smile with her. Alice Mason, parlor maid, now mistress of a nice little country property and with servants of her own—it tickled his humor and he could see that it pleased Alice.

"You're so good to me," she whispered, becoming solemn.

"Poof," he replied airily.

"You are." She said it fiercely. "You're the finest man in the world."

"That's what all wives say, especially when they want something. It's no use flattering me. I've no more money to waste on you. I'm going to have a brougham and another horse for me to ride into Reading every day. Think of that."

She fell silent. It was so easy nowadays to forget that he had been a captain in the 1st Lancers and was a first-class horseman. They drove into town and Henry stopped at his own shop to collect a bottle of good sherry, and they continued to the flat.

There he poured two glasses and they drank a toast.

"To Mereford, and the future," he said.

"To us, darling," she smiled, and they drank.

He poured two more glasses. "We'll be able to move next month, after Christmas, so we'd better have another toast—to 1895, and the happiest New Year of all."

"No more, you'll make me tipsy," she laughed, and they finished their second glasses.

Henry walked to the window and took a very deep breath, puffing out his chest as he looked at the little garden.

By jove, he thought with delight, I believe I've really done it. I've succeeded. It was something he had never dared to dwell on because at any time he might miscalculate and end up penniless, but now it seemed safe to say that he had succeeded on his own. What would his father say when he heard about Mereford? It would surprise him all right.

"I'm going out," he said, turning suddenly. "I don't

know how long I'll be, but don't start lunch till I come back."

"Where are you going?" Alice asked.

"To the bank, of course. Where else?"

He kissed her and hurried out of the room.

Chapter 6

Fʀᴏᴍ the beginning they had fallen in love with Mereford. By unspoken agreement they never referred to it as "Mereford House." Mereford *was* a house, and the white signpost with its black lettering said only "Mereford." It had laid its charm on them that first morning, under the worst circumstances, and the charm did not fade, not even when they were moving in, when there were decorators and carpenters, plumbers and electricians —for they were having electricity installed. For several weeks the place was in an uproar and the three of them lived virtually in two rooms upstairs.

There had been no difficulty about money. The bank manager had kept his word and had given Henry the full amount he wanted so that he did not need to take advantage of Robert Turner's offer. He was glad about this, because he liked Turner far too much to want to borrow from him. Borrowing from the bank was one thing—that was what business was all about—but borrowing from one's friends was an entirely different kettle of fish.

By the spring of 1895 the workmen were out and the grounds had been licked into some sort of shape. The drive was already tree-lined and to one side of this drive

Henry put an ornamental fountain in the center of a lawn, which would be a pleasant place for them to sit in the summer. The other side he turned into an elaborate rose garden. At the back of the house there was a walled vegetable garden and the rest of the ground was covered with trees, so that they had their own small private park. The arrangement suited them both very well and Henry spent more and more time in the garden in the evenings, helped by the five year-old Edward.

That spring they engaged their first servants. There were three of them—a cook, a housemaid, and a gardener whose job included looking after the small stables. Henry bought a smart brougham and two horses. Each morning he would set off on Starlight, the big chestnut, to ride into Reading, and he returned in the evenings in time for tea. On weekends they would go out together, shopping on Saturdays, exploring the countryside on Sundays after church. The Vernons became as familiar a sight in the country round Spencer's Wood as they were in Reading itself, a handsome couple with a pretty child. Seven years had passed since they first had come to Reading. Henry was now thirty-two, Alice thirty, and Edward at five was tall and sturdy and looked at least seven. The question of his education was now acute. They heard of a curate at Riseley, a mile or two south on the Basingstoke road, and called on him. He seemed satisfactory and Edward began to attend the private classes of the Reverend Mark Luke, along with three other boys of much the same age. They thought their tutor's name hilariously funny and invented a fictitious family for him, studded with New Testament names.

In July Lady Vernon arrived on a visit. This time they were able to offer her the hospitality of their home. She came on a Saturday morning, and Henry and Alice went to meet her. She was very old and frail now and had to be helped when she walked, but her spirit was unquenched.

She leaned on her silver-handled stick and looked up at the house, now basking in warm sunlight, its windows no longer expressionless but beckoning and friendly.

"You've done yourself proud," she said to Henry. "I had no idea."

"It was going for a song, Grandmama."

"I should hope so, else I might think you had robbed a bank. Well." She looked all around. "A proper property, indeed. I shall have to call you Squire Vernon. Now help me up the steps, boy. I want to see the inside of this fine house."

Alice would have been a good deal less than human if she had not derived special pleasure from sitting in her own drawing room while her own maid served tea to Lady Vernon, whose eldest nephew was a governor of the Bank of England. Yet there was nothing malicious in this pleasure. It reflected only a quiet pride in Henry's success.

Lady Vernon was fully aware of the piquancy of the situation, and enjoyed it almost as much as Alice. Edward was produced to be inspected by his great-grandmother, and then released to play in the garden.

"A fine boy," Lady Vernon pronounced. "He's got the Vernon look all right, but I'm glad to see he has your mouth and eyes, Alice. I saw his cousin John only last week."

"Did you? How are things there?"

"You won't have heard. Mary and John have returned to London. At the moment they are all living at St. James's Place. Oh, and James is a major now, Henry."

"I'm glad to hear it. So she's come back. I find that surprising."

"What is there between you and that girl? There's always something odd about it when you speak of her or she speaks of you. Are you sure you didn't know her before James met her?"

"Quite certain, Grandmama. I don't know what it is,"

Henry confessed. "It's an uncanny affair. She and I seem to understand each other without needing words."

"You make me jealous," Alice remarked in a tone which made it quite clear that she was anything but jealous.

"You needn't be," Henry smiled. "Why did she come back, Grandmama?"

"No one knows. For the boy's sake, perhaps."

"I think so," Henry agreed. "I feel sorry for Mary Lancaster. It's such a waste, but you mustn't tell anyone I said so. She's much too spirited for Jimmy. He needs someone meek and self-effacing who is content to manage the servants and preside over his table. Mary is unconventional."

"I met her sister, Joanna Hilton. She's a beauty," Lady Vernon said unexpectedly. "She came up to Town and both of them visited me and had tea."

"I'd like to meet the sister, and the father. They seem to be a remarkable family."

"They are. Now tell me, how are your affairs?"

"We've got three shops now, and they're doing so much trade that we need somewhere bigger," Alice said quickly.

"My goodness, has my grandson become another Mr. Andrew Carnegie?"

"I'll never be in that class, Grandmama, but Alice is right, the shops aren't big enough."

"I'd like to see them. Can we do that?"

"Certainly. We can drive into Reading this afternoon if you wish. Would you like to go inside any of them?"

"Of course I would. I wish to buy something. I would very much like to buy something from a shop owned by my grandson."

In the afternoon they went into Reading and she visited the shops and bought a lace tea cloth, which she assured them she would use from now on. She appeared to derive an unexpected pleasure from seeing the name Henry Vernon above the shops. This puzzled Henry who thought he knew her better. That evening before dinner he brought up the subject.

"Don't you mind my being in trade, Grandmama?"

"At my age one doesn't mind anything anymore. Happiness is all that matters—never forget that—happiness is everything. You've got a fine family, a fine house, and a flourishing business, and you are both very happy—so why should I object to your being in trade? I told your father once that all those gaudy soldiers and splendid viceroys and governors who rule the British Empire are only guarding a commercial enterprise. Poor Godfrey wasn't amused. It was too bad of me, but I've never been able to tolerate humbug. Besides, what was your alternative, answer me that? Were you to starve to death in dignity rather than work for a living?"

"I assure you I have no regrets."

"I'm glad to hear it."

"Grandmama, how is Papa?"

"He'll be fifty-nine next birthday, but you'd never guess. He's just the same as ever, a little quieter, much more lonely. He adored your mother. You see he's had a happy life too, even if in a different way. Now he feels a sense of loss—and of course, although he says nothing, I don't really think he likes having James under his feet all the time."

"I thought they'd get on famously together."

"Because of the regiment? James is a toy soldier beside his father. Your father is very fond of Mary. He was not pleased when she and James separated, and he blames James for that."

"Should I invite him here?"

"Yes, of course you should. Haven't you done so?"

"No. We've been rather busy since we moved in. Also, because James lives with him . . . I didn't want to make things awkward. You know Jimmy, Grandmama, he thinks I'm a cad and a bounder and utterly beyond the pale."

"Silly little boy," his grandmother snorted. "I'm disappointed in James. He's turned out badly."

"No." Henry shook his head. "He's turned out according to pattern. It's just that he's very inflexible."

"Give me a letter to your father and I'll take it back with me. Ask him down to stay with you."

She stayed for four days. On the last evening, after dinner, they sat talking in the garden, for it was a warm, balmy evening.

"I suppose you'll stay here now, make this your home. No more moves."

"We'd never want to move from here," Alice said quickly.

"I used to think St. James's Place was the center of the universe," Henry mused. "Everything was inferior to it—even Cleveland Row," he added with a laugh. "I had no time at all for the country. I've changed, you know. When I look round me here, at my own little bit of England, my lawns, my flowers, my trees, I realize I was wrong. This is the center of my universe now. Mereford means everything to us."

"I'm glad to hear it. Every family needs a home, a proper one where it can put down its roots. You've chosen a very beautiful one."

"We were extremely fortunate."

"You were," his grandmother agreed. "Well, I must go to bed. I tire easily nowadays. Help me inside please, Henry."

"Of course. Stay here, Alice," Henry said and helped his grandmother into the house and upstairs. He returned several minutes later and held out his hands. Alice got up and took them, and they walked hand in hand across the drive to the rose garden.

"That went off well, I think," Henry said with satisfaction in his tone.

"I was nervous, you know."

"Were you, my darling? Why?"

"She's rather a grand old lady and I haven't had much experience as a hostess, have I?"

"You did everything beautifully. I must remember to thank Cook tomorrow. I was a little worried about the food, I must confess."

"Not as much as I was," she laughed.

"It's a nice feeling," he said, changing the subject without warning.

"What is, darling?" she asked.

"To look at all this, and know that I've got something to hand on to young Edward. It isn't just for us, Alice. I want Edward to have a good home and a good business to inherit."

She paused and turned to face him.

"What's all this about inheriting? You're a young man, Henry, and look even younger."

"I know, but time passes, my sweet. It's nice to know that whatever happens Edward will be all right."

"Nothing is going to happen, as you put it, for at least another forty years. Look at your grandmother."

"Wonderful, isn't she? Oh, by the way, I have been meaning to tell you, but so much seems to have been going on these past few days. Last week I had an invitation."

"From whom?"

"Colonel Lavering."

"Who is Colonel Lavering, darling?"

"He commands the Volunteer Battalion of the Berkshire Light Infantry."

"What does he want?" she asked, puzzled.

"He wants me to accept a commission in it."

"Does he know about the Lancers?" she asked, startled.

"Not so far as I'm aware. I hope that secret is well

buried. I want to forget the past. I don't know much about
these Volunteer regiments—it seems to be pretty much of
a social affair. I told him I was rather long in the tooth to
be a subaltern, and he said he had a vacancy for a captain
coming up. He offered it to me."

"What did you say?"

"That I'd talk to you."

She stood silent, thoughtful.

"What do you want to do, Henry?"

"I don't know, darling. The army as such has no fasci-
nation for me now, and certainly not a Volunteer infantry
battalion. After the 1st Lancers?" he added with a chuckle.
"Dear me, no. Yet we're growing up in Berkshire, we're
becoming more prominent. I'm a businessman, a property
owner, and I haven't finished with my schemes yet. Things
are bound to come my way. I hadn't thought about the
army, of course. I thought that in a few years they might
offer to make me a justice of the peace or something of
that sort. Soldiering might not be such a bad idea, though
—Captain Henry Vernon of the Third, Volunteer, Battalion, the Berkshire Light Infantry." He laughed. "I've no
idea what light infantry are supposed to do, but I'm told
the uniform is quite nice."

"You must please yourself."

"I'll have to find out just how much of my time it will
take up, but in a funny sort of way I'd find it amusing and
. . . I don't know . . . satisfying, I suppose, a bit like being
reinstated. I can't explain."

"Then don't. Go ahead and accept if you wish. I don't
mind, Henry."

"That's all I wanted to know. I'll find out more about it.
The colonel of the regiment is Lord Thatcham, who
owns half of Newbury. You've heard of him—the lord
lieutenant. He was once a major in the Life Guards. It
might help with business, you know. There's a sort of
inner circle of people in this county—in all counties I

suppose—and the Volunteer officers here are on the fringes of that circle."

"Are you becoming a social climber, Henry?"

"No," he denied, shaking his head positively. "Not at all. I have no social ambitions whatever, but provided I don't have to get too deeply involved in outside interests, I'll consider anything that might help me develop the firm in the way we both decided it should go. After all, I'm only going to be a captain of the Volunteers. I thought the idea might amuse you."

"It does. The wheel turns full circle. The captain is a captain again."

"It has its attractions," he confessed, kissing her cheek.

On Tuesday, April 7, 1896, the day after Easter Monday, the manger of the bank received Henry Vernon in his office and offered him a sherry which Henry accepted. They discussed the state of the country and then the state of business in Reading, and finally, in his own good time, Henry came to the point. The bank manager listened and his eyes grew a little rounder.

"Six thousand, Mr. Vernon?"

"That should cover it."

"It's a great deal of money."

"My shops are worth that much. When have I ever made a mistake?"

"Quite so."

"The building alone is worth almost five thousand. It's brand new."

"I know, but do you think people will like it? Such a confused sort of shop."

"Nothing confused about it at all. The idea is that they can do more of their shopping in one place. Groceries, confectionery, cakes and biscuits, fruit, haberdashery, ladies' and gentlemen's clothing, children's clothing—all on three floors with a lift connecting them."

"What about your existing shops?"

"Number Eighteen can be turned into a furniture shop —it has the space; Number Forty-seven will become a tobacconist. I'd like to have it all under one roof but even that new building in Broad Street doesn't have enough room. I can only get half the building."

"It will mean alterations to your existing shops, won't it?"

"A certain amount, of course. I told you, I've got five thousand promised already."

The bank manager shook his head helplessly.

"Whenever you get established, you start off on something new. First there was Everett's and before you'd finished paying off that debt you bought your other shop—or shops, I never know which to call it. Now, just as you have cleared off everything and could reasonably look forward to a long spell of prosperity, you're risking it all again in a new venture."

"Not a new venture," Henry contradicted. "I'm growing, expanding."

"Where will it end?"

"In Broad Street, I hope, in Vernon's Universal Stores. That's going to be the name."

"Let me think about it. I'll keep these papers if I may. Can you call tomorrow at the same time?"

Henry nodded, smiling. He knew he had won. Within a week everything was signed, and the workmen began to move into the new three-story building in Broad Street. Reading watched, fascinated, until a week later the *Berkshire Herald* told the story. "Vernon's Latest Venture" the headline ran. "Modern Store for Town Center." People nodded, as though to say I told you so, and local businessmen wondered at Henry Vernon's daring and where he got the money from. Yet Henry's greatest piece of luck was not mentioned in the newspaper report—it was that he had purchased half the building and the land on which it stood, for six thousand, five hundred pounds. He had no insight into the future. He relied on common sense, and common sense told him that Reading was a growing, thriving town, that as London grew, so over the years would Reading, and that to own land in the center of town must be a good investment, even if it was only a very small piece of land accommodating half a building.

Once again Robert Turner had had a hand in things, and when he sat and thought about it Henry marveled at the way Turner had helped him so often. It was Turner who knew that the developer of the site was financially stretched to breaking point and desperately in need of ready money. They had wanted to lease the premises on a ninety-nine-year lease, but Henry had dug in his toes. The thought of six thousand, five hundred in ready money was too much for a speculator who had let things get a little bit out of hand. Reluctantly, but without hesitation, he sold the freehold.

Monday, September 7, was the opening day, and there was a special inauguration ceremony with all the local celebrities and notables present as guests. Lord Thatcham, a father figure in the county, spoke glowingly of the enterprise of Captain Henry Vernon and how he was helping to bring prosperity to Reading, and so declared open Vernon's Universal Stores. Henry had added an *s* to the *Store* because it sounded better and gave an impression of vastness.

Henry and Alice played host and hostess at a special lunch at the Thatcham Arms Hotel and the forty guests, who included a fair sprinkling of Henry's brother officers, drank champagne and ate caviar, served with *blinis* which they had never seen nor heard of until that moment. Indeed the *blinis*—thick buckwheat pancakes raised with yeast and served hot with sour cream—increased Henry's prestige enormously. The word went round like wildfire—"This is how they eat caviar in Russia." And it was true.

People spoke of that lunch for long afterward and in a certain stratum of Berkshire society there was a short-lived craze for caviar with *blinis* on special occasions.

That night he sat with Alice watching the sunset, a weak whiskey and soda by his hand.

"I've done it all," he said quietly.

"Have you? Are you sure?"

"I'm sure. We own the house and the land on which it's built. We own our half of the building which houses the stores, and the land on which that's built. We've got security at last. All we have to do is to sit back and reap the rewards. It's all over, Alice. I've achieved everything I set out to do when we left London. Of course I hadn't the remotest idea about a universal store—that's as much your doing as mine, more in fact. I wanted to make good, found a modest fortune, give security and comfort to you and our children. I think you and Edward will be safe from now on."

"Unless the firm goes bankrupt," she laughed.

"I won't say it can't, but I will say it won't. It only needs ordinary care and attention now."

"You're a remarkable man, darling, not at all like a simple cavalry officer."

"I wasn't a simple one, I was a cunning one. I married you."

They exchanged affectionate glances.

"I wonder how long you'll be able to sit still," she mused. "In ten years, perhaps less, you'll think of something bigger and better and you'll be raising mortgages or loans on all our property and buying bigger and better shops."

"I don't think so. I won't say the business will never expand—I hope it will, but in an ordinary way. I'm not forcing the pace anymore. I'll be thirty-four next year. I'm getting too old for excitement."

"You don't deceive me, Henry Vernon."

"I'm telling the truth. I have a feeling that I've done all I'm going to do in Reading. It's enough, isn't it?"

"Yes, of course. You know what I think of all you've accomplished, darling. What's this feeling you've got?" she added.

"I don't know how to describe it. For years—what is it now? More than seven years?—I've been working toward a fixed goal. Somehow when I drove that bargain over the stores, when I bought the land, I felt that my life's work was over. It's a very odd sensation, one I've never had before, not when I bought Mereford, not when I bought up my first shops. It has something to do with the land in the town center. This is the thing I had to do."

"You do sound odd."

"I know. Anyone would think I was an old man. I tell you one thing, I'm going to take it easy for a bit. We ought to go abroad for a holiday sometime. We've never had a proper holiday. Also, next summer, I'd like to go to Cornwall for a month."

"Why Cornwall?" she asked.

"Because my son is six and has never been to the seaside. He should be exploring rocky coves, catching crabs, fishing, swimming in the sea, behaving like a normal boy. He's becoming a stuffed dummy, stuffed with all that knowledge the Gospel Maker crams into him."

The Gospel Maker was Henry's nickname for the Reverend Mark Luke.

"He's no stuffed dummy. You don't hear about half the mischief he gets up to," Alice laughed.

"Perhaps you're right, but he should go to the seaside in the summer like other children. Maybe we can buy a cottage or something on the Cornish coast when we've had a look around."

"I like the idea," she agreed, "but we can talk about it later. Your father's coming to visit us again and that will keep me busy."

Henry nodded contentedly. Sir Godfrey had been to Mereford twice, and was due again at the end of the week.

"I'm going to take a week off," he said suddenly. "I deserve a rest."

"You certainly do," she agreed. "You work too hard."

"There's no need now." He let out a short bark of laughter.

"What is it?" she asked.

"I can't help it, I think these things. I was wondering what Holder would have said if he could have seen us today, entertaining the cream of county society to lunch, including the lord lieutenant, the high sheriff and the mayor. 'Captain 'Enery wot went to the bad,' " he concluded in a mock Cockney voice.

"Holder doesn't speak like that. He'd say, 'Captain Henry? We don't talk about him, Alice.' "

They laughed together.

Chapter 7

S IR GODFREY VERNON stood in the library at Mereford looking over the leather-bound volumes. It was a comfortable room, one in which he felt completely at home. There was a big fireplace with a wide steel fender and corner seats, leather chairs and a leather settee round the fireplace, sporting prints on the walls, a gleaming mahogany sideboard containing crystal decanters and glasses. On top of it stood a picture of himself in full dress, wearing his orders. Nearby, in a matching silver frame, was another of Adeline in Court dress. It pleased him that they should be the only pictures in his son's library.

He strolled to the window which looked out onto the side of the house, with a view of rhododendrons and trees beyond the beautifully trimmed grass, and then went to another window from which he could see the rose garden. This room and Alice's drawing room, the front rooms on the ground floor, were the nicest in the house.

Henry was virtually reinstated now, apart from James's continuing implacable enmity. There was nothing to stop him coming up to Town, although he never did so. He preferred the country. Sir Godfrey did not know that he blamed him for that. Only recently Her Majesty had asked him, one evening after dinner at Windsor, if he had heard from his eldest son.

"Yes," he had answered blandly. "He's back in this country now, Ma'am. He's set up in business in Reading."

"In business, Sir Godfrey?" his Queen had asked.

"Yes, Ma'am, but I'm glad to say he hasn't forgotten the army. He's a Captain in the Volunteers—Berkshire Light Infantry."

"I'm glad to hear it, Sir Godfrey. Did he prosper in . . . where was it? South America?"

"Yes, I think so."

"You must be glad he is in England again. It was very foolish of him to resign from the Lancers to go off like that. I'm glad it has all turned out quite well."

Sir Godfrey had smiled smugly. So that hurdle was over. The Queen did not pry into his affairs but there had been awkward moments in the past when she had asked about Henry, whom she still remembered as the extremely handsome young cavalry officer who had been presented to her.

He recalled his sovereign's words. Turned out quite well, indeed. It was better than that, it was a success story. Sir Godfrey had no idea where his elder son got his drive and ability—perhaps from his grandfather, Sir George, who had been lord mayor of London. Now all the boy had to do was to continue to live quietly and there was no saying where he would end up. Possibly as a deputy lieutenant, a justice of the peace, maybe even a knighthood. Would he get command of his Volunteer battalion? And always there would be Mereford.

Though he had only stayed in the house twice before, Sir Godfrey was a little astonished by how much it appealed to him. He knew that his mother felt the same. She spoke of it with great affection. Yes, Mereford was a gentleman's residence in every sense of the word. To think Henry had been turned out without a penny!

Time, the great healer, had dealt kindly with Sir God-frey. He had completely forgotten Alice, the parlor maid who had seduced his weak-willed son. This image had vanished. Alice was the mistress of Mereford, and it is true to say that Sir Godfrey never even thought of her as the woman who had been a servant in his own household for eight years. Yet a servant she had been, for as long as she had been a wife. Eight long years, from the age of fifteen.

When she came into the room, her evening gown sweep-ing behind her, he bowed with Old World courtesy.

"Alice, you look lovelier than ever."

"Thank you, Papa."

This was another triumph, persuading her to call him "Papa" as Henry did.

"Edward in bed?"

"Yes. He's growing so quickly that he tires easily. He's going to be tall, like his father."

"A fine boy. I'm glad I have a chance to talk to you like this, Alice. I hope Henry won't interrupt us too soon. I've brought you a message."

"From whom?" she asked, her curiosity aroused. She imagined it must be something from Lady Vernon.

"From Mary."

"James's Mary?" she asked, puzzled. She had never met Mary Vernon.

"Yes. It's a very odd message. When I told her I was coming here—she's always been interested in you and Henry, you know—anyway, when I told her, she said, 'Tell Alice that one day Henry will outshine us all. It hasn't come yet, but it will.' That's what she said."

"What does she mean?"

"Don't ask me. Mary says things like that, you know."

"Second sight?" Alice asked.

"I don't know, but I've told you what she said. I can't think what Henry is supposed to do, can you? Has he any plans?"

"None at all. He wants to take things easily now."

"Sensible fellow. I'm proud of that boy, but I can't imagine what Mary is talking about. How is he going to outshine us? It's a strange word to use."

"Perhaps he'll get a peerage," Alice laughed.

"I wouldn't put it past him."

"I was joking," Alice replied, shaking her head. "He isn't interested in things like that, Papa. He's only interested in his home and in us, his family. The strange thing about Henry is that he hasn't an ounce of ambition. All he's accomplished has been because he was driven by a desire for security. Money, power, social position—he doesn't care anything for them."

"I see. It's very mysterious. The main thing is that you're happy. One mustn't take Mary too seriously."

Even so, Alice brooded on this strange message. Had Mary some power to see into the future? She certainly impressed men, witness Henry and his father. Only James seemed to be indifferent to her, which was interesting, for James was married to her and presumably knew her better than anyone else. Perhaps that was an unfair thought. She wondered if she would ever meet Mary.

The year 1898 was a year in which many things of world importance happened. The U.S.S. *Maine* was blown up in Havana Harbor. Puerto Rico, the Philippines, and Guam were ceded to the United States. Mr. Gladstone died; the followers of the Mahdi were finally defeated at Omdurman in the Sudan; the Empress Elizabeth of Austria was assassinated and the Curies discovered radium. It was a year not without events in the Vernon family. Early in February Lady Vernon died in her sleep and her death was not discovered until her maid took in her tea the following morning.

This time Henry decided to take Alice and Edward up to London for the funeral. It was all very well avoiding awkwardness with James, but Lady Vernon had visited them frequently and they were closer to her than James was. Because James and Mary were still at St. James's Place, they stayed at Cleveland Row, his grandmother's house. It was nice to be fussed over by servants who had known him in childhood, and he walked over the big house, recalling memories of many years previous.

The first meeting with James was in his father's house on the evening of their arrival. They were dining *en famille* for the first time ever. The atmosphere was strained from the start, and James acknowledged Alice with a noticeable lack of courtesy. The children played together quietly in a corner while their elders fenced awkwardly with empty words. It was not a happy gathering and Sir Godfrey's temper was sorely tried. Even Mary, who had been so eager to meet Alice, was disappointed by the cloud of hostility that hung over them.

The funeral was held the following day. After it Lady Vernon's will was read. It was a simple document. She believed in people having money of their own, and therefore she had left ten thousand pounds each to Henry, Alice, and Edward, and to James, Mary, and John. The balance of her estate, about twenty thousand after everything else had been settled, went to Sir Godfrey. It was an eminently fair will, but James did not think so. In the privacy of their bedroom he ranted to Mary about it, calling it infamous and suggesting that his grandmother was a secret drinker.

Mary had suffered her husband for many years, and when the going had been too hard she had usually managed to get away from him for a bit. Now she lost her temper.

"You're like a spoiled child, James. What a stupid, silly thing to say, that your grandmother drank. Is nothing sacred to you?"

"Why else would she give money to that kitchen slut?"

"If you mean your brother's wife, she was a parlor maid not a kitchen maid, and she is no slut. Sometimes when I listen to you talking I wonder if you are your father's son."

"Meaning what?" he demanded furiously.

"That you have the instincts of the gutter," she replied cuttingly.

He was speechless and only just restrained himself from hitting her, and hitting her hard.

"If you feel like that," he countered stiffly, unable to think of a suitable retort, "why do you stay with me?"

"For my son's sake, of course, why else? You don't think I *like* you, do you?"

James was genuinely taken aback. He regarded her as eccentric, difficult, wayward, rebellious, and a great trial to him; but it had never occurred to him that she did not love him dutifully.

"What do you mean, you don't like me?"

"I despise you." She turned away as she spoke, flinging the words over her shoulder.

He grasped her arm and spun her round. As he did so, her hand flashed upward and she slapped him across the cheek. The sound was like a pistol shot and he took a step back, his face smarting.

"You'd dare to strike me, your husband?" he asked in a scandalized voice.

"God forgive me, you're not worth the effort."

His mouth twisted and he stepped up to her and grasped her by the throat and squeezed.

"Don't speak to me like that. Bitch."

"If you don't let go, I shall scream until help comes," she said coolly, and, when he had released her, added "and I shall see that all London knows that Major Vernon of the 1st Lancers tried to strangle his wife in a fit of tantrums over his grandmother's will."

"If that's how you feel, go away from here," he said.

"Why should I? You go."

"This is my home."

"It's mine too. If you don't believe me, ask your father."

"I don't understand you," he cried. "You say you despise me, you certainly act as though you do, yet you want to stay with me. It doesn't make sense."

"I am going to stay here with my son. I shall arrange to have a separate room. I'll see to that tonight. I married you in a moment of weakness for which I have never ceased to berate myself. I shall stay with you as long as your father is alive, for I think John should be near his grandfather. When your father dies, or when John grows up, I shall go away—and when I do I shall never see nor speak to you again."

"I believe you mean it."

"I do, James, believe me I do. I wish I'd never married you. I wish I could divorce you. As it is, I have to make the best of things. But don't call your brother's wife a slut in front of me again. She's more of a lady than you are a man, never mind a gentleman, you ridiculous little toy soldier. Now, I am going to see Holder about another room."

"You can't do that. The servants will talk."

"Let them. They'll have far more to talk about if I don't have a separate room. This is the end, James. Keep your distance in future."

To Major James Vernon it was injustice to the nth degree. Not only did his no-good brother, his low-born wife and their sniveling brat get ten thousand pounds apiece—the same amount as he himself got, he who upheld the family's honor—but on account of them his wife had insulted him and was now moving into a room of her own. Naturally enough, given all the circumstances, he blamed Henry for everything that had happened. It was all Henry's fault. He longed to say something to his father, but an unexpected onset of caution stopped him in time. He suspected that his father might be going soft in the head too, fussing over the unspeakable Henry. So, in his hour of trial, he had no one to comfort him, no one to whom he could turn, except his son. John was now almost eight and an obedient, docile child.

He found John in his own room playing with his toy soldiers and model fort.

"Enjoying your game, John?"

"Yes, thank you, Father."

"Who's winning?"

"The Highlanders." John was currently going through a phase of Highlanders versus Redcoats, and although he had not a drop of Scottish blood in his veins, he found his kilted soldiers more romantic than the others.

"You seemed to have a lot to say to your Cousin Edward today."

"Yes, Father. I like him."

"I'm sorry about that."

"Why?" John asked, interested by this unexpected remark.

"Because we don't really want anything to do with him and his father. Of course this is between ourselves, you understand?"

"But why?" John insisted.

"His father was a bad soldier. He had to leave the army."

"Uncle Henry? But he's a captain."

"Did Edward tell you that? He isn't a real captain. No, I'm afraid he had to leave. We don't talk about it. So you see, we mustn't make friends with them, must we?"

"But Mummy said I was to play with Edward."

"Mummy doesn't understand. Women don't understand these things. Soldiers do."

John nodded. He understood this sort of talk. "I'm going to be a soldier," he said.

"Of course you are. You'll command the 1st Lancers one day, young man. That's a promise. Meantime, be polite and do as Mummy says, but remember Edward and his parents are not nice people. Don't get friendly."

"I shan't," John agreed readily. "What did Uncle Henry do, when he was a bad soldier?"

"I mustn't tell you that. We don't mention him in the regiment, none of the officers ever speaks about him. Did you know that?"

"No." John was horror struck. What a terrible thing, to have been made to leave the 1st and have none of the officers ever mention your name again. Perhaps . . . he scarcely dared to think it . . . perhaps he had been a *coward.*

"Will you play with me, Father?"

"Of course. I'll take the Redcoats, shall I?"

John beamed. His father always said the right thing. It would be a gallant battle, but of course the Redcoats would lose.

The result was that on their last day the two children hardly spoke, Mary avoided her husband like the plague, and it was left to Sir Godfrey, Henry, and Alice to make most of the conversation.

Alice was dissatisfied with their London visit. She had not got to know Mary at all well and the atmosphere had been so strained that she had been uncomfortable most of the time. The only bright spot had been her encounter with the servants. She had not been quite sure what to do but her instincts were sound. She had asked Holder if she might visit them belowstairs. He had been surprised but had agreed.

It was odd to see them again, sitting round the table presided over by Mrs. Warden—Holder, John Rudkin, and Susy Wright. How often had she sat with them? Susy had long been the parlor maid. Alice knew that if she patronized them, or alternatively if she were familiar with them, they would despise her—indeed it was touch and go whether or not they would do that anyway—yet she had felt strongly that for her to stay at St. James's Place and not go down to the servants' hall would have been an unconscionable rebuff. Henry always went down to see Mrs. Warden and have a cup of tea with her.

"We are just having a cup of tea, Mrs. Vernon," Mrs. Warden said, addressing her with meticulous propriety as the wife of the elder son. Mary would be "Mrs. James." "Will you join us?"

"I'd like that very much, Mrs. Warden."

"Susy, go and bring the tea and look sharp about it."

Susy hurried off. Alice glanced round at their faces.

"Doesn't Mrs. James have a lady's maid?" she asked, surprised to see only the old familiar faces.

"Yes, but it's her afternoon off. There's a new kitchen maid, too, but she's sick."

There was a sudden pause as they all recollected some-one's afternoon off, years ago, and Alice smiled.

"Nothing seems to have changed here, but you must miss her ladyship."

"We do," Holder said, nodding gravely, "very much. Things haven't been the same."

"That they haven't," Mrs. Warden agreed. "Where are you living now, Mrs. Vernon?"

"In the country, Mrs. Warden, near Reading. We have a house called Mereford, about four miles out of the town. It is very quiet there."

"We met your son, Master Edward. Master John brought him down. They were after jam tarts, the little rascals."

"I know, Edward told me."

"Do you have any servants at Mereford?" Mrs. Warden asked cautiously and they all waited for the answer.

"Yes, a few. A cook general, a housemaid, and a gardener. That's all."

"Fancy that," Mrs. Warden exclaimed, startled out of

her composure. Alice with her own servants! If that didn't beat all. Master Edward had mentioned the cook, but she hadn't really believed it.

"Ah, here's the tea," Holder announced, glad of the distraction. Mrs. Warden poured and then cut some of her best fruitcake and offered it to Alice first. She stayed for as long as it took to drink two cups of tea and eat two slices of cake, and then she left them. By a miracle her instinct had not betrayed her. She had hit it just right.

"Well," Mrs. Warden said to Holder when Alice had gone. "Imagine. I thought she'd give herself airs and graces, coming back here where she used to work. Fancy her with servants of her own."

"I always said Alice was a most superior person," Holder replied.

"You said she was above herself," John Rudkin interrupted.

"Your tongue will get you into trouble one day, young man," Holder said peevishly. "I'm sure I said no such thing."

"I wonder why she come down here to see us like that," Radkin mused.

"Came down," Holder corrected automatically. "Because she is a lady, that's why. If she hadn't come down it would have been as though we weren't good enough for her any longer, so she came down, as nice and natural as you could wish. She looks well, doesn't she, Mrs. Warden?"

"What I don't understand," Rudkin said insistently, now over thirty and no longer so easily put down by his elders, "is how things turned out. You're always saying that people have to remember their place, and you're always on at Susy about not getting ideas above her station, but I remember when you first told us about Alice going off with Captain Henry. First of all you said she'd run away, then when Captain Henry never came no more, you said she'd run off with him, and you didn't half call them names, saying how wrong it all was. It seems to me she's done all right for herself."

"You're thirty years old and you still haven't got any sense," Holder growled. Mrs. Warden nodded and tutted her agreement. "Just because Alice was lucky doesn't mean that everyone else will be lucky. You stick to your own class, my lad."

"I bet she's glad she didn't," Rudkin said cheekily.

"That's enough of that," Holder said flatly, putting a stop to that particular flirtation with heresy.

Alice knew nothing of this conversation. She simply knew that she had surmounted the hurdle of revisiting St. James's Place. If ever she returned she would have no trouble with the servants. She and Henry talked quite a lot about James and Mary, for it was so obvious that everything was wrong with their marriage, but it was all guesswork and soon they dismissed London from their minds. There were too many things to occupy them at Mereford.

That summer they spent a month at a little place called Charlestown, on the edge of St. Austell Bay in Cornwall. It was one of the most carefree months of Henry's life. He forgot his business interests, forgot everything except the fun of living. They rowed and sailed and went for walks, ate mountains of good food, and read a lot. Edward developed an affection for crabs. He would search for them among the rocks and catch them and spend hours playing with them, probably much to the mystification of the crabs. He never killed one and he always freed them afterward, taking them back to their rocky pools. It was a month of warm sunshine, fresh sea breezes, and relaxation, and they grew quite tanned.

Henry made inquiries about a cottage, and they looked at several, but they did not buy one that year. They decided to leave it, and so it was never bought, but they could not see into the future, and it seemed to them that there was all the time in the world.

That summer Edward and Henry grew closer than ever before, and Edward was able to raise a matter which had been troubling him.

"Do you remember Cousin John, Father?"

"I certainly do," Henry laughed.

"When we first went to London he was nice to me, and then he stopped speaking to me."

"I noticed that," Henry answered patiently. They were sitting together on a cliff top, just the two of them, watching the waves on the shore beneath.

"I asked if something was wrong and he said you were a bad soldier and he didn't want to talk to me."

"Oh, did he?" Henry sighed. James had been doing his good works again.

"What did he mean, Father?"

Henry frowned and made up his mind. "I'll tell you, as much as you'll understand anyway. Your great-grandfather was a lord mayor of London and a Member of Parliament; your grandfather, as you know, is a general and a knight and a friend of the Queen."

"Yes." Edward nodded.

"So they're really rather grand people."

"I suppose so." Edward had never had this point of view put to him before.

"Your Uncle James and I were born at St. James's Place, where Grandfather lives now. It's a very grand house with lots of servants."

"Yes." Edward nodded again, still puzzled.

"Well, James and I went into your grandfather's regiment, the 1st Lancers. It's a terribly good regiment and you can't be an officer in it unless they want you and you have lots of money."

Edward understood this.

"Well, there was a maid who worked in the house, my mother's parlor maid. She was awfully nice, Edward. I fell in love with her, and of course everyone said it was wrong because she was a servant."

"Oh." Edward's face lit up as he began to comprehend. "Did they throw you out of the Lancers?"

"I resigned."

"That's silly! I say, does Mummy know?" he asked, giggling.

"It *is* Mummy," Henry answered slowly and deliberately.

There was a little silence. "Mummy was your maid?"

"My mother's maid, yes."

"You married her?"

"Of course," Henry chuckled.

"Then what's all the fuss about? Why did John say you were a bad soldier?"

"I don't know how to tell you, but I must try. Some people would say I was. Most people would have sent your mummy away after they were found out and hushed up everything, pretended nothing had happened. That's more or less what they wanted me to do. They said it was for the sake of the family and the honor of the regiment, and that we couldn't risk a scandal."

Edward frowned. "That's stupid."

"That's exactly what I thought, so I left home, resigned from the regiment and married Mummy . . . and here we are."

"Well, if that's all, I wish I'd punched John's silly head for calling you a bad soldier when everyone knows you're a captain."

"Listen, Edward, I hope it never happens to you, but one day you may have to decide between two things, and whatever you do people are going to say you're wrong. I believed the proper thing was to stand by the girl I loved,

so I had to go away from my home and all my friends.
Your Uncle James thinks I did a wrong thing."

"He's potty," Edward said with the wisdom of youth.

"He wouldn't agree, I'm afraid. He'd say you're a very
cheeky young fellow, which I may say you are. I've told
you all this because if ever you have to choose, choose the
right thing, *whatever* happens, then you'll be happy."

"Are you happy, Father?"

"Very happy. The happiest man in the world."

"I'm glad you left the Lancers and married Mummy,
otherwise I'd never have been born."

Henry ruffled his son's thick wavy hair.

"That's enough talking. I just wanted you to know what
happened."

"Can I ask you one thing?"

"Certainly."

"Did Grandfather approve?"

"Not at all. He was furious, but we're friends again
now. It was a bit difficult for him you know."

"Why?"

"Because he's a friend of the Queen. I mean, suppose
he's having dinner with the Queen at Windsor Castle one
evening, and Her Majesty says, 'Sir Godfrey, how's that
son of yours, Henry, who's a captain in the 1st Lancers?'
And poor Grandfather has to say, 'Oh, he left the army
because he ran away with the parlor maid.' Queen Victoria
wouldn't have thought that that was at all funny."

"Golly, no." Edward said, grinning. "*Did* she ask him?"

"Yes, I think so."

"What did he say?"

"That I'd gone off to South America to make my fortune. That was the official story."

"You mean Grandfather told the Queen a lie?" Edward
demanded, astonished.

Henry wished he had not embarked on this particular
piece of man-to-man education of his son.

"Sometimes—just sometimes, mark you—it's better than the truth. You see, Edward, she'd never have asked him back to dinner if she'd known the truth."

"Wouldn't she? Honestly?"

"No, definitely not."

Edward sat with knitted brows for several seconds.

"Silly old woman," he said at last. "Come on, Father. Let's go and catch some crabs before lunch."

Gratefully Henry followed his son down the winding path on to the beach below.

Chapter 8

THE last interesting event in 1898 was a surprise visit from Mary. She arrived at Mereford unannounced one morning in December while Henry was in his office in Reading. Alice, who had been in the morning room and had not heard the carriage arrive, hurried out into the hall to greet her visitor.

"Hullo, Alice. I hope it's all right my coming like this."

"Yes of course it is. Will you be staying?"

"I want to go back to London later this afternoon. Papa will be at home, and he likes me to be there." She too called the general "Papa."

Alice told the maid to bring them some tea and a few moments later they were sitting in her drawing room.

"I'm afraid Henry is out and he won't return till about five."

"It doesn't matter. I came to see you, not Henry."

Alice said nothing but was surprised.

"I felt we didn't really get to know each other when you came up for the funeral and I've been wanting to know you, really. So I came here to see you. James has no idea of course. He'd be furious."

"I wondered. Why risk it, Mary?"

"I don't do what James tells me." She stopped and smiled. "You and I are in the same boat, Alice. We've married into the Vernon family. I rather think you had the better of it, but I don't want to talk about James except to say that I don't share his opinions about this household."

"I didn't think you did."

The tea was brought in and the conversation was interrupted.

"Tell me why you came," Alice said when they were alone again.

"Curiosity. I've heard Papa talk about Mereford and I wanted to see it for myself."

"Then you should have come in summer when it is at its best."

"Perhaps, but I didn't want to wait. Are you happy here, Alice?"

"Tremendously."

"That's what Papa said. I think I'm a little bit jealous. Life at St. James's Place has a curious dual quality. It's such a splendid house and I love Sir Godfrey so much, but the rest of it is . . . well, not very nice."

There was a good deal of restraint about their conversation in the beginning. Alice knew that Mary and James did not get on well together and suspected what the cause of this might be, but she knew very little else. When she showed Mary round Mereford, however, the awkwardness vanished as they talked about the house. Mary was profoundly impressed.

"I know it isn't a very big house," she said as they came downstairs after an inspection of the bedrooms and Edward's playroom, "but it's a gem. I thought Papa was exaggerating. I do wish I could see the grounds in the summer."

"Then you must come back. Let me show you the library. The library and the drawing room are really the two rooms we use most, though I spend a good deal of time in the morning room during the day. The library is terribly masculine of course—leather and old prints, steel fender and things like that. Henry calls it his private club. We use it mostly at weekends when he is at home."

They toured the ground floor and arrived back in the drawing room.

"Would you like a drink before lunch?" Alice asked. "There's some sherry which Henry says is very good."

"Yes, please, I'd like a sherry."

"Perhaps I'll have one too, as it's a special occasion," Alice smiled.

She poured two small sherries and they sat together by the blazing fire.

"I've been wanting to ask you something," Alice said, sipping the sherry. "I wonder if I dare?"

"Please do."

"Do you have second sight or something?"

Mary laughed. "No. I get strange feelings about things, about people, and often I'm right, but I have no crystal ball. Why do you ask? About Henry?"

"Yes. It was Papa who told me that you'd made some sort of startling prediction about him."

"It wasn't a prediction really, it's just a feeling I have about Henry. I had it the first time I met him. Of course you must remember, Alice, that I was intensely curious about Henry and you, and thought about you a lot. That made a difference."

"Why should you think about us?"

"Isn't it obvious? I met the gallant Captain James who swept me off my feet, and he told me that he had a brother whose name was strictly not mentioned. After quite a long time I found out that the brother's name was Henry and that he had committed the unforgivable sin of running away with his mother's parlor maid. He'd had to resign from the regiment, which was pure heresy of course, re-sign from his clubs, and nobody had heard of either of them since. I lived with that situation for a long time. It was only when James's mother died that I met Henry, and you can imagine what an experience that was. Anyway, I had a very strong feeling that there was something about him, though I can't put it into words. He was the outcast, yet I felt—and still do feel—that somehow in the end he's going to win. I don't mean soon, and I don't know how he will do it. I may be dead when it happens. There's a strange feeling that when Henry left home he wasn't the one who suffered, but the family that suffered as a result. Something has been taken away from the Vernon family in London, and they won't recover from the loss."

She laughed self-consciously.

"But Henry and Papa are quite reconciled now, even if James is still awkward," Alice answered.

"I know. I told you I can't explain it. There's something else, quite separate. Henry is going to do something that will surprise everybody."

"I think that's what you told Papa, and he told me. Henry isn't ambitious, you know."

"Then I'm wrong. I'm only talking about feelings, Alice. I wish we hadn't got onto this subject, because I'm often wrong anyway. Papa thinks of me sometimes as if I were a gypsy at a fairground, telling fortunes. It isn't like that."

"It must be very uncomfortable."

So far as Alice was concerned one didn't need to have "feelings" to know that, when they had cast Henry out, the family at St. James's Place had lost considerably. She had grown to admire and even to love Henry's father, but Sir Godfrey and Lady Vernon had sent Henry away and the loss was theirs alone. He *had* won. His brother James was an ill-natured popinjay prancing about in Lancer uniform. He wasn't a real soldier like the general. James would never be a general and dine at Windsor with the Queen. James would be lucky if he were promoted beyond major. Henry's name, on the other hand, was known throughout the length and breadth of Berkshire, and although they didn't go out much in society, no more than they could help, he had floated naturally to the top so that it was nothing out of the ordinary for Lord Thatcham to drop in to see them or to invite them to his enormous stately home on the outskirts of Newbury. Alice doubted if James knew many people outside the closed circle of the Lancers.

She was glad Mary had come, and sorry that she could not wait for Henry's return, but at four o'clock Mary insisted she must go back. She had said very little about James and John, and Alice suspected that she was wretchedly unhappy. It was a great pity.

One evening Henry sat with Colonel Lavering in his office after a parade at the drill hall.

"I don't like the look of things in South Africa," Lavering remarked, lighting a cigar. "Things haven't been the same since the Jameson raid in '96."

Around the new year in 1896, Leander Starr Jameson, a friend of Cecil Rhodes, had led a raid from Mafeking into the Transvaal in support of the rights of the "Uitlanders." It was a complicated story. The discovery of diamonds in Cape Colony and gold in the Transvaal lay behind the troubles. The Boers, who were Dutch farmers and settlers and who had no interest in the mineral wealth around them, did not get along well with the mining prospectors who had flooded into South Africa. It was these mining settlers, temporary settlers as they were regarded, who were the "Uitlanders" and they had been denied citizenship rights.

Jameson had been forced to surrender and had been handed over to the British for punishment. He had been imprisoned for fifteen months but released early because of ill health, and had returned to South Africa. The ill feeling continued and tension was increasing. The Boers were more and more resentful of Rhodes and his undisguised imperialist ambitions. Henry, who took little interest in such matters, was surprised by the concern on Lavering's face.

"It's a local squabble, surely?" he said.

"I'm not so certain. It could turn into a war."

Henry considered that. Business was booming quite literally, and already he was feeling a little cramped for space in Vernon's Universal Stores. He did not think a war would affect trade much.

"Do you really think so?" he asked idly.

"Yes, which means there's always the chance they'll mobilize us. I think we ought to step up the training, Henry."

"Surely they'd never mobilize us?" Henry scoffed. "We're rank amateurs."

"Maybe, but that's what we're for, to be used immediately there's trouble, to reinforce the regular army. Anyway I'm not convinced that we deserve your scorn. The men are keen and at least they can shoot."

"That's true. Do you know, I'd never thought of active service."

"If it does come, you'll be invaluable to me. I hope you won't back out."

"Back out?"

"You've got a wife and a young son, and very important business interests—I don't think anyone would expect you to abandon them all to go chasing after Dutch farmers."

"Perhaps not, but I didn't join the battalion just to run away the first time I could do something useful. If they mobilize us, I'll be there with the rest of you."

"I'm glad about that, Henry. To me you're worth the rest of the officers put together."

"I honestly can't think why you say that, Colonel." Usually he addressed Lavering by his Christian name, off parade, but for once he felt awkward.

"I'm referring to your past service in the army."

Henry stroked his chin. "You know then?"

"I always have. I found out when I put your name forward for the vacant captaincy. A friend of mine in the War Office recognized your name and told me you'd been in the 1st Lancers. You can imagine how delighted I was about that. Apart from myself, you're the only officer who has done any soldiering at all."

"Peacetime," Henry said shortly. "It doesn't count for much, and I was twenty-five when I sent in my papers. That's a long time ago."

"The Lancers' loss is my gain," Colonel Lavering smiled. "A bit of a change for you though, from a crack cavalry regiment to a Volunteer infantry battalion. I've often wondered what you thought of us."

"I'm happy enough here. There's the makings of a very good battalion in us, if ever it does come to war. I've long since got over the prevailing feeling in cavalry messes that they alone lend tone to the British Army." He chuckled. "You know, I almost said something to you about having been a regular and then I changed my mind. It was too much like showing off, and in any case cavalry experience isn't as pertinent to the light infantry as the ignorant might think."

"No, but you're a trained, disciplined officer and a natural leader. I hope you didn't mind my mentioning the Lancers."

"Good God no, of course not." Henry laughed again. "I'm only grateful to you for not telling other people."

Henry did not venture any reason for his resignation and Lavering would never have dreamed of asking. He knew from his War Office informant that Henry had resigned of his own volition, not because he had been asked to do so, and that was sufficient for him.

They parted and a more thoughtful Henry went home. From then on he began to read the papers with greater attention to the news from South Africa, and it came as no surprise that on October 10, 1899, the Boer War began.

Like others, Henry expected the British to decimate the Dutch farmers. What, after all, could they know about war? But the Dutch farmers in South Africa were unlike their British counterparts who led smug, prosperous, well-fed lives. The war began with a series of shattering defeats which shook British confidence. On November 2, Ladysmith was besieged by the Boers and bottled up. Worse was to follow. Sir Redvers Buller was overwhelmingly defeated by the despised Boers at the battle of Colenso on December 15 and again at Spion Kop. There was panic, and units in England were mobilized and sent posthaste to South Africa to prop up the crumbling army there.

The mobilization of the 3rd (Volunteer) Battalion of the Berkshire Light Infantry took time. The 1st Battalion sailed during October of 1899, but it was not till the spring of 1900 that the 3rd was ready to go. By this time the news was a little more heartening. Kimberley was relieved on February 15 and Ladysmith on the twenty-eighth, but Mafeking—whose garrison was commanded by an obscure soldier called Baden-Powell, a name eventually to become a household word throughout the world in an entirely different connection as the founder of the Boy Scout movement —had been under siege since October 12 and had not been relieved. The war was now a matter of grave concern.

To most of the English the war in South Africa was a bit of a joke. Those crafty old Dutch farmers were making a fool of the British Army and it was necessary to send more troops out from Britain. Only a minority of Englishmen realized that the British Army was totally unsuited for the guerrilla type of warfare in which it was engaged. They were accustomed to great battles, not small, bloody engagements. Henry was among those who realized that going to South Africa was no joke, but he made light of it to Alice and to Edward, now ten years old.

Alice took to going into the office with him, for it was to her rather than to his senior manager that he entrusted the affairs of Vernon's Universal Stores and its two smaller offshoots.

One evening at the end of March they sat together after dinner, while young Edward got ready to go to bed. He dined with them now, very much one of the family. Henry poured himself a brandy and soda.

"If I'm away for any length of time, Alice," he said quietly, "go ahead and try to buy the shop in London Road as a going concern. I want a shoe shop. One day we must have a bigger store and get everything into it under one roof. The more shopping people can do in one place, the better, so get that shoe shop for me. You've got full power of attorney and I don't really care what you pay for it. It wouldn't hurt us to lose a little money for a year or so. We need gingering up," he added with a grin.

"Will you be away for long? Do you have to go, Henry?"

"That's two questions, my sweet. I think it might take a year to knock the spirit out of those wretched Boers."

"A *year!*"

"You must ignore those stories about the war ending any month now. I'm afraid this war will go on at least another year, and probably more. As for your other question," he said, "the answer is yes. I could choose not to go. There are younger men—though I'm only thirty-seven, remember—and I've got big responsibilities here, including you and Edward. I don't think people would pour scorn on me if I let the battalion go without me, but what would you think? And Papa? And Edward? What would Lord Thatcham and Colonel Lavering think? What would Robert Turner leave unsaid? I don't think I could stand his silence or my father's. But most important, what would I think of myself? You see, my dear, when I joined the Volunteers I committed myself wholly. I didn't have to join."

"You didn't join to fight," she said stubbornly. "You did it because you like the army and because it would be good for business."

He laughed and shook his head. "You have an uncomfortable tongue, darling. I agree that I wasn't thinking of wars when I joined the 3rd Berkshire Light Infantry, but I'm not a fool. I did know that soldiers had to do with wars, and that if ever there was a war I'd be asked to go and fight. Anyway, you don't want to worry too much; there will be no more Colensos and I may never see action. I'm quite likely to be stuck in a base camp for months. With all due respect to our men, we're hardly the cream of the British Army."

"I wish you weren't going."

"So do I. Who wants to spend a year in South Africa, especially when things might be quite interesting in Reading? You're going to have all the fun of branching out into shoes while I spend hours drilling in the heat."

She was far from satisfied, although he made light of things. War meant danger. When Henry had resigned from the 1st Lancers he had become a civilian, and it was ridiculous to expect him, twelve years later, to go off to battle as though he were still a soldier.

To Edward it was all an enormous adventure, and he was thrilled when Henry took him aside one day shortly before he sailed.

"Now look here, young man, I expect I'll be off in a fortnight. That means you're going to have to take my place. Do you understand?"

"Yes, Father."

"You're to look after your mother, behave properly, be

a man instead of a little boy. You may think it isn't so much fun, but in fact it can be more fun. You'll be the head of the household."

"Golly," Edward breathed, impressed by this argument.

"Yes, golly." Henry smiled. "That makes you think, eh? Now I may be gone for a whole year. I think the war will last that long. Maybe longer. Work hard at your studies, do as your mother asks, and look after my roses for me. Your mother loves roses, and that's why when we first got a garden I wanted to grow them. Now it's my hobby. You can give Maggett a hand in the garden sometimes. I want to hear good reports of you when I come back. You're a lucky young man."

"Why am I lucky, Father?"

"Because you're having a year's holiday from your father, that's why."

"But I don't *want* a holiday from you. Will you really be gone for a long time?"

"I'm afraid so, Edward. It isn't a matter of what we want."

"Can't you beat the beastly Boers quicker than that?"

Henry concealed a smile. He had a lot of sympathy for the Boers, which was very unfashionable of him, and he rather admired the way they were playing havoc with properly trained regular troops. It made quite a nonsense of all the peacetime army training. Even so, he would like to beat them as quickly as possible and come home. He had no heart for this war.

"I'll do my best, but it depends on others. I can't win the war single-handed."

"It would be fun if you could. I could go around saying 'My father won the war.'"

"I hope you wouldn't do anything so silly. You'd get your head punched by your friends for swanking. Anyway, I shan't, so let's drop that subject. Don't get any wrong ideas, Edward. I shall tramp about in the dust and heat doing drill till my boots wear through, and probably that's all."

This last remark puzzled and disappointed Edward. Then his face cleared. His father was being modest, of course. One didn't talk about heroics. Now that he was almost ten, he understood.

"Yes, of course," he agreed, almost patronizingly. "I do wish you could come home for Christmas, though."

"So do I. It will be strange spending Christmas in the heat and sunshine."

"I wonder if they have Christmas trees in Africa," Edward wondered aloud, and they were diverted into talking about other things.

The 3rd left Reading on Tuesday, May 29, 1900, watched by crowds in Reading's streets waving Union Jacks and cheering. When the battalion had gone, Alice and Edward drove back to Mereford in the carriage. People recognized them, and men raised their hats politely. Alice's chin went up a little. She mustn't show her feelings in public. When they arrived back at Mereford, they were surprised to see Sir Godfrey walking in the garden.

"Papa," Alice greeted him, "how did you get here and when?"

"I came up by cab. I was at the station watching them go. I knew the battalion was leaving today and I thought I'd come along."

"Then why didn't you come earlier, come here first?"

"I didn't want to intrude, Alice. I just wanted to watch."

"Henry will be so disappointed when he hears that you were here and he didn't see you."

"I said my good-byes to Henry in Town last week, as you know. I just wanted to be on hand when they left."

Edward interrupted them buoyantly, asking if his grandfather hadn't thought that his father was smart in his uniform, and telling him that he, Edward, was now the man of the house. They had to wait till Edward had finally gone off to play, for today was a day away from his tutor, before they could talk in private.

Sir Godfrey accepted a whiskey.

"How is James?" Alice asked.

"Much better." Sir Godfrey scowled.

The 1st Lancers had sailed for South Africa at the outbreak of the war, but one of their majors had not accompanied them. He had developed some mysterious trouble with his back which kept him at home, unable to sit a horse at all, far less sit one properly.

General Vernon regarded this back complaint, which in truth was a very genuine and painful one, with great distrust which turned to anger when the 1st went into action on the last day of March at an outlandish place called Korn Spruit. Here the Boers had ambushed a small column consisting of two batteries of the Horse Artillery, some cavalry—1st Lancers, 10th Hussars and some miserable mounted infantry, together with Roberts's Horse and Rimington's Guides. The guns had been saved, casualties had been ridiculously high, and the Lancers had received their first decorations, although they did not get any of the V.C.s which were awarded for the action. While all this was going on, the handsome Major Vernon was hobbling about the house like an old man, complaining that his back hurt.

James was sullen, Mary quietly contemptuous, and the general irritable.

"I think he'll be going out to South Africa next month," Sir Godfrey said. "I hope so."

Alice said nothing. She could imagine the situation quite well without words.

"Anything I can do for you?" the general asked her.

"No, thank you. Henry left everything in splendid order. I'll be looking after the firm till he returns."

"Yes, he told me. Sensible arrangement. I wish I were out there with them, you know, but I'm much too old—

too many years of being a staff officer. War's a young
man's business. Who'd have thought a lot of foreign farmers would give us so much trouble? There are going to be a
lot of awkward questions asked after this war."

"How is the Queen?"

"Old. Old and tired. She was eighty-one five days ago,
on the twenty-fourth. She can't go on for much longer."

"You'll miss her when she dies, won't you?" Alice
asked.

"Yes, I shall. I've been an A.D.C. since 1877, and that's
a long time I can tell you. I can't think why she keeps
me."

"Because she's a very sensible old woman." Alice smiled
and kissed his cheek. "She knows when she's on to a good
thing."

"What rubbish you talk," he said, obviously pleased.
He liked Alice. She always understood things, as Mary
did. His sons had married well, and that was a blessing.

And one of them was fighting for queen and country, as
the son of a general should do.

Chapter 9

WHEN Henry's letters began to arrive from South Africa, they bore out his predictions. The 3rd B.L.I. were in a base camp where they did little except drill and rifle practice. He did not like South Africa at all and was bored to tears. He filled most of his pages with requests for news about his stores. Only when writing to Edward did he manage to find amusing incidents of camp life to write about—and Alice suspected that he exaggerated them greatly to make them entertaining. She could sense the futility of the life he was leading.

In June, James finally sailed for South Africa, but not to join the regiment. He was being sent to a staff billet and General Sir Godfrey Vernon was livid but powerless to change the orders. He need not have troubled himself unduly. It would have done James no good at all sending him to the regiment. By the time he landed he had developed dysentery, and in October they shipped him back home again, unfit for active service. He was found a job in the War Office and promoted to lieutenant colonel. Sir Godfrey, who had never heard of a cavalry officer being promoted for having dysentery, preserved a chilly silence on the subject of James. The major of Lancers had failed, and it was left to the civilian-soldier son to represent the family in the war.

Alice was busy that summer, negotiating for the purchase of the shoe shop in London Road which Henry wanted to acquire. Robert Turner questioned her about it one evening when she was visiting him and his wife at their home near Erlegh Park.

"It's all part of The Plan, capital T, capital P, Robert," she explained. "The present store isn't big enough."

"I heard Henry say that but I didn't believe it. It's probably the most successful business in Reading."

"At the moment, yes, but now that we've begun to stock children's toys it's cramped, especially at Christmas. One day we'll have a much bigger store. The tobacconist shop will be absorbed into it as a department, and there will be a furniture department, and a shoe department. That's why we're buying the shoe shop, to learn about shoes."

"I suppose you know what you're up to, but what will you do with all these little shops you're picking up? Sell them?"

"Henry doesn't like selling. He says that if you have a decent shop on a decent site it is better to use it to make money than to sell it. We'll find something to do with them. Reading is expanding all the time."

"You're as much of a businessman as Henry," he said.

In her own way she was. It was Henry who had always provided the purpose, the sense of direction, but she understood almost intuitively what he was trying to do, and she had been far more of a partner than the normal woman of her time would have been.

Life at Mereford had settled down to a strange existence. Every morning Edward was driven to Riseley, where the Reverend Mark Luke continued to instill into his handful of pupils what was considered at the time to be an excellent education. Alice set off for Reading at nine each morning, and spent the entire morning at Henry's desk. Reading had at first been astonished and then amused. Mrs. Henry Vernon was playing at shops while the captain was away at the war. It was something of a joke until one tried to do business with Vernon's, then it was discovered that Mrs. Henry Vernon was a very tough character indeed. She spoke, thought, and acted as a man would have done. If she did not take advantage of her sex during negotiations and discussions, neither did she display any of its weaknesses. Word went round that Mrs. Henry Vernon was as tough as any man to deal with.

At noon she drove back to Mereford where she lunched at home. She never had any desire to dine anywhere else, quite apart from the fact that it really would have caused a scandal for a lady to lunch alone at a hotel day after day. She treasured the two hours she gave herself at Mereford, and she loved that moment when she turned off the road into the gateway and saw the house between the trees.

In the middle of the afternoon she returned to the office and at five o'clock she finished for the day. She drove home and spent the early evening with Edward, reading, playing games, gardening, whatever took their fancy. After dinner Edward went to bed and Alice would write to Henry. She wrote long letters, adding a bit every evening. At the end of each week she posted what she had written. She never went to bed without having written something.

She missed him desperately. After twelve years one tended to take things for granted, but now that they were separated she realized how much her happiness was dependent on his presence. She even missed him—and she blushed at the mere idea—physically. Yet, as she wrote to him evening after evening, and lay awake in bed afterward thinking of him, gradually she became aware of something strange—she was becoming accustomed to missing him. Sometimes when she thought of his return and allowed herself to imagine being in bed with him again, she felt unaccountably girlish and shy, just thinking about it. She hoped the war would not go on for too long. It would be terrible if he came back as a stranger.

But the war did drag on, a series of furious skirmishes and ambushes, and strange names appeared in the stately columns of the *Times*, names like Krugersdorp, Wolve Spruit—whatever a Spruit was—Mosilikatse Nek, Essenbosch Farm and Van Wyk's Vlei.

Alice and Edward did not go to Cornwall that year. Indeed they did not go away at all. Alice was far too busy, and Edward now began to take an interest in the stores. During his summer holidays he would go to Reading with his mother, and while she was busy in her upstairs office, he would help below. The staff got to like him, for he was a cheerful, pleasant boy. He began in the packing and unpacking department, helping to open up packages of goods as they arrived. Gradually, working to no plan, just "messing about" as he himself put it, he did other jobs— helping to price the goods and carrying them from the stores to the shop floor. His ambition was to serve behind a counter but he was too small, quite apart from being inexperienced. At first people suspected he was "playing" at helping, but soon he showed that he was serious. He would happily put in a full day's work, for which he received nothing other than the one penny pocket money he received every day anyway.

Alice was a little worried in the beginning that he might become a nuisance to people trying to get on with their jobs, but she need have had no fears. Nobody ever complained about Edward. If anyone had asked the boy—and nobody ever did, not even his mother—just why he loved working at the Universal Stores, he might just possibly have said because he felt that in some mysterious way he was helping his father. Then again he might not, because ten-year-old boys do not normally try to analyze their motives, especially in doing things which they enjoy.

The general came to see them again early in October, arriving on a Saturday morning. Alice allowed herself two days a week away from the office, Saturdays and Sundays, and was working in the garden. Edward was at a friend's house. She was cheered by the sight of the familiar tall figure, dressed as usual in a black frock coat and narrow checked trousers, with a gleaming stiff upright collar, gray top hat, gray gloves, and a silver-topped cane. She put down her trowel and walked over to meet him. They kissed.

"You're looking radiant, Alice. I thought you'd be tired."

"Work seems to agree with me, Papa, but in any case I spend the weekends in the garden. I get plenty of sunshine."

"Let's sit here on this bench for a moment," Sir Godfrey suggested. "It's a mild morning. I love the autumn tints on the trees, don't you?"

"Yes, you must come and have a look at the trees at the back in our little park. They are a positive blaze of autumn colors. What's the news from London?"

"Nothing much. Mary rolls bandages twice a week, and spoils me shamelessly. James is coming back, of course."

"Yes, you wrote."

"He should be here in a fortnight, perhaps less. A fine sort of soldier he turned out to be."

"He couldn't help it, though," Alice said gently.

"Perhaps not. I never had dysentery, but I remember there was a lot of it in the Crimea. Dreadful thing. It's a damned shame, Alice. All those years in the army and he's done nothing to justify himself. Mary used to call him the toy soldier, but please don't tell anyone you know. It infuriates James, naturally."

"John will be glad his father is coming back."

"Yes, and he's about the only one," the general said bluntly. "That boy dotes on his father."

"Perhaps James will be as brilliant a staff officer as you were."

"Not at all likely. He's got no tact, none whatever, and you need it on the staff. No, he'll never get anywhere. I'd always hoped one of them would become a field marshal. That was my burning ambition, you know."

"I didn't know."

"Oh yes, I wanted to be a field marshal. I don't suppose there will ever be a Field Marshal Vernon in the British Army."

"I shouldn't think so," Alice agreed, "unless it'll be John."

"I shan't live to see that. It's funny, isn't it?" Sir Godfrey mused. "You have your own private plans and dreams, and they never quite come off, so you transfer them to your children, and bless me, they turn out entirely differently. Do you know, now that Adeline's gone I'm afraid I'm going to turn into a crusty old bore one day, and everybody will avoid me."

"I don't think you need worry."

"You're kind to say so. What news of Henry? I haven't heard for a month."

"They're still in camp, but he says he is being attached to a Scottish regiment to gain experience. It's called the Highland Light Infantry."

"Is that a fact? Then he may see some action."

"I hope not," Alice said vehemently.

"What's that? Oh, I see. No, of course not. Who was talking about tact a few minutes ago? You mustn't pay attention to me, Alice. Still, it's a strange sort of war they're fighting out there, not like any other I ever heard of. There don't seem to be any rules."

He stayed for the weekend and was pleased when Rob-

ert Turner arrived on the Sunday after lunch, bringing his
wife and son with him. He had met Turner twice before
and had heard all about him from Henry, and he liked the
newspaper editor. Soon they were alone together in the
library, talking about the state of the nation. The talk
turned to the war, of course, as all male conversations did
in those days.

"How do you think it's going, Turner?" the general
asked.

"I don't know, Sir Godfrey, I really don't know. I suppose in the end we must win—at least they'll call it a
victory. I don't see how the Boers can resist forever and
we're much too proud to withdraw without appearing to
triumph over them. However, it may take quite a long
time yet. I'd give it another year at the very least."

"That's much as I see it myself. It's a wretched business."

"It's a futile one anyway," the editor replied.

"Futile in what way?"

"Because," Turner explained, "it makes no difference
what happens. The whole thing has been an enormous
waste of time and money, and a criminal waste of lives."

"Hey?" Sir Godfrey blinked and shifted in his seat. This
sounded like dangerous radical talk.

"When all this is over," Turner explained patiently,
"nothing is going to be very different. The war won't
achieve anything important for either side. It's just a
meaningless waste."

"Did you expect us to knuckle under to a rabble of
Dutch farmers then?" Sir Godfrey demanded a little heatedly.

"No, of course not. As matters stood we had no real
choice but to go to war. I'm not arguing about that, I'm
merely commenting on the futility of it all. You say we
had to go to war, and I understand that point of view.
Very well then, that means we're fighting because we had

to. *I'd* far rather fight to *achieve* something, and that's exactly what we shan't do."

"The Transvaal belongs to Britain," Sir Godfrey said stubbornly, "and this Orange Free State."

"I expect we'll get them, but for how long? How long can we hold them under if the Dutch farmers don't want it? Look here, General, you're a soldier and I'm a journalist. Neither of us is a politician, but it seems obvious to me that we are going to have to learn to get along with the Boers. We can't throw them out of South Africa. This is a damned funny way of making friends with them. I'm glad I'm not being asked to give my life out there. I'm not convinced it would be a useful gesture."

He had said the right thing in aligning them against the politicians. Sir Godfrey had the army officer's automatic distrust of politics and the men who deal in them. His job was to fight wars, not make them.

"When you put it that way, it does seem senseless," he agreed, "but as matters stand we must see it through."

Turner nodded. "I'm afraid so. I'll be glad when it's over and Henry comes home and we can forget about war and the talk of war."

"So shall I," Sir Godfrey agreed. "So shall I. Believe me."

Henry in South Africa had no time to philosophize about the roots of war, either in general or this war in particular. His military duties, deadly boring and calling for a minimum of intelligence, kept him busy by day, and the heat ensured that he was tired at night. The one thing that had made it all bearable was the thought of returning to Mereford, to Alice and Edward, and of taking up the reins of his business again. Most of all he wanted to walk in the grounds of Mereford with Alice, in the summer sun, admiring the roses, to see again the sun glinting on the long windows. He had three photographs of the house and he had almost worn them out already. Sometimes he would sit with a photograph of Alice and another of Mereford in front of him while he wrote the letters, which he found increasingly difficult to write.

For a few weeks, a month or two, he could find something to say, but soon the drab sameness of life robbed him of that, and how long could he go on saying "I love you" and "I miss you" without wearying her? How many different ways were there of saying that he longed for her? He was sure he had used them all several times. In fact letter writing was becoming a chore, not because he missed her less, but because he no longer knew how to tell her.

In October there was a welcome change to all this; he was attached to the 2nd Battalion of the Highland Light Infantry. Instead of the monotony of base camp life he found himself marching around the Transvaal from one unpronounceable place to another. This, he discovered to his surprise, was more uncomfortable and just as drab and wearying. One or two skirmishes enlivened matters, but they were unreal affairs. Two men were killed, but there was no noise, no shouting, no heroism.

There was very little to learn that could not be learned from any gamekeeper. There was no strategy in this war of ambushes. Only two things mattered—being able to blend into the background so that you were not seen, and being able to shoot with considerable accuracy.

Alice's letters brightened and lightened his life and he read and reread them. Obviously she was managing splendidly and he was delighted that Edward was behaving so well. The story of James's war amused him highly. He hadn't come across the 1st Lancers, although he knew they were around somewhere. It was ironic that the pompous James had never been with his own regiment. Henry would gladly have changed places with a cavalry officer. Being a light infantry officer was a wearying business, to say the least of it.

On Wednesday, November 7, 1900, two companies of the 2nd Highland Light Infantry were sent with a flying detachment to strengthen a column accompanying some guns. They left early in the morning while it was still cool and made good time, coming up with the column early in the afternoon. Henry was hot and dusty but he felt a wave of pleasure when he recognized the 1st Lancers ahead. They were part of the cavalry escort. They were near a place called Warmbad where, at the beginning of September, there had been a Boer ambush. Henry did not think it likely that lightning would strike twice in the same place. Indeed, so far as he knew, there was no real reason to suppose the Boers knew anything about the small column moving guns.

Suddenly, without warning, they were ambushed as they were crossing a drift quite near Warmbad, at a place unnamed on the map. Intense fire poured in on them. The heaviest fire seemed to be coming from the rear, and the rear guard under Henry's command settled down to fight off the attack.

Men began to fall and Henry had to steady the Highlanders who hated fighting against an enemy they rarely saw, and with whom they ached to get to grips, particularly with the bayonet. The engagement lasted half an hour until the main column was safe, then the cavalry came to the rescue of the rear guard, and drove off the Boer attack.

It had been a bitter half hour. Henry stood, streaked with dirt and perspiration, his pistol in his hand, his tunic torn, and watched as the cavalry charged past. He was just about to count his dead and wounded when, from a small gully to one side, a party of determined Boers opened fire. Four cavalrymen fell to the ground. Three of the horses scattered but one turned and galloped back. Henry caught the reins and halted it. He could see two of the men on the ground squirming under fire. Obviously they were alive, equally obviously they would not survive for long. He threw his leg over the horse and galloped up to them. The first cavalryman, a corporal, was shot through the thigh and in great pain. Henry flung him across the horse, mounted, and galloped back. Twice he returned under heavy fire, and twice more he brought back wounded men. He did not return for the fourth man, for he fell out of the saddle, wounded in the leg and the liver.

Henry Vernon did not die pleasantly. He was in agony and screaming. They hurried him ahead to the main column where, by pure luck, there was an army surgeon. He looked compassionately at the suffering man and wished that he had something to give him, but he had nothing. It was difficult to tell how serious the bullet in the liver was, but the leg would have to come off if Captain Vernon's life was to be saved. The surgeon had exhausted his meager supply of medicines in attending to the other wounded, and so, while hefty men held Henry down, the surgeon sawed off his leg.

Mercifully he lost consciousness, and he never recovered it. He died of his wounds an hour later. The column reached its destination safely, and someone began to make the reports.

The news was brought to Mereford by Sir Godfrey. Those concerned with personnel at the War Office knew very well that Captain Henry Vernon of the 3rd Berkshire Light Infantry was the son of General Vernon, for the general was perpetually asking for news of him. This was why, although he was not the next of kin, he received the news first and arranged to deliver it personally to Henry's widow.

He was packing a bag with some overnight things when James, in uniform, came home.

"I've just heard," he said to his father. "Henry's dead."

"I know. I'm going to Mereford."

"I see." For once James felt he could say nothing, although he disapproved rigidly of his father's visits to Mereford and had almost burst a blood vessel when he had discovered that Mary had been there too. "I wasn't sure. I came to tell you."

"He died fighting some sort of rearguard action—I haven't got all the details yet," Sir Godfrey remarked.

"I . . . er . . . if there's anything I can do you'll let me know?" James asked.

"Yes." Sir Godfrey could think of nothing whatever that James could do, but at least it was a civil, if insincere, offer. "I'll remember."

"You'll be staying overnight?"

"Yes."

He left James to his thoughts and was driven to the station where he caught the first train to Reading. As the cab drove him to Mereford he reflected on the irony of it all and remembered, uncomfortably, Robert Turner's words.

It was raining, a dull day, and growing dark. Moisture dripped from the black, barren branches of trees and there was a nasty chill in the air. The lights of Mereford beckoned through the gloom, among the bare black branches, as the cab clip-clopped along the drive to the big stone-pillared portico. Sir Godfrey paid the man and carried his small bag up the steps and rang the bell. After a few moments the maid answered.

"Sir Godfrey! Oh do come inside, sir. It's terrible weather."

"Yes, Ivy, it is. Is your mistress at home?"

"In the drawing room, Sir Godfrey. This way, sir."

She took his coat and hat, and ushered him into the drawing room, announced him, and withdrew. The general stood in the doorway. Alice, who had been reading with Edward, stood up, tall and erect, her beautiful hair piled high on her head. She looked at her father-in-law inquiringly.

"Come in, Papa. Come over here by the fire."

"Thank you, Alice. How are you, Edward?"

"Fine thanks, sir."

Sir Godfrey stood beside them, tongue-tied. Suddenly Alice knew, and she turned pale.

"It's news?" she asked very quietly.

He nodded. She turned to Edward who had missed the significance of the exchange.

"Leave us alone for a little while, Edward. Your grandfather and I wish to talk."

"Very well, Mother." He had stopped calling her "Mummy" and "Mama" ever since he had known his father was going off to war.

He gave them a bright smile before leaving the room, and Alice buried her face in her hands. Sir Godfrey put an arm round her shaking shoulders.

"It was on the seventh, near a place called Warmbad. They fought off an attack by the Boers and he was wounded and died a little later. That's all I know at present. I'm sorry, Alice."

He stood, his arm round her, while she cried bitterly. Her tears lasted for fully five minutes and then she wiped her swollen eyes and sniffed.

"I'm sorry. I've always dreaded this . . . always. Yet when it comes . . . you're never prepared. Why Henry?" she cried.

He almost heard her unspoken words, "Why not James?"

"There's never any answer to that question," he answered gruffly. "They say it's always the best who go. What will you do now, Alice?"

"What will I do?" She considered briefly, looking into the fire. "What can I do but carry on? There's Edward to think of."

"Will you sell the firm?"

"Never. It belongs to Edward. Henry had plans for it. I'll control it and look after it till Edward can run it himself. Henry did it all for Edward—the house, the shops, everything. He wanted to give his son security."

"I see. Will you need help?"

"What sort of help, Papa? Money? I've plenty of money."

"I was thinking of the business."

"I can run it better than any man."

He looked at her in surprise. It was one thing to keep an eye on things while Henry was away, but to take it on a long-term basis, while Edward grew up, was a most unusual step. Women didn't do that sort of thing. Somehow he did not imagine she cared much one way or the other what women "did."

"Look here," he said suddenly, "we're in the same boat, Alice. We've both lost someone we love. Would you like me to come and stay for a bit? James and Mary can look after St. James's Place. I could just as easily stay here and be company for you and the boy—and you'd be company for me."

She was about to refuse, and then she hesitated. Probably he felt greater need of her than she did of him. It sounded ludicrous, yet it was true. She, Alice Mason, the maid, was his only link with the things he loved. He was completely out of sympathy with James, and not even Mary's presence could make life at St. James's Place a happy affair.

"If you'd like to come I'd be glad," she said, not entirely truthfully. "What about the Court, though?"

"I can travel to Windsor from here quite easily."

"That's right," she agreed. "You can."

"Edward needs a man around the house. If you'll have me, that is."

She did not miss the slightly tragic ring about the last words. *If* she would have him, she thought with wry amusement.

"Of course I want you to stay here, Papa."

She wondered if he would try to interfere with the stores, if he thought, as other men had thought and would continue to think, that it was not a woman's work and that she could not do it properly. Well, time would tell.

"We'll have to tell Edward," she said suddenly, returning to the problem which presented itself most immediately.

"Would you like to leave that to me?" he asked.

She considered. "Perhaps that would be best," she said, nodding. "I might spoil it. You see, to me it is stupid waste."

He had no answer to that.

Chapter 10

BECAUSE of his position Sir Godfrey was able to get very full details of his son's death, and to get them quickly. He discovered that Henry had been recommended for a posthumous award of the Victoria Cross. He decided not to say anything of this to Alice yet, because obviously not all recommendations went through, but the mere fact that his son had been so singled out gave him tremendous pride. An even greater source of pride was that Henry had died not while attacking enemies, but while trying to save the lives of comrades. Bravery is bravery, but there are different ways of being brave, and Sir Godfrey took a special pride in this.

Before all this was known, however, there was a bitter little scene with James. James's first reaction to the news that his father was going to move out to Mereford "indefinitely" was one of relief. After all, St. James's Place would be his one day, and it would be nice for Mary and him to have it to themselves. Then, when he had enjoyed this momentary pleasure, he found time to resent his father's action. He spoke his mind the night before Sir Godfrey left.

"I really don't see why you want to go down to Berkshire, Papa," he grumbled. He had acquired an even more pompous manner since being promoted, and was now almost a caricature of a lieutenant colonel on the staff. "It seems to me that sometimes you forget the circumstances under which Henry left this house."

"No, I don't forget," the general said shortly, "but that was a long time ago. Your brother died fighting for his country. We can be proud of him. John has you, but young Edward has nobody. I think there should be a man about the house, for the boy's sake."

"You're going to stay for a long time, then?"

"I haven't thought about the length of my stay."

"It would have been a lot better if Henry had been with the Lancers. He was with the Highland Light Infantry," he added with an open sneer.

Mary jerked her head in alarm and saw Sir Godfrey go a beetroot red.

"Now you listen to me, James Vernon. You may think you are a hell of a swell, polishing a chair in the War Office with your elegant bottom, but your brother was a man. Everything he had, he got for himself. You got a commission in the 1st because of me; but Henry was a light infantry captain because they wanted him. Henry bought and paid for his own house. Henry created his own business. The name Vernon is a greatly respected name in Reading. Now I know your brother was thrown out of here years ago, and I know you've never recovered from the shock of it, but when you talk about the Lancers, ask yourself where their second-in-command was while they took part in the Boer War."

James now turned scarlet. "That's damned unfair," he complained.

"Now you know how it feels." He glanced apologetically at the silent Mary. "You've never given Henry the benefit of any doubt. If you don't mind, I'd rather not discuss your brother with you. I've tried to make allowances for you, James, God knows I've tried, and I find it increasingly difficult. I'll ask you to remember only that your brother died on active service, fighting for his queen. No soldier can do more than that—not even if he's in the 1st Lancers," he added with undisguised sarcasm. "Mary, I'd like a word with you in private before I go. Come through to the library with me, please."

James watched them with smoldering eyes but said nothing. Sir Godfrey closed the library doors and stood and faced his daughter-in-law.

"I'm sorry, Mary. I need to get away from here for a time. The atmosphere puts too much of a strain on me."

"I understand perfectly, Papa." She spoke with composure. She wore a white evening dress, cut low. She was always a dresser, he thought, and pretty as a picture. What a ghastly tragedy it all was.

"I hate leaving you alone with him, but if things go on much longer I'll say something I may regret—and what's worse I may say it in front of John. You should never belittle a man in front of his children. It's the final act of cruelty."

"Yes."

"Come to Mereford if you get the chance. I'm running away, you know that, don't you?"

"What?" She managed to muster a smile. "The general turning tail?"

"Yes. I feel guilty about leaving you. I'm very fond of you, Mary. It's a sad thing to say, but I don't enjoy my son's company. As he shows no sign of moving out of here, and Cleveland Row has been sold anyway, there's nothing for it but for me to get away for a bit."

"I wish you'd stop explaining, Papa. You don't have to."

"No, I never did with you. I'll tell you something, in secret. Henry is up for the Victoria Cross."

"Is he?"

He nodded and told her all that he had learned so far. "I don't know much," he concluded. "I'll find out more, but he's definitely being put up. He may not get it, you know."

"I think he will."

"It would be nice if you were right. To think that at one time I regarded him as a disgrace. That's one of the reasons I put up with James, you know. He took his cue from me, and I've only myself to blame. Don't say anything to James, whatever you do."

"I never do say anything to James."

The words were pathetic, he thought. He kissed her. Next day he went to Reading where Edward met him and they drove to Mereford, his manservant following with the luggage. Edward was delighted. His father's death had hit him very hard, but it was some consolation to have his grandfather staying with them.

It was just before Christmas, on December 18, that Queen Victoria said good-bye forever to Windsor. The previous day she had spoken to Sir Godfrey.

"We have been asked to consider your elder boy's name, Sir Godfrey, for the award of the Victoria Cross."

"I had heard, Ma'am, that his name would be submitted to you."

"I shall approve, of course."

"I have no words with which to thank you." He felt a lump come to his throat.

"You must be very proud of him, and you must take consolation for his death in your other son, who is also a soldier."

"Er . . . yes, Ma'am."

He did not see her again. She went to Osborne and there she died on January 22, supported by the arm of the Kaiser and not that of her elderly son. It was a strange omen for the future.

It was the end of Sir Godfrey's long term as an aide-de-camp. He was almost sixty-four now, and he relinquished all his duties. Nevertheless the new King, who had known the courtly old soldier for many years, did not lose touch with him. He was summoned to Marlborough House at the beginning of March.

"Look here, Sir Godfrey," King Edward said, rolling his r's and speaking with the guttural accent he could never lose, "it's about your boy's Victoria Cross. I'd like to present it at a private investiture. You served my mother for a very long time and she always spoke very highly of you. You know that. Isn't there a child?"

"There's a boy, Edward, now eleven."

"Edward, eh?" King Edward VII was pleased to approve. "Well I'd like to give the medal to the boy. I think your son would have liked that, wouldn't he?"

"There is no doubt whatever, sir."

"Then I'll let you know. It will be here in Marlborough House, an informal private investiture."

Sir Godfrey flushed with pleasure. This was a signal honor. There was no rule about investitures. The King could decorate people singly or in groups or in crowds, depending on his whim; he could decorate them where or when he liked. Nevertheless, in the unwritten order of things, a private investiture was a double honor. It was particularly touching of the King to wish to invest young Edward with his father's medal.

He hurried back to Reading and told Alice, who found it difficult to understand why the King of England should take any interest in young Edward. To her royalty were remote and godlike; they were there, but one did not expect to have anything to do with them. She had never fully grasped the fact that Sir Godfrey was almost like one of the family to Queen Victoria. However she was flattered and she and Edward went to London to buy new clothes. At eleven Edward was tall for his age and she had him fitted out with new striped trousers, a black Eton jacket and Eton collar, and a gray silk tie. He looked very smart.

It was at the beginning of May that the summons was received to attend at Marlborough House. Buckingham Palace was being extensively altered and improved, and was not fit to receive the King yet. Sir Godfrey traveled with them to the ceremony and they were shown into a small room. A few moments later the King appeared. He wore uniform. Originally he had not intended to change yet again, for he changed clothes so many times in a day that he grew weary of it occasionally. Then he had recalled that a small boy receiving a Victoria Cross on behalf of his dead soldier father would far rather be decorated by a king in uniform. Therefore he had on his field marshal's uniform, with scarlet tunic and blue trousers, medals and orders, and he was a most imposing figure. The lord chamberlain accompanied him, carrying a purple velvet cushion with gold cords and tassels, and on it the dull bronze cross with its drab purple ribbon, probably the world's most undistinguished badge of distinction, certainly the ugliest, and because of its very ugliness soon to become invested with a unique beauty of its own.

The lord chamberlain read out the citation, while Sir Godfrey and Alice stood behind Edward. Edward did not move a muscle and Sir Godfrey was impressed by the boy's composure. When he had pinned the cross to Edward's lapel, the King smiled suddenly.

"So," he said, "your name is Edward like mine?"

"Yes, sir."

"Do you know what the Victoria Cross is, Edward?"

"It's for being terribly brave."

"That is right. It is for being specially brave. It is the most important thing I can give to my brave soldiers and it comes before everything else. Once it was won by a boy called Andrew Fitzgibbon. He was a hospital apprentice, and he won it in China in 1860 at Taku Forts. Now listen carefully, Edward Vernon. Your grandfather is standing behind you wearing his uniform and on one of his medals is a bar which says Taku Forts 1860. So you see your grandfather was there when a boy of fifteen won the Victoria Cross."

Edward gasped and the King was pleased. He liked to be able to trot out little bits of information like this.

"Are you going to be a soldier and fight for me when you grow up?" the King asked.

"Yes, sir, if you want me to," Edward replied boldly.

"I hope we may live in peace, but if we have to fight remember the example your father has set you."

"Yes, sir."

His Majesty turned to Alice. He knew nothing of her, of course, except that she was the wife of General Vernon's eldest boy—and that she was pretty. He had an eye for a good-looking woman, and he was pleased with what he saw.

"Please accept our sympathy in your loss, Mrs. Vernon."

"Thank you, sir."

"I have only recently lost my mother, as you know. I understand how one feels."

"Yes, sir."

"Well, Sir Godfrey, look after them."

"I will, sir."

The King turned and left, followed by the lord chamberlain. Sir Godfrey unpinned the medal and put it into the small velvet-lined box which the lord chamberlain had slipped to him. He put it in his pocket.

Outside they were stopped by two reporters, and Sir Godfrey dealt with them and kept them away from Edward who was becoming a little bewildered. They set off to lunch at the Savoy.

"What did you think of the King?" Sir Godfrey asked Edward when they had ordered and were waiting to be served.

Edward considered. "He's very fat," he answered unexpectedly.

"I expect it's all the banquets, darling," Alice murmured, wondering if Sir Godfrey would be annoyed, but he was chuckling.

"He's very grand too," Edward added quickly. "I noticed one thing, Grandfather."

"What was that?"

"He hasn't got the Victoria Cross," Edward said, puzzled. It seemed strange that the King who awarded it hadn't given himself one.

"No and he never will have," Sir Godfrey agreed. "You have to win it in battle."

It dawned on Edward that in winning the Victoria Cross his father had done something the King of England couldn't do. He grinned his delight.

After the investiture life settled down quietly at Mereford. There had been a small stir when Robert Turner published rather a full account of the ceremony, but by now Reading had come to accept its local hero. They were much more surprised when it was announced that Vernon's, meaning Alice, had bought Bayne's the shoe shop. People wondered at her temerity. The interior was modernized and redesigned to become a typical Vernon shop, and people were pleased.

The weeks and months slipped past. Sir Godfrey went up to Town occasionally to visit his home, but he always returned the same day. There was no talk of his leaving Mereford. Then one Saturday in the late autumn of 1901 Mary came to see them. As usual they had no warning of her visit. It was obvious at once that she was agitated. When Sir Godfrey discreetly excused himself she asked him to stay in the drawing room.

"What I have to say concerns you too, Papa. I am leaving James again. This time I shall not return."

"Oh dear," Alice sympathized.

"I'm sorry," Sir Godfey said helplessly, "more sorry than I can say, Mary."

"So am I," she replied. "I hate the situation, but I can't go on with James. I should never have married him in the first place, but I have tried to make it work, I really have. You must believe me."

"Has something happened?"

"Yes, well, several things. You know my sister is married to Chris Hilton? Chris has a younger brother, Timothy, who works in the Foreign Office. He's very sweet and he's been in love with me for years."

They looked at her expectantly.

"He has asked me to go and live with him and I've agreed. He's got a little money and we intend to live in the country once he has resigned from the Foreign Office. There's a cottage in Gloucestershire."

"Oh," Sir Godfrey said blankly. This was unexpected news. One could not blame Mary, yet it was the very last thing he'd have expected of her.

"The day before yesterday I had to reprimand John for misbehaving. He turned on me. He said I wasn't a proper mother because I mixed with . . . well, I'd better not say it. He meant that I came here."

"What did he say?" Alice asked calmly. "You can tell us, Mary."

"He said I mixed with a harlot," she replied in a low voice.

There was a stunned silence.

"Of course he must have picked it up from James. I've known for a long time that James tries to impress all his own ideas on John. It hasn't been nice to watch."

"Good God," Sir Godfrey exclaimed, horrified.

"I had it out with James, and we had a terrible row. I'm afraid John heard, and no doubt so did the servants. I told James I wouldn't stand for it, and he told me to get out.

So I went to my father's and there I met Tim Hilton. He knew something was wrong and in the end I told him about it. He offered to marry me if I could divorce James. I've seen James and he has refused point-blank, so I'm going to do the other thing. I'm thirty-one now and I want a little happiness. I love Timothy Hilton and I'm going to live with him, divorce or no divorce. We don't care. He's got five hundred a year, and my father will help us."

"And John?" Sir Godfrey asked.

"I'm sorry, Papa, but I can't do anything about John now. It's much too late—he's James's son through and through. He has every prejudice of his father's. He's eleven and doesn't need much looking after when he's home from prep school. They can manage without me."

"What a ghastly mess," Sir Godfrey sighed.

Alice put an arm round Mary. "I'm so sorry," she said gently.

"I'm not. I'm glad it's happened at last. I've got a chance to be happy now, and believe me I'm not sorry about that. I may as well be honest and tell you how I feel."

"Quite right too," Sir Godfrey agreed. "Stay for the weekend, Mary, and we'll go up to London together on Monday. I'll go to St. James's Place and have a word with James about the future. You've got all your things out of the house?"

"All that matters. I've kept nothing I received from James."

They could see that she was overwrought, but by the following morning she had calmed down considerably and was her normal self again. Alice carefully avoided the subjects of James and John, and instead told Mary about the firm and how it was progressing. Mary was as interested and impressed as Sir Godfrey was, particularly by the capability displayed by Alice.

Nothing was said to Edward, who was quite accustomed

to the idea that his Aunt Mary always came to visit them on her own without Uncle James. He did not much like his uncle or his cousin, but neither did he ever think of them much. They were remote figures. They spent a quiet weekend together and on Monday Sir Godfrey and Mary went to London while Edward went to his private school and Alice went to the office.

Alice was surprised to find that Sir Godfrey was already at home when she returned.

"How did things go?" she asked when she had removed her hat, coat, and gloves and warmed her hands by the fire for a moment.

"About as I anticipated. I saw James at the club at lunchtime. He's perfectly happy with the arrangement. I don't think he minds losing Mary at all. He told me that she has run off with another man and called her a slut. It's a word he's overfond of using. I didn't say anything of course—I don't want to get involved in any arguments with him. I asked him about a divorce and he laughed and said he was damned if he'd divorce her so that she could marry someone else."

He sighed and went to pour himself a drink.

"When I said I thought I might stay on here for a bit, and asked how he felt about just John and himself at St. James's Place, he said he didn't mind at all. I'd already seen the servants of course, told them that nobody would lose their job; so I made it clear to James that it is my house and my servants, but he's welcome to live in it provided he doesn't try to get rid of any of my servants. Of course James is sublimely unaware of the existence of servants," he added with a chuckle. "His shoes get cleaned, the bed is made, food is served, and that is exactly what should happen. *How* it happens is a matter of no importance, but I had to make sure he doesn't do anything that would upset them. Oh dear. I saw John briefly. I think

James must have been telling him fairy stories about me too, for the child was extremely offhand, though perhaps I do James an injustice. Anyway, here I am again Alice, on your doorstep. May I stay on a bit longer?"

"It would really be much better if you stopped talking about it altogether," Alice told him. "You don't need to talk about going or staying. Treat Mereford as your home."

"Which it is," he laughed. "What a wonderful person you are. You've every right to order me out of the house."

"I think you're getting old," she replied firmly. "You talk such nonsense. Let's have no more of it. Now, Robert Turner is coming round this evening for an hour after dinner. Jean Turner and I will keep out of your way. Robert wants your advice."

"He does?" Sir Godfrey looked pleased. "What about?"

"It's something to do with army reform. He's writing a leading article. I think there has been something going on in the House of Commons."

"Ah, yes, there has. It's very civil of him to consult me. There's too much nonsense talked about army reform."

"I'm sure there is," Alice answered good-naturedly.

She had had an inspiration that day in the office. It had occurred to her that each counter had its own cash drawer, and that therefore it would be possible to cost each counter properly. She could find out if any were losing money—if the cost of floor space, related to rent, electricity, cleaning, and heating, plus wages and other overheads, was less than the gross profit each counter made. She was not quite sure what use she could make of all this information, if indeed there should prove to be anything of interest, but it would be fun finding out. Furthermore she would learn more about this store she controlled and owned. She was always learning something.

She went up to her large bedroom, which had its windows immediately above the portico, unbuttoned her boots, and sat down in a comfortable armchair. It was good to relax. She looked round the elegantly furnished room, with its high ceilings and two large gilt-framed mirrors. She liked her room. Her eye alighted on the silver framed photograph which stood on her dressing table. Henry in full dress Berkshire Light Infantry uniform, taken the year before the war had started. How handsome and how smart he was, and how terribly he had died. She had made Sir Godfrey tell her about it, against his will. It did not bear thinking about.

At least Henry's sufferings were over now. She wondered if there were really any truth in the Reverend Hugh Shobdon's confident assertions that there was life after death and that Henry was sitting in some celestial paradise right now, looking down on her. She rather hoped not, for her hair needed doing. How she missed him. She would never marry again, she knew that. She wanted no one else. She rose and picked up the photograph, peering at it intently as though trying to see something that wasn't there, perhaps even to bring life to the still reproduction of the man she loved. Then she sighed and put it down.

No use looking over one's shoulder, she told herself, no use at all. There were things to do, life had to go on. But it was no good, she could not avoid her moment of weakness. She was flesh and blood, not steel. Her eyes went round the lovely room again and she stood holding the edge of one of the curtains, feeling the expensive material against her cheek. How much had been given to her, so very much. There was her beautiful home, and downstairs were Edward and Sir Godfrey. So very much—the words kept running around in her head. She felt a foolish tear trickle down her cheek and brushed it away impatiently.

She had had her moments, and splendid ones they had been. This, all of it, was Edward's heritage, and she was its guardian. She put on her slippers and went to the door.

She must have a quick word with the cook about tonight's dinner, and arrange for coffee and brandy to be served to Sir Godfrey and Robert Turner afterward. There were no more foolish tears as the mistress of Mereford went downstairs. She was in full control of the situation.

BOOK II

Mereford at War
1910–1935

Chapter 11

IN 1910, the year that Florence Nightingale died, Mereford acquired its first car, an expensive, gleaming Daimler with much highly polished brasswork. Edward, who was to celebrate his twentieth birthday that summer, had been pressing his mother to buy a motorcar for some months, and finally she bought one as a birthday present for herself. Her birthday was on April 28, and on that Thursday the car was delivered shortly after breakfast, in accordance with her instructions.

Alice had taken a day off to mark the occasion, and Edward, who now worked in the family firm, was at home too. Together with Sir Godfrey they sat in the dining room, chatting. Alice had opened her presents, a small diamond brooch from Edward and a framed painting from the general. Edward's present involved a real effort on his part, for his father's will had left everything to Alice, and Edward had subsisted on pocket money till he was seventeen, when he started to earn a salary from the company. It was not, at the moment, a particularly handsome one.

The dining room was at the rear of the house, and so they did not see the car arrive. It was left to Ivy, the maid, to announce it.

"A man has come with a motorcar, ma'am," she told Alice. "He's waiting in the hall."

"Thank you, Ivy."

"Motorcar? Have you bought one?" Edward asked eagerly. "What sort, Mother?"

"Come along and see. You too, Papa."

They went out to inspect the glittering monster, Sir Godfrey leaning a little on the stick he carried habitually now. Alice signed the driver's delivery book and they walked all round the car, Edward exclaiming with delight. Then he turned to his mother.

"What about the controls? Is there a set of instructions?"

"We don't need one. I've been having lessons this past week."

"Well I'm blessed! *That's* where you've been going. Are you going to drive it?"

"Certainly I am, although you must do so too. We'll go for a spin now. Papa, you must come with us."

"Hm," Sir Godfrey grunted, "I'm getting a bit old for risking life and limb, but I suppose so."

"I've bought a scarf to tie round my hat, and I've bought a cap and goggles for Edward. You'd better put on your coat and scarf, Papa, for it can be quite drafty."

She produced the cap and goggles for Edward, who grinned appreciatively, tied a scarf round her hat, put on gloves, and climbed up behind the wheel. Edward turned the starting handle and Sir Godfrey sat rigidly in the back.

They set off at a sedate pace and for twenty minutes Alice drove along country lanes, startling the occasional pedestrian and having an encounter with a horse and cart. Then she changed places with Edward who drove them back home again cautiously and with much advice from Alice.

"It's wonderful, Mother. How splendid of you to get it without saying a word to us."

"That's my birthday present to myself," Alice smiled. "I can see that I'll have to share it with you. You can drive it into Reading in the mornings and I'll drive it home in the evenings."

"Aren't you going to engage a chauffeur?" Sir Godfrey demanded as he dismounted stiffly.

"Certainly not, Papa. It's much more fun to drive it oneself. We must teach you too."

"You're not going to get me driving one of these things," the ancient warrior said. "I'd end up in the middle of a field, or else I'd run over someone's pigs and we'd have a lawsuit on our hands. This is for young people."

"Didn't you enjoy it, Grandfather?" Edward asked.

"Oh, yes, I enjoyed it all right. Very exhilarating. Alice, doesn't it need to be looked after by a mechanic or something?"

"I've arranged for Edward to go to Morley's, the garage people, for a fortnight to learn about the engine. He can show me at weekends. I haven't time to go myself."

"What's the matter, are you economizing?" her father-in-law demanded.

"No, Papa. I just think we ought to learn to look after the car ourselves. It would appear that cars are going to replace horses, so we had better find out as much as possible about them."

"Replace horses? Rubbish. They're a novelty. I'm not saying a car isn't useful, but so are horses. People will always use horses. Imagine the farmers round here trying to tow their carts to market behind a car!"

Things were changing too quickly for the general, as he realized in May when King Edward VII died and George V was proclaimed. Sir Godfrey was seventy-three now. He had been born in the year during which Queen Victoria had come to the throne, and for sixty-three years she had been his monarch. Now, in the last ten years, there had been two changes, Edward and George. It was bewildering. The old order had gone.

And his personal life had changed. He had virtually lost contact with James and John, since now he rarely went up to Town. He was content to remain at Mereford with Alice and Edward.

He thought affectionately of Alice. If Henry had been full of surprises, then Alice was even more full of them. Who would have dreamed that a woman of such humble origins would have taken such a place in society, and more surprisingly, shown so much business acumen?

Like the people of Reading, he had become accustomed to this idea of a woman managing a company, one which employed over two hundred people. In the past few weeks they had even become accustomed to seeing Mrs. Vernon driving a car, her son sitting beside her on the front seat. It had become an accepted fact, locally, that Mrs. Henry Vernon was as good as any man. Even the women had ceased to resent this state of affairs—they were rather proud of her. Alice was supremely indifferent to what people thought. She was simply looking after her son's interests till he came of age.

Which would be next year, the general recalled, next July. He wondered exactly what Alice would do. Edward had now spent three years in the firm. He had worked behind the counter in all the shops, he had been a floor-walker in the stores, and now for the past seven months he had been assistant manager of the stores, working with a highly experienced manager. There wasn't much Edward didn't know about the business. The question was, did he have his mother's flair? Sir Godfrey wondered about that.

He admitted to himself only his disappointment that his grandson showed no interest whatever in the army. He never spoke of it, despite the fact that Edward's grandfather was a much decorated general and his father had been a captain both of Lancers and of Light Infantry and

had won the Victoria Cross. Obviously Edward would
have to take over the business Henry had created, but he
could still have been interested in the army. It was left to
James and John, in London, to carry on the military tradition Sir Godfrey had hoped to found.

Sir Godfrey decided to go out. He sent for Maggett, the
gardener and stableman, and ordered the carriage. Then
he went and put on a heavy coat and muffler. When the
landau was ready he set off to visit Robert Turner.

He was at home when Sir Godfrey arrived, and the two
elderly men sat down together with a drink.

"What's the news of the world, Robert?"

"Well might you ask. It seems nothing will ever shift the
Liberals. I don't like it."

Sir Godfrey chose to affect complete ignorance on polit-
ical issues. In truth he cared little for them, and in any
event he preferred to listen to someone like Turner. Today
the talk took a slightly sinister turn. Turner spoke of what
he called "creeping socialism," which he contrived to make
appear alarming.

"The trouble with the socialists," he pointed out, "is that
although they have such noble ideals, trying to help the
poor and the unfortunate—it's very difficult to argue with
them on those grounds—they want to overturn the existing order as well; and that, General, is just another name
for revolution."

"There will never be a revolution in this country," Sir
Godfrey exclaimed.

Robert Turner debated briefly whether to educate his
friend and point out that there had been several and that
they were on the verge of another. He decided against it.
Sir Godfrey would never understand the subtle changes
that were taking place.

"I hope you're right, but I'm thinking of the Continent.
There's no saying where this movement will end. I'm always afraid it will end in war."

"War? Between whom?" Sir Godfrey asked, raising his bushy eyebrows.

"War in Europe—Austria and France perhaps, or Germany and France. Germany is too fond of rattling the saber. I don't like it."

"Surely there's no risk of civilized countries going to war?" Sir Godfrey exclaimed.

"What is a civilized country?" Turner snorted.

"I hope you're wrong, Robert."

"So do I, General, so do I, yet sometimes I wonder where it will all lead."

"How can socialism cause a war?"

"As I said, by undermining and overturning existing orders. It may never come. I daresay I'm an alarmist, but I don't trust the Kaiser."

"He's a strutting jackass."

"A dangerous one. The man is hysterical and that's always dangerous. A war with Germany now—it would be a savage affair."

"What's all this got to do with England? Germany would never make a war against us."

"We could easily become involved if there was an upset in Europe."

"I don't want to see my grandson going off to war. I lost a son in South Africa and that's enough."

"I'm sorry," Turner apologized. "I shouldn't talk so much. As you said, it's not likely that England will find herself fighting other European powers."

He did not believe his own words and even Sir Godfrey took small comfort from them. The seed of doubt had been planted in his mind, and the thought of war disturbed him for many weeks.

Shortly after the New Year of 1911, while they sat in the drawing room after dinner one cold, dark, and very windy night, Alice looked up from a piece of tapestry she was embroidering.

"I'm going to make some changes, Edward. I want you to go to see Herbert Griffiths this week."

"Why, Mother?"

Sir Godfrey put down his book and took off his spectacles to listen attentively to mother and son.

"Because I believe he's ready to get rid of his half of the building in Broad Street and I want the whole building. His is the bigger half and we need it. I want to turn the whole thing into one large store. It means we can get everything under one roof."

"Griffiths will sell?" Edward asked.

"No, he'll never do that. He's never forgiven himself for selling the freehold of our part of the building. He made a mistake there. However, he will sell us a ninety-nine-year lease on his half of the building."

"If you sold your land to Griffiths, you might get the whole building free," Sir Godfrey suggested mildly and in ignorance.

Alice smiled and shook her head. "I'll never sell land, and certainly not that bit of land. It will be worth a lot one day, right there in the center of Reading. I'm happy to have the whole of the building and our own bit of land."

"Why do you want me to see Griffiths?" Edward asked, surprised that his mother was not going to handle the matter herself.

"Because as from Monday you will be managing director."

Edward flushed with pleasure.

"I want you to take over now. On your twenty-first birthday I shall make over the entire company to you. I shall keep nothing to myself." Edward opened his mouth and she held up her hand. "I'll stay on as chairman at a salary, but I intend to spend only one day a week in the office. I've been neglecting Mereford. It's time you took over and let me become a woman again. Anyway, your father and I always agreed that it would all be yours one day. When I die you'll have Mereford too, but meantime you will have Vernon's."

"I don't know what to say."

"Save it for Mr. Griffiths. Incidentally, I think it is time we turned ourselves into a limited liability company. I have been talking to the solicitors and accountants about it, and it is an overdue step. So, you will take over as managing director now, and you can share my office until July while I am still coming in full time. After your birthday I'll move my desk into a smaller office—there will be plenty of space when we get the whole building—and you'll be on your own, Edward. I'll be available for consultations, that's all. We'll have to talk about directors; also what we are going to do about the other small shops."

"What about money?"

"We've got quite a lot and the bank will give us more. I'd like you to change the name. I've never really liked Vernon's Universal Stores, although it served a good purpose at the time your father and I chose it."

"What do you suggest?"

"Henry Vernon, Son and Company Limited. After all, your father created the business and you, the son, are going to run it."

"I rather like the sound of that," Edward agreed slowly. "Besides, anyone in Reading who doesn't know what Vernon's is must have arrived on this afternoon's train. Yes, I like that, Mother."

"I'm glad."

"What are we going to do with the other shops if we move everything under one roof?" Edward mused.

"I want you to think about that and then when you have, we can talk about it."

Sir Godfrey, listening to them, was impressed. They were

supremely confident. Edward had the Vernon looks, the jaw, and the brows, but there was a lot of his mother in him. Alice's father, after all, had been a haberdasher— only in a small way of course and he'd never made any money, but perhaps that was where the business instinct came from.

During the next few months there were frequent discussions after dinner as they decided on the plans for the future. Edward secured the adjoining half of the building after rather a tense transaction. He had never negotiated and he was afraid of making a poor showing, but the terms were reasonable enough. He found discussions much easier at the bank, and the bank manager was suitably impressed by his young caller's decisiveness. Of course he had been briefed by Mrs. Henry Vernon that her son would be coming to discuss affairs and that he represented her now. Even so, he represented her well. The money was forthcoming.

Alice was rather pleased with Edward's suggestions about the smaller shops. Like her, he did not believe in giving up anything if it could be turned to good use somehow. He was going to have three empty sets of premises in the center of town. They were all due for modernization and redecoration. Edward suggested that they turn them into a bicycle shop, an educational and religious bookshop, and a gunsmiths and sporting goods shop. His mother agreed, especially with the bicycle shop. He was showing that he had learned the basic lesson which was to find a need or needs not being properly met, and then go ahead and meet them handsomely.

She began to sit back and think of other things. It was not in her nature to be idle. Her plans included the purchase of another five acres of woodland, the complete redecoration of the house, new electrical wiring throughout to provide better lighting, a garage for three cars, because she had decided to get rid of the stables, and modernization of the servants' wing which was really now substandard.

"Why three garages?" the general asked when he heard.

"Not three garages, Papa, one garage for three cars. I'm going to buy another car, and engage a chauffeur. You and I will share a car and driver, and Edward can have the Daimler to use to go to the office."

"What's the third garage for?"

"Guests, of course. Nobody wants to leave hundreds of pounds of valuable motorcar standing in the rain. It will be cheaper to build the larger garage now, rather than in several years' time when costs may have gone up. If we are going to have a garage, let's have one that will allow for expansion. It will be nicely screened by trees, and yet close to the house."

"It sounds like a lot of upset to me," he grumbled.

"It will be," she promised lightly, "but it will be worth it. Mereford needs attention."

"I like it as it is."

"I know you do, Papa, but you must remember that it is fifteen years since any work was done to the house and it's become shabby and a little old-fashioned. I want to make it brighter and more comfortable. I shan't spoil your room, I promise."

"My room? I'm a guest after all."

"We hope you'll never leave. You are a very special guest."

She reached up and kissed his leathery cheek and he turned away, moved by her manner.

"Next Saturday, the seventeenth, if it's another fine day, I rather thought we might drive to Henley," he said. "We could have lunch there by the river. My treat, Alice."

"That would be lovely. Why next Saturday?" She was thinking. June 17? Then her face cleared. "Oh, it's your wedding anniversary, Papa."

"My fiftieth. I'd always hoped to celebrate it with Adeline. You'll have to take her place."

"Fiftieth?"

"Yes, we were married in 1861—it was a Monday, I remember."

Alice smiled and kissed him again.

"It will be lovely to celebrate it together if that's what you'd like."

"Do you ever hear from Mary?" he asked suddenly, changing the subject.

"Not since the last letter I told you about. She owes me a letter. Why?"

"I just wondered how she was getting on, she and the baby."

"She's very happy, if you want my opinion, and the 'baby' is nine years old now. Nine last month, wasn't it?"

"Poor little fellow. His parents will probably never be able to marry. It's too bad of James to keep refusing to divorce her."

"I doubt if Mary or Timothy or young Timothy care very much. Mary never did worry about such things."

"Even so, it's awkward for the boy. I mean, you don't get an ordinary birth certificate if you're illegitimate. People can tell."

"Only if they see it," Alice pointed out.

"It means he can't really go into the army or into government service—oh, so many doors are closed. What will become of him?"

"I've no idea. You're very interested in him, Papa."

"It's funny, but as I grow older I think more of the young people. Of course Mary's boy is no relation of mine, there's no blood tie at all, yet somehow I always think of him as a third grandson—and I've never even seen him," he added with a smile. "Do you think Mary is really happy living in a cottage at . . . where is it?"

"Kemble. Warneford Cottage, Kemble, in Gloucestershire. I think so, Papa. She always seems happy when she writes. She adores Timothy Hilton and I know he's always been madly in love with her."

"It's a pity she wasted all those years on James then. She was never his sort."

"It can't be helped, can it? Would you like me to invite them here to visit us?"

"Would you?"

"Of course. Mark you I don't know if they'll accept, but I can try."

So she wrote to Mary and two weeks later received a reply. Mary would be delighted to come to Mereford for the twenty-first birthday celebration. She would bring young Timothy, but her husband—she always called the elder Timothy her husband—could not come. He was unwell. Alice told Sir Godfrey and he was pleased.

They arrived on Friday afternoon. Edward's twenty-first birthday was on Monday, July 24. They were having a small dance that night with only twenty guests, for Mereford was not a large house. The family, however, was celebrating privately on the Saturday beforehand. Without telling Sir Godfrey, and as a gesture of goodwill, Alice had invited James and John. After all, John would be twenty-one the next month and the boys were first cousins. There was no reply from St. James's Place, however, and no gift came for Edward. Alice's sadness at this continued coldness was offset by her pleasure when Mary arrived.

Mary, soon to be forty-one, was as vivacious and youthful as ever. She was dressed very stylishly. The two women embraced, and then Timmy—as the boy was known then —was inspected and approved. He was a sturdy, freckle-faced child with nice manners. Edward's old nursery remained just as it always had been, with its big rocking horse and its boxes of toys, and Timmy was sent there to amuse himself.

Sir Godfrey was equally delighted to see Mary, but soon went upstairs to the nursery and they did not see him again till dinnertime. Alice asked what was wrong with Timothy Hilton and learned that he had asthma and was always liable to attacks of bronchitis. His health had never been robust and he had not worked since leaving the Foreign Office to live in the country with Mary. He amused himself by producing little watercolors, some of which Mary brought with her as gifts. Nevertheless they were ecstatically happy.

"Do you ever see James or hear from him?" Alice asked.

"No. The last time was six years ago when he wrote to demand the return of a ring which had belonged to his mother. I wrote back and said I had nothing belonging to the Vernon family and that he had better ask Sir Godfrey. I've not heard since."

Alice nodded. It was in character.

"He's still only a lieutenant colonel," Mary laughed. "He never forgave me for christening him the toy soldier, but you must admit he proved me right."

On Saturday Robert Turner came to dinner, along with the earl and countess of Thatcham. The present Lord Thatcham was the son of Henry's old friend, and the money he had lent Henry had been converted into preference shares, so that Lord Thatcham was the only outside shareholder in what was otherwise a family business. Alice was content with the arrangement, for it did no harm to be associated with the Thatchams who, however far from brilliant they might be, were extremely important people in the county. There was a son, Lord Walter Paveley who was nearly twelve, and a daughter, Lady Elizabeth Paveley, the same age as young Timmy, but they had been left behind. Eight of them sat down to dinner and it was a cheerful, almost hilarious meal.

Watching her son, Alice wished that he knew some

suitable girls his own age. He seemed only to have male friends, and not too many of those. It was not that Edward was either shy or standoffish, he simply spent most of his time thinking and talking about the firm and did not go out often. Most of his acquaintances were older than he was. Yet he was handsome, Alice thought, with his fresh complexion, his thick wavy hair just like his father's, and his expressive mouth and eyes. She decided it was time to jerk him out of the rut he had got himself into. She did not know how she would do it, but do it she would. He must get about more and meet people. It was all very well, his preoccupation with Sir Godfrey and herself, his love of Mereford, and his interest in the company; it was flattering and commendable, but there had to be much more to Edward's life than this.

She watched him again at the small dance on Monday night. The guests were all young people between twenty and twenty-five, and included three or four presentable and even pretty girls, all socially acceptable. Edward was polite and charming, danced all evening, distributing his favors with mathematical exactitude, and singled out nobody for attention. It was, to put it mildly, frustrating and disappointing.

Mary could see what was in Alice's mind, and chuckled to herself.

"You'll have to be patient."

"I'm afraid so," Alice sighed.

"Men are exactly like horses—you can lead them to the water, and that's all."

"Your turn will come with Timmy."

"I suppose so, although it's not quite the same thing. Timmy isn't the head of a blossoming commercial empire, and he's a bastard, poor little scrap."

This coarseness shocked Alice, despite the fact that she accepted Mary as an unconventional person.

"There's no need for anyone to know," she said.

"His wife's going to have to know, isn't she?" Mary asked bluntly. "It's not the sort of thing it would be fair to hide. Some people are incredibly stuffy on the subject."

Alice swallowed. She had no desire to appear "incredibly stuffy," but it was *not* a polite subject. Then she smiled. Who was she to pass judgment? It was a difficult situation for Mary.

So Edward's coming of age came and went, disappointingly flat in some ways, and yet satisfactory in others. He now owned ninety percent of the stock, fully paid up, the expansion was forging ahead steadily, and for the first time for many years Alice was virtually free of the ties of the office.

Sir Godfrey had spent most of Mary's stay in the company of his "third grandson." He and Timmy got along famously. Sir Godfrey was good with young children. The old man and the child were sorry to part. There was no saying when they would meet again.

The epilogue to the birthday party came early the next month when Alice instructed Edward to buy a suitable twenty-first birthday present for his cousin, Cornet John Vernon.

"Why should I? I don't even know him. He certainly didn't remember my twenty-first, Mother."

"That is why," Alice said firmly. "Just because your cousin and his father are lacking in manners, there is no need for you to be the same. He is your first cousin. His father is your father's only brother. You must buy him something nice. Don't overdo it, for that would look bad —spend about ten guineas."

Against his will Edward did as he was ordered and bought a set of silver-backed brushes which, as an afterthought, he had engraved with the family's coat of arms. His father had never used their arms, and neither did Edward, although Sir Godfrey had them engraved on several things.

When he mentioned it to the general, the old man pulled his leg.

"I hope you had the arms differenced? Or did you just use the crest?"

"No, I had the whole thing, shield and everything. What do you mean, Grandfather?"

"Those are my arms, you know. James should difference them with a crescent to show he is the second son. I'm not quite sure what John should do—display a label on a crescent, I believe. You would simply display a label, as my heir."

Edward stared. "I had no idea. I know nothing of such things."

Sir Godfrey chuckled. "Then forget all about it. It doesn't matter anyway. I'm quite sure your cousin doesn't know anything about the subject either."

The silver-backed brushes were sent, but there was no acknowledgment.

"He didn't even invite me to his dance," Edward complained to his mother later on. "That was the least he could have done, especially when he knows I wouldn't have gone anyway."

He made a mental note to have nothing to do with the other branch of the family.

Chapter 12

ONE day about a fortnight after his birthday Edward received a message saying that a gentleman from America wished to see him. Intrigued, he asked that his visitor be sent in to his office. There entered a smartly dressed, stocky, energetic man with dark hair and a strong jaw, who shook hands vigorously.

"I believe this is your store, Mr. Vernon."

"That's right."

"My name is Forgan, Franklin Forgan from Chicago. I own Forgan Preston. Have you heard of it?"

"No, Mr. Forgan, I haven't."

"So much for fame," Forgan laughed. "It's only the biggest department store in the Midwest. I admire what you've done here. It's the best thing I've seen in England."

"You are on a visit?" Edward asked awkwardly.

"That's right, on holiday. I came to Reading to see the jail. I'm a great admirer of Oscar Wilde."

"Really? I thought he was out of favor."

"Great literature is never out of favor, Mr. Vernon. I have read everything of Wilde's that has been published. I visited him in Paris after his release from prison in '97 and offered him money, but he was very rude." He chuckled good-naturedly. "Yes, he was very rude. He was a bitter man. He told me, 'I have been to jail, Mr. Forgan, but I am glad to say I have never been to Chicago.' He was calling himself Sebastian Melmoth. That's after the novel by Charles Maturin. I must admit I'd never heard of it till I met Wilde in Paris, but I purchased a copy. *Melmoth the Wanderer* it is called, all about a man who sells his soul to the devil in exchange for prolonged life. Very horrific. It was typical of Wilde to call himself Melmoth following his imprisonment. He should never have been sent to jail, you know."

He stopped and grinned. "Now that's what I call a digression. I may have come here to see Reading jail, but I also came to England to have a look at your big stores in London. Very disappointing. You seem to be moving along the right lines here, though. I suppose there is no likelihood of your visiting Chicago is there, Mr. Vernon?"

"I'd never thought of it."

"If you should think of it, you would be welcome as my guest. You might learn a lot from us over in the States. We are a good few years ahead of anything in this old country."

"That's very generous Mr. . . . . er . . . Mr. Forgan." He had to glance at his caller's card surreptitiously. "I can't think what prompts you to make the offer."

"I like to see a man with the right idea. You're the only one I've come across in England. Come to Chicago, Mr. Vernon, come to see Forgan Preston. It will repay a visit."

Edward insisted that Franklin Forgan and his wife dine with them that night. Mereford was in something of an upheaval, for the workmen had moved in immediately after his party, but Forgan did not seem to mind. He admired the house and spent most of his time talking about commercial enterprise to Alice and Edward, leaving it to Sir Godfrey to entertain Mrs. Forgan. The Forgans had to leave next morning, but Alice did not forget them.

She checked up quietly on Franklin Forgan and discovered that he did indeed own Chicago's biggest store, also three of its not so big ones. It was rumored that he was a millionaire. It occurred to her that a visit to America might do Edward a world of good. He could not go right away, because he was much too preoccupied with the expansion of the store, but they decided that if all was well he could visit the United States the following spring.

Early in the new year Edward drew his mother's attention to an advertisement in the newspaper. The White Star liner *Titanic*, the last word in shipbuilding, was making her maiden voyage in April. If he was going to visit the United States, why not on the *Titanic?* They booked his passage accordingly, and wrote to Mr. Forgan to let him know the date of Edward's arrival. Mr. Forgan said he would come to New York to meet Edward and show him a little of that great city before taking him to the infinitely greater one—Chicago.

Once the decision had been made Edward grew enormously keen on the whole thing. He decided to spend a day or two in London before joining the ship in order to look at the larger stores there. Sir Godfrey and Alice saw him off at the station, and waved until he was out of sight. The house seemed deserted without Edward.

Edward stayed at the York Hotel in Ryder Street, which had been his father's favorite hotel. He enjoyed his three-day stay in the capital. He walked along St. James's Place, past 121, but he did not call at the house. He was merely curious to see what it looked like, for he had not been there since he was a child. On his second day at the hotel he bumped into a girl in the foyer. As he stood aside to let her pass, he was struck immediately by her looks. She had wonderful fair hair, and a pert, amusing face—not beautiful, but attractive and, more important, unforgettable. He wondered who she was. That evening at dinner he saw her come into the dining room with an older man and woman, probably her parents he decided. She was young, about his own age. In her evening gown she looked ravishingly beautiful. He stared at her until she looked up at him inquiringly, and he blushed and looked away. When he looked again she was eyeing him with interest. After several such optical encounters she smiled faintly and for no reason at all he felt happy.

After dinner he hung around outside the dining room and waited till the girl and her parents emerged. Of course he had no opportunity of speaking to her, but he watched them until they went upstairs, then he went into the lounge and asked for a drink. He had a sudden inspiration. He hurried back to the dining room and spoke to the headwaiter. That gentleman, pocketing a sovereign, smiled politely.

"Of course, sir. You must be speaking about Mr. and Mrs. Calvert and their daughter. Mr. Calvert is a counselor at the American Embassy in Paris."

Edward thanked the man and returned thoughtfully to the lounge. What was an American diplomat from France doing here in London? Was it possible that they too were joining the *Titanic* to sail to the United States on her maiden voyage? That would be a bit of luck.

More to the point, how to scrape up an acquaintance with the girl? His good fortune was in. He caught her alone next morning in the writing room. His heart beating, he went up to her boldly.

"Miss Calvert, isn't it?"

"Yes?" Her velvet eyes looked into his frankly. "I'm afraid I don't know you."

"My name is Vernon, Edward Vernon. I do hope you will forgive my speaking to you, but I thought I recognized you. You are from Paris, aren't you? From the embassy?"

"Yes."

"That's it. I was in Paris about a year ago, and you and

your parents were pointed out to me by a friend in the British Embassy. I forget where it was."

He had never been out of England in his life, nor did he know anyone at any embassy, but this did not trouble him in the least.

"About a year ago? That must have been in January last year, when I was visiting my parents."

"Yes. Yes, that's right. I remember I went over to France shortly after the New Year. May I sit down?"

"Please do, Mr. Vernon. What do you do?"

"Oh, I own a store—a department store."

"How interesting. You look much too young to be the owner of such a large concern."

"My father was killed."

"I'm sorry."

"Are you going to be in London for long, Miss Calvert?"

"No, I'm returning to the United States."

"On the *Titanic?*" he asked eagerly.

"Yes."

"So am I! What luck. Is your father leaving Paris?"

"Oh, no. They just came over for a few days to see me off. My father has only been at our Paris embassy six months."

"Ah, I see." Splendid, he thought, she would be traveling alone. Then his jaw dropped. "How long?" he asked awkwardly.

"Six months."

"Then I must have seen you more recently," he stammered.

"Please don't spoil it, Mr. Vernon. It was such a beautiful story, and it so nearly succeeded."

"But you . . . *you* said it must have been a year ago in January when you were visiting your parents."

"I know. I was testing you. You didn't pass the test."

"Well!" He grinned and she laughed. "The truth is," he

said, "I saw you yesterday and I felt I simply had to get to know you. I couldn't very well walk up and tell you that, could I?"

"Oh, I don't know." She smiled impishly. "It would have been very flattering. Are you really sailing on the *Titanic?*"

"Oh, yes, that part was true. I only made up the bit about Paris. In fact," he said with a grin, "I've never been to France."

"My mother is resting, and my father has gone to our embassy here in London," she said. "It's very nice outside. I'd love to go for a walk."

"Then let me take you. We could walk to Green Park from here. I can show you where my father was born."

"I'd love that," Frances Calvert replied. "I'll go and get my bonnet."

They walked down St. James's Street, crossed over into St. James's Place, past 121 which he pointed out to her, and then to the entrance of Green Park. It was a bright, chilly day and their cheeks were flushed, not entirely with cold. They managed to exchange a great deal of personal information in the forty minutes before they returned to the hotel where they found Frances's father looking for her.

"Oh, Papa," she said, "I want you to meet Mr. Edward Vernon. He's a great friend of Bobbie Heatherington at the British Embassy."

"Really?" Calvert smiled at Edward who tried to appear composed. "My daughter is very friendly indeed with Heatherington. A fine young man. You've known him long?"

"Since we were children," Edward assured him, wondering who Bobby Heatherington was.

"Are you in the diplomatic service, Mr. Vernon? The name seems familiar."

"No, I'm in commerce."

"He owns a department store, Papa. Isn't that clever?"

"Very. Frances, your mother has been worried. You'll excuse us, Mr. Vernon? Perhaps we could dine together this evening if you're staying at the hotel?"

He knew very well that Edward was, for he had been told that his daughter had gone out with one of the guests.

"That would be kind, sir."

Edward did not stop to examine his motives. He who had never really taken any notice of girls was suddenly flat out in pursuit of one. He thought Frances Calvert was the most beautiful, the most interesting, the most desirable of all God's creatures. He could hardly wait to get aboard the *Titanic* where he could enjoy her company minus the restrictive presence of her parents. Meantime, anything was better than nothing.

He managed to get through dinner with them without letting slip that he had never heard of Bobby Heatherington. Apparently satisfied that all was well, the Calverts went up immediately after dinner but allowed their daughter to remain downstairs with Mr. Vernon. They made their way to the lounge.

Frances Calvert was a tease by nature and she quickly discovered that Edward knew almost nothing about girls. He fascinated her with his good looks and his curious combination of worldliness and innocence.

"Perhaps on board ship we could sit at the same table— for meals," Edward suggested.

"Oh, I don't think that would be very proper, do you?" she asked, watching him.

"Wouldn't it?" He looked disappointed and she laughed.

"We could do it just the same. I wonder how one arranges it."

"Don't worry about that," Edward said confidently. "I'll arrange it."

He would too, she thought. She had learned by now that he was visiting Chicago as the guest of the owner of Forgan Preston. The Calvert home was in Chevy Chase, Maryland, and Frances had never visited Chicago, but she had heard of Forgan Preston. Everyone had.

"Somehow I've got to see you in America," Edward said. "We can't travel all that way together just to part in New York."

"I'll be staying with my sister and her husband at Annapolis."

"Then I must come to Annapolis."

"On what pretext?"

"Business," he said. "I can go where I like on business."

"You're persistent," she laughed and he took her hand.

"Where you're concerned, I'm going to go on being persistent. Consider that a warning."

She blushed and took her hand away from him.

"Are you angry with me?" he asked.

"No. No, I like you. You don't give a girl much time, though."

"I don't know much about girls . . ."

"I realize that, Edward."

"But I like you very much, Frances."

"I'm glad."

There is no saying what might have happened had they sailed on any other ship. The history of the Vernon family would have been completely different. But on the night of April 14 the unsinkable *Titanic* struck an iceberg . . . and sank. It was a night of horror, and so far as Edward was concerned it was a night of total confusion. It was only later that he was able to read all the accounts and piece together what had happened. He had no idea of most of it. The *Titanic* had twenty-two hundred souls aboard and lifeboats for half that number. Only seven hundred were saved—fifteen hundred perished. Among them was Frances Calvert who had got away in a lifeboat. Edward never found out what had happened to her, why she was not saved. It was a complete mystery. There was so much confusion that dreadful night that many stories remained untold forever. He himself was saved almost by an accident. He slipped and fell, knocking himself unconscious. Someone saw him lying on deck, blood streaming from a cut on his head, and called for help. He was passed by hand into a lifeboat which was on the point of being lowered. Had he not been a casualty it is doubtful if he would have got away. Luckily for him he was picked up by the Cunard liner, *Carpathia*, which was bound for New York. It was hours before he regained consciousness.

He suffered no ill effects from his fall, but it took him a long time to get over the death of Frances Calvert. It was so senseless and so tragic. The fact that he knew her for such a short time was immaterial—his feelings had run deeply. She was the first girl ever to arouse his awareness of the opposite sex, and he felt as though he had known her for years rather than a day or two.

In Chicago he did not talk about the disaster, and his hosts did not press him. Instead he threw himself into business. He was willing to learn and there was a lot to learn. In addition, he did not merely want ideas on how to run a big department store, he was interested in what was sold in America. His visit lasted for two months and during that time he ordered a great deal of merchandise for shipment to England. He and Alice had discussed this a long time before. If they were to sell goods imported from America, it would give variety to their stock. There were many things better or more conveniently produced at home, but Edward was on the lookout for new lines and he found plenty of them. He had no idea how people would react to them in Reading. It might cause a boom, it might cause a recession. There was only one way to test his judgment—put it to the test.

The results of his visit to the United States were not all apparent immediately. Certainly the new lines he had bought for summer and for Christmas proved to be fast-moving ones and he had established a new contact now with American suppliers. He had also made friends in Chicago, the most important of them being Franklin Forgan. It was from this visit that, later on, arose other visits, annual buying trips to America—but that was still years in the future. Many things were to happen before then.

It was typical of Edward that he never said a word to his mother or Sir Godfrey about the vivacious American girl he had met and fallen in love with so madly. Their brief meeting might never have happened, and if he was thoughtful and preoccupied, Alice put it down to the firm's affairs.

By the start of the summer of 1913 the extensive alterations and redecoration of Mereford were all over. There were two new cars in the garage, the stonework of the house had been cleaned at considerable expense, all the rooms were light and fresh and the servants' quarters were models of what such rooms should be. It had cost a great deal of money, but Alice had paid for it out of her own pocket. She had always saved money, and now it came in useful. Money was of no interest to her except for the use to which it could be put.

The new store was the busiest shopping center in Reading, and money was rolling in. They owed a lot to the bank, but it was obvious that in a few years they would pay off all their debts. It was a strange system, Edward thought when he considered it. You went into debt to expand and develop, then you made a lot of money and used it firstly to repay your debts and then put into reserve for future expansion and development. When that time came, you went back into debt again. It was a process of catching up and falling behind. Of course the company supported a large staff—and no one could complain that he was badly paid, for they all received much more than the going rate—and it kept the Vernon family in comfort. He and his mother both had good salaries as well as his shareholding.

That summer Lord Thatcham invited him to dinner one evening, and Edward drove to Pleasaunce, the stately Thatcham home just outside Newbury. Thatcham did not come to the point until after dinner, when Lady Thatcham had withdrawn and left them to the port and cigars.

"Edward, I had Lieutenant Colonel Allen to dinner the other night. He's the new C.O. of the 3rd Berkshire Light Infantry."

"The Territorial battalion?" Edward asked.

"That's right. It used to be the Volunteer battalion when your father was in it. They're very proud of him. He's their only V.C."

"I suppose they must be," Edward agreed.

"Allen is trying to find some new officers. He's worried about the international situation. With all this talk of war it's important to have the Territorial battalion at its best."

"That sounds sensible enough."

"He asked me about you. I said I'd mention it."

"He wants me to join the regiment?" Edward blinked.

"Why not? I'm joining."

Edward blinked again. Lord Thatcham must be nearly forty.

"That surprises you, I daresay. Allen thinks that it would help, that it would set an example, so I'm going to be a middle-aged subaltern. I've left my soldiering rather late, but you're just the right age for it. Why not come in with me?"

"I've never given it a thought," Edward said frankly. "I know nothing about the army."

"A young chap who can run a business as large and complex as yours could certainly contribute something worthwhile to the 3rd B.L.I. I thought that in view of your father's connection with the regiment you might react favorably."

"Well, yes. What do I have to do?"

"Write a letter of application to Colonel Allen and leave the rest to him."

"Is that all?"

"That's all. The regiment's a bit of a law unto itself in some ways. You'll get your appointment from the War Office, never fear. Naturally you'll have to pass a medical, but if I can, you can. Anyway it's old Doctor Haddow— he only counts your arms and legs."

"Is there going to be a war?" Edward asked.

"Don't ask me. I know nothing about it. Some say there must be, others say there can't be. It does look as though there is a certain amount of risk. Even if there isn't a war, it's rather fun being a Territorial, I think. They're a very decent crowd."

"Yes, well all right then. I don't mind."

"I can tell Allen?"

"Yes." Edward said.

So it was that very informally, over a glass of port and one of his noble host's best cigars, Edward Vernon joined his father's old regiment. When Sir Godfrey heard he was thrilled. Despite what Robert Turner said, the old man did not really believe there was any chance of a war in Europe. He considered that Robert Turner was a bit of a scaremonger, which was understandable as he had spent his life in pursuit of "news." Journalists tended to create news when times were dull.

Edward would have the best of both worlds. He could carry on the family firm and on weekends he could carry on the military tradition. It would be a bit of a slap in the face for James when his despised nephew became a second lieutenant, even if only in the Territorials.

Alice was not so pleased. The thought of Edward in the 3rd B.L.I. invoked memories she would rather have forgotten. She recalled all too clearly how Henry had regarded it as a bit of a lark, as something desirable from the social and business point of view, and as an amusing sequel to his resignation from the 1st Lancers. The lark had turned out to be a forgotten grave in the South African veldt and an ugly bronze cross in a little velvet-lined box. Alice did not want to give any more to the army. A husband was enough. It was not a subject on which she could talk to Sir Godfrey, so one day she went to see Robert Turner.

Turner was growing frail and forgetful as age began to take its toll. She was shocked by the change in him. After some general exchanges she came to the point of her visit.

"They want Edward to take a commission in the Territorials," she said in a flat voice.

"What, in the 3rd Berkshire Light Infantry?"

"Yes, Robert. He's agreed. He seems to think it's rather amusing, and all of a sudden he seems to have become aware of his father's military career. It's strange, for he's never shown any interest in it since he recovered from the excitement of the investiture."

"He's young," Robert Turner pointed out. "After all, I expect they've got Henry's portrait hanging in the mess, complete with V.C. Henry is a hero, don't forget. Edward would be inhuman not to be impressed. Why worry, Alice? It's harmless."

"I'm worried about war. If there's a war he might be mobilized like his father was. I don't want Edward to go off to war."

Turner thought. He did not want to tell her exactly what he foresaw. He compromised.

"There may be no war—in fact there probably won't be one."

"Are you sure?"

"Alice, how can any man be sure? I don't think there will be. If there *is* . . ." He paused to let the words sink in.

"If there is, it may be a big one, in which case it won't make much difference being in the Territorials."

"What do you mean?"

"It may end in conscription."

"Surely not!" It was an unthinkable idea.

"Well, if not, all fit young men will feel obliged to rush to the colors, and certainly Edward would. So, you lose nothing either way. Don't worry, Alice, Edward is going to be all right."

"If only I could be sure."

"We can never be sure of anything. I didn't have any children of my own, but I expect one never stops worrying about them, not for a moment, right up to the day of one's death."

"That's true," she laughed. "There was that terrible business with the *Titanic*. I almost died when I heard the news, and until I knew that Edward was safe I didn't sleep a wink. It was so terrible that I can't even describe it."

"I believe you all right, Alice, but you mustn't go on worrying about what may happen in the future."

"There's been talk about war. It scares me."

"It scares all of us, but it's unthinkable."

She went away, slightly reassured. If Robert Turner said it was unthinkable, then there was hope.

She didn't have a chance to discuss the subject again, for a week later he had a stroke and the next day he died. She and Edward attended the funeral of course, and Alice discovered that she had been named as an executor in his will. To her amazement he had left everything to Edward. He had no living relatives.

Robert Turner's death left her with a surprising sense of loss, because not only had he been a friend, but he was an important link with the past, indeed the only real link with those very happy days when she and Henry first set up house in two furnished rooms. And they *had* been happy days. As she thought back she knew that. There had never been any real unhappiness until Henry's death.

"God bless you, Robert," she whispered to herself, as the vicar intoned the burial service while she stood by the graveside. "God bless you, dear Robert."

Chapter 13

NOBODY at Mereford had ever heard of the Bosnian town of Sarajevo, nor indeed did they know much about the Hapsburg monarchy or the Archduke Francis Ferdinand, heir apparent to the Austro-Hungarian throne. At the time a young man called Gavrilo Princip shot Francis Ferdinand and his dumpy wife on June 28, 1914, it was a Sunday like any other, a sunny one which the family spent in the garden at Mereford. When they read about the assassination in the morning paper, it conveyed nothing. There was no feeling of destiny, of impending great catastrophic events. In fact, more interesting in the local morning paper was the news of Vernon's summer sale, which was expected to be a major event in Reading.

Lieutenant Colonel James Vernon was now fifty and due for retirement at any time. He had no medals, not a solitary campaign medal. He had missed out on the South African Medal, granted to all officers and men who had actually served in South Africa; since he had been sick on arrival and had never reported for duty technically he had never served. He had always been furious about this and about the fact that similarly he had missed out on Queen Victoria's jubilee medal and the two coronation medals for

Edward VII and George V. In James's opinion he should have had all four medals, but the fact was that he had been so consistently unpopular both in his regiment and at the War Office that when it came to allocating such things as coronation medals he was passed over. It was not, after all, as though he had had any direct participation in those stirring events. He had not.

A month was to pass between the assassination and the declaration of war against Serbia by Austria-Hungary on July 28 which actually precipitated the holocaust of world war. Another seven days would pass before England declared war on Germany, and a further eight before she declared war on Austria-Hungary. So on June 28 they basked in the summer sun and discussed the idea of going back to Cornwall for a summer holiday.

"I think August would be a good time," Alice said. "We could rent a house for the month and take some of the servants along with us. Papa, you really need a change. A month by the sea will do you good."

"The only thing that will do me any good is an elixir of life. I'm seventy-seven and I know it. Mind you," he added with a twinkle, "I'm not a bad-looking seventy-seven."

They discussed the pros and cons and eventually made up their minds to go back to Charlestown, but of course they never got there. When Austria declared war on Serbia all pretense was at an end.

"It's so unfair," Alice said to Sir Godfrey one evening when Edward was off with the battalion whose training activities had been speeded up. "Oh, God, must they have a war?"

"It may not come," Sir Godfrey said without conviction. "It may blow over yet."

"If Edward goes, I don't know what I'll do. I've given a husband, why should I have to give a son?"

There was no answer. "Edward will be all right," Sir Godfrey told her gruffly, but in his own heart there was a chill. Being a soldier and risking your own life was one thing, watching your nearest and dearest ones doing so was entirely different.

"Oh, Papa," she said, giving way to tears at last.

They stood together, the old man's arms round her shaking shoulders, his face screwed up with pain. They were helpless and they were acutely aware of the fact. The world in which they lived, this peaceful, pleasant rather cosseted world, had turned ugly and menacing.

On the day before war was declared Edward's battalion was mobilized. He made light of it as he said good-bye to them.

"We're only off to Salisbury, you know. I expect I'll be able to pop home for weekends. Nothing is going to happen, Mother."

"No, of course not," she agreed bravely, struggling to hold back the tears. "You'll look after yourself? Have you plenty of underwear and socks, Edward?"

"Any amount. Stop worrying about me. I can look after myself."

He was very smart in his uniform, wearing, of all useless things, a sword at his side. The general's heart filled when he beheld his grandson. At Edward's age he had gone off to his third campaign, in China, directly from India and the mutiny. War had been different then. He didn't like the look of this impending one at all.

Deakin, the chauffeur, drove Edward to the barracks where the battalion was assembling to be taken in trucks to Salisbury. As a subaltern, Edward had to accompany his men. He told Deakin to take the car home, and off he went to war which was declared the next day. For a month the 3rd Berkshire Light Infantry sat in Salisbury, and Edward did manage to get home on weekends. The first time Lord Thatcham gave him a lift home, and thereafter he had his own car at Salisbury. Suddenly everything changed. The 3rd was put under orders for France and all leave was stopped. Edward sent word that Deakin should come to collect the car, but before he could do so the 3rd was moved without warning and the next day they were in France. When Deakin arrived at the camp he found the car but no master. He hardly knew how to tell Alice.

The 3rd was at Mons on August 23 and at the Marne on September 15. By the end of the First Battle of Ypres, November 11, 1914, the 3rd B.L.I. had been decimated. There remained five officers and two hundred and seventy men fit for further action. The rest were mostly dead, some badly wounded. Edward had lived through the nightmare three months like a man in a daze. He had long since lost fear, just as he had lost hope. They had become automatons, going through the actions with scarcely a human feeling in their breasts. He sent home scrappy little postcards—"I'm well, hope you are too. The food is pretty awful." That was all he had time or energy or inclination for. Mereford was a million miles away. His mother and grandfather were shadowy figures. The only reality during this ferocious period was the memory of Frances Calvert. He could see her so clearly, without even having to shut his eyes. The thought of her sustained him in some peculiar way, although he was fully aware that she was dead. When the battalion finally came out of the line in mid-November, with white faces and staring eyes, human scarecrows, he found time to wonder why, when the going was toughest, he should have recalled Frances so vividly. In his own opinion it was her memory which saved his sanity.

They went back into the line in time for Neuve-Chapelle in March of 1915, a "reconstituted battalion." He had been given his second star now and was a full lieutenant. After Neuve-Chapelle they gave him the new award, the Military Cross, not so much for anything he did as for having survived. The middle-aged Lord Thatcham seemed to be rejuvenated by the war. He alone was cheerful among them, apparently enjoying it all. Because of his age and maturity he was now an acting captain and he too had the Military Cross. He and Edward sat in a little café one evening, clean and fresh for once, and drank some mediocre brandy.

"Didn't you tell me you had a cousin in the Lancers, Edward?"

"That's right, the 1st."

"They're in the line now, on the right of the Green Howards. They're lucky, they've got a quiet spot."

"Then John will be there too, I suppose. I haven't seen him since I was a kid. I wouldn't even recognize him."

"I used to think the cavalry were lucky, going everywhere on horseback," George Paveley, Earl of Thatcham, chuckled, "but the poor beggars are learning how to use trenching tools with a vengeance in this war. It must be a great blow to them." He brought up the subject at the front of everyone's mind. "I wonder when they're going to give us leave."

"We'll have to go to the Palace for these Military Crosses, won't we?"

"By jove, yes, that's a thought, but I expect they'll make us wait. We'll go together, Edward, and have a tremendous beano afterwards. Champagne—lashings of it."

Edward nodded without conviction. Beanos did not appeal to him very much, but right now the prospect of a jolly good party in London did have its attractions. He would rather be at home. He did not meet Lieutenant John Vernon of the 1st Lancers, for the 3rd B.L.I. were moved into another sector. The Lancers sat in their quiet corner of the line and kept their fingers crossed.

From April 22 to May 25 the Second Battle of Ypres raged, and the Germans used poison gas for the first time.

The battalion was in the thick of the fighting and once again casualties were high. By now Edward and veterans like him had acquired sharp instincts of self-preservation. Survival was as much an art as a matter of luck. Of course in the heat of battle it was almost all luck. Edward led an attack on a German machine-gun nest and he and his men wiped it out. He was rather surprised afterward to find that of the fifteen men he had started out with, only two were on their feet. This time they gave him the Distinguished Service Order.

Lieutenant Colonel Allen, Captain, the Earl of Thatcham, and Lieutenant Edward Vernon were all who remained of the officers of the 3rd Berkshire Light Infantry. All the others, all their friends from Berkshire, were dead. After Second Ypres, Allen was posted and promoted to full colonel and given a staff job. Thatcham was promoted again and made second-in-command to the new commanding officer, Lieutenant Colonel Michelmore. Edward was promoted to acting captain. There was nothing like a bloody war for rapid promotion, he thought.

In June, while the battalion was still re-forming, Thatcham and Edward went to London on leave. It was not their intention to spend any time in the capital—both were only too anxious to get home to Berkshire—but Thatcham had bumped into an old friend on the boat crossing the Channel, and they decided to spend just one night in London. The friend, Captain Warneford of the Artists' Rifles, was being met by his mother and sister. They arranged to meet for lunch at Scott's in Piccadilly. When they arrived, after a thorough cleanup at their hotel and looking fairly smart, they found Richard Warneford apparently surrounded by women. There was his mother, his sister, and two of his sister's friends, all of them from Wiltshire. There were introductions, champagne was ordered, menus were produced, and everyone settled down to talk. Edward found himself beside a quiet girl with dark hair and dark eyes, whose name had aroused his curiosity.

"Your name is Fownhope, isn't it?" he asked.

"Yes, Edwina Fownhope. I live at Castle Combe, near the Warnefords."

"I've never been to Castle Combe. Is it nice?"

"Very. We have a cottage just outside the village."

"I was interested in your name. My grandmother's maiden name was Fownhope."

"Was it?" Edwina Fownhope suddenly showed interest. "I wonder if we're related."

"Her father was a baronet."

"My uncle is the present baronet. I belong to the poor branch of the family," she added with a smile. "My father was a younger son—not that the family has much money anyway."

"Then my grandmother must have been your grandfather's sister. We're second cousins."

"What are you, a genealogist?" she asked.

"No. I've been working hard trying to solve the riddle, but I think I'm right."

"How strange, meeting like this in London."

"It's luck you decided to come up with your friends."

"The three of us went to school together, and Cicely Warneford thought it would be fun to see wartime London. Her brother coming home was the excuse."

"You're all going back to Wiltshire?"

"Tomorrow morning."

"Thatcham and I are going to Berkshire; we're practically neighbors. I live near Reading and so does Thatcham. Perhaps I could come to visit you? I mean, we're cousins after all."

"That would be nice. What's your name again?"

"Edward Vernon. I live at Spencer's Wood, about four miles from Reading. I've got a car."

"Have you? You must be rich."

He could not understand why she kept talking about money. Money was not very important.

"I've got enough for a car anyway."

"It would be lovely if you came to see us."

"You could come over to us too. My grandfather would love to meet you."

"Goodness, is he still alive?"

"Yes, he's seventy-eight or something. His wife was Adeline Fownhope. She died ages ago. I'm sure he'd love to meet you."

The smile she gave him drove all other thoughts out of his head. She was nothing like Frances Calvert, which is possibly why he liked her so much. Had she reminded him of Frances he might easily have ignored her. Instead she had a rather somber Botticelli look, yet when she smiled it was like the sun coming out. He was oblivious to everything except her, as his friend Thatcham noticed with amusement. It looked as though Edward had bitten the dust at last. Thatcham had often wondered at Edward's lack of interest in the opposite sex, knowing nothing of the brief encounter with Frances Calvert.

"Guess who that girl was," Edward said buoyantly as they walked back to their hotel after lunch.

"I have no idea."

"My cousin."

"Seriously?"

"Oh, yes, my second cousin. She lives at Castle Combe. It can't be more than sixty miles from Mereford. I shall visit them, of course. Her grandfather and my grandmother were brother and sister."

"Fancy that," Thatcham murmured dryly, thinking that the look in Edward's eyes had not been put there by any genealogical triumph.

"It was a strange meeting. I mean, it was your friend Warneford whose sister knew Edwina. If we hadn't met

Warneford on the steamer, I might never have met my cousin."

"That *would* have been a tragedy," Thatcham agreed, straight-faced.

They were in the garden eating strawberries and cream when the station taxi drove up the next day and deposited Edward and his luggage.

"Edward!" Alice ran toward her son and flung her arms round him. "Edward. Why didn't you tell us?"

"I wanted to surprise you, Mother."

"Let me look at you. How are you?"

She held him at arm's length and examined him critically while the general followed more slowly to meet his grandson.

"You're thinner," Alice complained.

"It suits me, don't you think?" Edward asked. It did too. He was older, more attractive.

Sir Godfrey stood and feasted his eyes, noting the three pips on each cuff and the bright ribbons on the left breast. He was enormously proud of his grandson. The two men embraced silently while Alice chattered.

"How long are you home for? Is that all your luggage? Have you any washing?"

"Help, Mother, one question at a time. I'm home for ten days starting yesterday, that is all my luggage and it's practically all for washing. I must go and buy new shirts and things."

"Ten days starting yesterday? But you've only got here today."

"Thatcham and I spent the night in London. Mother, guess who I met in London?"

"I don't know. Your cousin John?"

"No, of course not," Edward said. "John's probably in France. No, but I did meet another cousin."

"You have only one cousin."

"No, I don't."

"Do you mean Timmy? Did you meet Mary and Timmy?"

"No, Timmy's not a cousin. This is a real cousin."

Sir Godfrey and Alice looked puzzled.

"Edwina Fownhope. She's my second cousin."

"Fownhope!" Sir Godfrey was startled.

"Yes, Grandfather. I found out all about her. Her father is Guy Fownhope, the younger brother of the present baronet, Sir Giles Fownhope. Their father was Ernest Fownhope, Grandmother's brother."

"Bless my soul. I knew Ernest, of course, but we lost touch years ago. Ernest's granddaughter, well well."

"Yes, and listen both of you. They live at Castle Combe in Wiltshire, only sixty miles away. I'm going to drive over, and I've asked Edwina to come to visit us here also. I hope that's all right, Mother?"

"Yes, of course," Alice laughed, surprised at the excitement Edward was showing.

"You'll like Edwina. Wasn't it extraordinary finding a cousin like that? It was this chap Warneford you see, who's some sort of chum of Thatcham's . . ."

He embarked on a lengthy explanation while they listened with amused patience. When eventually he went inside to change into an ordinary suit, Alice turned to Sir Godfrey.

"His Cousin Edwina seems to have made a considerable impression."

"Yes, doesn't she?"

"I've never seen him so excited about a girl. I wonder what she's like."

"Well-known family anyway," the general said automatically. "We must wait and see. I expect he will have to go to London for an investiture while he's home."

"Go to London? Oh, dear."

"We can go with him. He'll have to go to collect his decorations, you know."

"I hadn't thought. Oh, Papa, time is so short. Only ten days and one gone already."

"Never mind. We must make the best of them."

Edward wasted no time in going to Castle Combe. After an early breakfast he set off the following morning and drove to Wiltshire. He arrived at eleven o'clock at the small two-storeyed house called Combe Cottage where Guy and Alexandra Fownhope lived with their twenty-two-year-old daughter. They made Edward welcome.

"What a splendid car!" Edwina exclaimed. "Will you take me for a drive?"

"Yes, it's a Daimler. Do you like it?"

"Enormously. I wish we had a car."

Guy Fownhope had any amount of charm and no money whatever. The words "shabby genteel" might have been devised for him and his wife, both of excellent families, both with expensive tastes, neither with a penny to their names. They tended to talk big and live small. Guy was always on the verge of some great financial coup, but somehow it never materialized and he lived on a tiny income from invested capital. Increasing taxation made life more and more difficult for the Fownhopes. Therefore they looked with a noticeable degree of interest upon this new cousin with the Daimler. It was impossible for Edwina to get about much in society. She had three close friends, but their brothers and their brothers' friends were disappointingly uninterested in her. It wasn't much fun being a sort of poor relative, and the girl had never had a chance.

When Edward suggested taking Edwina to Mereford, they agreed promptly and her mother even insisted on helping her to pack.

"Do you mean today?" Edwina asked, surprised.

"Er, yes," Edward agreed. He had not hoped to get such rapid agreement, but seemingly Edwina's parents assumed that he wanted to drive their daughter off at once. It suited him very well.

Not quite sure how it had all happened, Edward found himself driving back proudly along country roads and lanes till he hit the main road that led through Newbury to Reading. Edwina sat erect by his side, full of suppressed excitement. It was the most interesting thing that had happened for many years. She knew very well what her mother and father were hoping, but even if nothing came of this meeting, at least she was enjoying an adventure.

They arrived at Mereford at half-past six. It was still bright and sunny. Edward stopped the car at the beginning of the drive. He loved this view of his home.

"There you are," he said happily. "That's Mereford."

"It's charming. Have the Vernons always lived here?"

"No, no, my father bought it. It's only a hundred years old, anyway, but we love it."

"What a nice drive, and nice grounds. You're lucky."

"I know. My grandfather lives with us. He has a house in London but he hasn't lived there for years. My uncle uses it and Grandfather prefers this. He's going to be thrilled to meet you."

Sir Godfrey was, too. There was no family resemblance between this serious-looking girl and his Adeline, but the same blood ran in their veins. He and Alice made the girl thoroughly welcome. They hadn't really expected Edward to bring her back today, so a room had to be got ready hurriedly. They sat out in the garden and talked, and then Alice showed Edwina upstairs.

"What do you think of her, Grandfather?" Edward asked eagerly.

"A fine-looking girl. How did you like her people?"

"Very decent. They live in a very small house, but it's a nice one."

"What does her father do?"

"Nothing, so far as I can make out. He talked a lot about business, whatever he means by that, but I don't think he really does anything at all. Probably he buys and sells shares."

"The Fownhopes lost their fortune a long time ago. Your grandmother's father got through the last of it. I shouldn't think there's much left nowadays."

He did not add that there was an unstable streak in the family which luckily had missed his wife. He did not have very much regard for his wife's father or brother, now apparently dead.

"Anyway, Edwina's a jolly decent girl," Edward pronounced.

"Very."

"Aren't you glad I met her? I bet you were surprised to hear of the Fownhope relatives after all this time."

"Of course." Sir Godfrey patted Edward on the shoulder. "Now, tell me about the war. How are things going in France?"

Edward's face clouded. "If only you knew how difficult it was to answer a question like that. I mean there are the Germans in their trenches, and us in ours, with some muddy, bloody ground between, and every now and then we slaughter one another by the thousand in order to try to capture a bit of trench. Don't ask me what the purpose of it all is or what it will do to win the war. If we've got to beat Germany, how are we going to do it by decimating one another in the Flanders mud? Surely we've got to attack, to invade Germany, or else to destroy her armies? But we do neither. I don't see how it can go on for long. Flesh and blood can take so much and no more."

"It's bad, is it?"

"You've no idea."

Sir Godfrey looked mournful. From all he read it appeared that the war was going to be much longer than anyone cared to admit. If one considered the lengthening casualty lists, it was obviously simply a matter of time till everyone who had gone to France in 1914 was dead. The casualty rate was horrific.

"You haven't said anything about going to the Palace. Is the King investing you?"

"I clean forgot. Yes he is. Next week—twelfth July. It will make a nice birthday present."

"Do you remember going to Marlborough House years ago?"

"Of course I do. Nobody could ever forget a thing like that. I remember thinking how fat the King was."

"Now you're going on your own account."

"Strange, isn't it? I'd far rather be back here at work. I must manage to find time to talk to Mother about the stores. She's pretty busy, I imagine."

"Very. It seems business is brisk despite the war. How's your friend Thatcham?"

"Oh, he's grand. Do you know he's a major now? He'll be at the Palace on the twelfth to collect his M.C."

"That's rapid promotion."

"I don't think I ever mentioned it in letters, but out of all of us who went to France with the battalion, only three are alive, and only two are still with the battalion. Colonel Allen is on the staff now; Thatcham and I are still with the 3rd. Promotion is bound to be rapid under those circumstances. You won't tell Mother, will you?"

"Certainly not. I wish I could see the end of it all."

"So do I, Grandfather. Maybe they'll offer me a staff job one day. I'd like that. I've had a bellyful of the trenches. Any news of John?"

"John is still a lieutenant. You've overtaken him."

"Yes, but he's a regular. He'll catch up quickly enough."

"Did you come across the Lancers?"

"Not face to face, though they were near us at one time.

I think they've got a nice quiet spot at the moment."

"I was in London last month. There have been changes at St. James's Place."

"What sort of changes?"

"Young Rudkin joined up—he's in Mesopotamia, I think. Mrs. Warden has retired, gone to live with a younger sister in Brixton. Holder is still doddering on. He's the same age as I am and I won't allow James to get rid of him. Susy Wright is working in a factory—strange thing for a woman to do. Bless my soul, I always think of her as a girl, and she's a middle-aged woman now. We shan't see her again."

"So there's only Holder left of the servants?"

"Only Holder. He makes breakfast for James, can you imagine that? A comedown for Holder, believe me. James lunches and dines out. I suppose we really ought to sell the house, but I've left it to James in my will and I don't like interfering with the arrangement. It's much too big for him, of course, much too big. I can't think where he'll find servants after the war."

"Let Uncle James worry about that."

"I shall. I saw him last month. He's gone to fat. I'd never have believed it. None of our family ever got fat, but James has done it."

Edward paid scant attention. He was not really interested in his uncle and he had just caught sight of Edwina and his mother.

Chapter 14

Quite a party of them traveled to London together. There was Thatcham and his wife and their fifteen-year-old son Walter, Lord Paveley, Alice and the general, Edward and Edwina. Edwina had agreed to prolong her stay without a murmur, and there was no talk at all of her going home to Wiltshire. It was rather awkward because each person to be invested was allowed to bring two guests, and Edward felt bound to ask his mother and grandfather to be present, yet he also had an overpowering wish that Edwina should be there. She had told him quite bluntly that she didn't mind at all waiting at the hotel till they returned. The investiture was at eleven and they were celebrating with lunch at the York afterward, before returning to Berkshire in the afternoon. In the end he was forced to agree.

"I'll come to the next one," Edwina said brightly. "You must take your family to this one, Edward."

"All right, but I did so want you to be with me."

She gave him a special smile. Their friendship had progressed by leaps and bounds.

While she waited they went on to the Palace. The wartime investitures were austere affairs, and on this occasion the King was holding it in the open air, in the Palace courtyard. There was a platform with steps leading up to and away from it. On the platform was a table with all the awards laid out neatly. Only the secretary of the Central Chancery of the Orders of Knighthood and the master of the household were present, both in uniform. The King wore khaki service dress, with gleaming boots and spurs, and rows of gay ribbons on his chest. He was not tall or imposing, yet he had a most noticeable presence. As the long line of khaki- and blue-clad figures inched slowly forward, the King pinned on medals and said a few words to each recipient. Because of his D.S.O. Edward was fairly near the front of the line. When it came his turn the secretary handed the cushion with two crosses on it to the master, and read out Edward's name and the awards.

The excellent information service of the Palace had been at work. His Majesty had been briefed that this Vernon was the son of a holder of the Victoria Cross and the grandson of Queen Victoria's favorite and longest serving A.D.C. The King pinned on the two crosses, the D.S.O. with its red and blue ribbon, and the M.C. with its purple and white ribbon.

"This isn't your first investiture, is it, Captain Vernon?"

"No, sir."

"My father presented you with your father's Victoria Cross?"

"Yes, sir, he did. I was only a child."

"So now you've come back. Your grandfather must be very proud of you. Is he here today?"

Edward marveled at the attention to detail.

"He is, sir. With my mother."

"I share their pride. God bless you and keep you."

"Thank you, sir."

He saluted, turned right, and marched off and stood among the others, waiting and watching the rest of the investiture. The King had a fairly long talk with Thatcham too, for not very many earls went to the Palace to collect medals, and he had known Thatcham for a long time. After it was over, as they were on their way back to the York in a taxi, Edward told Sir Godfrey what the King had said.

"Fancy that," the old man murmured, delighted. "He asked about me. He's a great gentleman, you know."

Privately Edward tended to agree. He did not have his grandfather's intense reverence for the Royal Family, but he had been impressed despite himself. After his months in the trenches he had no illusions about the glory of warfare, yet, in some peculiar way, when the King had pinned on the medals it had all been worth it.

At the York he showed them to Edwina, and then handed them to his grandfather.

"Would you look after them for me, sir?"

"I will, my boy. Now, where's that champagne?"

It was a very gay party, only Alice and young Lord Pavely feeling at all out of it because they only had one glass of champagne apiece. The others had what Thatcham called a beano, and even Sir Godfrey was pretty much on the merry side. They were still in high spirits when they got back to Reading. Edward arranged to meet Thatcham on the nineteenth and to travel to Folkestone with him. This sobered him up a lot. His leave was almost over. In two days he would have to take Edwina home.

He took her out in the car before dinner and stopped in a quiet leafy lane.

"You realize you'll have to go home on Sunday, Edwina?"

"Yes."

"I've got to get back. I wish I didn't have to go."

"So do I, Edward."

"Do you? Do you really?" he demanded.

She nodded her head, her hands folded demurely on her lap.

"Edwina, I . . . er . . ." He fumbled for words, flushing. "Let's get married."

"When?" she laughed. "There isn't time."

"Couldn't we get a special license or something?"

"I don't think there's even time for that. Anyway, we can't get married like this."

He took her hands. "I love you. Don't you know that?"

It was a strange proposal, she thought. He hadn't even kissed her.

"I guessed, Edward."

"Of course I couldn't hope that you'd love me, but I'd be a good husband, Edwina."

She felt like laughing. How incredibly ignorant he was. "I do love you, Edward."

"You do?" He stopped and stared. "You *do?* Then you will marry me?"

"Later. We aren't engaged yet."

"We are now. Oh, Edwina."

He overcame his shyness and took her in his arms. She moved toward him willingly and their lips fused in a kiss. The passion of her response shook him a little.

"I love you," he said.

"Don't talk." As they kissed again she wondered. He was twenty-five in a few days' time. He would be spending his birthday in France with the army, yet he kissed like a child.

"We're engaged anyway, aren't we?" he demanded.

"Yes," she agreed.

"We'll go into Reading tomorrow, and buy a ring. It's Saturday and the shops will be open. Wait till our parents hear. Another Vernon marrying another Fownhope. It's wonderful, isn't it?"

"Yes, darling."

He sat silently. He had never been called darling by a girl, only by his mother. It was a new and very special experience. He could hardly believe his good fortune. He had rather expected that he would have to ask lots of girls before he would find one who wanted to marry him. Instead he had been lucky at the first attempt.

It did enter his mind vaguely that it might have been Frances Calvert he was asking. During lunch at the York he had thought of her rather a lot. It was difficult not to, in those surroundings. He dismissed these thoughts quickly. This was far more suitable . . . and she loved him. Just recalling the way she kissed made him tremble. He kissed her again.

They sat together in the car for quite a long time, embracing, not saying very much now that the decision had been taken. When she did speak, however, it was not of marriage.

"Edward, about the future, I'm not quite clear about the situation. Do you actually own this family business of yours?"

"Oh, yes. Are you wondering if I can afford to marry? I assure you it's all right, Edwina. I get my thousand a year from the firm. In fact I get it even while I'm in the army and can't spend it."

"A thousand a year!" The enormity of it impressed her. Her father had about four hundred.

"Yes," he nodded, misunderstanding, "but I don't pay for the house, you see. It's in my mother's name and she maintains it. That's why she gets more."

"Oh, she gets more, does she?"

"Lord, yes, she's the chairman. She built it up, you know. She knows far more about the company than I'll ever do. She takes two and I take one and she pays for the house and servants."

"So when your mother dies you'll have three thousand a year?"

"I suppose so, if I wanted it. I've never given it any

thought. It depends on the profits. At the moment it's doing well, but I'm never likely to have less than a thousand a year."

"Still, you *could* have a lot more," she insisted.

"I expect so. When we're married we'll live at Mereford. I'm not quite sure what will happen then, but you don't want to worry about money."

"I can see that."

"You won't want for anything, Edwina."

"You're very sweet, darling."

Again she had called him darling, and again he felt the little thrill at her words.

"We'd better go back and break the good news, and we'll have to tell your people too. Do you think they'll mind?"

"I'm sure they won't."

"When can we get married? Next leave?"

"Let's wait and see when that is."

"I want to marry you as quickly as possible."

"You're a dear man."

"Can I kiss you again?"

"Edward! You don't have to ask. We're engaged."

He grinned with delight before kissing her. He drove home, head in the clouds, and told Alice and Sir Godfrey the news with such excitement that they could hardly hide a smile. More champagne was produced, and they toasted the happy couple. Then they had dinner and all went to bed early after what had been a very exciting day.

Alice discovered that for once she could not sleep. She tossed and turned and at last about midnight she got up and went downstairs to make herself a pot of tea. She was in the kitchen when Sir Godfrey came in.

"Papa! What's the matter?"

"Couldn't sleep. I came down for some tea."

"I'm making some. I couldn't sleep either. I daresay it's

all the excitement—Buckingham Palace, champagne, the engagement."

"Yes."

"Is something wrong, Papa?"

"Nothing at all. What happens when Edward marries, Alice?"

"What have you in mind?" she countered.

"I was thinking of financial settlements."

"Normally I'd transfer the house to him on his marriage, but I think I had better wait till after the war," she said, looking a little unhappy.

"He won't want to wait till then to get married."

"No, of course not."

"I think you're wise. I wouldn't do anything at all about the house till it's all over."

"I expect you're right, but is there some special reason?"

"I don't want to introduce a note of suspicion, Alice, but I know my Fownhopes. Adeline was the best of them and quite unlike the rest of the family, as I discovered after I'd married her. They're a pretty grasping lot and they don't like being short of money. Have you noticed that Edwina talks of money a lot?"

"Ye . . . e . . . es, now that you mention it."

"Probably only because she's always short. What I'm trying to say is that you shouldn't do anything that would give her or her family any hold if . . . well, if Edward were killed. It's all right while everything is fine, but if Edward died before you . . . I don't know how to go on."

"You needn't. I understand."

"I hope you're not angry with me, Alice. I may be an old fool, but I mean well."

"You're an old darling. Here's your tea. Sit down there and drink it."

He smiled at her. "She's probably all right. She looks a thoroughly nice girl. I do not like the sound of her father and I know nothing about her mother."

"Funny you should say that," Alice smiled. "I'm not much looking forward to meeting them."

On the Saturday they wrote out notices for the *Times* and the *Berkshire Herald*. Edward enjoying the writing of them.

VERNON—FOWNHOPE. *The engagement is announced between Captain Edward Vernon, D.S.O., M.C., of the 3rd Berkshire Light Infantry, only son of Mrs. Alice Vernon and the late Captain Henry Vernon, V.C., of Mereford, Spencer's Wood, Berkshire, and Edwina Marion, only daughter of Mr. and Mrs. Guy Fownhope of Combe Cottage, Castle Combe, Wiltshire.*

"It's looks rather fine, don't you think?" he asked, kissing his fiancée's hand.

"Extremely."

"Now we must go and buy your ring. I've got my checkbook in my pocket. You must choose whatever you want, no expense spared."

"You angel," she murmured and kissed him in a way which caused him to turn scarlet.

"You're blushing," she laughed.

"Never mind, let's do it again."

Eventually she persuaded him that they had things to do, and they set out together. The ring she finally chose was a large ruby set in diamonds and emeralds. It was the most expensive ring in the shop, costing three hundred pounds. Edward signed the check without even thinking about it, and the ring was engraved while they waited. The look on Edwina's face when at last she wore it on her finger would alone have justified the cost.

They went back in triumph to Mereford for lunch. That afternoon as they strolled arm in arm on the lawns among the roses, Alice thought what a handsome couple they made, how perfectly they graced the house which she and

Henry had bought. Sir Godfrey thought how long it was since he had seen her looking so happy.

Next day Edward drove Edwina home. By arrangement they said nothing to her parents. Guy offered Edward a drink and he asked for a sherry. They sat together in the small lounge when suddenly Alexandra Fownhope's eye lighted on her daughter's hand.

"Edwina! Where did you get that ring? Guy, look at the ring she's wearing!"

Guy gaped. It was a beauty.

"It's on your engagement finger. Edwina, are you and . . . ?"

Edwina nodded happily and her mother let out a cry of pleasure. Guy Fownhope shook Edward's hand and re-filled his glass and was disappointed when Edward refused a cigar. Edward did not care much for smoking and hadn't had a cigar for a long time.

"This is great news. What did your mother have to say?" Guy demanded.

"As delighted as I hope you are, sir. We thought we might get married on my next leave."

"Yes, well we must talk about that. What a pity you have to go back."

"This war," Alexandra Fownhope remarked. "When will you be home again, Edward?"

"I have no idea. Perhaps not for many months."

"How tragic it all is. I hope you will take great care of yourself in France."

"How can he, my dear?" Guy asked, more sensibly. "We must just pray for his safe return."

Edward refused to stay for lunch, explaining that he had things to discuss with his mother, which was true. He had had very little opportunity to discuss the firm's affairs with Alice. Reluctantly they let him go, and with a farewell kiss from Edwina he set off back home, a supremely happy young man.

He and his mother talked shop all evening, and then next morning they waved him off at the station, where they met the Thatcham family. After they had returned to Mereford, Alice said to Sir Godfrey, "We ought to go to Castle Combe. After all, they have no car and we have."

"Yes I suppose so. Next week?"

"Why put it off?" Alice asked. "We can go on Wednesday."

"That suits me well enough," the general agreed.

On Wednesday they drove to Combe Cottage where they were not expected. Guy was reading his newspaper and Alexandra was working in the kitchen. They fussed over their guests effusively, and Edwina was told to get more vegetables from the garden for lunch. Sir Godfrey found himself deep in conversation with Edwina's mother, and he took an instant liking to her. Her father had been a naval officer who had been killed. She seemed a decent, sensible woman, rather plain but with a good figure.

Alice, meantime, was answering rather a lot of questions from Guy about Henry Vernon, Son and Company Limited. She answered most of them quite frankly, for Guy demanded no secrets, but his choice of questions interested her. Alice had had a considerable experience of the male sex, thanks to her innumerable business dealings, and prided herself that she could size up a man quickly. Guy Fownhope was a new type to her and she was not sure what to make of him. She only knew that he made her vaguely uneasy. This did not trouble her too much, for Edward was marrying the daughter, not the father or mother, yet before the afternoon was far advanced she thought how shrewd had been Sir Godfrey's advice. Guy was not a man she would trust with money. Worse, he gave her a permanently uneasy feeling that he was on the point of asking for a loan.

Alice was not sorry when it was time to drive home. By now she was in the habit of allowing Deakin to do most of the driving. She and Sir Godfrey sat in the back of the Daimler.

"Thank goodness petrol is short and we won't be able to come here often," she sighed.

"I saw you deep in conversation with Fownhope. What did you make of him?"

"Not my type," Alice said in reply. "I didn't like him very much, Papa."

"The wife is a pleasant woman. I got the impression that she was left in an awkward spot by her father's death and probably glad to marry anyone with pretensions to being a gentleman. Anyway there's no use in worrying about things. It's up to Edward. We must just see how it all turns out."

"I want Edward to marry and settle down. I'd like to have grandchildren of my own, you know. Edwina is a nice girl."

"Yes, she is. It will be all right, you'll see."

The following weekend Sir Godfrey went up to London for the day. He had a few things to discuss with James and he wanted to get it over. He did not think he had many years left. He telephoned his son and they arranged to meet at James's club shortly before lunch. Sir Godfrey was expected and was shown into the smoking room where James got up to greet him, cigar in hand.

He was fatter than ever, Sir Godfrey thought, and growing bald. It was too bad.

"Hullo, Papa."

"Well, James, how are you?"

"My back has been bothering me a lot recently."

"I'm sorry to hear that. The war will be keeping you busy."

"Yes."

"Just exactly what do you do at the War Office anyway?"

"I have to do with animals."

"Animals?" Sir Godfrey frowned and then voiced a sudden suspicion. "Supply and transport, you mean?"

"Well . . . er . . . yes."

"Good God. You haven't transferred to the Service Corps have you?"

"No, of course not."

"You work with them?"

"Yes," James said uneasily. "What was it you wanted to see me about?"

"Aren't you going to offer me a brandy?"

James flushed at his unintentional omission and beckoned to a waiter and gave the order.

"How's John?"

"He's gone out to Palestine with the regiment."

"Ah, so that's where they've gone, is it? Better than France, I expect."

"I don't know. The war extends to the Middle East."

"I suppose so. Got his promotion yet?"

"He's hardly due."

"Dammit, James, there's a war on."

"Yes, I read in the papers about Henry's son. I see he's engaged too."

"To a cousin, Edwina Fownhope. He's a fine young man that, a captain now."

"I saw that," James snapped. He did not wish to discuss Captain Edward Vernon, D.S.O., M.C.

Drinks came and the general sipped at his and refused a cigar.

"I'm too old for cigars. I'm seventy-eight. I shan't go on forever."

"You look very fit."

"More than I can say for you. You're fat. You should get rid of it." James flushed angrily but Sir Godfrey was sublimely indifferent. "I want to finalize my will," he said.

"I thought you'd made one."

"I have. I'm changing it."

"Oh?" James asked suspiciously.

"You can stop worrying. You'll get a copy of it. I'm not cutting you out, but I'll be making special provision for John. I shan't be coming to Town very often after this. I get tired too easily. I was at the Palace recently and it took it out of me."

James tightened his lips. He could guess why Sir Godfrey had gone to Buckingham Palace. That brat Edward with his decorations—a Territorial officer, too. It was too bad. It really was too bad. Nothing ever seemed to come right for him, or for John. He was torn between the desire to see his son covered with medals, and to know that he was safe—as he hoped he would be in Palestine.

"You needn't expect me to come to Berkshire," he said gruffly.

"I don't. I'm just letting you know how matters stand. You've managed very well without me all these years, so I don't suppose it makes much difference. I'm sorry things turned out the way they have."

"If you hadn't made such a fuss over Henry things might have been different. Just because he came home for Mother's funeral, you seemed to change, to dote on him."

"He was as much my son as you are. Did you expect me to turn my back on him forever?"

"It's the story of the prodigal son all over again, isn't it?" James sneered. "I've always wondered how any Christian could understand that parable. It's so utterly unfair, completely against all decent ideals. Henry was a prodigal son. You think more of Henry's boy than you do of mine."

"You always did oversimplify things, James. You turned me against you. You did it yourself, by your attitude to your brother and your wife."

"Leave my wife out of this, if you please."

"You're a fat, middle-aged fool, James," Sir Godfrey sighed, rising. "I'm sorry to say it, but you are. I don't think I'll stay to lunch after all. I've never pretended to be much of a religious man and I don't know a lot about Christianity and parables, but I do know a self-righteous prig when I see one, and you are one, James. I could forgive you that, but I suspect you've turned your son into another, and that was something you had no right to do. I'll make all the arrangements about the will and have a copy sent to you. It will simplify matters later. Just one thing. I want to be buried in the churchyard in Reading where there is a memorial plaque to Henry. Don't bring me back to London."

"That means I'll have to come to Reading," James exclaimed.

"It won't be like the Charge of the Light Brigade. You'll probably survive the ordeal."

"You've no right to put me in such a position."

"Frankly, James, I don't give a damn about your position one way or another. It isn't important to me. I'm only concerned with my own bones and what happens to them. Stay away from the damned funeral if you don't want to come."

"Then what would people say?" James muttered, biting his moustache.

"Poor James. There's no justice, is there?"

James stared thoughtfully at his father's erect back as the general walked from the room. That was exactly what he thought himself.

Chapter 15

THE New Year came and went. The 3rd B.L.I. was in the trenches in a quiet part of the line. Men died, of course, from snipers' bullets and from the occasional shell, but there was no wholesale slaughter. They learned to live with the mud and the lice and the boredom. Edward grew thinner and began to cough a little, but he and Thatcham were a cheerful couple and an inspiration to the other officers. They were both grateful for the respite from bloody onslaught. Edward wrote religiously to Edwina every week, and heard from her about once every three. He was well satisfied because, as he told himself, he had nothing to do but write anyway.

Early in the spring of 1916 Mary Hilton arrived at Mereford again, alone this time. To Alice's dismay she was dressed in widow's weeds.

"What's happened?" she asked Mary.

"Timothy, my husband. He died three weeks ago. I think you knew he wasn't very well, didn't you?"

"Yes, but I had no idea he was so ill."

"He hadn't been in good health for a long time, and then he caught a chill last winter and never really got over it."

"I'm sorry, Mary. He meant a lot to you, didn't he?"

"I loved him," she replied simply. "We were never able to marry, thanks to James, but it made no difference to anything. He treated me . . . the way a woman should be treated."

"And young Timmy?"

"He's at Eton."

"Eton!"

"Yes, my father arranged it. Timothy wouldn't accept any help for us—we lived quite well on his little bit, you know—but I insisted that Papa be allowed to help Timmy."

"I'm glad. How old is he now?"

"Almost fourteen. It will soon be his birthday."

"Papa never stops talking about him."

"I know. They got on so well together, didn't they?" Mary smiled. "I read about Edward in the *Times*. You must be very proud of him."

"I'd rather he were safe at home," Alice answered.

"Of course. I saw the engagement announced—that's when I made up my mind to come to see you. James's mother was a Fownhope, wasn't she?"

Alice explained the relationship and tea was served. Mary looked round the drawing room and out of the tall windows at the garden, the trees and hedges.

"Do you know, there's something special about this house. I don't know what it is. I think it's the nicest house I know."

"We've been lucky. We've always had enough to spend on it, and that's important. Houses need care and attention. I had no idea how much till we came here. It isn't really too big, you see—only twelve rooms plus the servants' wing. I've always been happy here. When I was young, never in my wildest dreams did I expect to live in a house like this."

"I like my cottage. It's small and rather untidy, but it suits me. Has anyone heard from James?"

"I gather you don't."

"No, James and I have nothing to say to each other."

"He's at the War Office. Papa saw him recently. I suspect they quarreled a little, although he didn't say so."

"I suppose John is in France with the Lancers?"

"No, they've gone out to the Middle East."

"Is he going to be another James—another toy soldier?" Mary asked, amused.

"I know very little about them, Mary. I don't bother to ask questions. They don't interest me."

"Nobody could blame you for that." She changed the subject again. "When will Edward be marrying—on his next leave?"

"I expect so. They really ought to wait till after the war, but I don't think they'll want to do that. Nobody does, nowadays. War is a sort of fever in the blood, driving people. Sometimes I think there are more marriages than casualties."

"It's natural, isn't it? Tell me all about the Fownhopes. What are they like?"

They sat and talked until Sir Godfrey returned from his morning walk. Then, while the old man fussed over his other daughter-in-law, Alice went to speak to the cook about lunch. She was surprised by the change in Mary. She had aged quite suddenly, and there were lines round her mouth and eyes which had never been there before. Perhaps it was Timothy's long illness and death; but she herself had lost Henry. She paused before a tall mirror in the hall and stared at her own face. It was curiously young and unlined. She smiled at herself wryly. What did it matter now? She had passed fifty and old age beckoned. She didn't feel old and she put in four very full days a week at the office, and still made all the major decisions. Quite unexpectedly she felt a tinge of annoyance with Mary and reprimanded herself severely for doing so.

Mary had never actually *done* anything. She had come out—it must have been back in '88, the year she and Henry had run away together—she had gone to parties till she met and married James; years later she had left James and had gone to live with Timothy. She hadn't *achieved* anything. Women, of course, weren't expected to achieve things, but she, Alice, had. She could look at Henry Vernon, Son and Company Limited, and see what she had accomplished. It gave her a good deal of pride to realize that she was not as other women were. Then the momentary sensation passed. "Don't forget your place, Alice," she chided herself, much as Holder the butler might have done many years ago, and when she rejoined Mary and Sir Godfrey no one could have guessed what uncharitable thoughts she had been thinking.

Edward came home unexpectedly, and this time he had two whole weeks. Neither Sir Godfrey nor Alice could get much sense out of him about anything—he had thoughts only for Edwina. He was determined to get married, and he swept away all opposition. He spent only an hour at Mereford before he had the car out and was driving furiously to Castle Combe. The next morning he had arranged a special license and there was a week of hurried preparation for the wedding.

It was a wartime affair of course, nothing grand about it. They were married in the church in Reading to which the Vernons owed rather nominal allegiance. The family had never been noted churchgoers. Edwina was dressed in white, and Edward wore khaki service dress. Thatcham had managed to get a few days' leave to be his best man. There was only a handful of guests, for their friends were scattered by the war; also, as Alice realized with surprise, they did not have many close friends. She herself had been too wrapped up in the family firm to bother about society, and Edward had taken his cue from her. The Fownhopes lived quietly because they were too poor to do anything else. There were about thirty people at the wedding and some of them could only be called "friends" by stretching the meaning of the word.

Of course none of it mattered. Edward and Edwina cared about nothing except getting married. There was a lunch at the Thatcham Arms Hotel, rather an austere wartime lunch. No caviar with *blinis*, Alice reflected, recalling Henry's little triumph on the opening day of the Universal Stores. Afterward the newlyweds returned to Mereford to spend their honeymoon there. Guy and Alexandra Fownhope were staying overnight. The Thatchams came to dinner and then disappeared, for he had only four days' leave and wanted to spend as much of it as he could with his family.

Guy Fownhope played true to form. They had come to Mereford on the day before the wedding, so that altogether they spent two nights. On the eve of the wedding Guy came to Sir Godfrey, worried.

"Do you know, the most awkward thing has happened. I've come away with no money and no checkbook, and I'm the bride's father! I wonder if you could lend me a hundred till I can write you out a check?"

"Certainly," Sir Godfrey said promptly. He had been wondering just how Guy was going to cope with the expense of the wedding. Now he knew the answer. "We'll go to the bank in Reading first thing in the morning, if that's all right."

"It's very decent of you. I can't think how I managed to overlook money. It was all the excitement, I expect."

"Naturally. Please don't give it a thought."

"I'll send you the money as soon as I get home," Guy insisted, and Sir Godfrey, who was a fairly good judge of human nature, knew that he would never see it. Overinsistence was a fairly reliable omen. Sir Godfrey did not ask why Guy wanted money. So far as he could see Guy had to pay out about thirty pounds in cash, and that was all; but he was far too much of a gentleman to raise the matter. If Fownhope was strapped, then he didn't mind paying out a hundred pounds, especially as it was his grandson's wedding; nor did he mention the subject to Alice who, on occasion, had a curious attitude toward money. She never let a debt slide. He supposed this might be because she regarded herself very much as the custodian or guardian of the family fortune. However, it proved also that one cannot make a gentleman out of a lady. Female thought processes were entirely different. Sir Godfrey was really rather pleased that a private bet which he had had with himself had paid off. Alice even remarked on it, saying that he seemed extraordinarily happy.

"Weddings always affect me like this," Sir Godfrey lied without a twinge of conscience.

They had only five days for their honeymoon, and Edward and his bride kept very much to themselves. They didn't get up till the middle of the morning, and they commandeered the library for their own use. It was obvious that Edward was deliriously happy, and the way he fussed over Edwina was really very sweet and not a little amusing. Nevertheless the war was a sad note underlying their happiness. Edwina was terrified that something would happen to Edward. Edward found it flattering. He had things to settle, however, and not much time in which to do it.

"Where will you live now, darling?" he asked her on the third day after the wedding.

"What do you mean?" Edwina demanded. She was brushing her hair and he was watching her with conscious pleasure. He would gladly have spent hours watching her getting dressed, with all that it entailed.

"You're married now, so you can please yourself. Would you like a little place of your own?"

"No, I think I'd rather go on living at Combe Cottage till you come home after the war."

"You wouldn't mind being with your parents?"

"No."

"I suppose it's different now. You're independent." He grinned. "Of course I shall give you a decent allowance and you'd better have a car although petrol isn't easy to get. You must learn to drive."

Edwina stopped brushing her hair. She had thought quite a lot about life with Edward after the war, when he was home again in the role of a wealthy businessman, but she had not thought much about the present. Somehow she didn't look upon it as a real marriage, not with her husband away from home all the time. An allowance and a car! That was going to make a difference.

"What sort of allowance?" she asked, trying to sound casual.

"You might as well have all of mine. I never use it anyway. A thousand a year should be enough, shouldn't it?"

She swallowed. A thousand all to herself. She'd never dreamed of so much.

"I expect that's enough," she answered, forcing herself to sound indifferent.

"We'd better buy you a small car for yourself. We could see about that this afternoon. We'll go into Reading, shall we? I'll give you your first driving lesson on the way."

"You darling."

"That's what I like to hear."

He got up from the bed and came over and hugged her. Her mouth sought his eagerly. He was so sweet, as well as being good looking—and now, apparently, generous. What a fantastic stroke of luck it had been meeting him that day in London.

"I can't think how you managed to stay single all this time," she murmured as they clung to each other passionately. "You were much too good to be allowed to escape."

"I was waiting for the right girl . . . you," he replied in a whisper.

"Lucky me. Aren't there any girls in France?" she teased.

"Only French girls," he replied quite seriously as though he were talking about street walkers.

"I thought they were something special. Haven't you ever been with one?"

He was looking at her in the mirror and she saw his eyes widen.

"Certainly not!" He sounded quite upset by the question, and for the first time it dawned on her that she had married a prude. He wasn't prudish with her, luckily—far from it—but his nature was prudish. She was so surprised by this idea that she could only stare back.

On the whole Alice was rather pleased to learn that Edwina did not propose to come to live at Mereford. She didn't dislike Edwina—in fact she rather liked her—but she felt instinctively that Edwina should be with her parents until she could come to live permanently with Edward.

She raised the question of Edwina's support with Edward and was glad to learn that he was making adequate arrangements for his wife. Edwina was really rolling in money now, for Sir Godfrey had given her a wedding present of two thousand pounds and had given a similar sum to Edward. He had not missed the gleam in Guy Fownhope's eye when he learned that his daughter had two thousand pounds, but Sir Godfrey was prepared to wager that it would not be easy to get Edwina to part with any of it. It would be interesting to find out if he was right. So Edward went back to France, and Edwina drove herself to Castle Combe.

Trouble began almost at once. Edwina was quick to

take advantage of her new independence. She was paying her parents a moderate sum for living at the cottage, and she considered that this discharged her liability to them. She went out and about, visiting friends in her car, and her shopping expeditions to Bristol became more frequent and prolonged.

Guy, who had conveniently forgotten to send a check to Sir Godfrey for the hundred pounds he had borrowed, and who would have surprised the general otherwise, began to hint heavily that he could always use a little ready cash and that it would be nice to be able to share the car. Edwina ignored the hints. Her mother, sensing trouble, said nothing, mainly because she knew that nothing would make any difference to father or daughter. When he failed to get any response to his hints about money, Guy tried different tactics. One morning, about two months after the wedding, he remarked casually at breakfast:

"Oh, Edwina, we're rather short of several things and I asked Littleton's to send us some wine and a few cases of spirits, and some cigars. I'm a bit short of the ready at the moment, so I asked them to send the bill to you. You wouldn't mind helping out temporarily, would you?"

"I shall send the bill back," Edwina retorted sharply. "It's nothing to do with me."

"But I can't pay it just at the moment. It's only a temporary arrangement."

"You should have asked me."

"There wasn't time."

She stared at her father and her mouth curled unpleasantly. "You don't expect me to believe that, do you? Look here, I give you two pounds a week, which is more than it costs to keep me here now that I buy my own clothes. That's all you're getting."

"You're forgetting about the years when we had to pay out for you, aren't you?" Guy demanded.

"What do you expect, free children?" his daughter asked

sarcastically. "It's your job to support your children till they can support themselves. You talk as though I owed you money."

"You went to a good school . . ."

"My uncle paid for *that*," she flashed back and he bit his lip.

"Well, never mind all that. If it annoys you I shan't order anything again."

"Order what you like so long as you pay for it. Don't expect me to pick up your debts, Father. They're your own business."

He found her attitude unforgivable. It was incredible that his only child, on whom he had genuinely lavished affection and love, should come into money and not spread a little of it around. She knew they were hard up, always had been and always would be. What had made her so ungrateful and selfish? he asked himself. The answer, which he quite failed to realize, was her upbringing. Money was an unpleasant topic at Combe Cottage, because it was always short. Now that she had independence and an allowance, she was not going to let anyone take it away from her. It was far too precious. She was quite correct in saying that two pounds a week more than covered her cost to them, and she did not consider that they had any further claim. Besides, it had always annoyed her that Guy never went without his whiskey and cigars, even if his wife and daughter had to make clothes last longer than most other women in their position.

They were too firmly attached to their own viewpoints. Guy sulked and Edwina simply ignored him. However, when she went to Bristol one day and did not return, matters came to a head. Guy was furious when she came home eventually.

"Where have you been? What happened?"

"I've been to Bristol. You knew that."

"But, dearest, you didn't come home last night," her mother said mildly. "We've been terribly worried."

"I met some people and stayed the night."

"Stayed where?" Guy demanded stung by her indifference. They really had been worried about her, imagining an accident with the car.

"At a hotel, where else?"

"Alone?"

"Naturally." She had got out of the car and stood facing her father calmly.

"Are you mad? You're married. You've no business staying alone like that in hotels."

"Oh, don't be silly. I was quite safe."

"It isn't done," Guy snapped.

"It is now, there's a war on. I wasn't the only woman alone in the hotel."

"Don't do it again, do you hear? I won't stand for it."

Edwina said nothing till they were in the cottage and Alexandra had gone into the kitchen to make a pot of tea.

"Look here, Father, you'd better understand that you have no control over me. I'm over twenty-one, married, and financially independent. You can stop talking about what you'll stand for. I'm not a child."

"What would your husband think, eh?" Guy demanded.

"I neither know nor care, but I don't suppose he would mind."

"While your husband is away in France I'm responsible for you," Guy insisted.

"You are *not!*" she shouted, stamping her foot angrily. "I shall do as I please."

"Have some tea," Alexandra suggested placatingly as she brought in a tray.

"I'll have a drink," Guy grunted.

"Yes, you would," Edwina retorted.

"What the devil does that mean?" her father flashed at her, stung by her tone. "Eh?"

"I would have thought you knew perfectly well."

"Are you suggesting that I drink too much?" he shouted.

"You used the words, not me." She laughed unpleasantly.

"Edwina, that's grossly unfair," her mother said heatedly. Guy drank, yes, and fairly regularly, but he had never been what was termed "the worse for drink," and nobody knew it better than his wife who had a horror of drunkards.

"Oh, you would stand up for him, Mother. He's got you eating out of his hand."

"I will not be spoken about like that," Guy shouted, thoroughly enraged. "You cheeky young thing, what you need is a beating."

"From you? Don't be silly." She sneered and he grasped her by the wrist and glared at her. Her reaction was to slap him hard across the face. He dropped her wrist and stepped back, dazed.

"Don't you touch me. I'm another man's wife."

"Edwina!" Alexandra screamed. "You've struck your father."

"It's about time somebody did. If anyone needs a beating, he does. Oh, I'm fed up with the pair of you."

She ran upstairs while Alexandra comforted her outraged spouse and poured him a very strong drink, torn between the knowledge that he had precipitated the whole disgusting scene, and horror at her daughter's unnatural behavior toward him.

Guy sighed and leaned his head against her. "I'm sorry, Alex. She gets on my nerves and has done ever since the wedding."

"Don't you think that she resents our expecting her to

share her money? We don't even know how much allowance she gets."

"You can see how much she spends. She's a selfish little brat. Besides, she really had no business staying in Bristol like that."

"If we'd had a telephone she could have called up and said she was staying, but we don't have a telephone."

"We can't afford one."

Alexandra was silent. If Guy did not insist on handmade shoes and shirts, and hand-tailored suits from one of the most expensive tailors in the country, if he smoked and drank even half what he did, there would be plenty of money. He owned the cottage and had no rent to pay, and an income of nearly ten pounds a week in 1916 was very comfortable indeed—but it did not allow one to live like a lord. She sighed again, helplessly.

Five minutes later they heard Edwina in the hall. Alexandra opened the door and saw her daughter struggling with three suitcases.

"Edwina, what are you doing?"

"Leaving, of course. I wouldn't stay in the house with that man."

Guy, who had joined his wife, blinked in sheer disbelief.

"Where are you going?" Alexandra stammered.

"I don't know. To a hotel somewhere to start with. I need time to think."

"But, darling . . ."

"It's no use, Mother. My mind is made up. I'll write."

Edwina turned and hauled her three cases out to the car, loaded them in the back, and drove off. Guy held his wife firmly by the wrist.

"Let her go," he said in a hard voice. "I'm glad to be rid of her."

"Oh, Guy, she's all we've got."

"Rubbish, we have each other, and I for one would

prefer to keep it that way. She's Edward Vernon's problem now, not mine."

When the car had disappeared from sight, he released his wife.

"I'm going to have a drink," he grunted and went back to the sitting room. Alexandra sighed. There was nothing else to do except sigh.

So it came about that Edward's next mail brought him a letter from the York Hotel in London. He stared at the address and then read the letter. It related at some length, and entirely from her point of view, how terrible things had been at home, what a fiend her father was, and how she had been forced to escape. She was now staying at the York, for it was really the only hotel she knew. Did he remember how they had lunched there at his investiture? She was looking for a flat but it was difficult to find anything suitable. The York was very comfortable and the food was excellent and really it was a convenient arrangement. She could easily afford it on his allowance.

There was not a word about Mereford, and the dazed Edward wondered why she had not gone straight there on leaving Castle Combe. He read the letter several times and waited for a week before replying. When he did, he wrote rather a short letter, saying that she should go to Mereford where she would be properly looked after. She could not, he pointed out, stay alone at a hotel indefinitely, especially in wartime London where anything might happen. He said nothing at all about her family or the quarrel, but he did write by the same post to Alice asking her to urge Edwina to go to Mereford.

When he saw her reading the letter, Sir Godfrey sensed at once that something was wrong and asked her outright. She handed the letter to him silently, and he scanned it.

"So they've fallen out at Castle Combe, have they? Probably over money."

"How can you possibly say that, Papa? She has plenty."

"That's the point. My guess is that Guy Fownhope has tried to borrow from her and been refused, so they have quarreled."

"Surely not!"

"I may be wrong—it's only a guess. What are you going to do? Go to see them or write?"

"I shall write to Alexandra and invite her here."

"No car."

"I can send Deakin."

"That's true. Are you going to write to Edwina, or shall I go up to Town and see her?" he offered.

"It's unfair to ask you to make the journey."

"I'm not in the grave yet. I can go if you'd like."

"Perhaps it would be better if you did," Alice said thoughtfully. "She might resent me a little."

"That's what I thought. I'll go tomorrow."

"I shall write to Alexandra tonight. Oh dear, Papa, all this upset so soon after the wedding."

"It's too bad," he agreed, "but it could be worse. I have a feeling that the less Edwina sees her father the better things will be for Edward and her—but don't ever say I said so. It's just a feeling. Guy Fownhope is not the sort of man Edward would like."

"Alexandra is nice."

"I know. She's a different matter. Blast it, I know they're happy, but why did he have to marry a girl who has a family problem? I think we've earned a little peace and quiet, you and I."

She smiled and patted his hand.

"There's no peace and quiet where children are concerned," she said.

Chapter 16

H<small>E</small> saw her from the doorway, sitting in a corner and almost obscured by a potted plant. She was talking to a young baby-faced lieutenant in the army, a boy in one of the Highland regiments, wearing a kilt. They were laughing happily and he saw her put her hand over the boy's. Frowning he walked slowly through the hotel lounge.

It was only when he stood close to them that Edwina looked up. Her eyes widened and she smiled.

"Sir Godfrey! I didn't know you were coming."

"There wasn't time to tell you. May I join you?"

"Of course. Let me introduce you. General Sir Godfrey Vernon, Lieutenant Neil Johnstone."

"How do you do, sir?" the boy said respectfully.

"Good evening. Are you on leave?"

"Yes, sir. This is my last night."

"Too bad. You're old friends, of course?"

"Oh no," Edwina smiled. "Neil and I met here in the hotel."

"I see." He did not see at all. "I wanted to speak to you privately."

"Of course, I'm sorry. Neil, you'd better leave us. I'll meet you at seven."

"Won't you dine with me tonight?" Sir Godfrey asked her. "I'm staying overnight."

"Oh, dear, I'd love to, but this is Neil's last night before he goes back to the trenches, and I've promised to have dinner and go to a show."

"It's quite all right . . ." the young lieutenant began.

"No, we'll do as planned. Sir Godfrey and I can talk later, after you've gone."

Sir Godfrey's mouth tightened but he said nothing and nodded politely as the young officer rose and took his leave.

"Well, how are things at Mereford?" Edwina asked, perfectly composed.

"They're fine. More important, how are they with you?"

"Staying here suits me perfectly. I think I shall make the arrangement permanent—until Edward comes home from the war, naturally."

"I don't think you should. Edward told us you were here and asked if we couldn't persuade you to come home to Mereford. It would be much more appropriate, infinitely cheaper, and less likely to give rise to comment."

"Money doesn't matter. I have a generous allowance."

"You could be saving it," Sir Godfrey pointed out a little coldly. "However, the main point is that it really isn't suitable for a bride to stay alone at a hotel, especially in London, especially . . ."

"In wartime," she capped his words with a charming smile. "Don't tell me. I've heard it before. Times have changed, you know. Women are no longer creatures to be locked up in the drawing room and produced at mealtimes. I prefer to stay here."

"Yes, well it isn't only a matter of what you prefer, is it?" Sir Godfrey asked mildly. "There is Edward to consider. He's sitting out there in the trenches, in danger and in acute discomfort, and it would be much nicer for him if you were to stay with us. I gather that you don't want to go back to Castle Combe."

"God forbid," she exclaimed, and smiled again. It was difficult to be angry with her, Sir Godfrey thought, she was such a vivacious girl. She had changed a lot since he had first seen her. She still had the Botticelli look, but she was much more effervescent than before.

"Quite. Then what is your objection to Mereford?"

"If you must know, it would be very dull for me without Edward. Life is much more interesting here."

"Are you talking about young officers on leave?" he asked bluntly.

"That's part of it, I suppose. I like company my own age, and they need company."

"Edwina, this is hardly the proper behavior for a bride."

"I'm doing no harm. Are you suggesting I'm behaving improperly?"

"It isn't only what you do, but what you appear to do. This could cause a scandal."

"How? Who knows where I am? Anyway, I'm quite sure Edward trusts me even if you don't."

Did he trust her? Sir Godfrey wondered. He didn't know. It wasn't his affair.

"You seem to have kicked over the traces completely since you were married," he pointed out.

"I never had the chance before. I was totally dependent on a father who was perpetually short of money."

"I can understand that bit all right. Look here, Edwina, I'm appealing to your common sense and good taste. Also, although living in a hotel might be amusing at first, it will soon pall. You won't feel the same way about it a month from now."

"Then I'll reconsider a month from now."

"What are we to tell Edward?"

"Why not let me tell Edward? He is my husband."

"I'm not going to make a nuisance of myself. You've promised that young fellow to dine with him and go to a show. I'll go and unpack and dine alone. I shall stay tomorrow, and we can talk again."

"If you wish, Sir Godfrey, but honestly I have no intention of coming to Mereford yet."

"Then you can turn your attention from boys playing at soldiers and entertain an old man."

"I would love that," she assured him with another smile.

It seemed that he couldn't get through to her. He was only scratching the surface, and the surface was hard and glittering. She was charming, respectful, full of fun, not at all the picture of a young bride pining for her husband away at the wars, and she was resolute. She dined with her young lieutenant of Highlanders, spared him a gay wave, and on their way out they stopped at his table and exchanged a few words. He did not see her again till after breakfast which she had in her room. By then Lieutenant Johnstone had gone.

He tried talking to her again, but he made no headway. They ended up by going out for a stroll in the park before lunch, lunching together, and then she saw him off at the station on his way back to Reading. As the train pulled out he stood with his head out of the window, waving to her. She was slim and erect, a delightful sight. It was really rather nice to be seen off by such a pretty young girl, yet he had to admit that his visit to Town had been a failure.

For once he picked his words carefully when talking to Alice. Normally he said whatever came into his head, so close were they to each other, but now he remembered that he was telling Alice about her new daughter-in-law. He didn't want to say anything that might bear unwanted fruit later.

"I don't understand," Alice complained. "I know you've told me, but I still can't quite make out why she doesn't come home to Mereford."

"Probably because it isn't her home. Alice, you're middle-aged and I'm an old man. We're no company for her. What she wants is Edward."

"Of course. I know *that*, but if we're no company for her, what company will she find in London?"

"I expect she meets other young people. She may have friends."

"Don't you know?"

"I didn't pry. I pointed out that Edward would be happier if she were here, but it made no difference."

For the first time Alice was disappointed in him. She had expected more. She wondered a little guiltily if he had tried very hard—or was it that he was too old? She regretted that she had not gone to see Edwina herself. Alexandra's visit, the following weekend, did not help much. Alexandra was loyal to her rather worthless husband, very fond of her daughter, and anxious not to do or say anything to upset the marriage—all of which meant that Alexandra really said very little. She succeeded, as a result, in leaving Alice with the impression that it was all Edwina's fault for staying at a hotel in Bristol; and from this Alice found it natural to wonder just what sort of girl Edward had married anyway, and what was behind this apparent fixation for staying alone in hotels. Although Alice and Henry had not married until four months after their first child was conceived, she was remarkably straight-laced. Edwina's behavior distressed her and she began to distrust her daughter-in-law. She reflected also on the garbled story about Guy and the wine and cigars. How unnatural for Edwina to refuse her father a temporary loan. Alice forgot her earlier opinion of Guy Fownhope as she considered Edwina's disloyalty and hardheartedness. She sent Alexandra a check for a hundred pounds but was careful to say nothing to Sir Godfrey.

As a result of all this Edward found it difficult to understand the letters he received from his mother-in-law, his mother, and his wife. In the end he did what anyone else would have done under the circumstances, assumed that his mother and mother-in-law had misunderstood the situation, and took Edwina's word for everything. It made him a little uneasy, her staying at the York, but she assured him that she was perfectly safe and capable of looking after herself, and that it was really much better for her to have the distractions of London to amuse her than to sit brooding in an empty bedroom at Mereford. After which Edward dismissed the whole matter from his mind. There were far more pressing realities near at hand. June 1916 saw the start of the Battle of the Somme, and the 3rd Berkshire Light Infantry was getting ready to move up to the front. Everyone was frantically busy.

In July he was wounded, shot in the leg. Unfortunately for him it was not serious enough to get him sent back to England. He was treated and convalesced briefly in France, which disappointed him greatly. It would have been nice to get home so quickly after his short honeymoon and to surprise Edwina by walking into the hotel. That would have to wait till later.

While he was in the hospital he received a letter from Sir Godfrey, whose handwriting was now very shaky, but who wrote to Edward once a month. This time he had news of James and John. James had finally been promoted from lieutenant colonel to colonel, and the announcement in the *Times* gave his appointment as "Supplies Liaison at the War Office." Apparently this was what he had been doing for years and it looked, Sir Godfrey wrote, as though he had been promoted *in situ*. It was an unexpected promotion, one for which James could thank the war. Indeed had it not been for the war he might well have retired some years before. The same Gazette had announced the promotion of John from lieutenant to captain. He was still with the 1st Lancers in the Middle East. Sir Godfrey had written to James to congratulate him, for he was meticulous about such matters, and it appeared from James's hasty reply that John was in some sort of base camp and, as Sir Godfrey put it without mincing words, "safely sheltered from war and talk of war."

The world was upside down, Edward thought. There was John, a young professional soldier brought up to an army career, only just promoted in 1916 for the first time since the war had started, sitting in the sunshine, no doubt thoroughly enjoying life in Cairo or wherever he was; and he, a civilian with no conceivable interest in a military career, was the senior captain in his battalion and twice decorated. It was all wrong. He felt rather sorry for his cousin. He considered writing to John, but dismissed the idea. He had not forgotten that John had ignored the twenty-first birthday present which had been sent to him.

It seemed that he was no sooner able to walk without a stick than he was back in the trenches. He was needed there, and once again the fury and despair of war closed over him and everything else became unreal. Nothing mattered except day-to-day survival.

They came out of the line in November. The British had lost over four hundred thousand men in one long and bloody battle. It worked out at about a hundred thousand a month, over three thousand, three hundred a day. The figures were meaningless, just as the sad, filthy, lifeless bodies themselves were meaningless. Any resemblance between them and human beings was, as the saying went, purely coincidental. Edward longed for leave, but there was no respite. The shattered battalion had to be licked back into shape again, ready for whatever the future held. Thatcham was finally posted away from them, to be given command of a raw battalion whose colonel had suddenly became ill and had had to be invalided back to England. It was remarkable for a man who was an elderly second lieutenant in 1913, but the Earl of Thatcham, at forty-two, was tough and resourceful. Edward was sorry to see him leave, the last link with the old prewar 3rd B. L. I. For a few weeks Edward acted as second-in-command until a major from the Indian Army was posted to them to replace Thatcham. Edward took an instant dislike to him and his desire to get home increased almost daily.

Christmas came and went, a Christmas of almost abject misery. It occurred to Edward that in some ways he would rather be in the line than out of it. There was less time to think then. It was not till February 1917 that his colonel sent for him and told him to take two weeks' leave. Overjoyed, Edward set off for England. What a surprise they would all get. His best uniform was a tattered and stained thing, and he felt a certain amount of perverse pride in his scruffy appearance as he moved among gilded staff officers on the steamer. Even so, his boots and belts gleamed with that dark, rich patina that comes with long usage and frequent polishing. He knew no one on the crossing, and indeed he knew very few people in France. They had a nasty habit of getting killed. When he arrived in London he hurried at once to the York where he presented himself at the reception desk.

"I'm Captain Vernon," he told the clerk. "My wife is here, I believe."

"Mrs. Vernon? In 141, sir."

"Yes, well, that's a single room I suppose?"

"Yes, sir."

"We'd better move into a double for my leave. Or, I tell you what, give me a double for two weeks, will you? She'll want her old room back, so she'd better keep it on. A double for me."

"Yes, sir."

"Where is my wife, do you know?"

The man glanced at the key rack and then at the clock. "I believe she may be in the bar, sir. Shall I have her paged?"

"No, no. Get someone to take my valise up to my room, will you, and my coat and cap? I'll find her."

"Very good, sir."

Edward did not see the man's worried look. He followed the notice which pointed the way to the cocktail bar. As he approached the glass doors he slowed down. He saw her at once, sitting on a tall stool, glass in hand, with four men round her, one a naval officer, the rest army. Plainly they were having a good time.

Edward pushed open the door quietly and went inside. The carpet was thick and made no sound, but they were all laughing so much that they wouldn't have heard him on a stone floor. He stood at the corner of the small bar, about six feet away, and asked for a whiskey. He paid for it and splashed it with soda, and felt the liquor bite at the back of his throat. He ordered another. Nobody paid any attention to him.

"Oh, Bobbie," he heard his wife squeal with delight, "you're a darling man. Isn't Bobbie a darling man?"

One of them was looking at Edward curiously and Edwina, noticing this, swiveled to follow the man's glance. She saw her husband, silent, expressionless, standing at the end of the bar watching her. Her jaw dropped.

"Oh, my God . . . Edward! Darling, why didn't you tell me? Here, help me down," she commanded one of her adoring escorts. "It's my husband."

There was a sudden silence as she rushed up to Edward and kissed him.

"When did you arrive, darling?"

"One drink ago," he replied woodenly. "Say good-bye to your friends, including darling Bobbie."

"I say, steady," a major said.

"Would you like me to thrash you here, or would you prefer to come outside?" Edward asked, and standing there in his stained uniform, his ribbons challenging them across the bar, his face dour and unsmiling, his height and breadth of shoulder rather daunting, nobody felt like replying.

Edward gave a little contemptuous smile, and then held open the door for Edwina. She swept out, flushed with anger. When they reached the foyer she turned on him.

"How dare you behave like that?" she demanded.

"Let's go into the lounge and have a drink. I feel like another."

"You've taken to drinking, have you?"

"Not noticeably. I found you with a glass in your hand, sitting in a bar like a tart."

"Are you calling me a tart?" she demanded dangerously.

"Not yet. Are you one?"

"Beast," she said, white with anger.

He beckoned to a waiter and ordered a large whiskey for himself.

"What about me?"

"You've had enough. Do you know something? I've been in a ferment all the way home. I've lived this scene a thousand times since I was given leave yesterday—how I would walk into the hotel, find you sitting knitting or sewing or something, here in the lounge, how you'd fly into my arms, how we'd hurry up to our room . . ." He stopped and shrugged. "Instead I find you holding court among a lot of uniformed camp followers."

"They're officers like you."

"Officers they may be, but I doubt if they are like me, my dear."

"Peter is the second-in-command, or whatever they call it, of a submarine."

"Then he should have more sense than to mess about with the wife of another officer. You know, I trusted you."

"Why not? Are you suggesting I've been unfaithful to you?"

"Have you?" he asked, cocking his head on one side.

"My God, you really are a beast."

"You didn't swear so much when I first met you. I don't like women who swear."

"I smoke too," she sneered.

"You don't surprise me."

"What does that mean?" she flashed.

"Never mind, it isn't important. We're going to Mereford. I was going to stay here with you in the hotel. I thought it might be fun, just the two of us alone. I had intended to go home for a couple of day visits only, but I've changed my mind."

"I'm not going to Mereford," she challenged.

"No? I am."

"Suit yourself."

"You're refusing to accompany me, your husband, on leave from France? You won't come home?"

"It isn't my home," she answered foolishly. She did not particularly want to face Alice, anticipating rigid disapproval.

"It's my home and therefore yours," he corrected sharply. "Don't forget that."

"Well, I'd rather stay here. Do you have to go?"

"It might be less embarrassing than meeting more of your . . . friends."

"Oh don't be *silly*, Edward," she said impatiently. "I live here, and they come into the bar. They all know I'm married. We cheer each other up. There's no harm in it."

"I don't suppose there is," he admitted, softening a little, "but it isn't very nice, is it?"

"What's wrong with it? Do you expect me to sit and mope?"

He did, he realized, but he decided not to admit it. "I'm sorry," he said, weakening, and she gave a little smile of triumph. "I wasn't expecting to find you having a party. I told you, I'd imagined it differently."

"But, darling," she said softly, putting her hand on his, "so did I. Do you think I haven't ached and longed for you? If I'd known you were coming it *would* have been different, but I didn't know. Today was just another day— another day without you—which had to be lived through somehow. They're company for me. We drink and laugh and sometimes go to a show or have dinner together, and I don't mind it all so much. There's nothing *wrong*, Edward."

"Of course not. I never believed there was. Ah, here's that drink. I've booked a double room for myself for a fortnight."

"Oh, goodie," she laughed. "That's more like it. Shall we have all our meals in bed?"

They exchanged glances and Edward drank his whiskey.

"Let's go up. I'm not hungry. I can wait till evening."

"So can I, darling," she said, taking his arm. "So can I."

He soon forgot the shock of finding her in the bar with other men. For one thing, he had undergone so many shocks since August 1914 that another here or there made little impression; for another, he was still wildly in love with her. Now that they had got over their little squabble, she was as loving and as much fun as ever. She knew a lot of people and introduced him to several, and they seemed nice enough. He allowed himself to be lulled into accepting the situation, because leave was short and what he wanted was the reassurance that she loved him. Less than ever did he think it was suitable for her to stay at the hotel, but he had no intention of provoking a crisis. People did unusual things in wartime. When it was all over they would settle down quietly and forget all this.

They went to Mereford after a week. It was not a successful visit. It started off well, for Alice and Sir Godfrey were surprised and delighted when they arrived together in a taxi, less delighted to discover there was no luggage. Alice was distressed to learn that they would go back to Town on the last train that evening.

Edward tried to explain that they wanted to spend his leave together, that they had had so little of each other, and that the war made things different. It was easy to agree with her son, but not so easy in her heart to accept his arguments. She lived for his letters and his infrequent leaves. Sir Godfrey saw how she felt and tightened his lips. It was too bad and it was not at all like Edward. The girl seemed to have bewitched him.

"There are things to talk about—about the company," Alice said lamely.

"Oh, Mother, you know you manage very well without me. I don't want to spend my precious leave talking about Vernon's."

"No. I'm sorry."

"It's wonderful to be home again. I've missed it all so much. Perhaps the war will end this year."

"Do you think so?" Sir Godfrey asked anxiously.

"I've no idea, sir. One hopes."

"Have you been fighting much?" Alice asked anxiously, and Edward blinked. Fighting was what it was all about.

"Not very much," he lied. "It's been quiet where I've been."

"No more medals, eh?" Sir Godfrey said brusquely.

"I've had my share, Grandfather. I'm all for a quiet life."

"I see your friend Thatcham has got his command."

"That's right, the 8th Herefords."

"He got a bar to his Military Cross."

"I didn't know that. Good for him."

"I thought you might have been there."

"Nowhere near them. We've got a new C.O. and a new Number Two. The C.O.'s not a bad sort, but Ellis, the

Number Two, is a fool—a dangerous one too. He seems to think the war is a game."

"Territorial?"

"No, he's a regular, an Indian Army type. It doesn't seem to have dawned on him yet that the Germans aren't a bunch of tribesmen. He's got an M.C. You'd think he'd know, but some people never learn. I'll be glad when it's all over. I'm going to have a three-month holiday before I go back to work. Edwina and I will go abroad—somewhere sunny, somewhere there's no mud."

He caught his mother's eye and smiled. "It's not the Germans, Mother, it's the mud. I'm more afraid of pneumonia than of bullets."

The joke fell flat, and so did the rest of the day. He promised to come back before returning to France, but it was a promise he broke. His time with Edwina was too precious and she refused to make the journey again, saying that it was dull and boring and that she didn't want to share him. He did not want to share her either.

He had overcome all his resentment about her friends and her gay life. Somehow it no longer seemed very important. When he asked her about her parents, she told him quite calmly that she no longer wrote to them and had not seen them since leaving Castle Combe. This sounded extremely callous, but he reminded himself that he didn't know the full story. No doubt they'd been nasty, and his mother's letter at the time had suggested that the quarrel wasn't entirely Edwina's doing.

She went to Folkestone with him to see him off, a gesture which pleased him enormously. As he walked beside her among the milling troops, he was proud of her. She was a striking young woman and he saw other men eyeing her appreciatively. This tickled his vanity.

They kissed good-bye.

"Take care of yourself, Edward. Come back soon."

"As soon as I can, you know that. I'm sorry it was such a short leave."

"You'll write?"

"Every week," he promised, "and you must tell me all about what goes on at the York. It will be good to have news of civilization."

"I promise," she agreed.

As he embarked she felt sad. She was wildly in love with him, enormously proud of him, and furiously resentful that he should be taken away from her like this. The worst of it was that she hated being without him. She knew that she would be laughing and drinking with other men that same night—not because she preferred them to Edward, but because she preferred them to the aching void his absence created.

She stamped her foot unconsciously and scowled. It was all unfair. A staff captain, seeing her, hesitated and then approached.

"Is something wrong?" he asked, touching the peak of his cap.

"No, no, nothing, thank you."

"Seeing someone off?" he asked, gesturing in the direction of the steamer.

"Yes . . . my brother," she lied. If she said "husband" he might go away.

"Too bad. Are you returning to London?"

"Yes."

"I can drive you. I have a staff car."

"Oh, can you really? That would be wonderful."

"Shall we go then?"

"I'd better wait till they sail. Is that all right?"

"Yes, I'll come back here, shall I?"

She gave him a dazzling smile. Then she saw Edward against the rail and waved. The glossy staff captain moved off. He had plenty of time. Let the brother go back to the war.

Chapter 17

A<small>T</small> the end of May, Captain Edward Vernon was transferred from the 3rd battalion to the 1st, the regular
peacetime battalion of the Berkshire Light Infantry. The
1st needed a new second-in-command and Captain Vernon
was the most battle-seasoned senior captain available, as
well as being a peacetime member of the regiment, one of
the few surviving ones. He was gazetted temporary major
and said good-bye to the battalion with which he had come
to France two and a half years before.

He liked his new battalion immediately. The 1st, like the
3rd, had only two surviving officers, but unlike the 3rd—
which had lost both Thatcham and himself, thereby having none of its original officers—these two were still with
the battalion. One was the colonel, Lieutenant Colonel
Maurice Seton, D.S.O., who had been a regular Army
second Lieutenant at the outbreak of war. The other was
Captain Donald Somerville, M.C., who had been a lance
corporal when they had sailed for France and had been
commissioned eighteen months before. They welcomed
Edward and the three of them, quite unconsciously,
formed a little inner circle in the battalion. Fortunately
this did not upset the other officers, and the 1st was a

fairly happy family. They were up to strength when Edward joined them. Seton told him bluntly that something was brewing and that they could expect trouble soon.

The trouble came quickly enough. On June 7 the 1st B.L.I. helped to capture Messines Ridge. Edward and Somerville were both wounded, neither seriously. Seton was killed, along with four other officers, ten noncommissioned officers and a hundred and forty-seven men. Messines Ridge was an expensive acquisition for the 1st B.L.I. Edward was put in temporary command for a month until a new colonel arrived. The following month he was notified officially of the bar to his D.S.O.

He managed to get away to Paris for a weekend, which was a welcome break. He luxuriated in a hot bath, ate a late breakfast, and found a convenient bar. It would have been more fun if Somerville had been able to get away too, but Somerville could not be spared. Edward's wound, a bullet through the hand, caused him no trouble. It would leave an unpleasant scar and it would be tender for a long time, but as it was his left hand he was not greatly concerned.

He was just starting on his second drink when he was aware of another officer coming into the little bar which he had chosen as having more character than the hotel. Automatically he noted the things one officer notes about another—the very smart, almost new uniform, the gleaming buttons, the lack of medal ribbons, the untired, unlined face—this one was out from England. Or was he? He had a deep tan. Perhaps from India. Edward waited till he was seated near him and studied the badges. The 1st Lancers! That was a surprise.

"Hullo," he said cheerfully, "have your lot been sent back to France?"

As the other officer turned, Edward realized at once who he was. He could not be mistaken about that face—it was too like his own. This must be his cousin John.

"That's right." John Vernon scanned the other's insignia and did not recognize it except for noticing the bugle denoting light infantry. "Vernon's my name."

"I know. It's mine too."

John Vernon looked again. Light infantry, D.S.O. and M.C., that face. Of course.

"Oh, so you're Edward."

"That's right. Have a drink?"

"Thanks, I will."

"How was Palestine?"

"Egypt actually."

"What's it like?"

"Rather decent." John did not want to talk too much about Shepheard's Hotel and the parties there. His cousin had probably been in France ever since the beginning of the war.

"Lucky you. I wouldn't mind some sunshine. That's what I intend to do when it's all over—go abroad to some warm country for three months."

"Good idea. Congratulations on your promotion."

"Survivor's luck."

John was silent at this reminder of the trench war. The 1st Lancers had seen hardly any action, not by design but entirely because of the capricious law of chance which governs such things. There had been comparatively few vacancies in the regiment, therefore little promotion. Even in wartime it was not customary for officers to be transferred from the 1st Lancers to other regiments, either cavalry or infantry. That would be something of a professional insult. Sometimes John could have wished it otherwise; and sometimes he was glad both that their own ranks had not been infiltrated by outsiders and that he had not been sent to some horrible wartime rabble of officers and men, one of the new battalions.

"Are you on leave?" John asked.

"Just a weekend off. I'm staying at the Meurice."

"That's funny, so am I."

"Then we must dine together. This calls for a celebration. I haven't seen you since I was a kid—when Great-Grandmother died, remember?"

"I remember," John said a little stiffly. "About dining together, I'm not free tonight."

"Oh, well, never mind, it doesn't matter. We'll have lunch anyway. Where are your lot?"

"I'm not sure. They arrived two weeks ago. I had to stay behind in Cairo to the last and I've only just got here. I'll be getting my orders on Monday morning."

"Make the most of Paris then."

"I intend to."

"I hear your father's a full colonel now."

"Yes, he is."

"Have another drink?"

"I don't think I'd better," John temporized.

"Nonsense, that's what we come to Paris to do. Another won't hurt. My treat."

Edward insisted on buying two more drinks. Conversation flagged. Neither wanted to talk about the war—it was as though they had been in two quite different wars—nor did they want to talk about their families. Officially they weren't on speaking terms.

Edward decided it was time to do away with all this. It was stupid.

"I'm glad I've met you, John," he said, suddenly warming to this long-lost cousin. "I thought I'd never meet you again. Here's to the war. Imagine our bumping into each other like this in a poky little bar in Paris."

"Quite," John said without enthusiasm.

"If it hadn't been for the war, you'd have been changing the guard at Buckingham Palace, or whatever it is your mob do in peacetime, and I'd have been in my counting-house pouring over the ledgers, eh?" Edward chuckled.

John's lips tightened. His cousin did not lack the common touch. Major indeed! Temporary, acting, Territorial, make-believe major. Didn't he know the difference between the 1st Lancers and the Household Cavalry? By long-standing tradition the 1st Lancers provided the sovereign's escort whenever the sovereign set foot in the City of London, that hallowed and exclusive square mile which was a law unto itself in all matters. Buckingham Palace, indeed.

"Another whiskey?"

"I must be going." John stood up.

"No, no, no. You must not go. I order you to sit down. Can't disobey your senior officer, now can you? Come along, John, this is a small celebration. Good heavens, we've only had a couple."

Edward was not in the least drunk. He was merely full of bonhomie and the desire to be friends. He had no idea why it should be so, nor did he care greatly. Family feuds were ridiculous things. Then he became aware of what John was saying.

"Senior officer? You must be mad. You're only a Territorial infantryman."

"Oh, my God, let's not start that sort of talk. I was only joking anyway."

"I'm afraid I must go."

"What's the matter?" Edward asked, suddenly suspicious. He grasped his cousin's arm. "Isn't a Territorial infantryman good enough for your highness to drink with?"

"I prefer not to discuss it. Let me go."

Edward's grasp remained firm.

"Well I do, you nasty young pip-squeak. I wasn't going to mention it, but you and the rest of the Butterscotch Brigade don't know what war is all about."

"What did you call us?"

"Butterscotch Brigade—you aren't real soldiers at all, you're chocolate soldiers, all of you. The 1st Lancers in-

deed! While you and your friends were playing polo or
whatever you did in Cairo, some of us were fighting here
in France. Don't you sneer at Territorials, my boy. If we'd
depended on the regular army to win the war, it would
have been over years ago—and the Germans would be in
London."

"You're drunk."

"Not in the least, nor shall I report you to your C.O. for
insurbordination or a hundred and one other military
crimes that would spell your ruin in that fancy mob you're
with. I hope you go up to the front soon, cousin. It's what
you need."

John managed to jerk his arm free.

"You ill-mannered boor," he said pettishly. "It's your
sort who give the army a bad name."

This was altogether too much for Edward. The resentment of years, which he had tried to smother under too
much good fellowship, the memory of the fact that this
gilded lily and his fat father had held his own father,
Captain Henry Vernon, V.C., in contempt, was too much.

He hit out, and as much by luck as by judgment he
knocked his cousin down. John sat on the floor, holding
his jaw, dazed and surprised.

"You struck me," he said disbelievingly.

"It's time someone taught you a lesson. It's so much
overdue that it may be too late to benefit you."

"I shall report you."

"Don't be fatuous. You've no witnesses and I'm a senior
officer. Go away. You annoy me."

"The barman . . ."

"Will swear you attacked me with a bottle, if I ask him
to," Edward said. "It's no use, Captain Vernon. You're a
natural loser. You'd better go and powder your nose."

John got to his feet and glared. Edward wondered if his
cousin were going to be man enough to hit back, but no.
With a curling lip John straightened his neat, well-pressed

tunic, picked up his hat and cane, and stalked from the bar. Edward chuckled to himself and ordered another drink. It seemed as though they were fated to quarrel. As a boy he hadn't liked John and now, as a man, he still did not like him. How could anyone be so infantile, at this stage of the war, as to sneer at men who had not been in the regular army in peacetime? Back in 1914 it had been the fashion, but in 1917 it was the sign of an arrested mentality.

He stayed on, drinking by himself for another hour, and then walked steadily back to his hotel where he joined a noisy crowd in the bar. He was in Paris to enjoy himself and enjoy himself he would.

He did not see John Vernon—who had changed hotels very quickly after their quarrel—nor did he hear anything further about the blow. He did not expect that he would. His cousin would have enough intelligence to work out that he could not come out of it well if there was an inquiry. Anyway John had no guts.

Edward did not mention his meeting in any of his letters home. Within a month he had forgotten it. At the end of September he got leave again, during which he had to return to the Palace to collect the bar to his Distinguished Service Order. This time he sent a wire to Edwina . . . and immediately afterward despised himself for doing so.

It was a different and in every way a more satisfactory homecoming. This time when he arrived at the hotel Edwina was sitting demurely in the residents' lounge. She kissed him affectionately.

"I couldn't come to the station, darling. You didn't say which train."

"I didn't know myself. It doesn't matter. How well you look," he told her, pleasure in his eyes.

"I wasn't sure how long you'd want to stay in Town, and the hotel is busy, but they'll let us have a double room for tonight and we can decide what to do when you've got your breath back. I expect you want to go to Mereford, don't you?"

This, coming from her, was a pleasant surprise. He had made up his mind to spend his leave at home—he couldn't repeat the performance of last time, nor did he want to. He had had many twinges of conscience over the way he had neglected his mother and grandfather. What he had not dared to hope was that she would meet him halfway like this.

"I do want to go home. I rather neglected them last time, you know."

"It was my fault. I wanted you to myself. I'm very selfish where you're concerned, Edward."

This was the sort of clever self-condemnation which was bound to arouse approval.

"You're very sweet," he said gently. "I don't deserve you. We'll telephone this evening if I can get through, and catch a train tomorrow morning. I'd like to spend the whole leave at Mereford."

"Yes, of course. I'll come back to London with you at the end of your leave and see you off at Waterloo."

"There, that's agreed then."

Alice was overjoyed when he telephoned, and even more delighted to hear that they were coming home. She met their train the following day. Just seeing Edward again gave her a pleasure so intense that it literally hurt. Toward Edwina she was warmly affectionate, but it was calculated rather than natural. She was Edward's wife and as such she would be treated, whatever private fears and doubts Alice might harbor.

"Your grandfather couldn't come," she told Edward as they settled down in the Daimler and Deakin drove them home. "He isn't ill or anything, but he's getting more and more frail and he doesn't go out so much. I'm always afraid of his catching cold, and it's been chilly this month."

"I didn't really expect him," Edward laughed. "By the way, I have to go to London for the day next week—another investiture. I thought I must take Edwina this time. Will you come?"

"No, I'll stay at home with your grandfather. You and Edwina go alone. It will be better for you that way. Are you well?" she asked anxiously.

"Fine," he said truthfully. His cough had gone and although he was thin and tired looking, he felt fit.

"Do you get enough to eat?" she asked next.

"Hardly ever," he laughed. "Food isn't the army's strong point, not in the front line anyway, but it's sufficient to keep us alive. You mustn't worry, Mother."

Alice turned to Edwina.

"How is London?"

"Very busy. Crowded."

"I suppose you have more company there than you'd have here."

"Yes, but I shan't be sorry when it's all over and Edward comes home."

"Nor will any of us," Alice agreed.

She wondered if it was imagination or if Edwina had grown sharper featured. She was a striking-looking woman. Alice honestly wished she could trust her daughter-in-law, but she found it difficult to accept that Edwina only lived in London because of the company there. Couldn't she have made friends in Reading?

She smiled and patted Edwina's hand.

"It's nice to have you back. You look splendid. Do you hear from your parents?"

"No, never."

There was an awkward silence at that. It seemed so unnatural, just as living at the hotel was unnatural. Alice put on a brave smile and talked of other things. When they reached the gates of Mereford, Edward told Deakin to stop.

"I'm getting out here," he said. "You go ahead. I want to walk."

"I'll come with you," Edwina offered.

"No, please, you go on with Mother."

The two women smiled as he got out of the car. Then as Deakin drove off, Edward looked all around, slowly. It was the second last day of September and the leaves were turning already. He walked at a leisurely pace along the graveled drive, savoring the sight and smell of home. All he wanted now was to get the war over and done with and to get back. He had never enjoyed the war—he had too much to lose to want to go off and fight, and in any case trench warfare was the most horrible thing devised by man. As the months went past he came to hate it more and more. Even the modest pride he had taken in his achievements—his promotions, his decorations—had gone. In the end they meant nothing. It would be sufficient for any man to live here, at peace with the world. He had changed his mind about going abroad, too. When the war was over he would have a long holiday here, working in the garden, getting to know his home again.

He came across Maggett the gardener sweeping leaves, and stopped to talk. It had been a lovely summer, Maggett said, and the rose garden had been a delight. He was going to make another vegetable bed at the back of the house, and next summer there would be a new fruit garden. They talked for ten minutes until Edward remembered that his grandfather must be waiting. He hurried the last short bit to the house.

Now the change in the general was more noticeable. The past few months had taken their toll. There were deep lines on his face, the flesh of his neck sagged, and the liver spots on the backs of his hands were more prominent; yet he was still as straight as a ramrod, though he walked very much more slowly. He was enormously proud of Edward and glad that the boy had come to his senses and was not spending another leave in London.

"Two D.S.O.s, that's something," he chuckled when the two of them were having a drink together. "Plus promotion. Second lieutenant to major in three years. It's not bad going."

"I'm a substantive lieutenant, temporary captain and acting major," Edward laughed.

"Never mind, you have the rank and the pay. You're Major Vernon. That cousin of yours is a captain on the staff, did you know that?"

"I didn't know he was on the staff. I thought he was with his regiment."

"No. I had a note from James. He never tells me much, but he mentioned that John was on Haig's staff."

"Lucky John."

"You've never come across him, I daresay."

"No," Edward lied. He was not particularly proud of his behavior at their one meeting in Paris.

"How's Edwina? No sign of an heir yet?"

"Well we haven't really had a fair chance, have we?" Edward laughed.

"I'd like to become a great-grandfather, you know. My time's short."

"Rubbish. You look very well."

"Don't talk to me like a family doctor, Edward. We both know I'm an old man teetering on the brink of the grave. I shan't be very sorry when the time comes. I'm tired, and that's the truth, but there are one or two things I'd like to see before I die—an end to this miserable war, you safely back home, and another generation of Vernons in the world. I don't want much, do I?" he added with a dry smile.

"Nothing unreasonable. You may get it all sooner than you think. Let's hope so anyway."

As it happened Edward was not sorry that they were childless. He did not want a baby to be born while he was away in France, a child whose growing up he wouldn't see. He would rather wait till the end of the war.

The time flew past. He and Edwina went up to London and she came to the Palace to see the King give Edward a bar to his Distinguished Service Order. It was another austere investiture with none of the splendor of peacetime. This time it was indoors, in the Marble Hall. They queued up in a corridor, a long khaki and blue line controlled by elderly ushers. The guests sat in rows facing the dais. Again the King was in khaki uniform, and to Edward it was a bit like a sausage machine. A man who, as a child, had been received privately by King Edward VII wearing the full dress uniform of a field marshal was spoiled perhaps. Maybe, he thought, others saw it differently. He took his place in front of the bearded monarch, received the bar to his decoration and was vaguely surprised when the King chuckled.

"Back again, Vernon?"

"Yes, sir." Edward smiled with pleasure.

"How is your grandfather?"

"Frailer, sir. He couldn't come to London this time."

"I'm sorry. Tell him I said that, won't you?"

"I shall, sir."

He bowed and turned away, ridiculously pleased. Sir Godfrey would be delighted by this message, and rightly so, Edward thought. The old man's years of devoted service to Queen Victoria had not been overlooked by her successors. It was something, after all, to have the King sending you verbal messages. It was never likely to happen to him, that was certain.

Somewhat to his surprise Edwina said she had been bored by the whole performance, and she was obviously irritated at having to sit through the whole thing until the last private had received his medal. She would rather have left when Edward's turn was over. Her reaction amused her husband. She was unpredictable and he rather liked that. The whole thing was a bit of a farce anyway, for there were thousands of people disintegrating in the Flanders mud who had done more to deserve their country's gratitude than he had. It wasn't as though he had saved his comrades' lives, the way his father had—that was different. He had fought and killed and survived. That was all.

He did not forget to tell Sir Godfrey exactly what the King had said, and the old general listened, his eyes glistening.

"That was handsome of him," he remarked. "Imagine his thinking of an old has-been like me when he's so busy, so burdened with cares. It makes me humble."

Edward realized that his grandfather's eyes were moist, and he moved away to stand by the window.

"I suppose you think I'm an old fool?" the old man asked.

"No. No, I don't think that at all."

"I was brought up to serve. It has always given me great pleasure to think I did so moderately well. I've never made any money, created anything, or provided employment for other people. Some would say it was a useless life, but it's been a satisfying one, you know."

Edward realized that he was listening to a man examining his whole philosophy at the end of his time, and he was silent. Some people would indeed say Sir Godfrey's life had been a useless one, but was it in fact? It depended entirely on your point of view and on your scale of values. Anyway it was obvious that only a small proportion of humanity could create anything or alleviate the world's ills. The vast majority served someone or something, and many of them served only to make other men rich. If his grandfather had not set the world on fire, equally he had done nothing of which to be ashamed, and he had lived up to his own highest ideals. Few men could say more at the end of their lives.

As his leave drew toward its end, he realized yet again that he was lucky in one respect. Edwina was the sort of loving and passionate woman he had always dreamed of without really knowing anything about women. Their days together were infinitely happy, and her tenderness toward him never ceased to astonish him. He felt so unworthy of her love. The only matter which troubled him now was her coldness toward her parents. He spoke to her about it on his last night.

"Shouldn't you go to Castle Combe?" he asked while they were dressing for dinner. "They haven't seen you for such a long time."

"I don't want to."

"Darling, what did they do to make you so relentless toward them?"

"I don't dislike them, I simply don't want to go back there."

"Then at least write to your mother."

"She could have written to me. What's more they know my address in London—your mother told them."

"What *happened?*" Edward insisted. "I don't understand."

"Nothing happened that you don't know about. My father is really a completely useless person and he thought when I married you that he could share my allowance. He'd have been a leech if I'd allowed him, so I left. There was a quarrel, but nothing terrible. I just don't want to have anything to do with them."

"It's such a fuss about nothing. You can't blame your father. Hang it all, no man enjoys being hard up. Don't you think you're making too much of it, darling?"

"Are you in a better position to judge than I am?" she asked a little stiffly.

"No, no. I'm just suggesting that you might be charitable."

"I'm not a charity, I'm their daughter. I expected them to get in touch with me, but they never did. It's better like this."

He was puzzled, wondering if there was more to it than he understood. He had no way of knowing that it was the implied threat to her independence which had driven her to implacable anger. All her life she had been dependent on them, forced to live as they decided, and all the time she had longed to be free. Her docile obedience had been the result of necessity. By nature she could not brook interference, and now she was her own mistress. It was as simple as that. Subconsciously she associated her parents with a form of bondage, and thus sought to avoid them. She herself had never troubled to reason matters out. She acted quite instinctively, and had no qualms about it.

Edward was troubled, but when she began to kiss him and he felt her arms around him again, he dismissed the matter from his mind. After all, he thought with relief, it was none of his business, was it?

Chapter 18

EDWARD'S war was over. After more than three years of the front line, two wounds, and three decorations, he received his reward. The fact that he was alive was a statistical impossibility, and someone took pity on him. He was transferred to the staff, where he found Thatcham a full colonel. Thatcham had had a most successful war. He was still full of fun and energy, and he and Edward had a grand celebration together. He was the only person to whom Edward mentioned his meeting with John, and probably he would not have spoken had he not had rather a lot to drink. Thatcham was amused.

"Silly young fool, sneering at Territorials," he grunted. Thatcham mirrored the common army rivalry. Just as the cavalry tended to look down on the infantry as their social inferiors, so the infantry tended to look upon the cavalry as useless ornaments who did less than their fair share of the fighting—and dying. It was usually a good-natured rivalry, but it was a real one nevertheless.

"Good for you, knocking the fool down," he commented, helping himself to another drink. "I've never seen you lose your temper, you know. Were you drunk?"

"No. In fact I've never been drunk. Normally drinking

doesn't interest me all that much, but once or twice when I've wanted to get rolling tight, I've tried and failed. I just get more sober. If I'd been a little drunk probably I'd have seen the funny side of things and not hit the ass."

"Ass is the word. Well, here's to the poor, bloody Territorial infantry, and here's to the 3rd Berkshire Light Infantry. Edward, my friend, we are the only two left. When this bloody war is over, do you know what you and I are going to do? We shall form up in threes—all two of us—and march from the station to the barracks in Reading. That's what we'll do."

"I wonder how many of the men have survived."

"We won't find out till after it's over. Seriously, you know, we ought to throw a dinner party for the survivors —you and I could pay for it."

"We'll do that—if it ever ends."

"Of course it will end. My God, it's 1918 now. The thing has to end soon. We'd have beaten them anyway, but with America on our side it can't go on much longer. I'm surprised it's gone on this long. It's over ten months since the Americans joined in."

"You know what the trouble is, don't you?" Edward asked.

"Tell me, Field Marshal Vernon."

"You can't win a war by sitting in trenches. This thing has been fought the wrong way. That's the trouble."

"Vernon for commander in chief."

They laughed and felt the warm, satisfying glow of a comradeship which has survived the stiffest of tests.

No sooner had Edward written to Alice to tell her to stop worrying about him because he was now a staff officer sleeping in a proper bed every night and eating like a turkey cock, than he received a letter from Edwina containing important news. She was going to have a baby. She had seen the doctor and he had confirmed it.

Edward did some quick arithmetic. The baby must be

due at the end of June or early in July. He had been home for roughly the first two weeks in October. He wrote to the general at once and then he and Thatcham had another party to celebrate with champagne—rather an inferior champagne but they did not mind much about that.

This was the nearest Edward came to enjoying the war. The tension of life in the trenches wore off and with it his disillusionment faded. It was not a bad old world, not really. What was more, there was hope everywhere. This year would see it through. He became cheerful and buoyant, life on the staff suited him, his job was well within his ability, his medal ribbons and rank meant that he was accepted everywhere as one who had proved himself, and his wife was going to produce a son at last. People noticed the difference in Major Vernon. He seemed like a new man.

Then one day the bombshell burst. It was a note from Alice. Edwina had moved to Mereford in April and had not been very well, but it was all over now. The baby had been born, a boy, seven pounds, fourteen ounces. He had been born on May 1. Edwina was going to be all right, and there was nothing to worry about.

When he had first read the letter at his desk, Edward had felt like shouting with joy, and then awful realization dawned on him. Suddenly he knew why the letter was short and stilted, why they had not written earlier to say that Edwina had gone to Mereford. The baby was not due for another two months! Suspicion gnawed at him all that day. Like most men he accepted certain basic facts without inquiring into them.

That night he went off alone and ended up with a girl in a bar. She was not pretty. She was gaunt, looked older than himself, and was rather surprised that the handsome major wanted to buy her drinks. She accepted readily and gladly. He would pay decently for her favors, and she needed the money.

Edward, however, showed no inclination to go home with her. He insisted on buying drink after drink, not getting drunk, just getting more morose.

"Chéri, why don't we go?" she pleaded. "It's late."

"There's no hurry, Ma'mselle. No hurry." He turned and faced her and she saw the agony in his eyes and wondered what was wrong.

"You're a woman. You must know about women."

"Of course." She laughed nervously.

"Can a woman have a child after only seven months?"

Her eyes grew wary. Why was he asking such a question?

"But of course."

"There's a girl. I met her seven months ago. She says I'm the father of her baby."

"A Frenchwoman?"

"No, an English girl."

"You could be the father. Don't you believe the girl?"

"I don't know. The baby is seven pounds, fourteen ounces."

"Pardon?"

"The baby. It weighs . . ." he calculated, "three and three-quarter kilos."

"A seven-month baby? No, Major, never."

"You're sure?"

"Quite sure." The woman thought she understood. "You met a girl seven months ago, for the first time? And now she says you are the father of her three-and-three-quarter-kilo baby? Is that right, Major?"

"That's exactly it."

"Then she lies. It is a nine-month baby—eight, just possibly; seven, never."

"Thank you. Another drink?"

"No. Let's go. You have nothing to worry about now. You can celebrate with me. Come home with me."

"Eh? No, no, not tonight." He saw the change in her

face and shook his head. "Stop worrying, I have a present for you."

He fumbled in his pocket and pulled out a bunch of francs. He handed them to her.

"Here, have that."

"I can't take so much."

She was a decent woman at heart. Her husband was dead, and she was alone in the world with three children to care for and a war to make life difficult. One had to do something, but she did not rob her customers.

"Take it, please. You've told me what I wanted to know."

"You don't want me?" she asked.

"I don't want to go to bed with you. Have another drink."

"All right," she laughed, relieved. "I'll pay though."

"Ma'mselle, you are a sport."

"Good."

He sat drinking with her till the place closed, then they went their separate ways never to meet again. He knew she had told him the truth. There had been no one else he could ask. It had to be someone anonymous. When he got back to headquarters he sat on the edge of his bed, head in hands. He'd consorted with a woman for the first time in France, and all he'd done was to pay considerably over the odds for the news that his wife had cuckolded him. He hadn't even had the ordinary guts to pay Edwina back with the Frenchwoman. He wasn't a man at all.

He lay awake all night, his thoughts black and bitter. Not only did he have to learn to accept the unpleasant fact, but he had to decide what exactly he was going to do about it. By morning he had made up his mind, but he was grim-faced and his eyes were lackluster. Thatcham, who was the head of his department, was astonished and sent him to see the doctor. Edward knew there was nothing wrong but he did not argue, indeed he even complained of a headache and sleeplessness and accepted some harmless tablets. He had to tell Thatcham the "good news" of course—not to do so would have caused considerable comment. They had a drink together, but Thatcham was not a suspicious man and he attributed Edward's lack of exuberance to the illness. Unfortunately, or perhaps fortunately, there was no question of leave.

Edward wrote to Alice. His letter was brutally direct.

"I am well aware what the birth of this child implies, nevertheless I shall consider him my own. There is to be no hint that anything is not as it should be and I must ask you not to air the subject with Edwina. Let her think she has fooled you, if she can be so naïve. In any event there is to be an absolute acceptance of young Jocelyn—the name I have chosen for him. In particular, say nothing to Grandfather. I am sure he can be more easily fooled than I can."

It was a tightly controlled letter and Alice, reading it, could have wept for him. The most difficult thing was to treat Edwina as though nothing were wrong. She had been surprised when the girl, pale and ill and grossly distended, had arrived at Mereford, and she had assumed automatically that there was likely to be a premature birth. When a full-term baby was born she had not known what to say. She had kept out of Edwina's way as much as possible. A nurse had been engaged already, and Edwina spent most of her time reading in her own room.

Sir Godfrey's delight was anguish to her. At long last his grandson had produced an heir, another boy. When he received Edward's letter on the subject he shed a surreptitious tear, for Edward had known how much this child would mean to the old man and had written an absolutely charming letter.

Edward's letters to Edwina were polite and restrained. He was glad to hear about the baby, delighted that they were both well, he was to be named Jocelyn and would be christened on his next leave, and he hoped Edwina would now settle down at Mereford and take good care both of herself and the baby. It was a letter in which the word love was not mentioned.

He came home for his last leave during the first week in November. His behavior gave away nothing. He acted as though nothing had gone wrong and Alice admired him. In the privacy of their room, however, he spoke harshly to Edwina.

"You can cut out the act, Edwina. Stop slobbering over me as though you loved me."

"What do you mean?" she asked, recoiling from the fury in his eyes.

"You know very well what I mean. I can count up to nine, you know. I don't know who Jocelyn's father is but I've accepted the baby as mine. The subject will never be discussed again. The boy will never know he is not my child and neither will anyone else."

"How can you say such a thing?"

"Oh, stop your silly pretending. I want to know who the father was."

"Never," she exclaimed, dropping her token pretense.

"I don't want to know for the obvious reason. I want to know what sort of blood the child is inheriting. Who was he? Tell me."

"I will not."

"Don't be silly. You're getting off lightly. You have a husband, a son, a home—nobody knows your shame except my mother. She will never reproach you—I've seen to that—so tell me who it was."

"His name was Erskine. He was a captain in the Scots Guards. He was killed three months ago."

"Very thoughtful of him, I'm sure. Did you tell him?"

"No."

"Who were his people?"

"His father is a surgeon in Edinburgh. That's all I know."

"Well, it's good enough. He sounds respectable, even if he wasn't honorable. Did you love him?"

"How can you ask such a question?"

"I'm curious," he said coldly. "After all, he may have been one of a long progression. I know now why you didn't want to live here. I should have guessed that day when I found you in the bar with that bunch of officers, but I was too moonstruck. I believed you."

"What do you take me for?" she cried.

"I won't insult your ears by telling you, but I'm sure you know the answer. I'll move into another room, of course."

"No."

"Did you expect me to stay here, to sleep with you after this?" he asked, astonished.

"I love you."

"You've a damned funny way of showing it."

"I was wretched, lonely. Donald loved me. He was the only one, but I didn't love him. It was you I wanted, but you were never there when I wanted you. You shouldn't have gone away like that."

"I shouldn't have gone away! What sort of silly joke is that? Do you think I started the war so that I could go off and get wounded and let a bunch of bloody Germans use me as a target for rifle and machine-gun practice? I had to go away, I had to crouch in the mud and get shot at and shelled; all you had to do was to live in comfort and style in London. You blame me for your immorality, which is cowardly, and you try to tell me you love me, which is an insult to my intelligence. I've told you, I shall never bring up this subject again. I shall treat you with the consideration and respect due to my wife. In return you will behave yourself, and devote yourself to bringing up Jocelyn. Nobody will ever know. My mother and I will never speak of this. Grandfather is a great big innocent. He thinks I'm the father."

"Oh, God," she cried, wringing her hands. "I *do* love you, Edward. I've never loved anyone else. I couldn't help myself. I know I was weak and I can't explain it, but it didn't mean anything. It was something I did—like a man might do when he's drunk. It meant nothing."

"I'm glad you think so. Now let's drop the subject."

"Have you no love for me?" she pleaded. "You can't have changed so much. You can't."

He stood and stared at her stonily. It would have been easy to succumb again, but he would never forget that moment in France when he realized that the woman he had loved and cherished had betrayed him.

"I despise you," he said with slow deliberation.

She stepped back as though he had hit her, and her face turned white.

"God forgive you," she breathed, shocked.

"You always did have a contorted sense of humor," he replied, and stalked from the room.

She flung herself on the bed and cried as though her heart were breaking. Anything, anything at all, would have been better than this desolation.

It never really occurred to Edward Vernon that there was anything wrong with his behavior. The possibility escaped him entirely. He was very like his grandfather—he had kept himself pure and virginal, waiting for the one woman in his life, and when he had found her he had had thoughts for no one else. He was almost physically incapable of being unfaithful. Her behavior, in his eyes, was the most outrageous thing since Judas. He considered that he was being generous to a fault. Her obvious desire to sleep with him, to return to their loving past, was quite ridiculous. How could any decent man have anything to do with such a woman?

Had he been able to understand her, had he been capable of realizing that a physical betrayal does not necessarily mean a mental one, and that she really had been driven to distraction—and beyond—by the lack of him, it would have been different, for he was a kind, generous, and forgiving man. Yet, because he himself could never have had an affair with anyone without being in love with her, he firmly believed that Edwina had loved Captain Donald Erskine. That being so, she no longer loved him and there was an end to it. They were civilized. They would behave properly. Jocelyn would have a decent home.

It is doubtful if Edwina could have explained things to him, even had he been prepared to listen. She was a creature of instinct and not given to putting her feelings into words. She went about the house stony-faced while he was meticulously polite and even considerate. Because Sir Godfrey could now no longer leave the house, Jocelyn was christened at home on Sunday, November 10, 1918. There were no guests, and there was no christening party. Thatcham and his wife were the godparents, but he was still in France and she was in Scotland. It was very much of a wartime christening, on the eve of the long-awaited peace.

The following day, Armistice Day, Edward and Sir Godfrey disposed of a bottle of good old port.

"You've got what you wanted," Edward chuckled. "You have your great-grandson, and the war is over. We've been lucky, you know. James, John, and myself—we all survived."

"James and John could hardly help surviving," Sir Godfrey growled.

"You mustn't be hard on them. We all take our chances

in a war. My short spell on the staff convinced me that all staff officers aren't fools."

"I'm glad about that," Sir Godfrey laughed. "I was one for years."

"So it's a happy ending. I must go up to the War Office. They may not send me back to France now. I'd like to get demobilized quickly and get back into harness."

"What about that three months' holiday?"

"I can manage without a holiday. Anyway, I'm having one now. I want to work."

He did, desperately, to take his mind off other things. Sir Godfrey looked at him with undisguised pride. This was a real Vernon.

Two days later Sir Godfrey died in his sleep. He was eighty-one. For Alice it was the eclipse of an era. She had gone into service at St. James's Place at the age of fifteen, in 1880. She had known the old man for thirty-eight years and for more than half that time they had been close friends. When she called him "Papa" it was more than a conventional manner of speaking—he had taken the place of her own father. Equally, because of Henry's death and James's estrangement, she had been quite literally a daughter to him.

Edward had to go to the War Office about extending his leave and also to see what the chances were of an early release to return to the family firm. He decided to go that day and to telephone James. When he had transacted his business to his satisfaction, having been told that he could go on leave pending demobilization, which he should request in writing, he managed to telephone his uncle.

"This is Edward Vernon," he introduced himself.

"Oh. What do you want?"

"I'm calling to tell you that Grandfather died in his sleep last night. The funeral will probably be on Saturday morning, in Reading."

"If you'll let me know the time of the funeral, I'll be there."

"I'll have to telephone you, in that case. Can you give me the number at St. James's Place? I don't know it."

James gave it and Edward thanked him. He did not ask about his cousin. He was glad to be able to hang up. On Saturday there was a small cortege from Mereford consisting of Alice, Edwina, and Edward, as well as the servants, all of whom had had a special affection for the old man. The Thatchams, who should have been there, were still split up and scattered so that they were represented only by two beautiful large wreaths. Timothy had measles, so that Mary and he were absent also. Twenty or thirty local people met them at the cemetery, and Alice looked all round for James. At last she saw him, arriving in a taxi, a few minutes before the service. He nodded rather curtly and stood by himself until it was all over. Alice went up to him.

"I'm sorry you couldn't manage to come yesterday and stay the night with us. Won't you come back for a glass of sherry?"

"No, thank you. I have to get back to London."

She gave him a somber look. He was stout, bald, and in his civilian clothes he looked like a tradesman. He was not an impressive figure. Edward, wearing uniform, was standing nearby, and he stepped forward.

"Won't you come for the reading of the will?"

"I have a copy of my father's will, which I have given to my solicitors. There's no need."

He stared at them, antagonism in his eyes. "Good-bye," he said in rather a loud voice, and turned away. Alice realized that his taxi was waiting. She turned to Edward and shrugged. She knew he had a copy of the latest will— Sir Godfrey had told her that he had sent it to avoid any unpleasantness when he died. She herself did not know what was in it. It had been drawn up by a local solicitor in

1915. They went back to the house, Edward poured sherry for his mother and Edwina, and they waited for the lawyer who arrived just before lunch. He was a brisk, cheerful man.

"I understand that Colonel James Vernon has a copy of the will. It is quite a simple one. Colonel Vernon gets St. James's Place and its contents, and Sir Godfrey's money is divided into three parts. One share goes to you, Mrs. Vernon; one goes to his grandson, John Vernon; and the last, a smaller share, goes to a young man called Timothy Hilton. I've been in touch with his mother and they know about it. There is a special note in the will, Mrs. Vernon, saying that he is leaving money to you rather than to your son because you made over to him your entire shareholding in Henry Vernon, Son and Company, and have only a salary now. He would like you to retire from the firm. What he says is, 'My daughter-in-law, Alice Vernon, has worked hard all her days, and done work of which a man could be proud. I would like her to enjoy leisure for the rest of her life and I hope she will use her share of my money to this effect.' "

"How much is it?" Edward asked.

"There are certain minor bequests to your servants here, but after everything is taken out, the three shares should be worth about sixty thousand pounds."

He refused to stay to lunch and hurried off to attend to other matters. Alice was very quiet. Sir Godfrey had never told her he was going to leave her any money, and she herself was not much given to thinking about finance. It had ceased to interest her in the personal sense, although she was intensely interested in the company and its affairs. She had expected a gesture, but not one to the extent of twenty thousand pounds.

"I think I'll take Papa's advice," she said to Edward during lunch. "I'll hand over everything to you and I'll retire completely from the company."

"It won't be the same without you, Mother. The staff will think the end of the world has come."

"I doubt it. They'll soon forget me when they have a young and vigorous man in the chair again. I want to do something with the grounds here anyway, and I've never had time. There are several things I'd like to change. Besides, I'm sure Edwina would like company. Isn't that right, my dear?"

"Yes, Mother."

"So it's settled. But what a strange funeral. Imagine James just looking in like that. I can't think why he bothered to come. And the Thatchams weren't here, nor Mary or John. It was all wrong, somehow, though I don't suppose Papa would have cared. He always said funerals were overrated. When will the plaque be put up in the church?"

"Next month, Mother. It will be beside Father's, on the south wall, close to the door."

"It seems so strange without Papa. He's lived at Mereford for so long. Everything is happening at once—the baby, the war over, and now your grandfather's death. It makes me feel old."

"You're only a girl still," Edward said with a warm smile. "Everything is going to be all right from now on. No more wars, no more upheavals, just a nice quiet life."

"I hope you're right," Alice answered without smiling. "I only hope Jocelyn doesn't have to go to war."

"Of course, he won't," Edward predicted confidently. "Wars are over."

Chapter 19

I T was ironical that a month after Sir Godfrey's death James's services to his country should finally receive recognition. He had spent the war working long hours at the War Office, and he had done a competent job rising to the rank of full colonel without getting a single medal, and was now made a Companion of the Order of the Bath. He was retired at the same time. As army careers went it was conspicuously undistinguished. The Great War came too late to help his career much, and he had missed all his chances in the Boer War.

Edward, now out of uniform and deeply immersed in the company, noticed the award in the *Times* and he thought that James had finally made the trip to the Palace. Well, he and James had kept the tradition alive. Would John? he wondered. All being well, there would be no more wars, so John would have to distinguish himself in peacetime service, which was much harder. He supposed that John was back with the Lancers, still a captain, and with limited promotion prospects.

Not for the first time it occurred to Edward that his father Henry had done the right thing in cutting loose and coming to Reading to start afresh. Every time he turned into Broad Street and saw the building with their name running along its front, he felt a little thrill. It represented solid achievement.

A few months later, in the spring of 1919, the newspapers carried an account of the wedding of Captain John Vernon of the 1st Lancers to Lucy Waterton, only daughter of Mr. and Mrs. Herbert Waterton of Eaton Place. It didn't tell Edward or Alice very much about the Watertons except that they managed to live in a certain style—Eaton Place is not for the poor of this world.

Edward's interest in these events was scanty. As the months passed he settled down into a comfortable routine. Each morning he rose at eight, breakfasted at eight-thirty, and drove into Reading at nine-fifteen, which got him to his desk in good time for nine-thirty. He drove himself nowadays in a new Rolls-Royce. Deakin had left them to go and live with his son in Bristol. At twelve-thirty Edward left the office to go to his club for a drink and lunch. He returned at two and stayed there till five. On the weekends he often went to Henley where he had a motorboat. He had given up the Territorial Army, despite pressure from Thatcham who now commanded the 3rd, Territorial, Battalion of the Berkshire Light Infantry and who had wanted Edward as his second-in-command. Edward considered the River Thames at Henley much cleaner and more desirable than the trenches in France and Flanders, and he developed quite an interest in his boat.

Edwina never accompanied him on these weekend excursions. She stayed at Mereford. It took her a long time to get over his neglect of her. He, of course, did not see it as neglect, but for the first month or two after his return from France, she had known real misery and loneliness. Her interest in the baby was at the best nominal. She did not like small children. Jocelyn had an expensive and competent nanny, he wanted for nothing where creature comforts were concerned, and he did not come into much contact with his mother. Edwina spent hours by herself, and nobody knew what she was thinking about during this time.

Eventually Edward bought a cottage at Henley, so that he could stay there on Saturday nights. He made friends locally among other boat enthusiasts, and they would meet at the Riverside Hotel for drinks on a Saturday night. They were a jolly crowd. He always returned early on Sunday evening, so that he was only away for one night each week.

Alice often wondered just how matters stood between Edward and Edwina but neither of them ever spoke on the subject and it was not in her character to ask questions. Now that she had more time on her hands, Alice had begun to cultivate a few friends of her own. They all lived nearby. There were the Thurloes and the Dennisons, for example, prosperous business people with whom she exchanged regular weekly visits.

In the spring of 1921, Edward started his annual buying trips to the United States. He was away for three weeks at a time, which subsequently he extended to a month or more. At the outset it was Franklin Forgan who saw most of him, but over the years he began to spend more time in New York instead of spending most of it in Chicago. He invited Edwina to accompany him, but she refused consistently. He accepted her refusal cheerfully, for in truth he had no special wish to take her along. His offer had been a polite gesture.

After he returned from the United States that year of 1921, he met Lord Thatcham in the club one evening when he dropped in for a quick drink before driving home to Mereford.

"I say, Edward, we've got some friends of yours staying with us—people called Hilton."

"Hilton? Mary Hilton? She's a friend of my mother's."

"Yes, and her son Timothy."

"What do you know about them?" Edward asked. Thatcham was his particular friend, even if he had refused to stay on with him in the Territorials after the war.

"Nothing much except that they're friends of yours. Elizabeth met Mrs. Hilton at some function or other in London. She belongs to the Lancaster family, the bankers."

"I know. She's also married to my Uncle James."

"I thought she had been married to some chap called Hilton?"

"No, James wouldn't divorce her. She left him years ago for Timothy Hilton. This is just between ourselves, but I think you ought to know."

"She is a friend of your mother's, isn't she?"

"Oh, yes, Mother and Mary Hilton are great friends as well as being sisters-in-law, though they don't see each other often nowadays. I only told you about Uncle James in case the conversation ever came round to the family. You don't want any awkwardness."

"Certainly not. Thanks for telling me. What about the boy, Timothy? Whose is he?"

"He's Timothy Hilton's son."

"Oh."

"Yes," Edward smiled. "He's rather illegitimate. My grandfather was very fond of him, but I don't know him at all. How old is he now?"

"Nineteen, nearly twenty. He's an artist—paints, you know. He and his mother live somewhere in Gloucestershire."

"Kemble," Edward agreed. "That's right. Why don't you bring them over this weekend? I shan't be going to Henley so we'll all be at home. They're staying with you, did you say?"

"Yes, Elizabeth invited them. It's some charitable thing they're mixed up in—orphans or something."

Alice was pleased when Edward told her, and on Sunday morning the Thatchams came for the day. There were half a dozen in the car which arrived—Thatcham, his countess, Lord Walter Paveley, his son, Lady Elizabeth Paveley, now nineteen and a beauty, Mary and Timothy Hilton. They made a merry party for lunch, stayed on to dinner, and did not drive back to Pleasaunce till after ten-thirty in the evening. When they had gone Edwina went up to her room.

"What a pleasant day," Alice said to Edward who was having a nightcap.

"Yes, very."

"Did you notice Timothy and Lady Elizabeth?"

"You mean the daughter?" The countess and her daughter were both named Elizabeth.

"Yes. They had eyes only for each other. I wonder if something will come of that."

"You're a matchmaker," Edward accused. "Anyway, would Thatcham let his daughter become too friendly with Timothy?"

"I don't suppose he knows that Timothy's mother and father weren't married."

"He'd be bound to find out, wouldn't he—if they were serious about each other? Anyway, he does know."

"Are you sure?"

"I ought to be. I told him myself."

"Why did you do a thing like that?" Alice demanded, taken aback.

"I wasn't thinking of Timothy and Elizabeth, believe me. It just occurred to me that Mary is still married to Uncle James, and I thought George Thatcham ought to know in case they ever talked about us. After all, he is my closest friend and Mary is my aunt as well as being a chum of yours, so it's reasonable to suppose our names would crop up. I didn't want him to put his foot in it."

"Yes, I see. It will be awkward if Timothy and Elizabeth fall in love."

"Really, Mother," Edward laughed. "Why should they? You're building a lot on one lunch."

"Lunch and dinner," she corrected. "I'm surprised you didn't notice it for yourself."

"I was watching Edwina. I haven't seen her so animated for a long time. She and young Walter kept one another amused. She's been so moody."

"I'd noticed. You shouldn't go away so much at weekends, not by yourself."

"I've offered to take her to Henley. I have that cottage there so if she doesn't like going on the river she needn't. There are other things to do, and Saturday nights are very jolly. She won't come—just as she wouldn't come to the States with me in April."

"I didn't know that."

"Edwina's entitled to live her own life, but the way she's almost gone into seclusion here isn't natural. You know that, Mother."

"Yes, I do. She should make friends of her own."

"Exactly," Edward agreed, "and she won't do it by sitting around. I must talk to her about it."

It was not in Edward's nature to put off anything once he had made up his mind. He finished his drink, kissed his mother good night, and went upstairs and tapped on his wife's bedroom door. She called to him to come in, and he did so. She was wearing a nightgown and combing her long hair.

"Hullo, what can I do for you?" she asked, looking at him in the mirror.

"I just came up for a chat. Did you enjoy yourself today?"

"Yes."

"Edwina, it's because I noticed you enjoying yourself that I came to see you. It's so long since I've seen you laughing."

"Whose fault is that?"

"Let's not start going into that."

"No, of course you'd rather not," she answered bitterly.

"Listen, you won't come to Henley with me at weekends, you wouldn't come to Chicago, you just moon about the house. Why don't you get out more? If you don't like borrowing my mother's car, I'll buy you one of your own." She had been without a car of her own for over a year.

"Will you?" She looked up sharply.

"Of course."

"I'd like that."

"That's good news. You ought to be getting about and meeting people. Even Mother has her friends whom she meets."

"I don't know anyone here. Still, Walter Paveley did invite me to the horse trials next week. I said I'd try to go."

"Just the thing. The Thatchams know everybody. When are the trials?"

"Friday morning."

"Then go. If you want a car I'll look around tomorrow morning. I could come home for lunch, and in the afternoon we can go and buy one if there's anything you fancy."

"Thank you, Edward."

"Look here, if you want anything, you only have to ask for it."

"You're very generous."

"Dammit, you're my wife."

She supposed that people seeing them might envy them, the successful and charming family at Mereford. Edward at thirty-one was young, energetic; war hero, head of a family business, possessor of a lovely home—he had everything. She, two years his junior, was certainly attractive and she knew it. She had filled out a little. She did not have what was regarded as the highly fashionable slim figure, nor did she want it. She suspected that men didn't like it all that much. She had a good, well-proportioned figure, and a young face. She was able to dress well too. How deceptive appearances could be, for Edward spent more and more time away from home, and she was acutely miserable.

Well, she thought when he had gone and left her to brushing her hair, it was time to end all that. What was sauce for the gander was sauce for the goose. She would take his advice and see if she couldn't make some sort of life for herself.

On Thursday a small car arrived at Mereford. Edwina, who was passing through the hall, stopped and looked out of the windows and received a shock. It was her mother. She opened the door before Alexandra could ring.

"Hullo, Mother. Come in. We weren't expecting you."

"I was going to telephone but I thought you might try to put me off, so I came."

"You have a car I see, and you can drive."

"Yes, we bought a secondhand one after the war." They went into the drawing room and Edwina rang the bell. "We really need one, you know, your father has gout."

Edwina tried unsuccessfully to smother a laugh.

"It's no joke. It is extremely painful."

"I'm sorry." The door opened and the maid came in. "Oh, Ivy, bring some tea, please, and tell Mrs. Vernon that my mother has called, will you?"

"Yes, ma'am."

When the maid had gone Edwina examined her mother critically.

"You're looking tired. Are things very bad at home?"

"Your father has had gout for four years. It's been severe this last year and now he's got bronchitis as well. He's a sick man, Edwina."

"I'm sorry."

"I came to ask you to visit us, for his sake."

Edwina was thoughtful. "I suppose I ought to."

"This silly quarrel has gone on too long. You're like Guy, you don't forgive. He wouldn't let me write to you. I kept hoping you'd write to me."

"It was your place, not mine," Edwina countered stiffly.

"Yes, just like your father."

"I suppose you're still hard up?"

"No, we manage all right. Some of your father's investments have done very well . . . at last. We have enough. Besides, he can't drink so much."

"Of course not. I have to go to a horse trial tomorrow. I've got a new car. I'll come on from Pleasaunce and stay for a few days if you'd like."

"We would like that."

"Well, that's settled." She smiled suddenly at her mother. "I'm glad you came."

Alexandra hid her surprise. She had not quite known what sort of welcome she could expect, but Guy was in a wretched state and recently had begun to ask to see Edwina. It wasn't too much to demand of their daughter that she visit them.

Alice came into the room, and while Edwina went off to fetch young Jocelyn the two older women caught up with their news. Alexandra stayed for lunch and drove home in the early evening before Edward returned. The weather was mild and bright, and Edwina and Edward walked in the garden in the evening. Alice had made a clearing in the small wood, and had built an arbor. It was a pleasant spot. Sometimes in summer they had a cold lunch taken out there for them. Now they sat on a rustic seat. Edwina told him about her mother's visit.

"I thought I'd go away for several days. I'm going to Pleasaunce in the morning anyway. I can go on to Castle

Combe and return some time next week. Is that all right?"

"Of course, it is. You need a break, my dear. Jocelyn will be all right with Miss Black."

"Yes, he will."

"Then take your time and don't hurry. How are you off for money?"

"I wanted to ask you about that. Most wives receive an allowance of some sort. I don't, because your mother looks after everything in the house. I know you're generous, and I have accounts in town I can use for clothes and things, but I have no cash. If I'm going to go out more, I really should have a small allowance."

"That's true. I ought to have thought of it before. How much would you like?"

"Twenty pounds a month?" she suggested.

"We can manage more than that. I'll make it five hundred a year. Of course if you need money for anything you only have to ask, but I can see that you ought to have pocket money of your own."

"Five hundred's far more than I dared to ask for," she said pleased.

She left next morning and was away for over a week. She telephoned on the following Friday in the evening.

"Where are you? At Castle Combe?" Edward asked.

"No, at Pleasuance. I spent last night here with the Thatchams."

"That's nice." He was surprised.

"Are you going to Henley in the morning?"

"Yes. I've got new engines in the boat."

"Then you won't mind if I don't come home tonight?"

"No. What are your plans? Have the Thatchams asked you to stay for the weekend?"

"Not exactly. I thought I might spend the weekend in Newbury. There's a good hotel."

"All right, if that's what you want. See you on Sunday?"

"Yes," she agreed. "How is Jocelyn?"

"He's fine. We're all fine. Have a good time, Edwina."

"I'll try."

He was really rather pleased about this development. It eased his conscience a little. Edward found life very satisfactory and he liked other people to enjoy themselves too. He told his mother not to expect Edwina till Sunday night.

"Is Mary still at Pleasuance?" Alice asked.

"No, she's gone, but Edwina says Timothy is still there."

"Oho," she smiled.

"There you go again. Perhaps he's friendly with Walter. They're about the same age, after all."

"I'm not convinced," Alice answered smugly.

"Of course I suppose Timothy's fairly well fixed for money," Edward mused.

"I expect they manage all right."

"His father was as poor as a church mouse."

"Money isn't everything," Alice pointed out.

"Perhaps not, but it helps enormously. The way wages and costs are going up, I'd say we're in for a thin time of it, even though our sales figures are always improving. I'd rather own a factory than a department store, you know."

"Are things serious?" Alice asked, faintly alarmed.

"Not serious, but they could be better. Thank goodness for that visit to Chicago. It will help enormously. We'll survive all right, but competition is getting much more fierce. We've had it all our own way in Reading for a long time. It's healthy competition of course, and it's good for trade, but it leaves me wondering what to do about the future. See if you have any bright ideas."

"I'm sure you have better ideas than I have," she laughed.

For the first time Edward was having to grapple with the problem of soaring turnover and a drop in profits. It was obvious to him that he would have to become increasingly cost conscious if he wanted to get the most out of the company. It was a new situation and one which interested rather than alarmed him.

When he returned on the Sunday from Henley, Alice had news for him.

"Edward, did you know that John had a son?"

"No, Mother. Of course I don't guarantee to read every announcement in the *Times*. Some days I don't have time to read any of it. When was this? How did you hear?"

"Mary referred to it in a letter. She said something about it being Robert's first birthday this month and about wondering how James liked being a grandfather. Of course Mary is the child's grandmother—one keeps forgetting about her and James after all this time."

"Robert, eh? A year old. I didn't know. Frankly, Mother, I'm not at all interested in James and his family."

"It's such a senseless business. We're all one family."

"Perhaps, but it wasn't this branch which made the trouble, it was my wretched fat uncle. When you think of it, it was ridiculous that Grandfather should live here for years while James was at St. James's Place, but the split was James's doing. Remember that business of John's twenty-first birthday? He hadn't the decency to write and say thank you. John is a stuck-up prig anyway."

"How do you know?"

"Well, I bumped into him in France."

"You didn't say anything."

"No, I didn't want to. We quarreled. He's a fool, you know. I'd rather not talk about it."

Alice sighed. The years mellowed her, but it seemed the younger generation was eager to keep the feud alive. She too blamed James. The years did not mellow him, far from it. He was like a character out of one of Mr. Galsworthy's novels, which she so enjoyed reading nowadays. She thought of her great-nephew Robert, and felt sad. Quite likely she would never see him.

In the months ahead, and during that splendid summer,

Timothy spent quite a lot of time at Pleasaunce, although Mary was content to remain at her cottage in Kemble in the heart of the countryside in Gloucestershire. Edwina, too, swung to an opposite extreme and disappeared regularly once or twice a month. Edward was surprised by how often she visited her parents.

He was at home one weekend when Alexandra telephoned.

"Can I speak to Edwina please, Edward?" she asked.

"But Edwina isn't here, she's with you."

"No, she left us yesterday morning. She forgot her handbag, and her checkbook is in it. I was ringing to let her know."

"I'll tell her when she comes. She must have dropped off at the Thatcham's on the way home."

"I hope she's all right."

"Don't worry about Edwina. She can take care of herself."

"Ask her to telephone, please."

"Yes, I shall. How is Guy?"

"A little worse. He has such terrible trouble breathing."

"I'm sorry."

"It can't be helped. Don't forget to ask Edwina to telephone me. Good-bye."

Edward hung up thoughtfully. Then he called George Thatcham.

"George? Edward Vernon. Is Edwina with you?"

"No, we haven't seen her recently. Wait a minute, I'm wrong. She called for an hour or so on Wednesday on her way to her parents' home."

"I see. I thought she was visiting you this weekend."

"No, sorry."

"Never mind. I expect I've got it all mixed up as usual. I have so many things to think about these days."

He began to feel faintly alarmed. Could she have been in an accident? Surely if she had left Castle Combe on

Friday morning, as her mother said, and had been in an accident, they would have heard about it long before now. No, she must have gone somewhere. He would wait and see.

Fortunately for his temper he did not have to wait too long. Edwina herself telephoned shortly before bedtime.

"Where are you?" Edward demanded irritably.

"Why, what's the matter?"

"Your mother telephoned to say you'd left your check-book and handbag at Castle Combe."

"Did I? I'm glad she rang. I hadn't noticed."

"Exactly. You left yesterday morning."

"I'm at Pleasaunce. I thought I'd drop in on George and Elizabeth and they asked me to stay. You don't mind, do you?"

"No." He could hardly believe his ears. She was lying to him. Why was she doing that?

"I'll be back tomorrow."

"Your mother wants you to call her."

"All right, I'll phone now. Everything all right at home?"

"Everything's fine here," he assured her dryly.

He hung up and puzzled over it. Why the mystery? Where was she, really? He could not think of the answer, but he woke early on Sunday morning, remembering that she had stayed twice at the Marlborough Arms in Newbury. It was only a slim chance, but without saying anything to Alice he got the car out and drove over to Newbury. He parked in a side street and walked to the hotel.

"Is there a Mrs. Vernon staying here?" he asked the reception clerk.

He consulted the register and shook his head.

"No, sir."

"Then I've got it wrong, haven't I? Many thanks."

He walked to the door. As he did so he heard a familiar laugh. Instinctively he ducked into the nearest doorway

and waited. It was Edwina all right. She came downstairs
with a man. Her hand was on his arm. So she was here
after all, and not under her own name either. His mouth
tightened and then he stared, amazed. He had recognized
the man. It was young Walter, Thatcham's son! Fortunately they turned away from him. He waited till they had
gone into the dining room before continuing to the door
and out to his car.

Lord Paveley? He was a child. Edwina was twenty-
eight, Paveley was twenty—eight years' difference. It was
odd, because he always looked on Paveley's father as a
contemporary, probably because of their service together
in the army. Even so, he thought with disgust as he drove
off back toward Reading, it was not too far removed from
cradle snatching. Paveley wasn't of age yet.

Edwina arrived back at six-thirty, and he noted her
flushed cheeks and the light in her eyes. She was blossoming, damn her.

"I'd like to talk to you upstairs," he said quietly.

"Very well, let's go up while I unpack."

He followed her to her room, closed the door and
leaned against it. She was chattering about the journey
and the weather, and then she stopped and looked at him,
head tilted to one side.

"What's wrong?" she asked directly.

"You made a mistake saying you were at Pleasaunce.
After your mother telephoned last night, the first thing I
did was to give George Thatcham a buzz."

"Oh, dear." She made a wry face, but seemed in no way
put out.

"This morning I remembered that you had stayed at the
Marlborough Arms in Newbury a couple of times. I went
along and asked for you. You weren't registered."

"So?" Her eyes were hard now. Obviously she guessed
what was coming.

"As I was leaving I heard you. I waited and watched. I saw you . . . and him."

"In that case there's nothing to say."

"Isn't there, by God?" he snapped. "Have you gone mad?"

"Not at all. You have your cottage in Henley, your weekends about which no questions are ever asked. Do you expect me to live like a nun? You refuse to share my bed. Am I supposed to become sexless to suit you?"

"Did you have to pick on my best friend's son, a mere boy?"

"He's a man, not a boy."

"He's twenty!"

"That's grown up, or didn't you know?" she sneered.

"My God, Thatcham would have a fit if he discovered his son was committing adultery with my wife."

"Oh, yes, appearances—that's all that worries you. Well Walter loves me, if you must know."

"You can't be serious about him."

"Of course not, but he makes a most diverting companion. He's so virile. He doesn't expect a woman to hug her pillow at nights."

"If you can't leave sex alone, can't you be discreet?"

"We are discreet, but if it troubles you, I'll drop him. There are other fish in the sea."

"Well, you've come out of your shell with a vengeance. I suppose after what happened in London, I was a fool to expect anything different."

"You selfish prig. You'll never understand," she flashed at him. "It was because you were taken away from me that I behaved as I did in London. I don't excuse it, but I told you before, I couldn't stand life without you. It's because you refuse to give me a normal woman's rights that I've had to turn to other men now. You've made me what I am, damn you, Edward Vernon. I worshiped the very ground you walked on."

"A fine way you had of showing it."

He would never understand, she realized, and it was a waste of time talking to him. Let him think what he chose.

"Would you mind getting out of here? Oh, and before you go, one thing—what about your little jaunts to Henley? Is it all boating, my dear?"

"There are no other women."

"If that's the truth, then you're unnatural. It can't last forever. There was nothing unnatural about you when we were first married."

"Doesn't it worry you being a harlot?" he asked wearily.

"My dear Edward, I don't accept money."

"No, you take mine. That makes it worse."

"Why?" she snapped back. "You don't want me. What does it matter about other men?"

"I'm not going to quarrel with you," he said patiently. "It wouldn't do any good. I'm thinking of Jocelyn, and Mother too," he added. "I must ask you to keep your sordid affairs well buried, and please leave the Paveley family alone. They happen to be friends of mine."

"Very well."

She waited till he had gone and then collapsed dejectedly onto a chair. Did he think she enjoyed it? Didn't he know she would far rather it were he? She loved him and she always would, and for all the good it did she might as well hate him, as he so obviously hated her.

She began to cry, not for the first time.

Chapter 20

EDWARD never inquired closely into his wife's movements after that, and he felt sure she was no longer having an affair with Walter Paveley. George Paveley, 7th Earl of Thatcham, was as modern and fun-loving as any man, but he would never have got over a shock like that. After that he and Edwina visited Pleasaunce together. In 1922 Alice's prediction came true. Timothy Hilton, aged twenty, married Lady Elizabeth Paveley, also aged twenty. They were married in Newbury and the place was crammed with guests. The bride and groom were going to live at Warneford Cottage, where apparently he liked working. The prospect of love in a cottage—a very well-furnished cottage with modern plumbing—did not daunt Lady Elizabeth in the least. Mary was moving out into another cottage in the village which she had bought with money provided by her father. Everyone was happy.

Edward and Thatcham did not refer to Timothy's illegitimacy again. It was a subject best left alone. Edward, however, was impressed that Thatcham, who was a traditionalist where his family was concerned, should accept Timothy so readily as a son-in-law.

With the passing of the months he thought occasionally of Edwina's taunt about it being unnatural of him not to have a mistress. It wasn't that he lacked the urge, but he had never come across any woman who affected him like that. He had a wide circle of friends nowadays, not only in Reading itself, where he was an extremely prominent citizen, but at Henley and even in the U.S.A. where the number of his acquaintances was growing rapidly. He knew it was almost certain that Edwina was still being unfaithful to him—he still thought of it in those precise terms—but she was so clever about it that soon he stopped thinking about it. It was a less pleasant fact of life, to be brushed under the carpet and ignored.

At the start of 1924 Colonel James Vernon, C.B., died at St. James's Place, London. It was January 21, the same day on which Lenin died, and the day before Britain had its first Labour Ministry under Ramsay MacDonald. There was change everywhere. The death of James affected Alice much more than she had expected.

She did not like James, although she was prepared to be friendly toward him, but he was Henry's brother. He was the only other survivor of that story which had begun in London so very many years ago before. She was fifty-nine now, only a year younger than the dead James. It was not really old, but it was enough to make her pause and think. It would be her turn next.

On impulse she telephoned the house in London and was told that Captain John and his wife were at home. She asked for John.

"Who's that?" he asked sharply. He had his father's voice, she thought.

"This is your Aunt Alice in Reading. I heard the news."

"He didn't leave you anything, if that's what you're concerned about."

She stared at the telephone blankly. Had she heard aright?

"I beg your pardon?"

"What do you want?" John demanded.

"I called to offer our sympathy and to ask if there was anything your cousin or I could do."

"Nothing whatever. Good-bye."

What an incredibly rude man, she thought as she hung up the receiver. What sort of hatred could make him behave in that manner? She had been considering going to the church service, if not to the funeral, but now she changed her mind. She told Edward what had happened.

"What do you expect? They're a funny lot in London. I've never cared for them. I hope you're not going to send flowers."

"It would be so rude not to," she complained.

"It would be a foolish gesture. They'd probably throw them away and derive a lot of pleasure from doing so. Ignore them altogether."

Alice sighed. Ignore them—what sort of advice was that to give about the family? Edward, however, had no difficulty in doing so. Business was bad, seriously bad. He had hived off the little shops—they were no longer an economic proposition—and all his effort and money were tied up in the stores. The return on his money was far less than he could have got if he had sold out and invested it all in gilt-edged securities. It was not encouraging, yet he hung on grimly. He would hand it on to Jocelyn, strengthened and improved, just as his father and mother had built it up for him. In July disaster struck—not Vernon's department store, but the Empire Bank. The bank collapsed. The depositors lost enormous sums of money, the Lancaster fortune was wiped out, and two Lancasters committed suicide. The City reeled under this catastrophe. Philip Lancaster, aged ninety, had a heart attack and died, almost penniless.

Alice wrote to Mary who responded by making a quick

visit to Mereford. She was gray-haired now, prematurely aged, looking older than her fifty-four years.

"It's almost all gone," she told Alice. "Timothy is lucky. He was given a wedding present of several thousand pounds to add to the money Papa left him, and it's invested for him by a stockbroker. His money wasn't in the bank. The rest of the family are more or less reduced to nothing. I've got a few thousands saved elsewhere—I suppose most of us have—but our capital was tied up in the bank. I'll manage all right; my cottage is paid for and I can live on capital—but there won't be anything for Timothy."

"Does he earn much?"

"About fifty pounds a year from his paintings. And there is the money Sir Godfrey left him. Poor Timothy. Elizabeth's family won't be able to help. They aren't rich and they've got Pleasaunce to keep up."

"It's too bad," Alice commiserated.

"James didn't leave me anything. I don't blame him for that, but I expect he left quite a lot to John. James wasn't short."

"The will was published. He left forty-seven thousand pounds, net."

"Lucky John, although it's not very much when one thinks what the family was worth once. Anyway they won't starve, neither shall I, but I worry about Timothy."

"Perhaps his pictures will sell better. Anyway, he isn't really penniless."

"No, I suppose not."

"Why doesn't he do illustrations for magazines or something like that?" Alice asked, thinking over the situation.

"I'll suggest it to him, but I don't understand art."

"Neither do I," Alice agreed.

"And you know, Timothy and Elizabeth are expecting a baby in about a month."

"How very nice, Mary. You must be so pleased."

"I would be if it hadn't been for this business of the bank."

Mary stayed for two days before going back to Gloucestershire, and Alice felt shaken. She had grown almost accustomed to the change which marked modern life, but the collapse of the bank was frightening. It hit at her sense of security. She began to take an interest in the department store again, and she and Edward often sat and discussed it after dinner while Edwina read.

Jocelyn was six now and went to a private school nearby. Edward had talked to his mother about his education, for really they had little experience of schools. Such places as the Reverend Mark Luke's establishment no longer existed and probably a good thing too, he thought. He had decided finally upon a new school which had opened nearby at Stratfield Mortimer, called Mortimer Hall. It was spoken of highly and was not too large. Edward had an instinctive distrust of large schools. Meantime, till Jocelyn reached twelve, other arrangements had to be made. He was a tall boy for his age, and very sturdy. He and Edward were enormous friends and the child compensated in many ways for the loss of real contact with Edwina.

Jocelyn was going through a "soldier" stage. One of the things Edward had done after the war was to have the various family insignia mounted in glass-fronted cases— Sir Godfrey's medals and the insignia of his orders of knighthood; Henry's Victoria Cross and South Africa medal, the smallest but in its own way the most impressive display; and his own string of medals. They were not for show—Edward would never have dreamed of putting them out for other people to see. That would have been very vulgar indeed. They were put away in a cupboard under one of the many glass-fronted bookcases in the library—family heirlooms to be kept, but not fussed over. There Jocelyn had found them and had insisted on being told all about them. Almost every day the child would go into the library and pull out the boxes to stare at their contents before going to his own room to play with his soldiers and his toy fort. He plagued Edward regularly to take him to the attic where all the uniforms and swords were stored away in trunks, amid mothballs. Edward indulged the boy's youthful enthusiasm, but he did not encourage it. Jocelyn was to follow in his footsteps, leaving school at seventeen to go into the family company.

At the end of August they received news of Timothy. He was the father of a daughter, Anne Hilton—but he was also a widower. Elizabeth had died quite unexpectedly and unaccountably in childbirth.

The Thatchams were distraught and urged Timothy to bring the baby and live with them at Pleasaunce. Timothy rejected them out of hand. Anne would live with her father at Kemble. He had engaged a local woman as a nanny. He passed out of the ambit of the family, as George Thatcham put it one evening after dinner when Edward and Edwina were dining at Pleasaunce.

"We never hear from him now. Not a word for four months. Hang it all, the baby is our granddaughter."

"It was a tragedy about Elizabeth," Edward commiserated.

"Yes, a frightful tragedy. I suppose they'll manage all right at Kemble. Mary lives nearby, to help the nurse and generally keep an eye on things. I wish they'd come here, but the fact is that they seem to prefer their own company."

Fate had not finished playing its tricks on the Vernons. A year later, in the winter of 1925, John Vernon was promoted to major. His pleasure in his promotion was marred by the fact that his hateful civilian cousin had been a major in 1917, eight years earlier. Then, a week later, he awoke one morning to discover that his wife Lucy had fled. She had run off with a band leader who had an engagement in South America. She would not offer any obstacle, she said in her abrupt note, if he wished to divorce her. In disgust he sold the house at St. James's Place and bought a very much smaller house at Hampstead, a four-bedroom villa.

The family at Mereford knew nothing of this at that time, nor would Edward have cared much if he had. He had no time for John.

Jocelyn went to Mortimer Hall in September of 1930. By now he had acquired Edward's enthusiasm for boats, and during the summer he liked to go to Henley for weekends. This meant that during term time he did not see much of his mother. If Edwina was troubled by this, she did not say so. Alice disapproved strongly, but as it was none of her business she tried to shut her eyes to the situation.

Edwina had stopped going away so often, and Edward assumed that she had grown tired of chasing men. He was not too far wide of the mark. Sex for its own sake meant nothing to her, but she was a woman who needed to love and be loved. At the same time this need was diminishing slightly and she was coming to love Mereford more. The house had put its spell upon her. The need for excitement, for reassurance, was not so strong. She took to sitting with Alice on summer nights, watching the lengthening shadows, and doing tapestry work at which she was unexpectedly skillful.

The following year John left the 1st Lancers, the last of the Vernons in the regiment. He was promoted to lieutenant colonel but given a job at the War Office. He knew he would never serve with the regiment again, and he was genuinely moved by this fact. Like his father he was a man of limited intellect and poor powers of expression, but in his dumb way he accepted that to serve in the 1st Lancers was the highest good fortune a man could have.

To add to his troubles, about the same time he lost most of his money in rash speculation. He had been listening to talk of killings on the stock market and had begun to dabble in moving money about, without really understanding how to do it. He woke one morning to discover that he had wiped out almost all his capital. He had his pay, and one day he would have his pension, but apart from that he had less than six hundred a year. It was all right at the War Office but how, he wondered, would he manage to send his son Robert into the Lancers? Even in these egalitarian days, one needed an income of more than six hundred a year to be an officer in the 1st—a thousand was the lowest figure on which one could do it decently. He did not know, of course, that Robert would never serve in the 1st Lancers, that no Vernon would do so again, nor that in less than fifty years the regiment would no longer exist, abolished in an economic "rationalization" of army regiments. He worried a great deal about money and Robert's future, and blessed the fact that it wasn't nearly so important to keep up appearances in the War Office as it had been at the regimental depot.

For a few years the two families went their separate ways, virtually untouched by outside events. In 1933 Adolf Hitler became the German Chancellor; and in 1934 the Chancellor of Austria, Engelbert Dollfuss—called the Pocket Chancellor because he was under five feet in height—was murdered by the Nazis. Shortly afterward Hitler became a dictator. In 1935 Italy went to war with Abyssinia and the League of Nations effectively demonstrated that it was ineffective.

During these years Edward continued to potter with his latest boat in the summer, and to play tennis with Jocelyn who had taken up the game, while surprisingly Edwina spent more time with her own mother at Castle Combe, and with her ailing father. Originally they had been an excuse to get out and to look around for amusement, but now when she said she was going home, she meant that she was going home and nowhere else. At the War Office John minuted files and sneered at warmongers and people who talked of war. The Germans were bluffers. He divorced his wife who had, surprisingly, stuck to her band leader.

At the tail end of the year 1935 John was walking along Oxford Street in a fog. He was much preoccupied with some trivial affairs of his department and not really noticing what he was doing. He bumped into another man near the edge of the pavement, staggered, and stepped out into the road. As he did so, he slipped and tumbled headlong into the path of a bus. It was all over in a second. He suffered nothing. The body was identified quickly and his housekeeper consulted. She told the police that Colonel Vernon was living alone. He had a son at boarding school. He had divorced Mrs. Vernon and she was not in England.

They were at a loss to know what to do till next day when the War Office looked up his documents and saw that he had recently changed his next of kin to Major Edward Vernon, D.S.O., M.C., Mereford, Spencer's Wood, Berkshire. Edward was notified.

After a short discussion they had John's body brought to Reading and buried beside that of Sir Godfrey. It was a pathetically simple estate to wind up. He had left everything to his son Robert, that everything consisting of a few thousand pounds. There was an annuity, but it died with him. There were some trunks of books, papers, and uniforms and that was all. Edward arranged for the Hampstead house to be sold and the money invested.

There was the problem of Robert.

"We can't leave him at boarding school after this," Alice said. "It would be cruel."

"I know. It means we have to have him here. There's enough room."

"Yes. He can go to Mortimer Hall later on, but I think

he should be a day boy at Granville, in Reading, for a term or two."

"I agree. I never expected that one of them would come to live here. Talk about a wheel turning full circle."

"That's no way to speak," his mother reproved him. "Robert is only a boy of fifteen who has done no harm to anyone. We must bring him up as one of us."

"I'll treat him like a son," Edward promised.

"That's what I'd hoped you'd say."

When Robert heard the news he seemed pleased. He had none of the usual Vernon characteristics and presumably took after his mother, not his father. He was fair-haired, of medium height, with a freckled face and rather a snub nose. He was very quiet. Like most boys of fifteen he was all arms and legs, just beginning to fill out.

Alice took him into Reading and bought him his new school uniform. Robert was more relaxed with her, more confident, and even asked questions.

"Are you really my aunt?"

"I was your father's aunt."

"Then you must be very old, but you don't look it."

"It will be the diplomatic service for you all right," Alice laughed, not displeased. "I'm seventy."

"Gosh, that's ancient."

"Thank you very much. I manage very nicely."

"Why did you never come to see us in London?" Roger asked. "My father never told me he had an aunt."

"Well, you know how it is—families go in different ways. This lot of Vernons came here to Reading and set up in business, and your lot stayed in London and were in the army."

"I don't want to go into the army."

"Don't you?"

"But I must."

"Why?" Alice asked.

"My father said it was my duty."

"Well, perhaps you won't have to go after all. What would you rather do?"

"I don't know. I like reading books."

"You can't do that all the time."

"I don't see why not. I bet some schoolteachers do."

"You could become a teacher, of course."

"I wouldn't like that. All the boys hate teachers. I don't want to be hated."

"None of us does," Alice agreed. "But somebody has to teach. Anyway, surely not all teachers are unpopular."

"I don't want to tell people what to do," Robert said, half to himself. "I don't want to boss people about. I don't like people very much."

"You don't mean that, Robert."

"Well, I don't hate them, but I just want to be myself."

Alice was a little troubled. Was it shyness? she wondered. Or did he feel a real gulf between himself and others? She hoped he was not going to be a difficult boy.

"What is Jocelyn going to do?"

"You are full of questions, aren't you? Jocelyn will be leaving school this summer and going to work in his father's office."

"I'd hate an office."

"I don't know what we're going to do with you then," Alice smiled. "Luckily we don't have to decide now."

She forgot about the conversation until one day a fortnight later she saw Robert, after school, standing in the drive watching Maggett's son, Young Maggett, who was now the gardener. He had been sawing some deadwood from a tree. Robert walked over to the gardener and spoke to him and then she saw him pushing the wheelbarrow for Maggett. Intrigued, she went out to the back and met them as they came round the side of the house.

"Mr. Maggett is making a bonfire," Robert said with some animation. "I'm going to help him."

"Good."

He put down the barrow and wandered over to her. "Aunt Alice," he said slowly, "I know what I'd really like to do."

"What?" she asked, wondering what was coming next.

"I'd like to be a gardener, then I could stay here all day and work in the garden. It's beautiful here . . . but I wouldn't want to be a gardener anywhere else."

"What a funny child you are," she laughed, and kissed him, putting an arm round his shoulders.

Robert looked up and laughed.

He's one of us, Alice thought happily.

BOOK III

The Family at Mereford
1938–1973

Chapter 21

IN 1938, to the disbelief of men like Edward Vernon who thought they had fought the war to end wars, war clouds were gathering menacingly on the horizon and there was mounting tension in Europe. Hitler, whom no one had taken particularly seriously five years before, was flexing his muscles in no uncertain manner. On March 13 Germany annexed Austria, to the great joy of the German people. Edward worried alone, however. Jocelyn, now twenty, had been working in the family business for three years. He was energetic and intelligent, and was the buyer for the department store. His spare time was taken up with tennis and dances, for he was a gregarious young man with many friends in and around Reading.

Robert, who had been a good pupil at school, had managed to get himself a place at London University, where he intended to study history. When Edward had asked him to what purpose, he had merely shrugged his shoulders. It was too early yet to make plans, he said. He remained a strangely aloof, rather solitary person. With the family he was relaxed and happy, but he avoided contact with outsiders, and he had never had any real friends at school. He had distinguished himself by becoming a prefect for one term only, in his final year. The headmaster wrote a short, apologetic but unsatisfactory note to Edward telling him that he had been forced to cancel the appointment. Edward naturally went to see him one morning to find out why. It wasn't a terrible sort of thing, but it was most unusual.

"It's not a punishment," the headmaster pointed out, in the privacy of his study. "I must make that absolutely clear. Robert has never had to be punished."

"Then what happened?"

"You know what the purpose of the prefect system is. It gives some of the boys a chance to exercise a little authority, to develop their characters and powers of leadership, and incidentally allows them a small part in the running of the school. Robert has been quite exemplary and it struck me that he was without enemies, and it seemed a good idea to make him a prefect. It turned out that in matters of discipline he is hopeless."

"In what way?" Edward asked, mystified.

"He can't maintain it. He can't use authority. What's more the younger boys soon found out. If you put him in charge of junior boys for five minutes, you can be certain that they'll be the noisiest lot in the school during that time, and probably end up fighting each other. It's my own fault. I ought to have known that the reason he has no enemies is because he is so aloof, so neutral. Anyway he was responsible for a number of boys out on a ramble one afternoon, and he returned minus four of them. We found them in a café gorging themselves. When I asked Robert about it, all he said was that he had told them to come along and they had refused, so it was none of his business."

"None of his business!"

"Those were his own words, not mine. The school captain came and spoke to me afterward and said the other prefects didn't like the situation much. It was undermining everyone's authority. What could I do? The fact is that Robert lacks any leadership ability and shuns responsibility. Yet he is utterly charming, intelligent, a hard worker, obedient—quite a model."

"In a negative way," Edward suggested.

"Not exactly. He can be positive enough sometimes, but never where other people are concerned."

"Did he have no explanation at all?"

"None other than what I have told you. I tried to point out that it was his duty to control the boys in his charge, but all he could say was that he had told them and they wouldn't listen. You see," the headmaster chose his words carefully, "I don't think he understands people. If a prefect said to him 'Don't do that,' he wouldn't do it and that would be the end of the matter. I don't think he fully understands that other people aren't like him."

"What's happened now that he's been demoted, as it were?"

"Strangely enough the boys appear to like him more, now that he isn't a prefect. I think he was becoming a figure of fun, but now that he's just one of them again, it's all right. There are times when I have to confess to myself in private that I don't always understand boys. Not too often, mind you, but this is one of those times."

In the end Edward said nothing to Robert about the incident, mainly because he did not know what he *could* say. Robert had done nothing wrong; he had merely failed to prevent other people from transgressing. He had warned them and they had ignored him. Edwina agreed that it was better to drop the matter.

In September of 1937 Robert went to live in furnished lodgings in London, where he had entered the university. It seemed that he was happy and contented there, going his inoffensive way, working as hard as he generally did.

As for Alice, she didn't even know there was a crisis in Europe. In her seventy-third year her mind had begun to wander, and finally she lost touch with reality. She was able to dress and undress, keep herself tidy, manage her food, and seemed to enjoy walking in the garden when the weather was mild enough. She had no real idea of what was going on around her, however, and had begun to live in the past.

Edwina was good with Alice. Now approaching forty-five, and a fine-looking woman, she was infinitely patient with her mother-in-law. Edward hid his surprise. He had no great opinion of his wife, yet she had a disturbing habit of surprising him. She was the only one, for instance, who seemed to understand Robert. It was to her that Robert sent his infrequent letters from London.

One evening in June, Robert telephoned and Edwina answered the call.

"Is that you, Aunt Edwina?"

"Robert! How nice to hear from you. How is London?"

"Grand. I'm ringing about the summer holidays. Could I bring a friend to Mereford for a week or two at the end of term?"

"You know you can. You don't have to ask."

"Yes, well this is a girl."

"Ah, is it? Tell me about her."

"There isn't much to tell. Her name's Sally Brown, she's the same age as I am, she's reading English, and she's got no parents. They're dead. She has an aunt in Broadway, but she's pretty old."

"Broadway?" Edwina asked. Geography had never been a strong point.

"Yes. It's in Worcestershire. It's fourteen miles from Stratford on Avon and about the same from Cheltenham. It's one of the pretty-pretty villages and rather dull for Sally, and the aunt is a bit of a bore. I thought it would be nice for her to come to us for a holiday."

"Yes, of course, if you wish."

"I knew you'd understand. She's very nice. You'll like her."

"I'm sure we shall. You'll let me know when to expect you, won't you, Robert? We'll have to get a room ready for Sally."

"Yes. How's Gran?"

He always called Alice "Gran," although she was his great-aunt.

"Robert, I think she's failing fast. She's become much weaker this spring. She still gets up every day and she seems to be very happy—so far as I can tell, that is. One rarely knows what she is thinking about."

"Poor Gran. She's not in pain, is she?" He had a horror of pain and suffering.

"No, no."

"And Uncle Edward?"

"Busy, and gloomy."

"About the war?" Robert asked.

"Yes, he's certain there will be one."

"It's his generation—they see war as the answer to everything," Robert assured her airily. "I was talking to one of my lecturers the other day and he says war is out of the question. Don't worry. Anyway, Uncle is well?"

"As always. He still potters about in his boat every weekend."

"Jocelyn?"

"This is the tennis season, so Jocelyn divides his time now between the office and the tennis club."

"That only leaves you," Robert said.

"You know me—nothing ever goes wrong with me," she replied placidly. "I'm going to Austria later this summer."

"Going *where*?"

He heard her laugh as she repeated, "To Austria. An old friend of mine has a house for the summer at a place called Hallein. It's close to the border of Germany, near

Berchtesgaden, which is very pretty. It's also close to Salz-burg. I thought I'd go for three weeks in August."

"Isn't it a bit risky with all the trouble in Austria?"

"Oh, that's only politics. My friend says everything is normal."

There was nothing in her voice to betray the fact that this was a very special holiday. Her friend was Walter Paveley. Since she had known him, he had married, had two children, and had recently been divorced. Edwina had been surprised to receive his letter inviting her to Austria for a holiday. At forty-five she had few illusions—possibly there would never be another such invitation. She was not yet so old as to be indifferent to the opposite sex, and Edward still slept in his own room. Soon it wouldn't mat-ter, but right now the prospect of what she amusingly thought of as "a little summer sunshine to brighten up the winter years" was not without its attractions. She intended to go, whatever happened.

They chatted for a few moments and then hung up. She went into the drawing room, lit a cigarette and poured herself a sherry. Robert and a girl was an interesting situa-tion. Of course the boy was too young to be serious, a mere eighteen. She wondered what sort of girl attracted him. A few minutes later her son Jocelyn burst into the room.

Jocelyn was tall and strong, dark-haired, with a nice mouth. He wore his tennis clothes under a blazer and had a towel wrapped around his neck. He glowed with good health and animal spirits.

"Hullo, Mother. At the bottle?"

"Join me?"

"Not sherry, thanks. I'll have a gin before I go and bathe. When's Father coming home?"

"Soon I hope. He said he'd be here in time for dinner."

"He'll be late. He always is. I'm hungry, but never mind."

"Robert has just been on the telephone."

Jocelyn brightened. He and his cousin had become good friends during the years since Robert had come to live at Mereford.

"How is he?"

"Very well. He's bringing a girl home from London at the end of term, to spend a holiday here."

"Robert? A girl? He's only a kid."

"He's only two years younger than you are."

"And chasing girls already! I wonder what she's like."

"Exactly what I was wondering. Anyway, you leave her alone, she's Robert's friend."

"Oh, I've no time for girls—not unless they can play tennis, and most of them aren't much good at that."

He was very boyish, she thought. But then so had his father been, the long-dead Captain Donald Erskine. It was odd, but she couldn't really remember what Donald had looked like. Jocelyn did not take after his father in appearance, but after herself—which was just as well or it might have made people wonder.

Rather to Jocelyn's surprise his mother kissed him gently.

"That's right," she said cheerfully. "Leave the girls alone till you're older."

"It isn't a question of age," he laughed. "I'm simply too busy with other things. Besides, keep it to yourself, but most of the girls round here are crashing bores. They've nothing to talk about."

How refreshing, she reflected, to find a young man of twenty who thought about girls in terms of people to be talked to.

"Probably you haven't given them a chance," she said.

He drank up his gin and put down the glass.

"I must go change. I shan't be long. What's Robert's girl's name?"

"Sally Brown."

"Very distinguished. One of *the* Browns, I assume?"

"Give the girl a chance, darling. Maybe she's a charmer."

"I was only joking. See you."

He went off and left her to her own thoughts. They were not unpleasant ones. She was thinking that life here at Mereford was singularly cosy and sheltered. Edward could have divorced her twenty years ago, but he hadn't. He was considerate and attentive. It was expecting too much to look for affection in him when he believed he had been betrayed. He had played fair. He did not interfere with her, he gave her a generous allowance, she had always had her own car, and she had gathered a small circle of friends with the passing of the years. She was really very lucky indeed. It would have been nice to have a husband passionately in love with her—but that was not the way things were. She was rapidly becoming philosophic.

She went upstairs to Alice's room, tapped on the door, and went inside. Alice was in bed. She went to bed every afternoon.

"Everything all right?" Edwina asked, raising Alice with one hand and fluffing up the pillows behind her. "Are you going to get up for dinner?"

"I think I'll have it in bed."

"All right. What can I get you?"

"Nothing, thank you, Edwina."

She was really no trouble, Edwina thought. Alice began to struggle to get out of bed, and she helped her.

"I shall sit by the window and look out at the garden. It's so lovely at this time of year. I could spend hours watching the garden."

Could and did, Edwina thought, amused. She helped Alice to put on her dressing gown and to sit in the easy chair by the window which overlooked her beloved rose garden, planted by Henry so many long years before.

Alice settled herself comfortably in her chair, put her feet up on her embroidered footstool, and crossed her hands in her lap.

"That's all, thank you, Edwina. Is Edward home yet?"

"No, he's still at Henley, but he should be home soon."

Alice nodded. "I wonder if he will bring Mr. Turner to tea."

"Who?" Edwina asked, taken off guard.

"Henry, of course, bring Robert Turner." Edwina realized that her mother-in-law had slipped back in time again. She gave Alice a little pat, straightened the bedclothes, and went down to tell the cook that the mistress would have her dinner on a tray in the bedroom. Alice did not hear her go. She was thinking of her husband, Henry.

She gazed out at the beautiful rose garden, with its large circular plots and its long side beds, the turf a lovely deep green, the soil fine and dark and friable. They had many more varieties of roses now than she and Henry had had in the beginning, although the great center display was of red and white roses, to remind her of him.

Sometimes he was very real to her, very near. She could feel his presence. She had the feeling that she could talk to him, but when she did there was no answer. This always disappointed her. Only this morning when she had woken up he had been standing by her bedside in the uniform of the Berkshire Light Infantry. When she had cried out with joy and stretched out her hand toward him, he had gone suddenly, leaving her sad and a little lonely.

Yet she was not unhappy, far from it. She wore a little smile now, as she looked at the garden. Henry would be home soon and they would walk in the garden together.

Sally Brown was a vivacious, blue-eyed blonde, with long slim legs and a truly marvelous figure. *Stunning* was the word he used in his thoughts. It was the highest accolade he could bestow on a girl at that particular phase of his life. Sally was certainly stunning, and what's more, she was friendly. They all liked her. She had few clothes and obviously not much money, but she was a thoroughly nice person. Robert naturally enough had eyes for nothing and no one else.

Jocelyn wondered how on earth Robert had managed to meet Sally, for Robert was still as remote from the rest of humanity as he had been in his schooldays. He had few personal friends at the university, as Jocelyn knew from talking to him. He lived in a little world of his own, and Jocelyn was pleased that he had finally fallen in love. Perhaps Sally would be good for him. Perhaps she would give him that interest in the rest of the human race which seemed to be so terribly lacking sometimes.

"What do you think of her?" he asked Jocelyn when the cousins were alone and Sally had gone upstairs with Edwina.

"She looks very nice. How did you manage it?"

"We're good friends."

"I can see that. She's here, isn't she? Are you serious about her?" Jocelyn demanded.

"What, at my age? With no job in sight? I've only just finished my first year, you know. I can't afford to be serious about anyone."

"You've got some money."

"Not enough to live on for the rest of my life. I have to get a job."

"Then come into the firm."

"I'd be no good at it, Jocelyn, you know that."

"What will you do then?"

"Sell motorcars. There's money in that."

"That's a funny thing to go to university for."

"I only thought of it recently. I want to give Sally the best of everything."

"Ah, so you *are* serious."

Robert colored a little. "It's up to Sally, not me. I haven't said anything to her yet. She'd think me mad."

"Maybe, maybe not. You can't really sell motorcars, Robert."

"I bet I could. I don't just mean any old motorcar—Rolls-Royces and Daimlers and things like that."

"You're joking. You must be."

"Not really. I don't want to work in an office. There's a chap I know who is going into the Colonial Service. That sounds fun but you have to go and live in Africa or some awful place like that."

"Come on, admit it, you don't know what you want to do."

"I admit it," Robert answered cheerfully. "I have **no** idea whatever. So how can I possibly be serious about Sally?"

"How much money *do* you have?" Jocelyn asked, interested.

"Fifteen thousand pounds, that's all. It's invested at four percent. It brings in six hundred a year."

"That's not bad, is it?"

"No, not if you want to live in a council house, but I want something better when I get married. A decent house would cost me more than five thousand, probably. That would cut my income down to less than four hundred. Eight pounds a week is too little. I must have more."

"I can see that." Jocelyn himself worked for a nominal eight pounds a week, but he lived free at Mereford, and one day the house and the company would both be his. He wouldn't like to have to look forward to eight pounds a week for life.

"Perhaps I could go into politics."

"There's no money in that."

"I'm not so sure. I'd be offered directorships and things. How to get to the top in commerce without climbing up the ladder—the sideways move, they call it. Start off as a director."

"You do have funny ideas," Jocelyn laughed.

"Well, they're only ideas not to be taken seriously. I wonder if Sally is ready. I said I'd take her out for a run. I'm borrowing your mother's car."

He and Sally spent most of their time together, away from Mereford. It was a lovely summer and they took picnic lunches away with them. She was going to Broadway in August, and Robert was acutely aware of time passing quickly. One day they were sitting by the bank of the river, near Sonning, the car parked under a tree. They had eaten and were watching the water flowing past.

"Can I come to see you at Broadway, Sally?" Robert asked.

"I don't know. There really isn't room. It's only a tiny cottage."

"I could stay at a hotel. We could go out together in the car. My aunt will lend me her car, I expect."

"I don't know, Robert. That would be expensive."

"It doesn't matter." He thought for a few minutes. "Sally, I've been thinking about money. I've got a little, you know."

"Yes, you told me."

"It brings in six hundred a year."

"You're supposed to be saving that."

"I am. I was thinking of what will happen in another two years when we finish at university. If I drew out five thousand pounds it would leave nearly twelve thousand, for my fifteen thousand is growing all the time. In two years it should be near to seventeen thousand."

"Yes?" she asked uneasily.

"We could buy a house."

"We?"

"Yes, we. I want to marry you, Sally. Haven't you guessed?"

She nodded silently.

"I love you, Sally. We'd have nearly five hundred a year, and I could get a job. You wouldn't have to work."

"I'm going to be a teacher."

"You don't have to be one. You could be a wife instead. If I had a job at five pounds a week it would give us nearly seven hundred and fifty—call it eight hundred."

"Call it seven hundred. It's nearer, and you'd have to pay some tax."

"Oh, very well. We could live on that."

"We could live very handsomely on that," she laughed. "Have you any idea what other people live on?"

"Then it's all right?"

"What?" she asked.

"We can get married."

"It's not as simple as that, Robert. I'm not sure I want to get married."

"I thought you liked me," he said naïvely.

"I do, but that's not the same as marrying you," she laughed.

"What's wrong?" he asked, looking wretched.

"We're both too young to be talking like this. Leave it until two years from now and we'll see how we both feel then. You may have met someone you like more."

"That's ridiculous," he cried. "I love you. You can't change a thing like that."

"Then you shouldn't mind waiting."

"Is there something wrong? Don't you want to go on seeing me?" he asked, distressed.

"Oh, Robert, you are stupid today. Of course I want to see you. I just think we shouldn't talk about getting married."

"At least you're my girl."

"Yes," she agreed slowly.

"Do you like my family?"

"Very much."

"Of course they're not my own family—I mean, my mother and father are dead. At least," he corrected again, "I don't know where my mother is. I haven't heard. My father's dead. I don't have to live here."

"I don't know what you're babbling on about," she laughed. "They're wonderful people and it's a lovely house. You're lucky."

"Yes, I know. You could make me luckier."

"Robert, it's going to be very boring being your girl friend if you're going to talk like that all the time. Let's forget about getting married."

"Sorry."

He didn't know whether to whoop with joy or to feel miserable. He had all the impatience of youth and wanted her to commit herself to marriage. Waiting was a repugnant idea. Yet she liked him, that much was plain. She wouldn't drop him for some other man, he was sure.

When she leaned over and kissed him very softly on the mouth he was totally unprepared. It was the first time they had kissed, although they had been going about together for five or six months. Indeed his backwardness in this respect alternately impressed and infuriated her. He was no wolf, but it would be reassuring to know he was no mouse either.

He soon demonstrated that he was no mouse and she had to stop him after several minutes. He spent the rest of the day in a sort of daze.

There was an air of unrest in the house that evening, for Edwina was leaving for Austria the next morning. She had decided to go a few days earlier than planned, because she was just a little worried about leaving Alice. There was no particular cause for concern, but she knew that Alice's condition could change at any time, and she could become helpless. She had briefed the servants very thoroughly and given Edward instructions about his mother.

"I can't think why you're going away if you're so worried," Edward grumbled mildly.

"Because I need a holiday and a change. I've been looking after your mother for a long time, and it becomes a strain after too much of it. Also I may not get a chance like this again."

"Damned if I see what's so special about Austria."

"It's a very beautiful country."

"It's full of Germans. They're all Nazis there now."

"Really, Edward, I don't care if they're revolutionaries. I'm going there to enjoy the scenery and a quiet life for three weeks."

"You must please yourself. I hope you do enjoy it."

"I shall."

"Later on I might take some time off. I've always wanted to go back to Cornwall. I had one holiday there with my father, and I've never forgotten it."

"It will depend on your mother. I don't see how we can both go away and leave her, and I'm a bit apprehensive about taking her anywhere. We'll see how things are when I come back. You may have to go to Cornwall by yourself."

"Wouldn't you mind if I did?" he asked casually.

She looked up and frowned. "Why should I, Edward? It's your life. I don't expect you to go without a holiday because of me. I'm not doing so."

"No, I suppose you aren't. You're like a stranger, Edwina. We dine together in the evenings, and that's all really. I go to Henley at weekends all summer, and in the winter there always seems to be something cropping up."

"We have a little bit more than just dinner together," she smiled, "but not very much, I agree. I have my friends, and you have yours. You like Henley and I don't."

"When I am at home, as often as not you're upstairs with Mother."

"Do you object?" she asked, raising her eyebrows.

"No, of course not. I was just reflecting on what a strange life we lead. You're a fine-looking woman, Edwina. Did you know that?"

"I like to flatter myself that I don't positively look forty-five."

"You look about thirty-five, and better than most that age."

"I hope you're not making improper suggestions," she said coolly. "I don't think I could stand that after being neglected for years."

He turned quite red while she lit a cigarette with amusement.

"Certainly not," he said stiffly.

"I'm glad. I'd hate to be disappointed in you."

"Disappointed? What do you mean? Do you find me repugnant?" he asked.

"I don't find you at all. I've learned to ignore you—I had to learn that twenty years ago. It was your doing, not mine. All I meant was that it would disappoint me if you abandoned your purity of thought, word, and deed after all these years of righteousness."

"I can't think why you're being sarcastic."

"Can't you? Well I'm certainly not going to quarrel with you, Edward. You are a most exemplary husband in every respect but one, and I am very grateful to you for it. I think we were talking about your going away to Cornwall by yourself. You certainly ought to get away. You need a holiday as much as I do. You should look after yourself better."

"I live a life of ease and luxury."

"You still need a change."

"I often wonder what you think of me," he mused.

She shook her head, bewildered, wondering what on earth had caused him to talk like this after years of avoiding every thing contentious.

"I really don't think we ought to keep up this conversation," she said, eyeing him watchfully.

"Why not? We're husband and wife."

"Edward, you told me many years ago that you despised me. Eventually I decided that I despised you too. Time mellows us all, but what we think of each other is something better not discussed."

"Edwina, sometimes I wonder if I love you," he said unexpectedly. "I don't want to lose you, and I don't want any other woman. Never have. You're my wife and I'm damned if I want to change it. Is that love?"

"Are you asking me? You know, Edward, I decided years ago that as soon as Jocelyn was old enough to manage without me, I would leave you. I meant it too. I used to look forward to the day when I could pack my bags and go—separate from you, possibly get a divorce. It was only Jocelyn who kept us together. I've done my duty. Jocelyn knows nothing about his real father, and never will. Now, however, I'm middle-aged. Where would I go, and why? I've come to love Mereford. This is my home. So I propose to stay."

"I'm glad to hear that," he said with a friendly smile.

"It's not for your sake. It wouldn't matter to me if you never came home. I'm thinking of the rest of the family, and the house, and myself. Not of you."

"Are you serious?" He sat up and scowled. "Wouldn't matter if I never came home?"

"Edward dear, you can drop dead at any time you wish. I shan't mourn for you. You killed any feelings I had a long time ago. What's the matter, does the truth offend you?"

"I find it difficult to understand you." He got to his feet angrily. "That is a terrible thing to say. I've always treated you well."

"You treat the servants well too. You're a nice man. I just don't happen to be interested in you any longer. For

God's sake, let's not have any more stupid talks like this, shall we? There's no reason why we shouldn't get through the next twenty years as pleasantly as we've got through the last, so long as we don't wallow in false sentimentality. I've done my duty, Edward, just as I admit you have. That should be enough for both of us."

"Yes, but talking like that—telling me to drop dead."

"I did nothing of the sort. I wouldn't dream of telling anyone to do so. On the other hand if you do, don't expect tears from me. You've never given me any affection—you reserve it all for your boat, and any girl friends you may have in Henley. Oh, and some for Jocelyn too, and your mother and Robert—in fact for anyone except me. I'm quite accustomed to the situation. I'm not complaining."

"You're a hardhearted bitch," he said.

"If you think crude language is going to accomplish anything, you disappoint me. I'm going up to see your mother."

She gave him a calm, cool look, and left the room. He got up and poured himself an unusually large whiskey.

Dammit to hell, he thought furiously. She is an attractive woman, very attractive. Why does she have to be so cold-blooded? As in the past, the ridiculousness of his own behavior never crossed his mind. He was a thoroughly nice, kind man who was the soul of honor and probity, always did his duty with a good grace, and frequently thought more of the welfare of others than his own.

How could he possibly have earned such contempt from her?

Chapter 22

WHEN Edwina returned from Austria there was no noticeable change in Alice. She went through each day in a sort of dream, perfectly content with things. She liked to spend the mornings in the garden, sleep in the afternoon after lunch, and read in her room in the evenings. She was rereading the works of her favorite author, whom she always referred to meticulously as *Mr. Galsworthy*. Her favorite character, strangely enough for one who had begun life as a servant, was Soames Forsyte. Instinctively she understood Soames, and she had nothing but contempt for Irene. Irene, in Alice's simple philosophy, needed a good shaking.

Shortly after Edwina's return, Edward made what he thought of, a little inaccurately, as a last attempt at reconciliation. It puzzled him that he was finding his wife increasingly attractive. It was beginning to irk him that she was his wife in name only. Had he taken her roughly in his arms, kissed her passionately, told her that he had been a fool for years, and made some very improper but legitimate suggestions, there is no saying what might have happened. Edward wasn't that type. He made his approach obliquely.

"About Cornwall," he said one evening after dinner. "Yes?"

"I've managed to rent a small place in Charlestown for a fortnight only. I left it a bit late. It's a fortnight starting next weekend."

"That sounds nice."

"Would you like to come with me?"

"No, I don't think so, thanks."

"Mother's all right, isn't she?" he asked a little sharply.

"Yes. She seems a little more frail but she's remarkably cheerful."

"Then she could be left to the servants, couldn't she? After all, Jocelyn will be here too."

Edwina saw her chance and ignored it. It was not her nature to seek excuses. It would be simple enough to make an excuse of Alice, but the reason she wanted to stay at home had nothing to do with Alice. So instead she said, "They could look after her easily enough, but I'm not coming to Cornwall."

"Why not?" Having won one point, Edward was irritated at not having won the argument.

"Because, Edward, I'd rather you went alone."

"That's plain enough, isn't it?" he demanded heatedly.

"I hope so." She spoke mildly, perhaps disinterestedly.

"Don't you care about me at all?" he burst out.

"I thought we'd decided not to have these pointless conversations."

He gave her an angry look and became silent. He felt thwarted and unhappy and he did not know how to cope with the situation. He told himself bitterly that she was an unnatural woman and always had been. She hardly ever went to see her parents nowadays, although her father was now in a wheelchair. That proved she was unnatural.

In Cornwall, however, his moodiness disappeared, and he saw life again from the philosophical, slightly detached viewpoint he had acquired assiduously over the years. He sailed a bit, walked for miles along cliff tops and beaches, ate heartily, and slept like a child. He returned in great good humor on September 25. Even the current crisis could not spoil his pleasure.

"Your mother is in bed all the time now," Edwina told him when he had unpacked and come downstairs for a drink.

"Oh? I'd better go up and see her. She's worse?"

"I don't know. She's weaker and doesn't want to get up. It's so hard to tell with her. The doctor has been twice but there's nothing the poor man can do. She eats and sleeps perfectly well, never complains, isn't in pain or anything—she's just a tired old lady."

"You've been marvelous with her," he remarked, and surprised Edwina who had not been expecting compliments.

"She's always been very good to me."

"She's a wonderful old woman. I'd hoped she'd last a lot longer."

He finished his drink and went up to Alice's bedroom. She was propped up against several pillows and a book lay on the cover of the bed, ignored. She looked at him searchingly as he came into the room.

"Henry? What time is it?"

"It's Edward, Mother. It's just after teatime. How are you today?"

"I'm very well my dear. Why don't we go for a drive to Bramshill and walk on the common before dinner? You get out the trap while I get ready."

"It's Edward, Mother," he said in a louder voice.

There was a quick look of disappointment in her eyes and then she smiled.

"Dear Edward. How are things at the office?"

He leaned over and kissed her and then sat on the side of the bed.

"I've been away in Cornwall on holiday. I've only just come back. Jocelyn has been looking after the office."

"I remember. Edwina told me. Why wasn't Edwina with you?"

"She didn't feel like it. She wanted to stay at home."

"She's a good woman, Edward, despite what happened in London all those years ago. She's been a fine wife and mother, and she's very good to me. You must be kind to her. You should try to understand her, Edward. There is no evil in her."

It struck him as amusing that after so very many years he should try to understand his wife. It was a bit late for that, surely. He smiled at his mother.

"Of course," he agreed pleasantly.

"I thought you were your father," she said in a moment of lucidity. "I wait for him every day, but he never sees me. One day he will."

Edward put a hand over hers. He had only a vague idea what she was talking about. He did not know how often she saw Henry, how often she spoke to him, how he always went away unseeing. He only knew she was becoming old and fanciful.

"Is there anything I can get you?" he asked gently. "Anything you'd like?"

"I'd like a little fish for dinner tonight. Not meat, fish."

"I'll ask Edwina to speak to Cook."

"You're a fine son."

"I can't imagine why you think that," he laughed.

She sat silently, busy with her thoughts, and he kissed her and walked quietly from her room. It troubled him that she should take to her bed like this. A nap in the afternoon was one thing—to be expected really—but to spend all day in bed was totally unlike her.

He told Edwina about the fish and then Jocelyn came home. When they had greeted each other happily they went into the library to talk about the company. They had decided to build a restaurant on the roof of the building, and Edward had schemes to make the ladies' department more exclusive and to compete with the West End establishments in London. There was good money in expensive clothes.

On Friday, September 30, Neville Chamberlain, the Prime Minister, arrived triumphantly in London from Munich. The Czechoslovakian crisis had brought real panic to England. The Air Raid Precaution system came into full wartime readiness on September 25, and on the twenty-sixth schoolchildren were evacuated to safety in the country, hospitals were cleared and made ready for casualties, and people in London were registered and fitted for gas masks. Even trenches were dug in the London parks.

Now came the hoped-for relief. Chamberlain stepped out of the aircraft which brought him home from Hitler's four-power conference, triumphantly waved his piece of worthless paper and spoke of peace with honor and peace in our time. England, recovering from the shock of "Black Wednesday," September 28, went wild. Only two days ago there had been complete chaos in Paris as people fought to get out of the city, while in London everyone had dug feverishly. Now they accepted the miracle. There would be no more wars. Everyone was happy—except of course Czechoslovakia . . . and Austria . . . and the Jews . . . and a handful of thinking people throughout the world who were not entirely fooled by Hitler and who attached no mportance to his promises.

Edward Vernon did not know what to think. This sudlen reversal, this rapid withdrawal from the edge of the byss, did not ring true to him. He would have liked to ılk to Alice about it, the way they used to talk about ıings, but Alice was sublimely unaware that there had been any crisis. She never read a newspaper or listened to the radio. She had the Forsyte Saga and a life of Queen Victoria and they kept her wonderfully happy.

Edwina was cynical and there was no point in talking to her. She thought cheerfully that Hitler had found the secret of success. He did what he wanted, and knew that the other great powers would never dare to go to war again. Hers was not a flattering view of international politics. Germany would never declare war on the other major European powers, and they in turn would never declare war on Germany; so Hitler could safely gobble up the little countries he wanted and who had, after all, considerable German elements in their populations. As for the Jews, their only sensible course was to get out of a country that obviously did not want them. That Hitler was an unscrupulous man was beside the point. One had to face facts. Edward had long since given up trying to have a rational discussion with his wife.

Jocelyn had the optimism of youth. When they discussed events that Friday night, after Chamberlain's return, Jocelyn reassured his father.

"People don't want war," he said. "Hitler doesn't want war. There are all sorts of problems in Germany, and as far as I can make out half the trouble was caused by the Treaty of Versailles. Hitler is simply trying to get what rightfully belongs to Germany. Anyway, right or wrong, I don't believe he's a warmonger."

"Right or wrong? Is there any doubt about that?" Edward demanded.

Jocelyn shrugged. He was inclined to dismiss the affairs of foreigners as being of no real interest.

"I don't know," he answered, a little bored. "One never knows whom to believe."

Edward gave up the battle. He had an uneasy feeling that war had not been averted at all, that it had merely been postponed temporarily. He hoped most sincerely

that he was wrong. He did not want to see Jocelyn and
Robert go through what he had gone through. Modern
war was no joke.

The following afternoon, while Jocelyn was off taking
part in a mixed doubles tennis tournament; while Edward
was at Henley; and while Edwina sat in the garden by
herself, enjoying the sunshine and thinking a little nostal-
gically about Walter, Lord Paveley, who had given her
such a very satisfactory holiday in Austria, one she would
never forget . . . Alice got out of bed. For a moment she
steadied herself with one hand, and then put on her dressing gown. She could see the sunlight streaming in through
the window overlooking the garden. She put on her slippers with some difficulty, her thin hands shaking as she did
so. Then she went to her dressing table and made a half-
hearted attempt to brush her long thick hair, now completely white. That done, she shuffled to the chair by the
window and sat in it. How beautiful everything was. The
drive swept in a broad curve toward the gate, which was
out of sight. The hedges were a dark, rich green, and the
trees were thick and luxuriant. She could see Edwina sitting in a canvas chair near the fountain, a table by her
side. Dear Edwina, she thought. What a pity she should be
alone on such a day. It was too bad of Edward, always to
be going off. Edward had never recovered from that business of Jocelyn. Men were such prudes. They were
shocked so easily. Women were much tougher and more
resilient.

She sat looking at Edwina for several moments, and
then her glance strayed, as it was bound to do, to the other
side of the drive. There the rose garden was a blaze of
colors. There were such lovely roses nowadays, and colors
that had not existed in her youth. Edward didn't have
much time for the garden and left it to Maggett. She
hoped Jocelyn would learn to love it. Mereford was not
just a house, it was not even just a home, it was a whole

way of life, where people learned to be tolerant and contented, where beauty softened attitudes. It was a happy
place. She did so hope that Jocelyn would come to love it,
for Mereford needed love. She must speak to him about it
later on, when he came home from wherever it was he had
gone.

Then she saw him walking in the garden below—Henry.
He was not in uniform today. He wore a striped blazer
and carried a small trowel in his hand. She recognized the
old blazer he always wore in the garden on weekends
during the summer months.

"Henry," she called in a quavering voice. "Henry, darling."

This time he heard. He turned his fine eyes on her and
smiled that old smile. Tears welled into her eyes, tears of
pure joy, but she could still see him quite clearly down
below in the garden, through the mist of her tears.

"Alice," he answered. "Come and walk in the garden,
Alice."

She struggled out of the chair and took one joyful step
forward. At long last they were together again.

It was Edwina who found Alice. She went upstairs to
get a scarf because a slight breeze had sprung up. Automatically she opened the bedroom door and looked in.
Alice was not in the bed, nor was she in her chair. Edwina
looked all round, puzzled, and then she saw the body on
the floor.

"Mother," she called in alarm and ran to Alice's side.

She saw at once that it was too late, that it was all over
for Alice. There was a smile on her face. Her head was
within a fraction of an inch of the wall, but she had not
hit her head when she fell, that much was plain. Her heart
had given out at last. Edwina picked her up, surprised how
light Alice was, and carried her to the bed, where she drew
a sheet over her. There were things to do. She telephoned

the doctor at once, and then tried to contact Edward. Obviously he was out on such a fine afternoon, for there was no reply from his cottage at Henley. Then she telephoned the tennis club and after a delay Jocelyn was brought to the telephone.

"Hullo, Mother," he said a little breathlessly. "Is something wrong?" He could not think why she should interrupt a game of tennis.

"Yes, I think you should come home. Your grandmother is dead."

"Oh, poor Gran. Yes, I'll come at once. I'll just let them know. Somebody will have to take my place."

Edwina consulted her little leather-covered notebook and found Robert's telephone number. She rang that and his landlady answered. Robert was out, but she would ask him to telephone as soon as he came back. There was nothing else Edwina could do now but wait for the doctor. Edward would have to take charge of the arrangements.

It was evening before she managed to get hold of Edward at the hotel bar where he was drinking with his friends. When he heard the news he was stunned, but he hurried home, driving as fast as he dared. Robert arrived next morning.

Alice's death left a tremendous gap in life at Mereford, for Alice and Mereford went together in everyone's thoughts. It took weeks for things to settle down again and Edward never afterward felt really comfortable at Mereford. There was always that feeling that something was missing.

That Christmas was the last peacetime Christmas they would know for many years, although nobody really believed it, not even Edward. Robert had brought Sally Brown back for the holidays. Her aunt was in the hospital. He had finally bought a small, cheap secondhand car, and they intended to visit Sally's aunt during the holidays. The five of them contrived to make a merry party of it, and even danced to the gramophone on Christmas Eve. They had been invited to Pleasaunce on Christmas Day and to stay for a few nights, but Edward had no heart for it and had refused politely. For some reason which he did not understand fully himself, he wanted to make it a family Christmas at home. He didn't mind Sally, but he did not want to see a lot of other people. They ate and drank more than usual, and on Boxing Day went for a long drive in the country. Then Jocelyn went off to stay for a few days with friends, and Sally and Robert made themselves scarce, so that Edward and Edwina found themselves thrown together rather more than usual.

"I think next spring I'll spend a few extra weeks in America," Edward said suddenly. "All these visits and it's always been business. I've really seen nothing of the United States. I want to go to San Francisco."

"Why San Francisco?"

"Because I've heard so much about it and I'd like to see it for myself."

"Why not?" she agreed pleasantly. "How long will you be away?"

"I don't know. Probably two months—April and May, I think."

"I suppose Jocelyn can manage for two months without you?"

"Of course he can. Sometimes I think Jocelyn understands the business better than I do. He's so like my mother. What will you do while I'm away?"

"I may go away too, now that there's nothing to hold me here. I'll have to talk to Jocelyn about it," she said. "I might go to Scotland."

"Doesn't it always rain up there?"

"That's a point," she laughed. "I've never been to Scotland. I'd like to see it, even if it does rain."

"You . . . er . . . you know you can come to America if you'd like," he said diffidently. He was only going through

the motions again. He didn't really want her, any more
than she wanted to come with him.

"Thank you, but another time perhaps."

He nodded, relieved. They were interrupted by the
summons of the telephone bell. Edward answered it and
called Edwina.

"It's for you. Your mother."

She took the call and came back looking thoughtful.

"Is something wrong?" he asked.

"Yes, my father has just died. I'll have to go to Castle
Combe, I'm afraid."

"I'm sorry. Shall I come with you?"

"No, I don't think so, thank you. You stay here. I'll let
you know when the funeral is to be. You and Jocelyn
really ought to come to that."

"Yes, we shall."

She packed a suitcase, gave a few instructions to the
servants, and set off alone in her car. When she arrived at
Combe Cottage she found her mother unwell, suffering
from a heavy cold. Next morning she was worse and by
evening she too was dead, struck down by a bad attack of
pneumonia, with complications which Edwina only dimly
understood. How unfair it was, she thought. Alexandra
was only sixty-eight. Guy was different, for not only was
he a little older but for years he had smoked and drunk far
too much. Her mother had always been healthy and
strong, yet she had been denied even a few peaceful years
on her own, relieved of the burden of an ailing husband.

There was a double funeral on a bleak, cold day. The
Fownhope relatives were present, but none of them really
knew each other and there was a good deal of awkwardness. Edwina was glad when they came back to Mereford,
a silent, depressed little party. She had not been close to
her parents, had not particularly liked her father, but
somehow she felt very alone now that they had gone. She
did not understand herself, nor why she should feel like

this. She really despised sloppy sentimentality. It was a pity about her mother, but Alexandra had chosen her own life. Once, years before, in a sudden surge of affection, she had offered to let Alexandra have some money if she wanted to go away and leave Guy and make her own life. Edwina was sure Edward would help with a few thousand pounds at the very least. Alexandra had refused firmly. Combe Cottage was her home and there she intended to stay, come what may. So what could one do?

The weeks slipped past and great events filled the newspapers. In February Britain recognized the Franco regime in Spain. In March, Hitler played his next card and annexed Bohemia and Moravia. Lithuania ceded Memel to Germany. The anti-Polish campaign began in the German press. April saw the end of the Spanish war, and conscription was introduced into Britain, just the day before Hitler vehemently repudiated the Anglo-German naval agreement, together with the Polish nonaggression treaty. In May they began taking sides, ominously. Britain signed agreements with Turkey and Poland, France signed an agreement with Turkey, and Italy and Germany made a pact. All the danger signs were returning. Little men who had floundered and bled in the mud of Flanders wondered if their leaders had gone mad. The leaders went their own way joyfully. There was no place in the firing line for presidents, prime ministers, or foreign secretaries.

Edward in America was glad to be away from events in Europe. They seemed more detached and less important from the other side of the Atlantic. He transacted some very satisfactory business, met his old friends in Chicago and New York, and newer ones in Pittsburgh, and finally went off to San Francisco on his own, intent on nothing more than a pleasant and relaxing holiday. Instead he had a shattering experience. He fell in love.

He was staying at the St. Francis in Union Square, which had been recommended by friends back East, and on the second day he received a telephone call inviting him to a cocktail party that evening at a house on Clay Street. He did not know his host or hostess. They had been asked by one of his Chicago friends to contact him and look after him. They were charming people but in any event he did not need much looking after.

When he arrived they talked to him for several minutes and invited him to a dinner party the following night, and then his hostess took him off and began to introduce him to some of the other guests. He was talking business to a group of three men when, over someone's shoulder, he saw her, a beautiful dark-haired woman with great dark eyes and a superb figure, momentarily standing by herself. As their eyes met she gave him a small friendly smile and his heart turned over.

About two seconds later he had disengaged himself and pushed his way over to her side. He took a deep breath.

"Hullo," he said feeling foolish, expecting the rebuff.

"Hullo." She was smiling again.

"I saw you alone, and I thought . . ."

"I know. I'm glad. I'm Grace Montgomery."

"I'm sorry. I'm Edward Vernon."

"I've heard about you. You're on a visit from England."

"That's right." He became bold. "It's noisy and crowded. Do we have to stay here?" he asked abruptly.

For a split second she showed surprise and then she put a hand on his arm.

"I suppose not. Where would you like to go?" she asked.

"I don't know. I don't know San Francisco at all. I'm staying at the St. Francis. How about that?"

"Perhaps you'd better come to my place for a drink."

"That would be nice."

"Let's slip out, then. We can get out without being seen if you follow me."

She led the way and they escaped. She lived in a pretty

little plaza, an oasis of quiet garnished with trees and flowers, not too far from Union Square. It was delightful and he admired it. Her home was an elegant old house and he learned that the Montgomerys had been in San Francisco for generations and that she had been brought up in this house.

"You must have thought me rude," he apologized over a drink. "Coming up to you like that, unannounced."

"Not at all." Her smile was infinitely lovely. "I think I willed you to do it. I don't really like cocktail parties."

"Why me?" he asked.

"The interesting stranger from abroad."

"Have you ever been to England?" he asked her.

"Many times."

For a little time they talked about their travels and then about his friends in the Midwest and the East, but it was obvious to them both, without anything being said, that something very special had happened to them.

"I ought to tell you," he said abruptly, "that I'm married."

"I'm divorced," she replied wryly.

"I'm sorry about that."

"It doesn't matter, not now. I got over it a long time ago. Harry played around with other women, and latterly it became obvious and also intolerable; so I divorced him."

"My wife did much the same, but instead of divorcing her I moved into another room years ago."

"That must be very unsatisfactory."

"It is. I suppose if there had been someone else, someone I wanted to marry, I might have done something about it."

"Hasn't there ever been?" she asked, raising her eyebrows.

"No. Oh I've kept my eyes open—hopefully." He laughed self-consciously. "There were a couple of women. I tried to have an affair with each of them, but it just didn't work. I think perhaps I was trying too hard, or maybe they just didn't find me attractive. It all sounds pretty stupid, I'm afraid."

"No, no, it doesn't."

"Somehow things drift along without you really noticing it. I'm forty-eight now."

"You don't look it. I'm thirty-five."

"And you certainly don't look *that*." He laughed. Then he sobered. "I wish I'd met you a long time ago."

"I wish you had too," she agreed softly.

They said nothing. After a few seconds he put down his drink and gathered her into his arms. She did not resist him. She came to him gladly. It was as simple as that. They were completely in love with each other.

Afterward he became very quiet and she asked him why.

"I'm not asking about your husband. I don't think I want to know about him, but I wonder what sort of misbegotten creature could marry you and then chase after other women. It's like being told that St. Francis of Assisi secretly pulled the wings off flies."

"What a quaint way you have of putting things, darling."

"I mean it. It's incredible. I can't conceive what sort of man would do it."

Three days later he moved out of his hotel into her house, for the remainder of his stay. There was a dreamlike quality about their relationship, something very precious, almost fragile.

"You'll acquire an evil reputation," he laughed when he woke up in her bed on the first morning.

"I don't care," she said smugly. "The Montgomerys survived the earthquake in 1906, so I guess I can survive a little gossip. Anyway people probably don't gossip as much as we like to think."

"I didn't know what love was till I met you," he confessed.

"Isn't it funny?" she answered. "When I saw you at the cocktail party I knew just by looking that something special was going to happen."

"I knew at once that I had to talk to you."

"Same thing," she laughed. "Love at first sight. The genuine article. What shall we do today, darling?"

They did lots of things together. They ate at the Blue Fox and at Jack's, and he sampled the Chinese food in Chinatown. She introduced him to the streetcars and the cable cars, and to the seafood in the restaurants and stalls of Fisherman's Wharf. They drank briefly in jazz joints and piano lounges and laughed a lot together; but mostly they stayed in her house, just getting to know each other, "savoring ourselves" as she expressed it with picturesque simplicity. It was a process which gave them unending joy.

He was filled with a childlike wonderment that she could possibly love him. That he should have fallen in love with her was normal and natural. She was the most beautiful and also the nicest woman in the world. She was made to be loved. He had no illusions about himself, however. He was middle-aged, not very handsome by any standard, nobody could possibly call him a good catch and the fact that he was married made it all just that much worse.

Yet she did love him and she showed it in every possible way. Their sojourn together was the stuff of which dreams are made: idyllic, happy, totally fulfilling. They even liked all the same things—there was almost no divergence whatever in their tastes.

The main problem was that he had no intention of leaving England and coming to live in America. He had his home and his work in Reading. He spoke of Grace coming to Mereford, of offering Edwina a divorce, although in truth he had no idea how Edwina would react to such a situation. Grace, who had visited England a good deal more often than he had visited America, was equally wedded to San Francisco and her house there.

"Poor Edward," she said, stroking his hair one evening as they sat together. "We'll simply have to have an affair. You won't leave Mereford, and I certainly won't leave San Francisco. Perhaps it's better this way. Probably we won't suffer any disillusionment."

Edward at forty-eight, almost forty-nine, wasn't so happy about having a transatlantic affair. It was apt to prove physically as well as mentally exhausting after a few years.

"If you won't come to London, I'll have to think about it," he said quietly. "I'll be back next year. I'll come for three months—four weeks of business in the East, and the rest of the time here."

"That sounds marvelous, darling."

"It's so long to wait. Couldn't you come over before then? In the autumn, say? Do some shopping or something?"

"I'll think about that," she laughed. "How would you explain coming to London to see me?"

"I don't know that I'd bother. Edwina and I live very much our own lives. Right now she's in Scotland—probably with a man. I never ask."

He said it casually, unaware that Edwina was playing out her affair with Walter Paveley. She was growing too old and placid to continue this sort of life. She had looked upon Austria as a last fling, and she was determined that very definitely this would be the end of it all. It had been good while it lasted, and it was fitting that it should all end with Walter, who seemed hardly to have changed with the years. So while Edwina was firmly convinced that the time had come to give up, Edward was just embarking on a middle-aged love affair.

"Come in October," Edward suggested. "It's a nice

month. I'll take a holiday and we can go away together and explore some of the English countryside before winter sets in."

"We'll see. If I can't manage it, there's always next year here."

"You sound very . . . I don't know what word I want. Cheerful? Resigned? You don't seem to mind waiting."

"Darling, I mind terribly," she laughed, "but I'm old enough not to struggle against life. We've got to take it as it comes."

"I suppose you're right," he shrugged. Then he laughed suddenly and kissed her, and they both put aside these practical problems which were such a nuisance to them.

Before he left her, however, he raised the question of the future once again. It was their last night and they were sitting together in semidarkness. They had been silent for a time, for the parting was a painful wrench to both of them.

"I still want you to come over to England in October," he said hesitantly.

"You know it's practically certain."

"I was going to add that whether you do or not, I shall return next year. When I do, either I will come here to stay beside you, or I will come to take you away with me. One or the other."

"You've made up your mind then?" she asked softly.

"Yes." He nodded, his eyes fixed on hers. "I don't care how it's done, but I'm not going to lose you. Somehow we'll settle all the problems. They aren't serious ones anyway. If it means my leaving England, I'll leave. My son can take over the business. My wife will have the house and plenty of money. She's had her lovers—why should I sacrifice my own happiness? I've waited for this for a long time, Grace."

She put a hand on his. "I know, Edward. We'll do

whatever has to be done. Would you really give up your whole life in England just for me?"

"Without a qualm. It's no sacrifice. I love you, Grace."

"I love you too, darling."

They kissed intensely, as though they would never see each other again.

Edwina did not need to be a mind reader to see that something had happened. Edward was an entirely different person. His walk, his mannerisms, his whole air had changed somehow. She waited, interested to see what would happen. It did not take him long to come to the point one summer afternoon. They were alone at Mereford. Robert, Jocelyn and Sally had gone off to Cornwall together, just the three of them. Mereford basked in the summer sunshine and there was a sense of ineffable contentment which Edward found poignant.

They were having tea together on the lawn.

"I may be taking some time off in October, having another holiday," he said casually.

"I see. Are you going away again?"

"I expect so, if I take a holiday at all—it isn't settled yet."

"Goodness knows you work hard enough during the week," she said pleasantly. "You could afford to take things easily but you rarely do. You earn your holidays."

"It's not that I'm tired. I may have a friend coming over from America."

"I understand."

"A woman."

"Really?" She glanced at him with new interest. This was a change.

"Yes. I want to marry her but there are certain problems."

"Is that how you think of me?" she chuckled. "As a problem?"

"No, it isn't just that. She doesn't want to come and live in England."

"I see your difficulty. How long has this been going on?"

"Only this year," he answered and she nodded. She had guessed as much. "You've no cause for complaint," he added defensively. "I've never interfered with you."

"I'm not complaining, although I may do so if you try to turn me out of Mereford."

"Are you suggesting I leave?" he asked, surprised.

"I haven't really had a chance to think about anything. I suppose you could hand over the company to Jocelyn and go and live in Chicago or wherever it is."

"San Francisco."

"Ah. Well, San Francisco then. I can't see what's stopping you."

"It isn't so easy, giving up everything."

"What is it you want to do? Divorce me and send me away?" She was watchful now.

"I don't know, Edwina. You make it sound very brutal."

"It isn't pleasant. I've had my affairs, as we both know, but I never suggested divorce or anything of that nature. You're turning everything upside down. It's bound to seem brutal."

"Well, there it is. I'm not a womanizer. I think you know that. If I had been I'd have had plenty of time to amuse myself with countless affairs. I've never cared about another woman. This is the first time and neither of us expected it to happen. It just did."

"You don't have to defend yourself. It doesn't matter, but in any case I believe you implicitly. She must be a remarkable woman."

"She is."

"I'm glad for your sake that this has happened." she

told him unexpectedly. "It's just a pity that it looks like disrupting life here."

"There's no hurry. She may not come over in October. I'll be going to America for three months next year. We can wait and see what happens then."

"Of course. Thank you for telling me, Edward."

"If we did part," he said quickly, like someone taking a dose of unpleasant medicine, "and you left Mereford, I'd see that you were all right. There's plenty of money. You'll never want."

"Thank you," she replied gravely.

"If I did go away," he said hesitantly, toying with the idea, "would you stay on here and look after the place for Jocelyn?"

"Probably. I wouldn't fill it with my passé boy friends anyway," she added with a sudden laugh.

• "I didn't think you would. Well, it's something to think about."

"It certainly is," she agreed.

Chapter 23

EDWARD had upset her far more than Edwina let him see. It was not a matter of grudging him his belated fling. She had always been astonished that it had not happened before. It was the prospect of upheaval, the possibility of going away that depressed her. Why couldn't he be like a Frenchman and take a mistress discreetly?

Then they both forgot about the future as events in Europe rushed on relentlessly. Britain reaffirmed her pledges to Poland, Germany signed a pact with Russia, Japan broke away from the Anti-Comintern Pact and finally, on Friday, September 1, 1939, Germany invaded Poland. All hope of peace was gone. On Sunday the third, Neville Chamberlain broadcast to the waiting nation. At 11 A.M. he said that the country was now at war with Germany, although the official start of the war was 5 P.M. There was compulsory military service for all men aged between eighteen and forty-one. The very next day, Monday, the liner *Athenia* was sunk by a U-boat, and the Royal Air Force bombed the Kiel Canal. The war was on.

Robert had come home from London on Sunday evening, bringing Sally Brown with him. On Monday he and

Jocelyn went into Reading and joined the army. They had their medical examinations the same day, took the oath, signed the Official Secrets act, and came home to lunch. It was all very quick and easy—except for Edward. He wanted to do something but he was too old, and someone had to look after Vernon's. Robert and Sally disappeared for an hour before dinner, and were silent during the meal. When they had finished the last course, Robert spoke quietly.

"Sally and I have news for you. We've talked this over and we're going to get married. Right away. We're under age, but we'd like your consent. Sally will get her aunt's easily enough."

"I see." Edward was taken aback. "I don't know what to say."

"Congratulate them," Edwina laughed. "You look as though they'd announced a funeral."

"You're so young," Edward objected, then he caught Jocelyn's eye and shrugged. "I must be getting old. Of course it's congratulations. I hope you're both going to be happy. Jocelyn, go and get some of that Madeira of my father's will you? Sally, what will you do? Stay at university?"

"That seems rather silly. I don't know what to do."

"Why not come here?" Edwina suggested.

"Come here? Could I?"

"As a matter of fact you could help me. There's a small holding about a mile away which Edward bought a few months ago when the old man who owned it died. He thought it would be a kind of hobby for me. If you could come here we could cultivate it properly and grow food for the war effort. It's too big for me to manage alone if I want to work it seriously. My original idea was to lay it out with trees and shrubs, but think of the food we could grow."

"That sounds marvelous. Are you sure you really want me?"

"Of course we do. Isn't that right, Edward?"

"Yes," he agreed with feeling, "your place is here with us till Robert comes home."

The emphasis of his words was not lost on Edwina who concealed a smile. Edward never forgot, which was no doubt a very useful asset in business. Jocelyn returned with the wine, two bottles of it, and they drank and toasted each other and the future. Jocelyn and Edward kissed Sally.

There was a certain amount of chaos in Britain. When Robert and Sally were married three weeks later, he and Jocelyn were still not in uniform, but fate was not kind to Robert. Two days afterward they received their papers to report to the barracks of the Berkshire Light Infantry. Robert's honeymoon went by the board.

They received their uniforms and began their training. Although they were only minutes away from home, they were not allowed out of camp for the first month. There were inoculations, vaccination, hours of drill and hours of spit and polish, and they were confined to camp. It all struck Jocelyn as ridiculous. Just before the end of their recruit training the commanding officer sent for them. He saw Jocelyn first.

"I'm putting you in for officer training, Vernon. Your name is a well-known one in the regiment. We're all tremendously proud of your father and grandfather."

Jocelyn, recalling the bullying of the sergeant major and a certain sergeant, wondered at their manner of showing how proud they were. He was quite prepared to accept the fact that they hated him. However he looked polite and remained rigidly at attention.

"You'll be going off in about a fortnight's time. Meantime I'm making you an acting lance corporal."

Jocelyn blinked and looked pleased.

"Thank you, sir."

"There are no guarantees about what happens after officer training, but I shall put in the strongest possible request to have you sent back to us when you are commissioned. Your place is here in the B.L.I."

"Thank you, sir," he repeated, and then as the interview was over he saluted smartly and marched out.

Robert had much the same treatment. The colonel knew he was Jocelyn's cousin, and therefore related to that branch of the Vernons which had so graced the regiment. He knew also that Robert's father, grandfather, and great-grandfather had been regular officers in the 1st Lancers. Indeed he could not imagine what Robert had been thinking about, going to the university instead of to Sandhurst.

They got a weekend pass and drove to Mereford where Jocelyn proudly displayed his single stripe. Robert and Sally promptly went off together, and Jocelyn and Edward sat in the library and shared some malt whiskey Edward had received as a present on his last birthday. He was very fond of pure malt whiskey. They talked about the war and the Army and the B.L.I. It gave Edward a funny feeling to see his son in uniform like this, but he was proud of him, proud of that single stripe and the fact that he was going to do his officer training at once.

"I'll look after things for you," he promised. "When you come home you'll find the company in a healthy state. I only wish I were coming with you."

"You've had your share, Father. It's my turn now."

"I hope you have a nice quiet war. I mean it. Leave the glory to those who want it. War is a damned unpleasant business, mostly boring, sometimes bloody. Probably you won't enjoy it much."

"Thanks for the warning," Jocelyn laughed, "but it's too late now. I'm in it."

Edward grinned. "You shouldn't have joined, as they

say. Well, more whiskey? How is Robert getting on in the army?"

"Poor Robert."

"What do you mean?"

"Robert just naturally does everything wrong. He's hopeless at drill, and he's dreamy. He forgets things. He's lucky not to have been put on a charge. Perhaps he'll make a better officer, but as a private soldier he's an awful flop."

"I'm sorry to hear that."

"He's just not cut out for it, that's all. He does his best to please, but it's never good enough. He isn't even a good shot. He's very lucky to be accepted for officer training. It wasn't on merit."

"Oh, dear. Well, he may settle down yet."

"I expect so," Jocelyn said without conviction.

That Sunday, while they were still on leave, there was a telephone call. The caller asked for Alice.

"Who's calling?" Edwina asked, taken aback.

"Mrs. Hilton."

"Aunt Mary? This is Edwina."

"Hullo, Edwina. We're at Reading Station—Timothy and Anne and me. I wondered if we could come and see you, and perhaps stay for a night?"

"Yes, of course you can. What luck your arriving now. Everyone will be pleased."

"We're on our way home from Paris. We've been there for over a year. We thought it might be a good idea to visit you before they clamp down on rail travel. We may not be able to come next year."

"That's a thought." Edwina was taking it all in. This was what had happened, was it? They had wondered, when Alice died, why there had been no response from Kemble. Nobody seemed to know where the Hiltons had gone.

"Can I speak to Alice please?" Mary asked.

"Mary, I'm afraid I've got bad news for you. Mama died a year ago."

"Oh, no! We didn't know."

"We tried to contact you but we couldn't find out where you were."

"We went to France in June. Timothy wanted to work there, you see, so we shut up both cottages and took Anne with us. It was so good for her, learning to speak French. Of course we have to come home now because of this stupid war. A year ago, you say?"

"She died on the first of October, 1938. Oh and your grandson Robert, John's boy, is staying with us still. He's married. His wife is here."

"So much happening."

"Robert and Jocelyn have joined up. They're in the army. They're both at home today but they have to go back to barracks before midnight tonight. You'll hear all the news when you come. Are there any taxis?"

"Yes. We'll come at once."

Edwina routed out Edward and told him, then she went to give orders about rooms. Four bedrooms were occupied, but luckily that left two spare. They would have to be dusted and aired, the beds made up and hot water bottles put between the sheets. Luckily there was plenty of food in the house and they had a store cupboard groaning with tins, most of them bought from their own grocery department. Edwina had bought two chickens only the previous day. She made arrangements about lunch and dinner, and warned Jocelyn and Robert.

The Hiltons arrived at midday, and there was a confused chorus of greetings. Then Mary managed to get a proper look at Robert.

"Well, Robert, you're married."

"Yes," he replied. He had never called her "grandmother," although she was. Now he didn't know how to address her.

"Introduce me, please. I want to meet my grandson's wife."

Sally was introduced and Mary kissed her. She said all the usual things, but her eyes were on Robert in his uniform. Edwina thought she saw pain in Mary's expression.

"What's going to happen to you, Timothy?" Edward asked Mary's son. "Are they going to call you up?"

"They can't," Mary said sharply. "He has a bad heart."

"I do have a heart condition," Timothy admitted with a slow smile. "I wouldn't say I have a 'bad' heart. I may live to be a hundred, according to my doctor. I doubt if I could pass an army medical though."

He was thirty-seven, Edward reckoned. They wouldn't bother with him if he couldn't pass his medical.

"They might find me some sort of job. There must be something an artist can do, even if it's only putting camouflage paint on tanks."

"You keep out of it," Mary advised firmly. "Let younger, fitter men do their bit."

As she said it she caught Robert's eye. He grinned at her, and Sally, who was watching, did the same.

"Well," Mary said lamely, "what good would Timothy be to anyone?"

They went into the drawing room for drinks before lunch. Jocelyn found himself beside Anne. He looked at her appraisingly. At fifteen she was already striking, a tall girl with glorious fair hair, deep blue eyes, and a mischievous mouth. She looked older than her age. He liked her on sight.

"You're Anne, aren't you? I'm Jocelyn."

"Yes I know."

"A sort of cousin."

"Not a real cousin," she smiled, "just a pretend cousin."

He nodded and grinned. It was true. She and Robert were cousins, but there was absolutely no blood relationship between her and himself.

"How was Paris?" he asked. "Do you drink?"

"Paris is wonderful, but we won't see it again now till this dreadful war is over. I drink wine and sherry."

"I'll get you some sherry."

"Thank you."

She was very self-composed, he thought. While Edward and Edwina brought Mary up to date on all the family news, and Timothy talked quietly to Robert, Jocelyn chatted with this "pretend cousin" of his.

"What will you do now you're in England? Go to school?"

"I don't think so. We're going back to Kemble. I could go to school in Cirencester, I suppose, but I'd rather not. I'll stay at home and look after Daddy, and I can study in my spare time."

"Oh, that's right—your grandmother doesn't live with you, does she?"

"She lives in a cottage a bit farther along the road."

"Does your father paint much?" Jocelyn asked. He knew very little about art.

"Yes, he's very prolific," she assured him with composure. "He had several exhibitions while we were in Paris. The critics were kind to him. Do you know Paris?"

"No, I don't."

"What a pity. It's so civilized."

Is it? he thought with amusement. She's fifteen and she's telling me! Yet he did not mind. There was something haunting about the girl.

"Will you be going to see the Thatchams?" he asked her. "Your mother's people?"

"I think so. Grandma wants to. We haven't got a car yet."

"We've got three here at the moment. One of them's mine, but I'm not using it. Robert and I go to and from camp in his old wreck, so you could borrow mine. Things are going to be difficult when petrol rationing hits us and the more cars one has the better. We ought to get a ration for each of them—I hope so, anyway," he added with a grin. "Meantime, mine is sitting in the garage."

"Do you know," Anne said seriously, "it's rather nice coming here. It's almost like coming home."

"Yes, isn't it?" Jocelyn agreed with enthusiasm.

All during lunch he found he could hardly take his eyes off her. She sat opposite him, so that it was difficult to avoid looking at her. It was incredible to him that he should find a fifteen-year-old schoolgirl a subject of so much interest. Of course these days girls didn't always look their age, but there was a serenity about her which was rare in one so young. That, together with the special quality of her smile, and her really beautiful hair, made her altogether a memorable person.

"How do you like the army?" she asked him.

He considered the question carefully before replying. "I don't think anybody could really like it," he said slowly. "It's all right in small doses." He laughed. "That must sound silly. What I mean is that it's boring and uncomfortable and sometimes unpleasant, yet it has strange qualities all of its own. It's so completely unlike anything else."

"Will you be going to France?"

"I expect so, sometime. Robert and I are going off on officer training."

"Good for you," she said approvingly.

"It's not really much of an achievement. They are short of officers. Anyone with a decent education, who knows how to behave, is automatically selected. It seems funny that I might be commanding soldiers when I'm such an absolute beginner."

She laughed with him.

"I'm sure you're being modest," she said.

"Not at all. The fact is that I look stupid."

"Pardon?" she asked, puzzled.

"I must do. That's why they've picked me for officer

training. You see, in the infantry every time you attack
you put all the second lieutenants out in front and they
mostly get killed. Nobody minds, for they're about the
most useless things in the army. Of course if they are
lucky enough to survive, you promote them and they grow
up into proper officers. But they have to be lucky. Not
clever; just lucky."

"You're not joking, are you?" she asked shrewdly.

"Not entirely. It works something like that."

"I thought it might."

They exchanged a long sober look, and he could see
concern in her eyes. He immediately regretted having mentioned second lieutenants and their wartime life expec-
tancy. It wasn't the sort of thing to discuss over a meal.

"Will you like being back in England?" he asked awkwardly by way of a change.

"I don't know. At the moment it all seems strange. I
shall miss Paris. The war has changed everything, hasn't
it?"

"Yes, of course."

"I wonder what life will be like afterward?"

"After the war, do you mean?"

She nodded.

"The same as before."

"No." She shook her head. "Things never go back to
what they were. Whatever it is, it won't be the same."

Her wisdom surprised him. He had never thought about
it, but he knew she must be correct.

"Perhaps it won't last long," he ventured.

"Do you believe that?"

"I don't know what to believe," he confessed.

"It seems to me," she said seriously, "that people don't
take all the trouble to start a war, just to call it off. Do you
know what I mean? Once you start, it's almost bound to
last a long time, unless of course you happen to win
quickly."

He did not know what to make of her. He had rarely had so much to consider in one conversation. In his experience people generally dealt in clichés and banalities, except when discussing something of specific interest, such as shop or family matters. Polite conversation was just a complicated system of saying almost nothing. Anne was different.

"Of course," he remarked with a quick smile, "if the war lasts for a very long time, people like me will get promoted—the ones who survive. All the regulars will be killed off and we'll have a civilian army, with civilian colonels and generals trying to run the war. It might be an improvement at that," he added with a chuckle.

"You'd make a very handsome colonel."

"I can't quite see myself as a choleric colonel. Nothing so elevated."

"Are they choleric?"

"No. It's a joke we made up one night, a few of us on guard duty, talking about the officers. Rather like the Twelve Days of Christmas, you know? We had six simpering subalterns, five cunning captains, four meddlesome majors, three choleric colonels, two blustering brigadiers and one geriatric general. That was as far as we got. We didn't know what to do about the regimental sergeant major."

She laughed. "I like it. I shall write it down."

"What on earth for?" he demanded.

"Because it's funny." And because it will remind me of you, she thought to herself.

Afterward they went for a walk together and she told him about their life in France. It was obvious that she adored her father, but in a lighthearted, rather irreverent way.

"Is he a good painter?" Jocelyn asked, prompted by real curiosity.

"Yes, I think he is. Only good. Not great."

He gave her a startled look which she did not appear to notice. She was immersed in some thought process all her own.

"He's what I call a nice painter," she said at length. "He paints pleasing things and paints them well. His paintings make life happier. Not all painters see their art in those terms. His paintings will be giving pleasure as long as they survive. They won't come and go with fashions. There will always be people who will like them. But I wouldn't call them important."

"I see." He did not. He did not see at all. She was talking Greek to him, but he did not want to admit it. He was absolutely certain that what she said was the truth.

They ended up by having tea in a café. Later that night, in bed, he thought about her for a long time before going to sleep. She was the most remarkable schoolgirl he had ever encountered, and he wished that she were older.

Anne had no such dissatisfied feelings about their ages. He was exactly right, she thought; not too young, not too old. She wished they were not going to bury themselves in the country. She might not see him again for ages, which was indeed a great pity.

At the end of his training, Officer Cadet Jocelyn Vernon was commissioned and gazetted to the 1st Battalion of the Berkshire Light Infantry. He was a little disappointed not to be sent to the 3rd, but his father had been second-in-command of the 1st for a time, so it wasn't too bad.

Officer Cadet Robert Vernon was not commissioned. He failed, and failed fairly miserably. When it came to such things as cleaning boots and buttons he was on reasonably safe ground because other people were sitting on the edges of their iron bedsteads, polishing like mad, so he didn't forget. When it came to drill, however, he was hopeless; and when he was allowed out of camp, he invariably forgot the time and came back late and was charged with being Absent Without Leave. He became the bane of his company commander's existence. That gentleman knew very well why Officer Cadet Robert Vernon had been sent to them, and his sympathy was all with Robert, but it was hopeless. No matter how hard one tried to look the other way, and even the N.C.O.s recognized that Robert meant well and tried to help him, he had a happy knack of getting into trouble which could not be ignored. He had intelligence and nothing else. Had circumstances been different he might have made a useful officer at the War Office, but he was much too young for the sort of appointment in which brains meant more than officer-like qualities, and he had come into the army through the wrong door. He was a private in the 1st B.L.I., and so he returned to the 1st B.L.I. as a private where, by sheer accident, his platoon commander was his cousin, Second Lieutenant Jocelyn Vernon.

Jocelyn had been given commissioning leave and had told them all about Robert. It was a sad state of affairs, considering Robert's ancestry. His father, grandfather, and great-grandfather, Sir Godfrey, had all been regular officers in the 1st Lancers, and Robert could not even get a commission in the infantry. What would they have thought had they been able to see it, Edward wondered with amusement, remembering particularly how arrogant James and John Vernon had been.

Jocelyn, on the other hand, took to soldiering naturally, although he never pretended to be in the least bit interested in the army. He was that rarity, a born infantry officer. From the beginning he showed qualities which impressed his commanding officer, not only qualities of leadership and ordinary ability, but he could look at a map and see terrain as though he were standing in front of it. In exercises he knew better than anyone how to make good use of ground, and he was a born strategist. There was the makings of a really fine officer in him, and his

C.O. regretted that he had gone into the family business, important though that might be in the commercial life of Reading, instead of joining the B.L.I.

Jocelyn had a problem in his cousin. It was far more difficult for him to turn a blind eye to Robert's little blunders than it was for another officer, because he had to make it clear to himself as well as to others that he was not playing favorites. Jocelyn was intensely interested in the handful of men who made up his first command, and he knew that Robert was a weak link. If they went into battle Robert could endanger them all, and being an infantry battalion it was likely that they would go into battle— indeed they might be off to France any day.

One morning Robert and two other men were sent off in a truck to collect some crates from a supply depot several miles distant. They collected the supplies and on the way back they made a detour to a pleasant little inn where they had several beers and some pork pies and sandwiches. Like most soldiers they were permanently hungry.

It was a harmless enough exploit except for the fact that they were spotted by two military police passing the pub. That turned the harmless exploit into all sorts of heinous crimes, such as misuse of service transport, making an unauthorized journey, and conduct prejudicial to good order—and all aggravated by the fact that on the charge sheet the offenses were prefaced by the awful words, "While on Active Service."

Their punishments were quite light. Robert and one other man received seven days confined to barracks, and the driver, who was in charge of the vehicle, got fourteen. Nobody except Jocelyn gave the matter much thought, but Jocelyn contrived to see Robert alone afterward.

"That was a stupid thing to do," he said. "Imagine parking a truck outside a pub on a fairly busy road."

"I know. I warned the other two but they wouldn't listen."

"Whose idea was it?"

"The driver's, but we were all hungry and the beer didn't go amiss either."

"I'm sorry you got seven days, if you were against it anyway."

"Oh that?" Robert laughed. "Think of the money I've saved in the past week. I don't mind. It was worth it, in fact."

"Worth it? Do you mean you'd do it again?" Jocelyn was trying to follow his cousin's thinking.

"You don't seem to understand. I was against going there. I knew it was breaking their stupid rules. All I'm saying is that I enjoyed it and it was no hardship to be confined for seven days. The food here is so ghastly that any chance for a snack is welcome."

"Look, Robert, I know you think the rules are infantile. Lots of them are, but surely you can see the necessity for them? You can't run an army by letting people do as they please. It wouldn't work."

"Wouldn't it? It works in shops and factories where you can't put adults on stupid charges. Why not treat soldiers like adults?"

"You know the answer to that. We're training for war, not playing at Boy Scouts. Don't you realize what you've done? You don't have a clean record anymore. When your name comes up for promotion, they look at your crime sheet to see what sort of soldier you are."

"Really." Robert laughed. "Is that meant to worry me? You don't think I care about promotion, do you? Let's finish the war and go home. It's all so completely childish and infantile."

Jocelyn stared at him and sighed. "You really don't see anything wrong with what you did, do you?" he asked.

"Frankly, no. We only went a mile or so out of our way."

"Suppose we were advancing in France, and I sent you

to do something—something important? What would happen if you took an hour off to do something else?"

"I wouldn't do that," Robert denied indignantly.

"You had a chance to prove that point several days ago, and you failed. If you can't be trusted here, who's going to trust you overseas?"

"Oh, don't be so righteous, Jocelyn. That star on your shoulder has gone to your head."

Jocelyn colored at the injustice of the remark and dropped the subject. It wasn't the fact that Robert had got seven days which troubled him. The army was run on childish rules that wouldn't be tolerated in any decent public school, and he himself knew the feeling that just being alive was almost grounds for being put on a charge. It was the deliberate disobedience of a sensible rule designed to conserve petrol, and the subsequent attitude, which troubled him. Robert, far from feeling contrite, thought the army should alter its rules.

Robert was no criminal, but Jocelyn was forced to the conclusion that either he was ridiculously irresponsible, or else he simply lived in a world of his own which bore little resemblance to the real world. Either way he was becoming a serious problem in the platoon. One simply couldn't depend on him.

In the end he spoke to his company commander who sent him to the C.O. The colonel heard him out in silence.

"In your considered opinion Private Vernon should be posted to other duties?" he asked, expressionless. He was wondering how Jocelyn felt about what he was doing.

"Yes, sir."

"Would you be prepared to put that in writing?"

"Yes, sir." The question surprised Jocelyn, who nevertheless did not blink.

"I'll have to see Private Vernon, you know. He's going to have to find out just why he's being transferred."

"I realize that, sir."

The C.O. shook his head sadly. "Very well. You don't surprise me. In fact it won't really surpise anyone." He did not go on to say that what would surprise everyone was that Jocelyn had had the guts to go through with the unpleasant business. The C.O. had been wondering how to go about removing Robert without upsetting his cousin. It had been a mistake putting them in the same platoon, but it had been an accident and once done it would have been very pointed to undo it.

The same day Robert was sent for, given a chance to defend himself, which he was unable to take since he had no reply to what he recognized as the truth, and was told that he would be sent to a holding unit for reallocation.

"Couldn't I stay with the B.L.I., sir?" he asked sadly. "In the quartermaster's office, perhaps?"

"I'm sorry, but we have no vacancy at the moment. I tell you what, though, I'll put in a good word for you. You might get back to one of the other battalions eventually. You'll have to go on some sort of course, you realize that?"

"Yes, sir."

When the battalion sailed for France, Robert did not go with it. He was doing a stores course. The 1st B.L.I. arrived in France in time to get caught up in what was a retreat. Holland, Belgium, and Luxembourg had been invaded by the Germans. The British began to retreat. On May 29, the 1st had to fall back from Ostend, where they had been holding out for several days. Jocelyn and his platoon were the last to leave, and their casualties were heavy. Jocelyn himself acted as a machine gunner and received a couple of grazes which did him no harm. They kept going until they arrived at the beaches of Dunkirk.

So much for glorious war, Jocelyn thought sadly as he looked at the beach which was literally crowded with soldiers and a sprinkling of airmen. It hasn't been going five minutes and we've bloody well gone and lost it. He watched the relief operation with wonder as boats, little boats, bigger boats, paddle steamers, Royal Navy ships— anything that could float—came across the Channel to pick up six, sixty, or six hundred men, as the case might be. All the time the Luftwaffe was breaking through the R.A.F.'s desperate defense of the area to drop bombs on the boats and machine-gun the beaches. Dunkirk was no health cure, that much was plain.

What he did not know, as he waited for his turn to get away, was that on the first of June a trim launch from Henley called *Seabreeze* had been sunk by a direct hit just before it reached the beach.

Edward Vernon had no warlike intentions. He considered himself an onlooker and had resigned himself to that role. He was surprised therefore when a friend, Bill Enright, came round to the house one evening with the news that most of their friends at Henley were taking their boats downriver where they were planning to help with the withdrawal from Dunkirk. He was on his way to Henley. Did Edward want to come along?

Edward did not need to think twice about it. He agreed at once. Everything was in a mad hurry, of course. People all over the south of England were dropping what they were doing, making their way to their boats, and setting off for France. He packed a few hasty items in a duffel bag and came down to find Edwina waiting for him.

"You're off then?" she asked, not really surprised.

"I must go. We're needed. It will only be for a day or two and then I'll be back."

"Edward, what exactly are you going to try to do?"

"Our whole army in France is in retreat. They're stuck on the French beaches and we need every available boat to go and rescue them. They're surrounded by the Germans."

Edwina bit her lip. "That's no job for civilians."

"My dear, I fully agree, but it's a case of everybody lending a hand. It's an emergency."

"You did enough in the last war, Edward. You shouldn't be asked to risk your life like this."

"My dear, Jocelyn may be on that beach. Anyway there probably won't be any danger when it comes to the point. I know I don't have to go but I don't think I could live with myself if I didn't. Everybody who can is offering his boat. Besides, *is* it so important? It hasn't been much of a marriage for either of us."

"Of course it's important and what about that woman in San Francisco? I thought you were in love with her? I don't want to see you hurt, Edward. It may sound funny when we both agree that our marriage is a mock, but I'm very fond of you and I do care what happens to you."

"Thank you." He took her hand, not without feeling. "That was a nice thing to say. So far as Grace is concerned, she obviously had to postpone her visit. However she may come over here at the end of the summer. If she does, it will be because we've decided to live with each other come what may. I wasn't going to tell you this yet, certainly not standing in the hall, but as you've brought it up, I suppose this is as good a time and place as any."

"I had no idea." Grace, she thought. That was the other woman's name. He had never mentioned it before. She wondered what Grace was like.

"We've only just made up our minds about it. So you see there's no real need to worry too much about my safety, because I'll probably be moving out of Mereford in a few months, leaving you alone. Besides, people like me don't get killed. Only the good are taken."

"Who said you aren't good?" she demanded.

"Lots of people would deny it hotly," he joked. "Now I must be off, my dear. I'll send word as soon as I can, but I don't suppose the whole thing will last more than a day or two. And please don't worry about me. I'll be all right."

They looked into each other's eyes, and she came dangerously close to tears for no reason that she could define. She told herself that she was being a fool, but she could not convince herself. Then he grinned and winked, and before she knew it, he had gone out through the door.

"Good-bye, Edward," she said to herself very quietly.

She did not say good-bye because she had any fear for his life, but because she was acknowledging that the marriage was indeed over—if it had ever been anything else! Nothing would ever be the same again. Edward, who in his funny way had always been faithful to her, had found someone to love; she who had not been faithful had no one. Life could be cruel.

Edward and Bill Enright were among the last to leave Henley. Eventually, when they had filled in some forms at the other end, they were allowed to fuel up and set out. As he stood at the helm, Edward felt pleased with life. All round him were other little boats, some expensive, some cheap, some grubby, some spotless, all with their civilian owners staring ahead toward the French coast. Already they could hear the sounds of war—the gunfire, even the rattle of machine-gun fire, and there were vapor trails in the sky.

This was more like it, Edward decided happily. He might be an old has-been of nearly fifty, but there was life in him yet. What a story he would have to tell Jocelyn when they met. Jocelyn was over there somewhere. It would be rather fun if he picked up the boy. As he approached the coast and could see better, he was astonished by the thousands of human figures on the beach. At the water's edge were orderly queues of men, patiently waiting to file into whatever it might be, motorboat or something larger. Every now and then a German aircraft played havoc with them, and then there would be a lull and the withdrawal would continue. There were boats streaming past him in the other direction, each with its cargo of tired, dirt-streaked, often wounded men.

He had no premonition of death, no warning of its approach. He was fixing his eye on the particular spot on the beach where he would run in his launch, and, because of the noise around him, he did not even hear the aircraft approaching.

Chapter 24

JOCELYN was allowed to go home. He had to buy new uniforms, and in any case he had earned some leave. It was only four days, but it was enough. He arrived at Mereford in a taxi, still battle-stained and tired. Edwina, seeing him getting out of the car, ran to the door and down the steps.

"Jocelyn. Are you all right?"

"Fine, Mother, fine. Just a little tired. Can I have a bath?"

"Can you have a bath! You can have ten. Have you any luggage?"

"No luggage. Just what I stand up in."

"Then come in."

While he had a bath and changed into a sports coat and flannels, she had a hot meal made for him and opened a bottle of wine. He came downstairs looking much better and quite cheerful despite the dark rings round his eyes.

"Was it bad?" she asked, handing him a drink.

"Pretty awful. Where's Father?"

"He went off with the boat. Three days ago."

"Oh. Yes, of course, I suppose he would. Have you no news of him?"

"None."

"Well, the little boats are working miracles. I wish I could describe it. A whole army is being taken off that beach under the noses of the Germans, and they can't stop it. Those men in the little boats, by God, that's really something to see. I bet Father's in the thick of it, loving every minute."

At that very moment a telegram was on its way. Bill Enright had seen it happen. He himself had been wounded and put in the hospital on his return to England, but he had finally managed to get the doctor to let him send the news to Mereford. It arrived just as Jocelyn was finishing his meal. Sally and Edwina were sitting watching him as he ate ravenously. The doorbell rang. Edwina jumped up and ran out into the hall, and saw the uniformed telegraph messenger standing in the doorway. He offered her the telegram and the delivery book. She signed and slit open the buff envelope.

"No reply," she said dully and turned away.

She walked into the dining room, her feet like lead. This was the end of it all, the end of a strange marriage which had not been entirely unsatisfying. Edward was gone. They looked at her expectantly, and their expressions changed as they guessed.

"It's Edward," she said heavily. "He was killed. The telegram is from Mr. Enright. I expect he'll come to see us."

There was a hush. All three of them sat speechless, not moving, as it sank in. Then Jocelyn got up and put an arm round Edwina's shoulders.

"I'm sorry," he said lamely.

She got up and left the room, and Sally and Jocelyn exchanged miserable glances. Edwina walked slowly upstairs and into Edward's bedroom. It was a room she rarely set foot in. Now she viewed it as a stranger. She touched the bedspread, and the pajama case on the pillows. These were the pajamas he had worn the night before he had left. He would never wear them again.

She wandered over to his chest of drawers. There were some silver-framed photographs on it—none of her, she noticed. That was understandable. She opened and closed drawers, looking at his shirts and socks, his handkerchiefs and underwear. On his desk she saw an envelope lying where he had left it. It was sealed and ready for the post. It was addressed to a Miss Grace Montgomery at an address in Pacific Avenue, San Francisco, California, U.S.A.

She took the envelope down to the morning room and sat at her desk, and began to write a short note.

> Dear Miss Montgomery,
>   I have just heard that my husband, Edward, has been killed at a place called Dunkirk where he was helping to pick up British soldiers from the beaches. I found the enclosed in his bedroom and I am sending it to you with the news of his death. I am very sorry for you both.
>
> Yours sincerely,
Edwina Vernon.

She put envelope and note in another envelope, addressed it, and put it in the hall for the next post. It was the least she could do for Edward, this last small service. She wanted desperately to cry, but she could not. Tears did not come easily to her at the best of times, and now when she would have welcomed their relief, they stubbornly refused to provide it. Instead she wandered about the house silently.

After dinner, when Sally had gone up to her room, she detained Jocelyn.

"I know you're tired, darling, but we must talk. Do you know anything about your father's will?"

"Yes," Jocelyn said. "He told me before I went to France. He's left the business and the house to me, but there's some money I can't touch while you're alive. You get the interest. Also I must let you stay here—not that there's any problem about that. I couldn't quite see why he put it in."

He wouldn't, she thought. Edward was being kind, making absolutely sure that whatever happened she should stay at Mereford which she had come to love so deeply.

"He may have thought that when you married you'd want me to go," she said mildly.

"Throw my own mother out of her home?" Jocelyn snorted. "Not likely. Nothing will change so far as you're concerned, Mother."

"What about the company while you're away at the war?" she asked.

"Oh, lord, I hadn't thought about that."

"Do you have a good manager?"

Jocelyn considered. "There's an excellent accountant, we have really good auditors, and we've got some good senior men, too old to go off to war. Father made John Boag acting general manager when I went into the army. I think he's all right, but of course he had Father sitting on top of him."

"What's the best thing to do? I'd offer to help but I know nothing about it."

"I'll have to see Purcell, the accountant, I think. I'd better do that sometime tomorrow. As a matter of fact, if I made Purcell and Boag joint general managers it might just work. Purcell understands finance and Boag knows how to run a department store and how to buy. I can arrange it so that all expenditure over a certain amount has to be approved. I'll work out something."

"It's so unfair giving you worries at a time like this," she remarked.

"I don't mind, really. The army isn't very intellectual. It will be good to have the firm to think about in quiet moments."

He went into Reading the next morning, arranged about the newspaper notices of Edward's death, attended to a few affairs at the office, and broke the news to the staff that Edward had been killed at Dunkirk. Then he telephoned the Thatchams and wrote to Mary Hilton in Kemble. Later he remembered the boat club at Henley to which his father had belonged, and telephoned the news to them.

Bill Enright arrived that night, just as they were finishing dinner. He had been discharged from the hospital. The Dunkirk operation was over now. Enright accepted a drink and told them what had happened.

"I'm afraid there's no doubt about it," he said. "Edward is dead all right. You must accept my assurance of that fact."

He did not explain in detail. He had tried to pick up the body, but when he got there, it was half a body, severed by the blast just below the ribs. The blast had played funny tricks. Edward's face was unmarked. Enright had let the hideous thing in his hands slip back into the water, and finished his run to the beach.

"Yes, of course, we understand," Edwina answered. "I'm glad the bomb missed you."

"It rocked the boat, that's all. Glad to see you got away all right, Jocelyn. Your father would have been thankful about that."

Jocelyn agreed. Enright stayed for perhaps half an hour and then went off to his own home. Edwina produced half a bottle of malt whiskey.

"Your father was always particularly fond of this. I think we might have one."

They drank silently to Edward's memory.

The battalion re-formed. It took time and recruits had to be trained. It would be a month or two before it would be even approximately ready for active service again. Jocelyn was surprised to be sent for by the colonel one day. He walked in and saluted.

"Hullo, Jocelyn. Good news for you. You're getting your second pip."

"Thank you, sir." The promotion pleased him. He felt less like a new boy now.

"And something else. That was a good show you put up at Ostend. This has come."

It was a notification from the War Office congratulating him on his award of the Military Cross.

"It's in tomorrow's Gazette," Colonel Crofts told him. "Well done."

"Th . . . thank you, sir," Jocelyn stammered.

"You look surprised. Sergeant Filson gets the D.C.M."

"I'm glad about that. He deserved it."

"Drinks all round in the mess at lunchtime . . . on your bill, of course."

"Damned unfair," Jocelyn grinned. "On my birthday I expect people to give me presents. What's the difference?"

"If we bought people drinks every time they won a medal, we'd have so many heroes the war would be over in a week, before regulars like me had got our promotion. We must keep the war going."

Jocelyn laughed and left. Fantastically enough, the war was going on despite the debacle in France. Things were black—they could hardly be blacker. Italy had declared war on Britain and France, Paris was occupied by the Germans, and the war in France was finally over. The French had signed an armistice. The Channel Islands were occupied, so part of the British Isles was in the hands of the enemy. It was a sobering thought.

Yet the spirit of the country was resolute and there was little talk of defeat. It was remarkable. Jocelyn went into town, found a tailor, had his M.C. ribbon sewn on and his extra stars put on his shoulder straps, and returned to the mess where his brother officers ceremoniously "wet" his new finery at his own expense. When he contrived to get home on the weekend, Edwina frowned at the purple and white ribbon on his left breast.

"What's that, darling?"

"The Military Cross, Mother."

She knew almost nothing about the army, but she did remember the Military Cross from the first war. Edward had won it, she recalled. It was for heroism against the enemy.

"How did you get that? Jocelyn, were you in the fighting?"

The question surprised Jocelyn. Where else did she think he had been? He did not yet appreciate fully the power of the human mind to rationalize itself out of unpleasantness.

"It was nothing much."

She looked at him for a long moment.

"That's not true. What happened?"

"We were the rear guard at Ostend—my platoon, that is. We held up the Germans while the others got away."

"I see. You weren't wounded?"

"I got a graze, two actually, but nothing much."

"Where?"

"Ribs and thigh—nothing you'd notice. Anyway, it was really quite easy."

He had killed men, she thought sadly. This was what you brought them into the world for, so that they could grow up, become men, and then go and kill other women's sons. It was so senseless and stupid.

"While Robert sits in camp somewhere in England," she said softly.

"Please don't say that, Mother, and especially not in front of Robert or Sally. He does his best. The war isn't over yet."

"I wish you'd get married. I really do."

"What, with a war on?"

"Why not? Live as much as you can, while you can."

"I believe you're trying to drive me into some woman's arms," he laughed. The only woman, he thought, that he really knew was his almost cousin, Anne Hilton. Most of his friends had wives and sweethearts to write to, but he wrote almost solely to his mother. He had taken some photographs in France and now had copies. He sat up late that night, decided to write to Anne at Kemble, and sent the photographs.

After all, he thought as he got into bed, it was someone to write to.

Her reply moved him.

> Dear Jocelyn,
>
> It was so nice of you to write to me. I love getting letters, but I never do get any. I hope you will write often, if you have time. I did enjoy the photographs, especially the one of the goat drinking the beer. I am glad you have been to France, although probably it isn't so nice now.
>
> I am sending a photograph of myself. It isn't a very good one. I really look much older. Can I have one of you, please, in uniform? I would like that very much. Not a little snap, but a bigger one which I can put in a frame on my dressing table. Would you mind that very much?
>
> Grandma and Daddy send their love, and Grandma asks if you see Cousin Robert at all? Is he in the same bit of the army? Or another bit? It is a pity you can't come to visit us at Kemble. Do you still have the car you lent us? It was a nice car. I wish we had a car because I hate going to Cirencester in the bus, but Daddy says it would be no good because we wouldn't get much petrol. I said I don't want much petrol anyway, just enough to go to Cirencester to the cinema.
>
>   Your loving pretend cousin,
>   Anne (Hilton)

The letter amused him, especially when she asked about "bits" of the army. Why not, he asked himself? The 1st Berkshire Light Infantry was only a "bit" of the army, when all was said and done. He surprised himself by going to a photographic studio and having a portrait taken. He sent it to her with a longer letter, and began a pen friendship which kept him amused and occupied during many a dull evening.

Robert's war lacked excitement. His intellectual ability made it child's play to pass the simple army courses he attended. He was now an acting corporal in stores at a recruit training school. He had applied several times for a transfer to the B.L.I. and still hoped he would get it. He felt guilty about being at a recruit school. Normally he would have suggested that Sally come and live near the camp, but because he hoped to be moved, he preferred that she stay on at Mereford. The mellow old house was far more pleasant for her than any dingy lodgings in the grimy Midlands town near his camp; and in any case she was very involved now in developing the small holding, which was just beginning to produce a fair crop of vegetables and chickens from the long line of hen houses Edwina had had erected earlier that summer.

Robert heard from Sally about Jocelyn, and occasionally from Jocelyn himself, although the cousins did not write very frequently. It irked him that Jocelyn should be covering himself with glory while he, Robert, skulked in safety. He was glad his Uncle Edward was dead. At the same time he rather despised himself for these feelings, because logically war was a stupid waste, and to show proficiency at it was completely unimportant and unworthy. As the months passed he began to cultivate a sneering attitude toward the war, the fighting forces, and anything and everything connected with them. Only by doing so could he still the small voice which reproached him with failure.

Early in 1941 the 1st B.L.I. sailed for North Africa. Jocelyn spent a short embarkation leave at Mereford, and wrote and told Anne that he would be going away. Her reply both pleased and touched him. In it she said,

> I do hope you will write whenever you can. I look upon you as a real cousin, you know. Robert never writes. Sometimes life here is dull. Kemble is a small place, and Daddy is wrapped up in his painting. Often he goes away—he's become a war artist, I think. As for Grandma, she is old and feeble. She has changed a lot during the past few months. She is well over seventy now. So, as you can imagine, not much happens. I do love getting letters—and writing them. I promise always to reply.

He realized now that she was a lonely girl. She was over sixteen, would be seventeen later in the year, and she was buried in the country with an elderly grandmother and a father who, from the sound of it, was no company for her. It was too bad, and he made up his mind to write as often as he could. He was beginning to enjoy writing.

Edwina was quiet for the first two or three days of his leave. Jocelyn said so one morning, while Sally was out shopping.

"It's going to be dull when you go," she replied with a quick smile. "Your father's gone, and now you're off overseas. It only leaves Sally and me, with very infrequent visits from Robert."

"I suppose it isn't very gay," he said sympathetically.

"It isn't just that, darling. I don't mind a quiet life, but it's becoming lonely. I like Sally, but she's a lot younger than I am. I suppose we're two lonely women, but at least she has Robert's leaves to look forward to."

"But you have the small holding to run."

"Yes, I know, but I'm not terribly interested in that and at the moment there isn't enough to keep us both busy. Anyway, I've got a sudden urge to join up."

"What!"

"You sound astonished. Why not? I haven't got one foot in the grave yet, you know. I'm only forty-eight. They'd take me."

"What would you join? The A.T.S.?"

"No, the army uniform doesn't suit women. I'd rather like to be a Wren."

"Are you serious?" he asked.

"Yes, I am. Sally can run Mereford, with Cook and Mrs. Hobson to help her."

Mrs. Hobson was an elderly housekeeper, as old as the cook. They were the only servants left at Mereford now, and as Edwina often said to Sally, they were lucky to have them, especially as they were both so devoted to Mereford.

"That's true. If you put it like that, you might even enjoy being a Wren. You're glamorous enough," he added with a grin.

"Thank you for the compliment."

"I mean it. You don't look nearly old enough to be my mother."

"You must have been reading about how to make friends and influence people, but I appreciate the sentiments behind your inaccurate remarks."

"Have you said anything to Sally?" Jocelyn asked. "She may not be too thrilled at the idea of being left with so much responsibility."

"Not yet. I wanted to speak to you first."

"If you're asking my permission to abandon the old family homestead, permission is granted," he laughed. "There is, as someone said, a war on."

"If you'd objected I shouldn't have gone. It is your house, after all, and I have a duty to look after it."

"Dear Mother." He kissed her lightly.

"Is everything all right at the office?" she asked, lighting a cigarette. She was the only one in the family who smoked, and since Edward's death she smoked more heavily than before.

"Yes, it seems to be working out all right. The auditors are very good—they keep a watching brief on things for me. So far as I can see we can sell virtually all we get. Trade flourishes. Taxation is awful, though. Sometimes I wonder what we're fighting for."

"If you men would worry about that *before* you started wars, there might be fewer of them."

"You're a feminist."

"Not at all. I'm just pointing out the facts of life."

Edwina was in no great hurry to discuss her plans with Sally. She said nothing, not even after Jocelyn had sailed. At Easter Robert came home very pleased with life. He was now an acting sergeant, "with pay" as he pointed out gleefully to Sally, and he had been transferred to the Berkshire's regimental depot outside Reading.

"I'll be able to live out," he told them, grinning like a Cheshire cat. "Think of that. I can come home at night, most nights anyway, just like an office worker."

"Oh, Robert, how lovely," Sally exclaimed.

Edwina decided that her moment had come. She told them of her plans. They were surprised, but to her question about the house and small holding, they gave a unanimous answer. Sally would stay and look after it all till Edwina and Jocelyn came home again.

"I've thought a lot about it," Robert said. "The life of a camp follower is no fun really. It's much better for Sally to be here. It's a nice place for her to live and a nice place for me to come home to. I expect I'll be at the regimental depot for quite a long time. If I do move, it may be overseas. At the moment there's no prospect of that. There are five battalions in the regiment now, plus a training battalion, so the depot is kept busy."

"What's your job exactly?" Edwina asked.

"Looking after stores, and issuing them. It's what's

known in the army as a 'cushy job.' Quartermasters tradi-
tionally go short of nothing."

"Do you enjoy it?" Edwina asked.

Robert and Sally exchanged amused glances.

"Not in the least. It's a life for morons. However, as I
have to be in the army, I'll admit that there are worse
things than being a quartermaster sergeant. I'll be glad
when it's all over and we can settle down to a normal life
again."

"What will you do when that happens?" Edwina inquired, interested. "You won't want to go back to being a
university student."

"I'll have to find a job. There will be plenty going."

"And plenty of people looking for them," Edwina
pointed out.

"I must take my chance along with the rest. Thank
goodness I'm not totally dependent on a job. I'm thinking
of buying a house."

"What?"

"Well, prices are down because of the war, so now is the
time to buy. The trouble is I'm not sure where to buy. My
best bet for a job may be London and I'm thinking of
looking for something there. It ought to be an investment."

"It might get bombed."

"I know, that's what's holding me back. I'm still thinking about it, though. There's no hurry—the war will probably go on for years."

In April of 1941 that was a fair statement to make.
Greece and Yugoslavia had just been invaded by the Germans. The British had withdrawn from Bardia, although
Tobruk still held out. Unknown to them, Jocelyn was in
besieged Tobruk. All war news was strictly bad news, and
the world wondered how long Britain could hold on.

After Robert's leave, Edwina began to pull strings quietly. Eventually she was interviewed by a naval captain at

the Admirality. It was a sympathetic interview. She was the cousin of a baronet although she had not seen him for years and almost never wrote to him. He, as good fortune would have it, was already serving as an officer in the Royal Navy. She was also the widow of a First War hero who had given his life at Dunkirk taking over one of the little boats which had made possible the evacuation of the bulk of the B.E.F. These things were in her favor, as was her keenness. Even so, she was forty-eight, she had never worked in her life, and she possessed no qualifications of any sort. What could they do with her? Would she like to be a welfare officer? If nothing else offered, she would. So after a short discussion it was settled. She would do her officer training, and if she passed she would be posted as a welfare officer. If she failed, she would almost certainly be discharged. There were no vacancies for middle-aged, untrained, unqualified Wren ratings.

Two days after Pearl Harbor, Tobruk was relieved. That same day, December 9, Edwina Vernon became a Wren officer and was posted to the south coast of England. Also on the same day Robert was confirmed in his rank of sergeant and became war substantive instead of acting paid. As he pointed out to Sally, it didn't bring any more pay, but they couldn't bust him now without a court-martial.

They both thought that was rather amusing.

Chapter 25

JOCELYN and Anne Hilton kept on writing. She got more news of him than anyone else. She was the first to hear that he had been awarded a bar to his Military Cross for bravery in April 1941, although the award was not announced until after Tobruk had been relieved. Early in 1942 he was promoted to captain.

In May he heard from her that Mary Hilton had died. Timothy was now in uniform of a sort, as an official war artist, and was hardly ever at home. Anne had taken a job with a local farmer, to help the war effort working on the land. He tried to imagine her in Wellington boots, wearing a headscarf and thick woolly jumper, carrying buckets of pigs' swill, but could not. She had been such an elegant and self-composed young woman when he had last seen her. She sent him photographs occasionally, and it dawned on him gradually that she was no longer a child, but a woman and, judging by the snapshots, a desirable one. His snapshots to her were the usual wartime ones showing him and his friends celebrating Christmas under a blazing sun, or standing beside a camel, or posing outside a tent.

On October 3 he won the Distinguished Service Order at Alamein, doing what his grandfather had done in South

Africa—saving the lives of wounded comrades. When the award was announced, he wrote and told Anne with some justifiable pride.

He was especially pleased to have been singled out for an act of mercy similar to that of his grandfather, Captain Henry. He and his father had often talked about wars and medals, particularly when he was a boy and interested in the family's collection of honors. Edward had always been a little disparaging about his own awards because, as he said, there was nothing very noble about killing other men, and bravery under fire was expected of soldiers. Edward had always distinguished between awards for ordinary heroism, especially under attack, and the other kind which involved saving life, rescuing guns, and similar deeds.

A lot of this had stuck in Jocelyn's mind. He shared some of Robert's cynicism about life in wartime, although his cynicism had a different basis and was not the result of personal frustration. Like his father before him, he had seen too many heroes die unhonored and unsung to attach too much importance to bits of tin and gaudy ribbons. If he could do his duty, his conscience would be clear and that was all he really wanted.

Despite all this it was undeniably pleasing to be able to write and tell Anne that he had got his D.S.O. It was illogical, but it was a fact. He only wished that he could get leave in England to see her again. She would be a stranger to him after so many years, years in which she had been transformed from schoolgirl into woman.

The news from home, when it came, was good. Edwina was already a two-striper, the equivalent of an army captain, which amused him greatly. She was in Portsmouth where she seemed to enjoy the bustle of navy life. Robert was at the B.L.I. depot, still in the stores, and he and Sally were having the best war of all. It was just like Robert having a job in an office in town. Nothing had changed much at Mereford, Sally wrote, though she was tremendously busy with the small holding. She had a full-time Land Girl working for her now, and even Robert was pressed into service on weekends and during his leaves.

Sally was a good source of local news. Lord Thatcham's son, Edwina's friend Lord Paveley, was an intelligence officer in the R.A.F. Lady Thatcham, among other things, was a Red Cross organizer. She saw Sally occasionally and befriended her, and once again there was a certain amount of coming and going between Mereford and Pleasaunce.

Edwina, rather surprisingly perhaps, had struck up a friendship with Grace Montgomery in San Francisco. When she had forwarded Edward's last letter to Grace she had not really expected any response. Instead, less than two weeks later, she received quite a long letter in bold handwriting on expensive notepaper. In it Grace said,

"It was very kind of you to forward Edward's last letter to me. I know he had told you of my existence and that you know how we met and fell in love. I find this letter very difficult to write, partly because I'm unused to the role of 'other woman' and partly because I know very little about you. Edward did not say much and I never asked.

"We have heard about Dunkirk over here, and it was like him to go when he did not have to. I don't wish to be impertinent but I do think we share the same loss. You were his wife for a long time, and I can assure you that he never said anything unpleasant about you to me. There must be many, many bonds between you of which I will never know anything.

"I am not sure what I am trying to say to you. I feel very tempted just to tear up this letter, yet because Edward loved us both I shall mail it and hope that it doesn't upset or irritate you. I intended visiting England later this year —in fact I was coming over 'for the duration,' to be with Edward—but now I shall stay here where I have always belonged."

Edwina read the letter several times before replying.

Like Grace, she too did not know whether just to drop the whole affair, which seemed the most sensible as well as the simplest thing to do, or to respond to what was so obviously an act of friendship. In the end her heart overruled her head. There had been much affection but no love between Edward and herself for years. This woman had given him the love he had never had with her, which he might have had under other circumstances, and which in fact she had wanted to give him in the beginning. Her reply was generous.

"You have no idea how glad I am," she wrote, "that Edward found happiness before he died. Our marriage held together because there was no reason to break it up, that is all. Immediately before he left for Dunkirk he told me that you would be coming to England and that when you did he would leave me and live with you. So I knew what to expect.

"Obviously I had known of your existence for some time but that was the first positive indication that he had made up his mind to choose between us. I was very fond of Edward. Nobody could be married to him for long without being fond of him. I would have been sorry about the change but there was an obvious need for change. To tell you the truth, I was a little bit envious because I had never found any other man I wanted to marry.

"Believe me, I grieve for you. I have my home, my son, my own friends, and my loss is really nothing compared with yours. I would so much like to meet you. I feel no bitterness, as you must have realized if you have read this far. Perhaps after the war we can meet. I keep thinking that we are two lonely women and that we have something important in common—Edward."

After that they exchanged letters regularly, and Grace sent food parcels to Mereford. She heard all about Edwina's joining the Wrens and the frequency of their letters increased. It was a surprising friendship and a remarkably warm one considering that they had never met and had no immediate prospect of meeting.

Then, about six months after Pearl Harbor, Grace wrote to tell Edwina jubilantly that she was now an officer in the Waves, the American Wrens. There was much lighthearted comparing of their relative experiences. Edwina kept Grace's existence a secret. Nobody knew of their correspondence and she never mentioned Grace's name to any member of the family. It was not because of Grace herself, but because of Edward. What Edward had done in the United States was strictly his own private affair, and not even Jocelyn was told. Edward was dead and his past had died with him.

In the early summer of 1943 Edwina wrote triumphantly to Grace, who was then at the naval base in San Diego, that she had at long last been posted overseas. This was what she had wanted more than anything because, as she said, it was frustrating to be a sailor and not see the world. It was a letter full of high spirits. The truth was that in the Wrens Edwina had found something she had always lacked without ever being conscious of the fact— an outlet for her energies and her abilities. For the first time she had a job worth doing, and did it well. Joining up had changed her whole life, and she rejoiced with all her heart that she had done so. She felt useful, and it was a new and pleasant sensation.

She spent a short embarkation leave at Mereford, helping Sally. They turned very brown under the summer sun which, as Edwina pointed out, was good because she would like to arrive with a tan and not have to go through the distressing and painful business of turning red and peeling.

She put down her fork one afternoon and sat back on the grass and looked at the house.

"It's funny," she said to Sally, "life takes some strange turns."

"What exactly are you thinking of?" Sally asked, stopping work.

"I was thinking about Mereford. When Captain Henry and Alice bought this place, before the turn of the century, the last thing they would ever have expected was that James's family would become its custodians, yet you are Robert's wife and you are in sole charge here. I wonder what Henry would think. He must have been quite a remarkable man."

"I don't know much about him."

"Of course not, you wouldn't. Edward used to talk about his father—in his own quiet way he worshiped him. He was a cavalry officer back in the 1880s, a dandy, living the gay life. Yet he came here with no job and no income, he started up a business that supports us today, and he bought Mereford—and he did all that in a pretty short time too. Then, having shown what a clever civilian he was, he went off to the Boer War and won the V.C. It's such a pity he was killed."

"From the way Robert talks," Sally said slowly, "I often think he wishes he had been born into this side of the family."

"I don't know. Robert doesn't often talk about the family, but he never mentions his own mother and father, never. If I try to talk about them, he changes the subject. Does he know what happened to his mother? She ran off with a band leader, didn't she?"

"Yes, she did, and that is literally all I know about her. If Robert has ever heard anything, he certainly hasn't told me. Sometimes he talks about his great-grandfather, the old general, but that's about all."

"How odd. I think he's been happy here."

"Oh he has," Sally assured her.

"Has he ever done anything about buying a house?"

"No, although he always says it's a pity the house in

Hampstead was sold after his father's death. I think he wants to buy another house there if he can."

"I don't know London at all, really, just the West End. Is Hampstead nice?"

"Quite nice, yes. Robert says it will boom after the war. It's like a suburb and yet it is fairly close to central London."

"He may not work in London."

"I know. He says if necessary we could let the house and make some money out of it."

"That's an idea. Have you and Robert ever talked about having a family?"

Sally nodded. "Often. He wants to wait till the war's over. I'm not sure I agree, but that's what Robert wants."

"Well, perhaps it won't be so long now," Edwina said cheerfully.

In truth things were looking up. Starting the previous September, the Germans had been halted at Stalingrad, the Allies had invaded North Africa with Rommel in full retreat, the U.S. Air Force had begun its daylight bomber offensive against Germany, and the German armies in Russia had been put to rout. This very month Tunis and Bizerta had been captured by the Allies, and the R.A.F. had carried out the fantastic dams raid and seriously disrupted German war production in the Ruhr.

Early in June, Edwina sailed in a large convoy for Malta. No one knew at the time, but the invasion of Sicily was imminent, and troops were being sent out in readiness. She was posted to Naval Headquarters, Malta, and was looking forward to seeing the beleaguered island.

When they passed Gibraltar the convoy came under heavy attack. The Germans knew about it and were determined to inflict as much damage as possible. They spent practically a whole day at action stations and they were tired when night fell and they could turn in. The convoy raced on through the hours of darkness. At dawn it was sighted by a small submarine pack and without warning the U-boats struck. One, two, three transports were hit. In Edwina's ship everyone rushed to battle stations. She herself had just set foot on deck when two belated torpedoes hit them amidships. The clumsy vessel broke in two and sank with incredible rapidity.

Edwina found herself thrown into the water, one of the lucky ones. She swam as fast as she could away from the stricken ship whose bows and stern were now pointing skyward. At last she found a broken spar and clung to it. The water was not too cold but she had lost her life jacket when she had been flung into the sea. She clung gratefully to the floating wood and saw the ship disappear from view, taking most of its complement with it. There was nobody else in the immediate vicinity.

After what seemed like a long time she heard a faint sound and saw a launch in the distance. She shouted and waved frantically and was quickly spotted. Several minutes later she was being pulled aboard by two sailors. There were a number of other waterlogged figures—all men, she observed. She wondered what had happened to the Wren draft, a hundred of them all told.

"Where are the other Wrens?" she asked the coxswain.

"I haven't seen any, ma'am." He had spotted the badges of rank on the shoulder straps of her shirt.

"Look out," somebody called suddenly.

They all followed his finger skyward, and there was an aircraft, flying toward them low over the water.

"Down, everybody," the coxswain yelled.

They flung themselves flat, and then they heard the awful sound of machine-gun fire. Bullets thudded home all along the center of the launch, from stern to stem. Edwina felt hammer blows on her back, and knew she'd been hit. Then the pain began, terrible nightmare pain. Gradually she realized that the bottom of the launch was punctured and that the water was rising. She tried to raise herself. The pain was less intense now. She looked all round at the limp, blood-spattered bodies. Two or three were moving painfully. The launch was only just afloat. She could see no other vessel in sight, but in the distance were the sounds of gunfire. Would help ever come? she wondered.

When the destroyer finally managed to locate its missing launch, there were no survivors, just a lot of waterlogged corpses in a half-sunken boat. One of them was a woman, the only woman they had seen. The other Wrens had all gone down with the transport.

Lists of identified casualties were promptly signaled to the Admiralty in London. There busy people in offices wrote out telegrams and signals. In due course, Captain Jocelyn Vernon was sent for by a saddened commanding officer.

"It's bad news, I'm afraid, Jocelyn," he said bluntly, for there was no way of sweetening this pill. "The worst."

He handed Jocelyn the signal which had come in. Jocelyn, fear in his heart, but really thinking more of Robert than Edwina, took it and read.

"Inform Captain J. Vernon," it began. The words blurred as he saw his mother's name. Dead! How could she be dead? He was aware that the colonel was speaking.

"Here, have this, Jocelyn."

It was a glass of brandy. Jocelyn knocked it back and made a face. It was strong stuff.

"Thank you, sir."

"Sit down. Take your time."

"It's all right, sir."

"I'm very sorry. Isn't your father dead too?"

The colonel had not been with them in France. He had been transferred from the Wiltshire Regiment just before they came to Africa.

"Killed at Dunkirk, sir. Funny isn't it? Most people are

losing their sons, but I've lost my parents. It's upside down."

The colonel was silent. Jocelyn had another small brandy, stood up, and saluted. He marched out stiffly. That night he wrote to Anne, and when he had poured out his grief to her, he wrote to Robert, and to Sally. He didn't even know if they had heard yet. If Edwina had given him as her next of kin, nobody might tell Sally at Mereford. His letters to them were rather short and unsentimental. By now he felt quite numb.

His letter to Sally crossed one from her. It was a pathetic letter and it spoke of personal tragedy. Sergeant Robert Vernon had been convicted of theft and sent to prison for two years. Because his offense was not just a military one, but involved civilians, he had been tried by a civil court. He had been dishonorably discharged from the army—the soldier's worst possible punishment.

His arrest had come out of the blue, just when they were particularly happy together. Recently he had bought quite a nice house in Hampstead and put it in Sally's name. He had got it for just under four thousand pounds —less than a quarter of the capital that had accumulated from his father's legacy. It was a large, four-bedroomed house in nice grounds, not far from the heath. They were even talking about having a baby before the war ended. He was slowly coming round to her point of view. There was no reason to expect a move from the depot, where he was firmly entrenched now, and theirs was a singularly pleasant war.

She was surprised when he didn't come home one evening, and telephoned the depot. The reply was evasive but she got the impression he had been put on unexpected night duty. Then a strange sergeant arrived on a motor bicycle and introduced himself as a friend of Robert's.

Sally invited him in.

"Is something wrong?" she asked.

"I'm afraid so, Mrs. Vernon. Robert won't be home for a few days. He's under close arrest."

"Under what?"

"Close arrest. There's an investigation going on. Eventually he'll be put under open arrest and probably you'll be able to see him then. I think they'll let him come home in the evenings."

"What are they investigating?" she asked, incredulous.

"A pilferage in stores, it seems."

"Robert? Stealing?"

"Oh, I'm not saying *he* was mixed up in it, Mrs. Vernon. This is a big one; there's a lot of stink involved. Several people have been arrested and detectives are questioning them. After the investigation they decide who to charge—if anybody."

"I am sure there's been a mistake," she stammered.

"I expect so," the sergeant agreed quite cheerfully. "You see, Bobbie being a Q.M.S. he's naturally suspected."

She had never heard him called Bobbie before.

"What was taken?" she asked as he finished the drink she had given him.

"Various things. Blankets, underwear, socks, crockery, cutlery—lots of things civilians want."

"But why?"

"The story is that they were being sold to civilians locally, and some say there was a firm in London involved in buying blankets and other things in bulk."

It seemed incredible to Sally that this could be true. She spent a miserable five days until Robert showed up one evening, his shoulders drooping.

"Hullo, Sally. I know you've heard. I'm sorry."

"It's all right though, isn't it?" she asked, kissing him hungrily. "You're free now?"

"Not exactly. I'm under open arrest."

"Robert, what's happened?"

He accepted a drink and told her. He was coming up for

trial. He hadn't himself done anything, but he had turned a blind eye to another man who was working a nice little racket.

"Why?" she asked, unbelieving.

"He needed the money, and I didn't think he was doing much harm. There's so much stuff goes to waste in this ridiculous army that if somebody can solve his problems, and at the same time let people have a few things without coupons, so much the better. You'd be amazed at the waste that goes on."

"But, Robert, *stealing!*"

"That was his business, not mine. I didn't steal anything."

"You're a sergeant; you should stop things like that."

"Give the game away you mean? What sort of man do you take me for?"

She wondered if she was sitting with a stranger. Was this Robert? Mixed up in a theft?

"What's gone wrong with you?" she demanded.

"Nothing." He got up and poured himself another drink. "Look, it's a stupid, wasteful war. Money and goods are being squandered every day—to say nothing of lives. War and waste are the same thing. So why should I get all worked up if someone wants to do a bit of pilfering?"

"Who were they?"

"Two chaps I know. A corporal and a private. The corporal is in bad financial trouble—or he was. I expect it's all right now. I think they made about twelve hundred pounds out of it, between them."

"While you just stood by?"

"I didn't help them in any way."

"Then why have you been arrested?"

"Because I should have stopped them, that's why, and I think they don't really believe I wasn't taking money. They suspect the others are trying to cover up for me."

There was more to it than he told her, for he had passed

several indents for goods intended for the civilian market. They had been forged and he knew it, but he had let them go, and the goods had been snaffled on arrival and disposed of for a reasonable price. It might have gone undetected had they not overdone it—someone at a supply depot wondered at the number of blankets the B.L.I. was demanding. Of course officially they weren't demanding any, as the quartermaster captain knew only too well when he heard about it. He, unfortunate man, was in almost as bad trouble as Robert, whom he had trusted. He was a singularly lax officer.

In the end Robert, the corporal, and the private, plus a driver and four civilians, were convicted. The judge spoke scathingly of their terrible crime, committed in time of grave national emergency. He wanted to make an example of them and he both said so and did so. They never proved Robert guilty of an active part, but everyone knew that he must have permitted, if not actually encouraged, the theft. The judge took great delight in talking of Robert's betrayal of the trust reposed in him by the army authorities.

Jocelyn heard the news with a heavy heart. Several Vernons must be rotating rapidly in their graves, Jocelyn reflected. Robert, a sergeant, convicted of the theft of army stores. It was incredible. He believed Sally implicitly when she said that Robert, foolish and deluded Robert, had taken nothing for himself. He had no need of anything.

He wrote to Sally several times but he found it difficult to sympathize in words. It was Jocelyn who told Anne Hilton, for Robert had not written to her for a very long time, and Sally and Anne did not correspond.

"What a terrible year it has been for you," Anne wrote. "First your mother killed and then Robert being sent to prison. It will be worse, because you are out there in Africa, out of touch with everyone. Will they never give you leave, Jocelyn? How I would like to see you again. It is nearly four years since we met, when Grandma and

Daddy and I came back from Paris in 1939. I was a fifteen-year-old brat then, quite insufferable. I can't understand why you wrote to me at all in the first place. If I remember correctly I was completely patronizing toward anyone who had not lived in Paris. What awful little beasts children are, aren't they? Would you like me to go to Mereford and visit Sally? I can, you know; I'm overdue for a holiday."

Jocelyn thought about that. There was no reason why she should or shouldn't go. Robert was her first cousin, so she had a right to visit his wife, and, of course, as far as Jocelyn was concerned, she could go to Mereford at any time. In the end he left it up to her. She did visit Sally, and wrote to say that it had been quite a successful occasion.

"She is very subdued and doesn't really understand what has happened. It will be a long time before she gets over this. However she isn't so much angry with Robert as astonished at his stupidity. She won't leave him, I'm sure of that. I wonder what I'd do if my husband went to jail? I can't imagine. She visits him once a month—that's all she's allowed, it seems. He appears to be quite well, but of course he hates prison. I can picture what sort of life it is in a prison, so I'm not surprised that he is in low spirits."

At the end of the year Jocelyn was promoted to major and sent back to England. He was to go to the 4th battalion, re-forming in Reading, as second-in-command. He forgot about Robert. From Southampton he sent a telegram to Anne announcing his arrival in England. Two days later he was given twenty-one-days' leave, which was long overdue. He telephoned her and then set off by train to Kemble.

She met him at the station, a tall young woman with uncommonly nice legs and a heartwarming smile. He saw she wore hardly any makeup, and was relieved. He did not care much for highly painted women. He kissed her cheek, but she laughed and kissed him on the mouth, and to his amazement he was mildly embarrassed.

"How well you look," she exclaimed. "You're so brown. Smart too—uniform suits you."

"Thank you for all the compliments. I won't tell you how you look. It would swell your head too much."

She gave a little curtsy and he followed her out to a muddy station wagon.

"It isn't mine," she said as they got in. "I borrowed it. How long can you stay?"

"A week?" he suggested tentatively.

"That would be lovely."

He was being put into Mary Hilton's cottage, now empty. He would eat his meals at Warneford Cottage, where Anne was living alone at present. Timothy was in Scotland, she said, doing something for the War Office.

"How was Mereford?" she asked as she drove the short distance to the cottage.

"All right. I only spent one night there with Sally, a flying visit."

"I'm flattered that I take precedence over Mereford," she chuckled. "Sally okay?"

"Yes. How grand it is to be back in England, to see real English countryside again after endless sand and blazing sun."

"What a pity you've come in winter."

"I don't mind. I like the winter."

"Don't you feel cold without a coat?"

"Not a bit of it. We're tough, we Vernons."

She pulled up outside a low cottage with a small garden in front, surrounded by a wooden fence and a hedge. It was quaint and tiny, but when he went inside he realized that it was warm and comfortable, and a cheerful fire burned in the grate. There was quite a large garden at the back.

"So this is where you live," he said, looking round.

"No," she laughed. "This is where you live. This is Grandma's cottage. I'm just down the road."

"This is nice. All for me, too."

"To sleep in. I hope you'll spend the rest of the time with me. I want to hear all about what has been happening. You look much better than your photographs."

More than four years of war had fined him down. At twenty-five he was a splendid-looking man. He gave her a quick smile and then dumped his luggage upstairs in the bedroom she had got ready, and together they completed the journey. Warneford Cottage was slightly larger, even more nicely furnished and decorated, and while he walked round the little sitting room looking at pictures, she made tea. She brought it in and put it down on a long, low walnut coffee table. She stood up and looked into his eyes and smiled.

"Home at last," she said, and he nodded.

Chapter 26

THEY sat together in the flickering firelight and his arm was round her waist. Her head rested on his shoulder. They had no idea what time it was.

"I wish this could go on forever," he murmured.

"So do I, but at least it can go on for a week," she laughed.

"Longer. I've got three weeks' leave. We can talk about my leave later. I don't think we need to say much to each other, do we?"

"No," she said. "I don't think so."

"I love you, Anne. I want to marry you."

"I know. I feel the same."

Their coming together had been instinctive, almost inevitable. They knew, without saying anything, that all day they had been thinking the same thoughts. After supper, when they had washed up, they took their coffee through to the sitting room. He took her in his arms and kissed her. It was the most natural thing in the world.

They sat silently for quite a long time. They needed no words. Just holding each other like this was sufficient. Lazily he stirred, bent, and kissed her lovely mouth.

"One must be practical," he murmured. "You're what, nineteen?"

"That's right."

"Then you need your father's permission, and he may think you're too young."

"Not Daddy. He isn't like that."

"I'm glad to hear it. How soon can we tell him?"

"I'll post a letter to him in the morning. It would be nicer not to announce the engagement until he's replied."

"Of course," Jocelyn smiled. "The thing is, when do we get married? This leave, next leave, next summer—I thought all girls wanted to be June brides?"

"The sooner the better, I'd say," she answered happily.

"I agree. This is mostly disembarkation leave. I've got accumulated leave to come. I expect I could get another two or three weeks in May or June, or we could just go ahead and get married now."

"I'd like to get married now. I could come to Mereford to live and you'd be able to get home occasionally, wouldn't you?"

"Yes," he agreed, but he was thinking of Sally. It would be harrowing for her to have to watch their happiness during her own misery.

"Let's do that then."

"We could see about a special license tomorrow, but we'll still have to have your father's consent."

"I'll write tonight before I go to sleep, don't worry. The letter will go off by the first post."

"That's settled then."

"I'll have to give up my job on the farm. They may make me take another job at Mereford . . . oh, of course, I could help on the small holding."

"What will your father do if you're not here?"

"He doesn't work here now and hasn't for months. I expect it will be all right. The studio is lying almost empty."

They spent an idyllic few days till a telegram arrived from Timothy. He did not believe in brevity.

OF COURSE GET MARRIED SOONEST POSSIBLE. I WILL
BE BACK AT WEEKEND WITH TWO HOSTAGES. LETTER
IN POST. LOVE TO YOU BOTH. TIMOTHY.

"What does he mean by hostages, I wonder?" Anne
asked, but they could think of nothing.

They borrowed the same station wagon from the farmer
she worked for and went to Cheltenham to buy an engagement ring, and Jocelyn wrote out notices and sent them to
the *Times* in London and to the local paper at home, the
Berkshire Herald. He wrote to his commanding officer,
and telephoned the news to Sally. On Friday evening
Timothy arrived.

"There you are," he said brightly. "So you're Jocelyn.
I'd forgotten what you look like. I've been hearing all
about you for a long time now. Well, is everything fixed?"

"We've got the license," Anne said triumphantly.

"Splendid. I'm glad. My letter did the trick did it?"

She nodded while he fumbled with his suitcase.

"Hostages," he said proudly, holding up two bottles of
whiskey. "All the way from the Highlands of Scotland."

"What were you doing there, sir?" Jocelyn asked.

"Don't you 'sir' me, please. The name is Timothy. It
was very hush-hush, a special training establishment. I've
been doing official drawings and things. All quite ridiculous but it keeps me busy and sometimes gives me delu-
sions that I'm helping the war effort."

He poured three drinks and they toasted each other.

"When's the wedding?" Timothy demanded.

"Whenever you like," Jocelyn answered.

"Monday morning then?"

"We need two witnesses, don't we?"

"Don't worry about that. Anne has lots of friends to
choose from. It's quite painless. Church weddings are different, of course. I went to one of those and I didn't like it
at all. I don't know what your plans are," he went on,

pouring more drinks. "I thought you could get married on Monday and then on Tuesday we could all go to your home, Jocelyn. You'll be anxious to see it again and I'd like to meet Robert's wife. I could stay for a night or two."

"Stay for as long as you please."

"No, I must get back and make arrangements to have someone keep an eye on the cottages while I'm away. I don't think I'll be going for a few weeks, but one never knows. It's a funny job, this one I've got. They send for me when they want me."

"Would you like to live with us at Mereford?" Jocelyn offered.

"Goodness no, I get on far better by myself. I won't pretend I shan't miss Anne. Obviously I shall, but I'd far rather be on my own than come and park myself with you. I can manage all right."

He was so full of infectious good humor that one could not help liking him. Next morning they managed to speak to the registrar on the telephone and he agreed to marry them on Monday morning at eleven. It was as simple as that.

They went to the registrar's office and about ten minutes later it was all over. The lack of ceremonial did not trouble them in the least. Wartime marriages of this sort were quite fashionable.

They traveled to Mereford the next day, and while Timothy talked to Sally, Jocelyn and Anne went up to what had been Edwina's bedroom, which would now be theirs. It was the main bedroom and had its own dressing room. Jocelyn took her in his arms as soon as they were inside the door, and kissed her.

"Welcome to Mereford, darling."

"I love you," she whispered.

He looked at her proudly. "Oh, Anne, it's all so right. Don't you feel that?"

"Yes," she agreed.

"We're going to be very happy. I know it."

"I hope so, darling." She did not voice the fear in her heart. Jocelyn felt invincible, but she would not know peace till the war was over.

Their time together at Mereford was less than they had hoped for, and Jocelyn was glad that they had not waited till May for another leave before getting married, for before the end of May all leave was stopped and soon the battalion moved to the south coast.

This was it. It was obvious when they saw how many troops were massing. On June 6 the 4th B.L.I. was part of the invasion force which landed on the beaches, on what went down in history as D day. Three days later the battalion was involved in fierce fighting at Caen, and Jocelyn won his second D.S.O. His letters to Anne were short and hurriedly written. She learned to live with fear now, and when his award was announced she felt no pride, only increased fear. He must be involved in heavy fighting.

The 4th battalion fought its way through Europe. In September they were in Holland and Jocelyn won his final decoration, his third Military Cross, in Antwerp. By now he was the most decorated man in the regiment, with two D.S.O.s, and three M.C.s. He was sent home at the end of the year, ostensibly to attend an investiture, but he had a suspicion that he would not see the battalion again. He had Christmas at Mereford and, to their surprise and delight, so did Robert. It was one year and four months since he had gone to prison, and he was due for release because he had earned full remission of sentence for good conduct.

Sally went to meet him and bring him home. Considerately Jocelyn changed out of uniform, although this was, strictly speaking, against regulations. It would not be exactly tactful to parade his rank and his medals in front of his less fortunate cousin.

The change in Robert was alarming. He was thin and

wasted looking. Jocelyn asked Sally about it as soon as he could get her alone.

"He's had tuberculosis. He'll be all right and it could have been a lot worse. They won't call him up, though. He's home for good."

"I'm glad."

"Jocelyn, he wants to move out of here."

"What? Why?"

"I think he wants privacy, to be on his own. He wants to move into the house in Hampstead. Would Anne mind if I left? Would she take over running the market garden and the chickens and all that?"

"No, no, of course she won't mind. It isn't that, but are you sure? Mereford has been your home for so many years and you've looked after everything for us ever since Mother and I went away."

"It will be a tremendous wrench leaving, and I love the house very much, but can't you understand how he feels, especially with you on leave? He likes you, Jocelyn, I know that, but your mere existence is a reproach to him just now. He sees himself as a failure, a disgrace. He needs peace—and love."

"Of course, Sally, how stupid of me. I'll explain to Anne. When will you go?"

"Soon. Anne knows all about running the small holding, so probably we'll leave tomorrow and stay at a hotel until the house is ready, then I'll come back and fetch the rest of our things."

"That's quick. I'm very sorry. You won't lose touch, will you?"

"Of course not, Jocelyn, but he must get away."

"Yes. You're sure he's all right now? His health?"

"He needs rest, good food, no worry. He'll be better soon."

On Friday December 22 they moved to London. It was so close to Christmas, but as Jocelyn explained to Anne, Christmas was the last thing Robert wanted to spend with them. Because Timothy had been sent out to India for a few months, from where he bombarded them with amusing black and white drawings of the Indian scene, they spent their first Christmas together, just the two of them. When it came to the point, they preferred it this way.

Jocelyn's news was good. He had already been told that after his leave he was to take over command of the 3rd B.L.I., at the depot. He would be gazetted lieutenant colonel at the beginning of January, before his leave was up. It was a real triumph for him, to command the battalion his father and grandfather had served in with such distinction. It was the highlight of his war.

He quieted Anne's fears.

"The war will soon be over now. I expect I'll go back to Europe, but don't worry about me. It will be one long victory parade."

"I get so frightened when you're away. I wish you didn't have to go."

"Take heart. It is positively against orders for lieutenant colonels to get themselves killed. If you disobey, they court-martial you."

"Idiot," she smiled.

His prophecy proved true, however. They went back to Europe shortly after Jocelyn assumed command, and on March 6 the 3rd Berkshire Light Infantry marched into Cologne and at their head was Lieutenant Colonel Jocelyn Vernon, D.S.O., M.C., the proudest officer in the British Army. The end was very near now. On April 30 Adolf Hitler and his mistress perished together, and on May 8 it was all over. The war against Japan still continued, but nobody was too worried about that. With the entire effort of America and Britain directed against it, Japan could not possibly last for long.

Jocelyn never went to the Far East. The 3rd battalion remained in Europe for a short period of four months after V.E. Day and returned to Britain in October. There was a points system for demobilization and Jocelyn had accumulated quite a healthy number of points, which meant a correspondingly low release group number. Early in 1946 he handed over the depleted battalion to a major and came home for good, hung up his greatcoat, and forgot the war. In two trips to Buckingham Palace he had collected five decorations, all of them what was known as "good" ones, well earned. He had risen from private to lieutenant colonel. He felt that the family tradition had been safeguarded. He had done his bit. He was only sorry that Robert, well-meaning but misguided Robert, had had such a ghastly war.

Life was not easy for Sally in Hampstead. Robert was doing nothing at all. The income from his capital supported them with some difficulty. He sat about the house, reading newspapers, listening nonstop to the radio, grumbling about life in England. There was a good deal to grumble about in those austere days, but Robert had less cause than most. It was Sally who had to queue for food, who had to try to manage on their income, who had to bear with his incessant mutterings. The fact was that he was sorry for himself. In the end she felt she could take no more of it.

"Don't you ever stop to think how lucky you are?" she asked him one day when he was being particularly difficult. "Don't you? Because you are lucky."

Her aggressiveness startled him. Sally was good-natured and long-suffering and he had come to expect that she would put up with anything from him.

"Lucky? If you'd been in jail, you wouldn't talk about being lucky. You've no idea what it's like."

"I haven't been in prison, no; and I am aware that it isn't a home from home. I'm also aware, without having taken part in a battle, that you might have been much worse off at Anzio or Arnhem. You could have been a fighting soldier, not a crooked clerk."

"Crooked clerk." The enormity of this unjust description—made deliberately although he did not realize it—staggered him. "I did nothing wrong," he said hotly.

"You condoned it. You allowed it to happen. Like the story of the Good Samaritan, you passed by on the other side and pretended it wasn't happening. Only in your case it resulted in a prison sentence. There you were safe, warm, fed, and looked after. That was your punishment, while good soldiers were sent into battle to be killed or maimed."

"How dare you talk to me like that?" he flared.

"It's time someone did, Robert. I'm not troubled by the fact that you went to prison. I don't hold it against you. You yourself aren't a thief. You're just an irresponsible fool, and I happen to love you. What does trouble me is the sight of you sitting in a chair all day, doing nothing, grumbling grumbling grumbling. Why don't you go out and do something? Why don't you work?"

"Who'd give me a job?"

"Then go and dig in the garden and grow things. I'm fed up with the sight of you, and more than fed up with the sound of you."

His jaw dropped. Self-pity is of course an insidious thing, and he had been indulging himself more and more. This attack was exactly what he needed, but he did not accept it with equanimity.

"If that's how you feel, perhaps I'd better go out."

"Yes, and take some garden tools with you."

"I'm going for a drink," he said grumpily.

The little clash, displaying as it did unaccustomed temper on Sally's part, did have some good effects. Robert stopped grumbling aloud, but he remained apathetic and Sally worried a good deal about him. He did not seem to be interested in anything, and although he obediently did do quite a lot of work in the garden, he did only what he was told.

Sally wondered how long it was going to take him to recover from his prison sentence, and Robert feared he was going to go through life like some sort of zombie, a perpetual burden to her.

The transition from war to peace was not difficult for Jocelyn. His family business was waiting, his house was waiting, and his wife was only too anxious for them to begin to make their life together. Jocelyn threw himself into his work. Staff was coming back from the war, there was reorganization to be planned, and the future of Henry Vernon, Son and Company to think about. It kept him happy without making him too preoccupied. He looked forward to every day, but he was always thankful to come home in the early evening to be with his wife.

She began to teach him a little about art, and they got into the habit of going to London quite frequently to the galleries and to exhibitions. They also went together to concerts. Anne was astonished to discover that her husband had never been to a concert. He enjoyed classical music—in fact he enjoyed almost any music—but he had always listened to it on the radio or on records. She soon put that right.

They visited Robert and Sally once only, but it was not a relaxed or happy evening. Robert was moody, declined an invitation to Mereford, and rather pointedly did not invite them to come to Hampstead again. His main topic of conversation was money. He had spent rather a lot decorating and furnishing the Hampstead house and talked as though he were a pauper. Jocelyn contrived to get Sally alone in her kitchen and found out that Robert did not work at anything, and that the income from his remaining money was about five hundred a year. They were living a bit above that, and he was drawing a little on his capital.

She told Jocelyn not to worry, and there was no time to discuss the situation properly.

Jocelyn had his own business worries, although on a much grander scale. The days of low taxation and high profits from department stores were over. Jocelyn owned ninety percent of the shareholding. Lord Thatcham still owned ten percent, and indeed it had been a splendid investment when one considered how many times over the Paveleys had received back the five thousand pounds they had lent originally. Jocelyn settled forty percent of the shares on Anne at once and made her a director. It was not, he explained, that he expected her to work for a living, but as his wife she had certain rights, absolute rights to a stake in the company which supported them. As a director she could attend meetings and ask questions.

Anne was highly amused and wrote to tell her father that she was now a baptized follower of Mammon.

The company had always accumulated large reserves, and Jocelyn began to spend these now on modernizing the store from top to bottom. In 1946 he spent a month in America and another in Canada and came back full of ideas. Anne went with him and contributed her own suggestions. They paid themselves directors' fees of a thousand pounds a year each, and from the joint profits they received, on average, another four or five thousand a year. Taxes played havoc with what should have been a handsome income. Jocelyn could have done many things, of course. He could have doubled their salaries, increased dividends, bought a car on the company and used it privately—but he did none of them. He had always been taught by his father to plow back as much as possible. His rule was to put money in reserve every year and not take it all out in profits. Even so, a total of six or seven thousand pounds in 1946 was a very good income.

Anne turned her attention to Mereford, encouraged by Jocelyn. One by one the rooms were redecorated, new color schemes chosen, oil-fired central heating was installed, new carpets were bought, and the place underwent a considerable change. It cost a lot of money, and it took time because things were in short supply. Jocelyn applied the same principles to his private money as he did to the business. Something had to be put in reserve every year. Mereford would make demands on them in years to come and they had to have the capital accumulating. Of course all during the war money had been building up at a very gratifying rate and he had quite a considerable private fortune now. Like his grandfather, Henry, who had started it all, he was never quite certain that he had enough. "A little more" might easily have been his family motto.

By August of 1946 Anne's suspicions were confirmed. A baby was on the way. This pleased them so much that they promptly went off for a holiday to Mawnan in Cornwall, and while they were there they bought a cottage. Mawnan was on the estuary of the Helford River, near a promontory gloriously named Rosemullion Head. It was not too far from Falmouth for shopping. There was rather a tenuous Cornish tradition in the family—his father and grandfather had both liked the county—but visits had been few. Now Jocelyn had his own cottage there and this pleased him enormously. His experiences in North Africa and in Europe had taught him how much he loved England, and by buying a little house on the Cornish coast, he felt he was increasing his stake in the country.

England, after all, was what it was all about. His great-great-grandfather had been a lord mayor of London. What had he, his father, and his grandfather fought for, if not for England?

"Next Christmas there'll be three of us," he said to Anne that Christmas of 1946. "I'm glad about that."

"And I'm glad you're glad," she replied with a little laugh.

"What shall we call him?"

"I don't know. I have no special preferences."

"I've always liked David," he ventured.

"It's nice. Is it a family name?"

"Not so far as I know, not a single David in the family. Does it matter?"

"No." She shook her head. "If you like David, David it will be."

"If it's a girl, we'll call her Anne, like you."

"No."

"Why not?" he demanded. "It's my most favorite name."

She laughed. "You are funny sometimes. What does 'most favorite' mean?"

"What it says. I'm sure it's good English. Anyway you understand it all right."

"Not Anne, please. Something nicer."

"Nothing is nicer," he said stubbornly.

"I liked your mother's name."

"I disagree. Her mother's wasn't too bad, Alexandra, but I don't like Edwina."

"Well, we'll see," she said placidly.

They had a fall of snow at Christmas, and carol singers came to the door. The scene was almost Dickensian, Jocelyn thought as they stood in the doorway, their arms linked, listening to the singers and the lights reflecting on the snow. Inside everything was warm and bright.

On the twenty-first of February Anne gave birth to their son David. Timothy had come to Mereford to celebrate the event, and afterward he was going abroad. He wanted to paint something new and was going to Barbados for a few months. He was delighted when it was all over and he and Jocelyn were celebrating with champagne.

"I'm a grandfather. I don't feel like one."

"You don't look much like one," Jocelyn said.

"I'm only just forty-five, that's why. Of course I don't look like one."

"Well, here's to you, Grandpop."

"Don't you grandpop me, young Jocelyn. More champagne?"

He stayed at Mereford for three weeks and then went off, and Jocelyn and Anne became absorbed in their son.

In 1948 bread rationing ended. This momentous event, which occurred on July 29, was accompanied by a change in Robert's fortunes. His mother died. Nobody had heard anything whatever about Lucy Waterton for years, not since she had left John Vernon and gone off to join her band leader. They had not married and it seemed that she had not been content with him. Some years after John's death in 1935, which apparently she had heard about, she had married a well-to-do factory owner. Her second husband had been prosperous when she met him and the war had made him rich. His factory turned out contract work for the Ministry of Supply, and when he died in 1946 he left his widow a fortune. She died in 1948, and even with two bites out of the cherry by an avid Treasury anxious to collect duties, Robert became a wealthy man.

He first heard about it when a letter from his mother's solicitors in Birmingham arrived for him, addressed care of Mereford, for she had lost contact with him completely. Jocelyn had forwarded the letter. Sally saw Robert's face as he read it and asked anxiously, "Is something wrong, darling?"

"My mother's dead. Apparently she's been living in Birmingham. I haven't heard of her for years. The solicitors have asked me to go to see them. I'd better telephone to let them know I've received the letter." He paused for a minute and then said, "I wonder what she was doing in Birmingham? I thought she was out of the country."

Robert telephoned, made an appointment, and went to see them. There he visited his mother's house in Edgbaston, collected several things he wanted to keep, and put the rest up for auction with the house. It was then that he learned he would probably receive a little over a hundred thousand pounds after payment of all duties and debts. The amount took his breath away.

He returned to Hampstead and told Sally.

"I can hardly remember her," he said wonderingly, "and she's made us rich."

"Where did she get all the money?"

He told her about his mother's second husband, or as much as he had learned in Birmingham.

"What will you do with it all?" Sally asked.

"I don't know. With what I've got, it makes us really very independent. You must do all you want to this house, make it exactly as you would like it. As for me, I don't know."

She could see a new light in his eye. He even seemed to stand straighter.

"Perhaps I can start some sort of business of my own. My prison sentence is a handicap when it comes to job hunting, but it won't stop me hiring myself." He laughed and she realized how rare laughter had been recently.

"I'll find something to do, and I'd better see about investments. I must go into the City tomorrow. Dash it, I haven't got a decent suit. Have we any clothing coupons?"

"Quite a lot."

"Enough for a suit?"

"A suit and a coat if you want them."

"I'd better see about them tomorrow while I'm in town. You understand we're no longer short of money? Better get yourself whatever you need, if you have the coupons for it."

She kissed him. "All I need is to see you snap out of your misery."

"Yes, well I suppose I have been a bit low," he said, not really paying attention. "I wonder whom to see. My grandfather dealt with Everard's. Perhaps I'll try them. I ought to take a fresh look at this whole matter of investment. I'll telephone them."

She smiled as he marched back to the telephone. This was a welcome change.

A few weeks later she went to Mereford, and Jocelyn and Anne got the whole story from her. She arrived in a new Citroen, and looked very smart and fresh. She was full of her news. Robert had not been able to accompany her, because he was busy. He was starting up a small estate agency. With the growing housing shortage, it seemed there was a good future in the property market. Sally was delighted now that he had something to absorb his attention.

Jocelyn and Anne shared Sally's relief that the hard times were over, although as Jocelyn told Anne after Sally had gone, the nearest they had got to poverty was a very nice house in Hampstead and ten pounds a week. There were worse fates.

In 1949, with no sign of a brother or sister in the offing for young David, they went to America again, taking David along with them. They stayed for six weeks in the spring and thoroughly enjoyed themselves. Anne was disappointed that she had not yet gotten pregnant again and she was a trifle envious of Sally who was awaiting the birth of her first child.

Sally's pregnancy had completed Robert's rehabilitation. It seemed it was all that was needed to transform him, and he fussed over Sally like an old hen, much to her amusement. He kept buying her expensive things which were not rationed, such as bottles of anchovies, and pickled walnuts which she particularly liked, two paintings which she had admired, and finally a gold bracelet which he produced one evening about ten days before she went into the expensive London nursing home where she was to have her baby.

"What's this for, darling?" she asked.

"For you. To show you I love you."

"You do know that it's only a baby I'm having, don't you?" she asked, giggling. "People are always doing it. They don't get gold bracelets."

"My wife does."

"You're sweet. You really are. If you keep this up, I shall insist on having a baby a year."

"I'm not sure I could go through it all again. I mean," he said hastily, "I'm pleased of course, but it's a bit of a strain. Are you feeling all right?"

"I always feel all right," she laughed. "You know that."

"Oh, I got some pure lemon juice. It's in the kitchen."

"What for?" asked Sally who disliked lemon juice.

"I read in one of the Sunday papers that it's good for you—when you're pregnant, you know."

"Darling, if you're going to believe all you read in the newspapers, we'll have to have an extra house to put everything in. Besides I don't like lemon juice."

"I think you ought to have it. Just a little. You could drink tea afterward to take the taste away."

"All right," she said. "To please you, I'll have some at night. Please don't buy anything more."

"You know," he said, "it's funny, but when I'm walking in the street and I see all those people scurrying about, I have this tremendous urge to stop them and tell them I'm going to be a father. I have to fight it. I'd be locked up if I did it."

"Serve you right too. They're probably all married and have children of their own."

He kissed her. "I know, but I can't help it. I shall be glad when it's all over. I'm getting nervous."

"You silly man."

He sat and hugged her. How could he explain his fears to her? She seemed to think having babies was natural. Deep down he was petrified.

She went into the nursing home on the evening of May 27, and the next day, the twenty-eighth, their son was born. When Robert was told that mother and child were both not merely well, but *very* well, he practically fainted with relief. He haunted the nursing home till Sally and the baby were allowed home, and there he continued to fuss over her, not even letting her make a cup of tea if he was around.

By the time Jocelyn and Anne returned from the United States, some ten days after Sally came out of the nursing home, he had calmed down a little. They had written to Jocelyn and Anne telling them the news, and of course they drove to Hampstead almost immediately on their return. The baby was to be called Roger, and while the two women fussed over him, Jocelyn and Robert had a couple of drinks to celebrate the great occasion.

It was when they were driving back to Mereford that Anne asked Jocelyn:

"Why are they calling him Roger, do you think? I was going to ask Sally and then, for some stupid reason, I felt I didn't want to pry. Silly, isn't it? Anyway, Roger and Robert is very confusing. Was that Sally's father's name?"

"Roger is the old devil who started it all," he chuckled. "You really must read that genealogy in my bottom drawer, along with the medals, the patent of arms, and other dubious claims to fame. Roger Vernon was a merchant born in 1782. He had two children, George and Hester. Sir George became lord mayor of London, and Hester died unmarried. Sir George was the father of Sir Godfrey, and he was Captain Henry's father, then came my father and then me. How funny of Robert to remember. I didn't think he even knew about Roger. I got the family tree from my father, who got it from Sir Godfrey."

"It's an odd thing," Anne said pensively, "there's been only one girl in the family—Hester. There were no others, were there?"

"No. In fact it's pretty much a family of only sons. Sir George had a son and daughter, and Sir Godfrey had two sons, but everybody else has had only one son. It's a miracle the family has survived, especially when you think of all the wars we've been through."

Anne bit her lip.

"I wish we could have more children," she said rather sadly.

"Dear Anne." He put an arm round her, and with his free hand tilted her chin and kissed her very tenderly. "We try. That's all we can do. Thank God we've got each other, the three of us. You mustn't take it to heart."

"Sometimes I feel I've failed you."

"What utter nonsense, my darling. Do you really think that the 'family' matters, in the abstract sense? What matters is ourselves, that we are happy, that we live fulfilled and useful lives, that we go on loving each other. That's what matters. There's no particular merit in perpetuating the descendants of one Roger Vernon born in 1782, merchant in London. None at all."

"You don't believe in links with the past?" she asked curiously.

"Very much. You know, when I went to those two investitures to pick up my gongs, I had an uncanny feeling that a lot of Vernons were peering down at me from the clouds. Mind you, they were pretty short, sharp, and sweet ceremonies, like shelling peas. The King must have got very fed up with it all. Anyway, what I'm saying is that one needs to maintain a sense of proportion. We, us, the present, are what matters—the rest may or may not be interesting, but it's hardly crucial."

"I still wish we had more children," she said stubbornly, returning to her original point.

"Let's look after the one we've got," he answered, kissing her again. "That's the big job now."

Chapter 27

IN August 1951 Sally and Robert changed the pattern of events. Sally gave birth to a girl. Robert telephoned Mereford with the news.

"Congratulations," said Jocelyn who took the call. "What are you going to call her?"

"Valerie."

"Valerie Vernon. It sounds well."

"Why don't you and Anne come to see us? It's been a long time."

"I know. Since David was born we haven't been coming up to London as often as we used to."

"Why not come this weekend and stay for a couple of nights?"

"We could manage that. On Friday then?"

"We'll expect you."

When Jocelyn told Anne, he said, "You know, just talking to him on the telephone you notice the difference in him these days. I don't know what it was, whether it was the money his mother left him, or Roger's birth, or perhaps both, but he's changed enormously."

"I think he took a long time to grow up, that's all," Anne answered.

"How do you mean?"

"From what you've told me and from what Sally has said plus what I've seen myself, I'd say he was very immature for a long time. He just didn't grow up. He couldn't understand why he was put in prison. It was the final injustice of the grown-ups toward him."

"Jailed for being Peter Pan?" Jocelyn joked.

"I suspect a lot of people are."

"You may be right," he said thoughtfully. She still retained this ability to say things that made him think. "I never considered it in those terms. I just called him irresponsible."

"It was the same thing in his case."

"It's gone now anyway, whatever it was." Jocelyn laughed. "Now that they've got *two* children he is quite blasé."

Anne's face clouded and Jocelyn could have bit his tongue. He changed the subject as quickly as he could. Not for the world did he want to hurt Anne's feelings. On Friday they set off with four-year-old David in the back of the car, and drove to Hampstead.

Robert seemed much more relaxed than he had been in recent years, as though he had finally learned to live with his own past. He helped Jocelyn with the two suitcases and all the loose odds and ends. Sally was waiting in the sitting room, and she and Anne went upstairs to see the baby who was asleep after her six o'clock feeding.

"You're looking well," Jocelyn said to his cousin, and indeed it was hard to believe that Robert had been unfit for military service only a few years ago. "Feeling all right?"

"Yes, and the doctors say the TB has gone. I'm as sound as a bell."

"You and Sally have broken the record at last."

"How do you mean?"

"Well it may never have occurred to you, but we haven't had any girls in this family for a long time."

"Neither have we, come to think of it. The grandparents didn't have a sister?"

"No. The last female Vernon was old Sir Godfrey's Aunt Hester, and she was born in 1812, the year of Napoleon's retreat from Moscow. That's a long time ago."

"My God, yes. Are you sure of your facts?"

"Quite sure. Sir Godfrey left my father the family tree and I've got it now. I keep it up to date. It isn't a very brilliant one, I'm afraid, but what am I to do with it? I can't very well throw it in the dustbin."

"No. I'd like a copy of it sometime."

"Right-oh. What do you think of this Korean business?" Jocelyn asked, changing the subject.

They talked earnestly about the Korean War which seemed now to have settled down to becoming a long-drawn-out affair. It was incredible that there should be a war again, so soon after the last one, even more incredible that a bunch of peasants in a tinpot country neither of them had ever heard of should be holding the U.S. Army at bay, even if they did have some help from the Chinese.

Then Sally and Anne came down and joined them, and Robert poured sherry and handed round the glasses. He had a prosperous look now, and was putting on a little weight. He told Jocelyn that business was good despite restrictions and a general shortage of money. Britain was going through a period of postwar austerity. Although clothes rationing had ended in 1950, there was still a shortage of many things in the shops, sweets were rationed, and it was compulsory to carry identity cards. There hadn't been a clean break with wartime conditions, as many people had expected. Jocelyn and Anne really enjoyed their annual buying trips to America, and Anne had been disappointed to miss two when David was a toddler.

That weekend saw the end of the slight estrangement between the two families. It had not been a serious one, but it had been there and they had all known it. The change in Robert was quite startling. He was much more talkative and much happier than they had seen him for years.

It was during that weekend, too, that Robert gave his daughter her nickname of Vivvy. Her initials were V.V. Sally was indignant, but nevertheless Vivvy stuck, and before long Sally was using it herself.

The two families settled down to what they had always wanted, quiet, uneventful lives, and there was much visiting back and forth between Mereford and the lovely house in Hampstead.

During the years of David's childhood a strong bond grew between him and his father. He was a remarkably uncomplicated child, mischievous, but not difficult. He had a pleasant disposition and never gave either of his parents any real cause for worry. He was in fact a very ordinary boy, and Jocelyn was content that it should be so.

David occupied a very special position in Jocelyn's eyes, for as matters now stood David would one day inherit the family business. Jocelyn had always regarded the company as something which he held strictly in trust for those who would follow him, his descendants. From an early age David was accustomed to being taken to his father's office, and he was also familiar with the store and most of the people who worked there.

Jocelyn saw himself in his son. Anne did not, but she was too wise to say anything at that stage. Anne noticed that David, although he responded to all his father's suggestions, did not show any spontaneous interest in the business. Knowing Jocelyn as she did, she was afraid he would see David as he wanted to see him, not as the boy really was, and she feared that one day he would be bitterly disappointed.

Meantime Jocelyn showed David how to fish, bought him his first roller skates, his first two-wheel bicycle, taught him how to row, and reveled in his son's boyhood. When David was ready for school of course none but Mortimer Hall was considered. Jocelyn's old school was now a minor public school, rather a good one and much larger than it had been in Jocelyn's day. It had almost two hundred boys in 1959 when David entered the school.

It was fairly obvious by now that they weren't going to have any more children and gradually Anne came to accept the fact. It seemed such a pity to her that they, who had plenty of money and a large house, together with a real wish to have a large family, should only have one child while other people bred like rabbits and lived in consequent poverty.

When Jocelyn tentatively suggested adoption, Anne was flatly against it. She would never be able to treat an adopted child in exactly the same way as her own child, and she knew and admitted it. That being so, it was better to drop the subject. Rather relieved, Jocelyn agreed.

Jocelyn was going through a period of considering the company much more critically than before. He was over forty and David was thirteen, and in a few years David would be coming into the office. He had to consider what he was going to hand on to his son. It was no use waiting till he was sixty-five and then thinking of all the things he might have done earlier. The time to think was now.

In 1960 he opened his first branch, a big department store in Newbury, not too far from Reading. There was enough trade to support both establishments. The new store had a large grocery and provisions department on the ground floor which was run on the latest American supermarket lines. Jocelyn's aim was still to cater for all tastes except the poorest—he would allow nothing shoddy to be sold from his premises. His main market was the working middle class, but Jocelyn never ignored the people with lots of money, and he catered to the ones with expensive, even luxurious tastes. The new store tied up all his capital and put the firm into debt, but it was sound enough. They were bound to make money.

It was at Christmas, 1960, that David, now approaching fourteen, dropped a minor bombshell. He had been with Jocelyn visiting both stores and doing some Christmas shopping while he was at it, because, like all the Vernons of Mereford, David did not believe in spending his money outside the family business. Jocelyn was driving home from Newbury, David in the front seat beside him.

"Well, how do you think the stores are coming on?" Jocelyn asked.

"They're super," young David assured him. "I do like the new one."

"It's a more modern building. I wonder how many stores we'll own by the time you're managing director."

There was a pause and then David said in a small voice, "I don't want to be managing director."

"You mean you'd rather be chairman?" Jocelyn laughed. "You'll have to start at the bottom as I did, and as my father did."

"No, I didn't mean that. I want to fly airplanes."

"What of it? You want a pilot's license?"

"I do want a pilot's license," David said, brightening. "I want to start taking lessons when I'm sixteen. Of course I'll be too young for a license, but I want to learn then and study for all the exams, then when I'm old enough I'll get my license. Besides, it will be much better if I can actually fly when I go to Cranwell."

Jocelyn's hands gripped the steering wheel of the Jaguar and his knuckles whitened.

"Cranwell, eh?" he asked, controlling his voice.

"Yes, Father. I want to join the Air Force, as a pilot."

"They may not take you."

"I'll work hard." Indeed he was considered bright at school, despite his dislike of it. "I think they'll take me."

"I see. I'd expected you to do what I did, come into the firm."

"I don't want to," David said in a subdued voice.

"No? Well that's different, isn't it?" Jocelyn made himself sound cheerful. After all, he thought, it was a craze.

"You're a good sport. I thought you'd be furious," David chuckled. He was a self-composed young man who treated his father as an equal.

"Did you? That's not flattering."

"I didn't mean it that way. After all, great-grandfather started the stores, didn't he? I thought you might be set on my coming into the office."

"I was a bit, but you must please yourself."

"I wouldn't sell the business or anything," David promised magnanimously. "I expect we could pay somebody to look after it, couldn't we?"

"We can talk about that later. Ah, home at last."

The big gray Jaguar turned into the drive. They saw Anne's little runabout parked in front of the house, and she was standing beside it with parcels in her arms. Jocelyn brightened at the sight of her, so slim and erect, smiling a welcome as they pulled up behind her.

"Hullo, you two." Her cheeks were flushed and her eyes were bright. "Been shopping too? I didn't see you at the store."

"We went on to Newbury," Jocelyn explained as they got out.

"Mummy, isn't it super? Father says I can take flying lessons so that I'll be able to fly before I join the Air Force."

He ran on ahead of them, and Anne turned to Jocelyn, her look inquiring. He shrugged and gave a rueful smile.

"What can you do?" he asked as they fell into step beside each other and walked toward the columned portico. "Who can compete with a jet plane nowadays? My grandfather, bless his old heart, started off with a single little grocer's shop, and now we have two big, prosperous department stores—and we lose out to an aluminium gadget that can break the sound barrier. There ought to be a law against it."

She waited till they were indoors and then gave him a quick kiss.

"Don't take it too much to heart, darling. It will all work out for the best."

"I suppose so. Bless you for trying to comfort me."

His feeling that the sane old world of prewar had gone forever was reinforced after Christmas, which the three of them spent together quietly. On December 31 the farthing ceased to be legal tender. Jocelyn could remember very clearly going into a shop with a penny, spending a farthing and getting three farthings change. That was a long time ago, in the late twenties when he was still a child, but he could remember it and he had a sudden longing for the old days. Things happened far too quickly now. People even talked about flying to the moon. Sadly it occurred to him that perhaps department stores were really rather old-fashioned.

A lot of their links with the past were disappearing about this time. Timothy had decided that he liked warm climates and painted better in the sunshine. He was still moderately successful, certainly able to support himself comfortably by his work. He would never be a bright star in the artistic firmament, but making a living from painting was more than most people could boast. He had bought a small house in the Bahamas, partly because there were no taxes and partly because it enabled him to visit the United States easily. He had discovered and fallen in love with Vermont and spent part of each year there, painting.

Old Lord Thatcham was dead and Walter Paveley had succeeded to the earldom. He too no longer lived in England but in Switzerland. Only the dowager countess of Thatcham lived at Pleasaunce now, and she was old and infirm and did not receive visitors.

Jocelyn and Anne had new friends of their own age, usually business people Jocelyn had met in Reading. For the most part, however, they liked to sit at home in the evenings listening to classical music on their new stereophonic sound equipment, or to go walking. In summer they drove deep into the countryside and walked for miles. They were a very close pair, and neither felt the need of outside distractions.

In September 1961 David received a surprise. Robert had consulted Jocelyn about Mortimer Hall and as a result had entered Roger. Jocelyn however had said nothing to David. He liked to spring surprises on the child, and Anne humored his whim.

It was their custom to drive David to Mortimer Hall at the beginning of the term and then go on for tea to a little country tearoom about four miles away. As usual at the school there were scores of cars parked in the big tree-lined courtyard, and boys and parents were milling about. Suddenly David caught sight of a familiar figure and his jaw dropped. He tugged at his father's arm.

"I say, look who's here," he said in a disbelieving tone.

Jocelyn glanced to where Sally and Vivvy were standing beside the car watching, while Robert and Roger struggled with a school trunk instead of waiting for one of the elderly school porters to come and unload it. Jocelyn grinned and David caught him at it.

"You knew!" he accused.

"I thought it would be a nice surprise."

"Some surprise," David snorted.

"You don't sound pleased."

"Well, he's only a newt." Newt was the Mortimer name for a new boy, and it was invariably spoken with the deepest scorn.

"Nevertheless you can come and say hullo to him."

"You'll be able to keep an eye on him, won't you?" Anne asked brightly, and with quite natural lack of understanding.

David swallowed and made a face at his mother's back. Really. How could his mother be so incredibly stupid? He wouldn't even *see* his cousin. One didn't associate with newts; they were unspeakable.

Meantime there were joyful sounds of reunion.

"Hullo, everybody," Jocelyn said gaily. "Hullo, young Vivvy. Isn't she looking lovely, Anne?"

"Come and say hullo to Vivvy, David," Anne said firmly.

David, who was glaring at his cousin, not out of any dislike for him but because he was a newt, looked round. He was confronted by a ten-year-old who was almost as tall as himself, a very composed young lady indeed, with long brown hair and an amused smile on her patrician face.

"Oh . . . er . . . hullo," he mumbled.

"Hullo, David. What have you got in your bag?"

"Rugger things," David answered, forgetting to be superior. He was playing rugby football for the junior fifteen this year, and was secretly proud of the fact.

"Why don't you take Roger along and show him where to go and what to do?" Anne suggested to her son.

"Yes," Robert said, secretly relieved. "We'll say goodbye now, old man. You go with David."

He wanted to get the good-byes over. Dutifully Roger shook his father's hand and allowed his mother to kiss him, but broke away quickly in case anyone was watching.

" 'Bye, Vivvy," he said to his sister, avoiding her eye. " 'Bye, Uncle Jocelyn and Aunt Anne."

He picked up a small suitcase of overnight things, for his trunk wouldn't be properly unpacked till next morning, and looked at David hopefully.

"Come along then," David said. " 'Bye, everybody." He gave Vivvy a thoughtful look and stomped off, followed by Roger. When they reached the master standing by the main entrance, they stopped.

"Hullo, sir," David greeted him easily.

"Ah, David Vernon. Welcome back, Vernon."

"I've got a newt sir. He's my cousin Roger."

"Another Vernon?"

"Yes, sir."

"Then we must find a guide for him."

David was relieved. He was afraid that because Roger was his cousin the system might break down. Second-year boys provided guides who looked after the new boys. David was now third year. He had done his duty as a guide a year ago, just as he had done his year as a newt. He did not wish to associate with either class again.

The master beckoned to an unsuspecting boy whose mouth drooped but who approached.

"Littleworth, you're a guide this year, aren't you?"

"Yes, Mr. Somerville."

"Then you can take charge of this newt. His name is, er, Roger Vernon. He's Vernon's cousin."

David colored. That had been unnecessary. It was wrong to associate him with the newt. Littleworth, however, retained his lugubrious expression.

"All right, sir," and, turning to Roger, "bring your case and I'll take you to your dorm."

Roger looked hopefully toward his cousin, but David turned away. With a shrug, Roger followed his guide. David saw some friends.

"G'bye, sir," he said to the master, and rushed off.

Meantime Jocelyn was inviting Robert and Sally to tea. "There's a delightful little place about four miles away. It's called the Peter Pan which sounds absolutely awful and off-putting, but it's really extremely nice. We always go there when we've dropped David at school. Not many other parents do because it's not on a main road. If you'd like to follow me, I'll lead the way."

"It seems so funny going away and leaving him," Sally said anxiously.

"It's all right," Anne promised with a reassuring smile. "You soon get used to it."

They drove to the tearoom, a quaint little place which served excellent meals as well as morning coffee and afternoon tea. Jocelyn and Anne were known at the Peter Pan and greeted with smiles. They all settled round a large table in a corner, near a lovely diamond-paned window, and ordered tea, hot buttered toast, scones, and cakes.

"Everything's fresh," Anne told Sally. "We make pigs of ourselves here. We come quite often in summer and have had dinner here twice. It's very nice. Now what's the news? Where are you sending Vivvy?"

"She still goes to school in Hampstead," Sally replied. "Next year she's going to Cheltenham. They say the academic record is good."

"Are you looking forward to that, Vivvy?" Anne asked.

"Yes, Aunt Anne."

"I never went to boarding school," Anne said.

"Neither did Mummy," Vivvy replied coolly, "but Daddy and Uncle Jocelyn both went to Mortimer, didn't they? Just like Roger and David?"

"That's right."

"I'd rather go to Cheltenham," Vivvy continued. "I'm glad there are no boys there."

Jocelyn and Anne exchanged amused looks.

"You'll be all alone there, darling," Sally reminded her. "Roger has David at Mortimer."

"Yes, I expect they'll be great friends, but I'd rather meet new people," Vivvy countered.

Jocelyn and Robert exchanged knowing looks. They had been through this particular mill together. It would be nice if Roger and David did become great friends, but it wouldn't be for the next year or two. The age gap that separated them was far too great.

Chapter 28

DAVID's determination to join the Royal Air Force did not waver. What was more, within three years he had infected Roger with it. Robert and Sally were at Mereford for a weekend in June when Robert mentioned it to Jocelyn.

"It's extraordinary, but Roger is mad keen on the Air Force. He brings it up in almost every letter. He's only just fifteen, of course, so he may get over it."

"Do you want him to go into it?" Jocelyn asked.

"I don't know. I'd rather hoped he'd manage to get to Oxford or Cambridge and do something really worthwhile with his life."

"What's worthwhile?" Jocelyn wondered. "Didn't Roger tell you where he got this R.A.F. craze from?"

"No."

"How odd. It's almost certainly David. They're quite friendly nowadays."

"Yes, that's surprising. Usually cousins at school are like brothers and rarely speak to each other. So it's David behind this flying thing, is it?"

"Yes. David's having flying lessons this summer, and he's applying for Cranwell next year."

"I see. I had no idea."

"Well, I've never talked about it much. At one time I rather hoped he'd forget it."

"Of course," Robert said sympathetically. "You had plans for him in the firm, didn't you?"

"I did. It makes the whole thing seem rather futile now. It's always been a family affair. Do you know, I'm beginning to lose interest."

"You shouldn't do that."

"I know, but it's true just the same. What a headache children are. How's Vivvy?"

"She's fine. She likes it at Cheltenham."

"Good school?"

"It seems to be. It's got a good enough reputation."

"I know. It's one of the few girls' schools I've ever heard of," Jocelyn laughed. "That, Roedean, and Benenden."

"She's been at college almost two years now. Time passes."

"It does. I'm branching out, you know—another big store."

"Really, where?"

"In Oxford. It should be ready by Christmas and open early in the New Year, but what's the point of it all?"

"Doesn't it give you any satisfaction?"

"A little, but it's not the same when there's nobody coming up behind you. I'm moody today. A drink is called for."

His moodiness lasted, although it was an eventful summer in its own way. They took David along to the flying school and enrolled him there, and before long they were beginning to feel involved in his progress. He turned out to have a natural aptitude for flying and his instructor was very pleased with him.

He spoke to them one day, while David was changing out of his flying suit.

"He'll do well in the R.A.F. I wish I had more pupils like him. It's a pleasure instructing him. Does anyone in the family fly?"

Jocelyn shook his head. "Nobody."

"Did you and Mrs. Vernon never think of it?"

"What, flying? At our age?"

"Speak for yourself, darling," Anne laughed. "I'm not that old. Still, my husband's right, you know. Isn't it something you have to do when you're young?"

"Not at all."

"I'm not terribly interested," Jocelyn said slowly.

"What about gliding? That's real fun. It's my hobby."

They laughed at that. He flew for a living and glided for a hobby. They discussed it for a time and in the end they agreed that all three of them would pay a visit to the nearest gliding school and have a trip in a glider. To their delight they loved it, and both of them joined the gliding club. David followed suit a fortnight later. All summer they flew—David had his regular lessons in power aircraft and all three of them went gliding. What particularly pleased Jocelyn and Anne was that it was something they could do together. When they both went solo, Jocelyn promptly bought a twin seat glider.

Talk all that summer was about flying. In their forties, Jocelyn and Anne had found a new and passionate interest in life and one which they were able to share with David. Roger was green with envy when he heard all about it at the beginning of term. Robert and Sally were amused but thoughtful as the four of them sat having tea together at the Peter Pan.

"We may as well say good-bye to dreams of Oxford," Robert remarked wryly. "When Roger hears all this from David, that will clinch the matter. Nothing on earth will keep him out of the R.A.F. now."

That was true, but what really settled it was when David

entered Cranwell in 1965. He wrote to his cousin at school, and Roger's mind was now finally made up. He was committed to following in David's footsteps.

Immediately after Christmas, David went to Hampstead for a few days. Roger monopolized him for the first day of his stay, asking endless questions about Cranwell and about flying. School had suddenly become incredibly child-ish and stupid, and he wished with all his heart that his schooldays were over. Vivvy was neglected by them both and not very pleased.

She expected to be neglected by her brother, whom she treated with friendly contempt, he being a mere schoolboy. She did not expect to be neglected by David. However her chance came. She caught David alone on the second eve-ning, about half an hour before tea. Roger, much to his disgust, had piano lessons during school holidays and he was out of the house.

"I think you're mean," Vivvy said unblushing.

"I am? Why?" David asked, taken aback.

"You've talked to Roger for a whole day now, without stopping. It's very rude of you. I might as well not be here."

"I didn't think you'd be interested. We were only talking about the R.A.F."

"What's it really like to fly?" she asked.

"I don't know how to explain. It isn't like anything else. I love it."

"Does anyone get killed?"

"No. You have to do something absolutely stupid to get killed."

"Don't the wings ever fall off, or anything?"

He laughed. "No they don't."

"I'd like to fly. Why aren't you wearing uniform?"

"One doesn't. Not off the station and off duty."

"What a pity. I thought soldiers wore uniform all the time."

"We aren't allowed to go out in uniform unless we're on duty," David said truthfully.

"And I thought you wore uniform most of the time. I'd love to see you in it, with all your brass buttons and everything. Have you had your photograph taken?"

He flushed. "Yes, I have."

"Can I have one?"

"Good lord, what for?"

"None of my friends have got cousins at Cranwell."

"You don't mean you want to take it to *school*, do you?" he asked suspiciously.

"Coll, not school. Yes of course."

"Must you?"

"Are you shy or something?" she asked.

"No. Oh, all right then, I'll post a photograph to you."

"Not here. Send it to me at coll."

"If you say so."

"I'll tell them all you're my boyfriend. I shan't say you're my cousin at all. I'll say you're a wonderful pilot I met in a nightclub."

"Go on, what would you be doing in a nightclub at your age?"

"I look eighteen sometimes," she flashed. "Anyway I'll say we're secretly engaged."

He stared at her and then laughed. "You had me believing you."

"You tease very easily, but seriously, I would love a photograph of you in your uniform."

"You shall have it. I promised. Only I shall write on the back, 'To my cousin Valerie,' and everybody will know who I am."

"Don't you dare call me Valerie. I hate it."

"Sorry."

"I wish girls could do interesting things like joining the R.A.F. and learning to fly."

"You could be an officer in the W.R.A.F."

"And fly?"

"No," he admitted.

"There, it's a man's world. We ought to be allowed to fly."

"You're only a girl."

"Indeed? Do you know what George Bernard Shaw said?"

"No," David confessed.

"He said, 'Think what cowards men would be if they had to bear children. Women are an altogether superior species.' That's what he said; and you say I'm only a girl. The fact is that you're only a man."

"It isn't I who stop women being pilots. During the war in fact lots of girls flew in the A.T.A. They ferried everything from flimsy little Tiger Moth biplanes to Spitfires and Lancasters, and probably even flying boats too. They had a super uniform."

"Did they? I didn't know that. I'd like to do a job like that."

"Would you really?" He found her interesting for the first time. Up till now he had taken her pretty much for granted.

"Yes, I would. I suppose I'll end up by getting married and doing the dishes for the rest of my life."

"No!" He was vehement. "Get married, yes, but do the dishes, no. Not you."

She gave him a little smile, pleased by the way he had said it.

"I'll have to marry somebody like you, then, shan't I?"

"Ah, but I'm going to be a bachelor," he pointed out.

"Beast." She said it without rancor. "Will you come skating with me tomorrow? To Queens?"

"If you like. I'm not much good."

"It doesn't matter. Just the two of us."

"We can't ditch Roger," he protested.

"Why not? He's only a silly schoolboy."

"Roger comes too," David said flatly, and would not be persuaded otherwise.

It was a short visit, six days altogether. It was obvious to David that Roger was now only technically a school-boy. In many ways he had already outgrown school. It was not an unusual thing. School life was irksome to him and he longed for the more functional and directional discipline of Cranwell for, as he confided to David, he had made up his mind to join the R.A.F. too.

After he had returned to Mereford for one night prior to going back to Cranwell, David discovered that he thought more and more about his two cousins. It was a great pity Roger was younger. They could have had a lot of fun together at Cranwell. And it was a pity too that Vivvy was a girl or rather, he corrected, a pity that girls weren't allowed to come to Cranwell. That *would* have been a party!

The new store in Oxford opened that year and almost at once it was suggested to Jocelyn that he open another in Swindon, where there was plenty of scope and where a Vernon's store was needed. He talked to Anne about it before making up his mind.

"It's beginning to run away with itself now," he said. "Apart from the money it's costing—and it's frightening me a little to tie up so much and go so deeply into the red—I feel I've lost control of the situation . . . and for what, darling?"

"Why don't you sell out then?" she asked.

"Sell out?" He got up and poured a drink for himself and stood with the glass in his hand, thinking. "That's a new idea," he replied, turning to face her. "What would I do with myself?"

"You'd find something."

"It goes against the grain to sell a family business."

"Isn't that what people are doing nowadays? Isn't the day of the family business about over anyway?"

"That's true. We've got a devil of a lot of outside shareholders now. It's becoming a struggle to find the money to maintain a majority shareholding. It's a pity we had to go public, but that's progress for you. I don't know, darling. It would be different if David were going to take over from me, but there's no hope of that now."

"What will you do?"

"Go ahead in Swindon, I suppose. Certainly I can't sell out at the moment. I can't even retire—there's nobody to take my place. I must do something about that. I shouldn't have to shoulder the whole burden the way I do. It's my own fault, and it's because of David again. After the war I took everything back into my own hands, thinking I was building up his birthright. Oh, darling," he smiled, "I feel like a middle-aged failure."

"Failure? Why?"

"Because at forty-eight I don't know what to do with myself. I've lost interest. That's failure, isn't it?"

"Then you should look around for something else, train somebody to take your place, retire from the business, and, if you feel like it, sell your shares."

"If I retired I would sell them. I wouldn't have all my money invested in one company which I didn't control anymore, or which one of the family didn't control."

"What would you do with the money?"

"Play for small, absolutely safe dividends. That money represents several lifetimes of work. We wouldn't need to go for big returns on it. We could afford to be conservative."

He thought about it a lot in the months ahead. In 1967 David received his wings and was commissioned. Roger was entering Cranwell as his cousin left. It was sheer bad luck that David did not win the Sword of Honour for his year, but this didn't trouble him. He wasn't really ambitious, rather to his parents' surprise. He merely wanted to fly.

In February of 1968, Mereford came alive. Neither Jocelyn nor Anne had had any special sort of celebration on their twenty-first birthdays, and they decided to make it different for David. They planned a dance for him. About forty people were invited, and Jocelyn booked rooms in hotels in Reading for most of them, since few could stay at Mereford. The vast majority of the young men were fliers and one, Roger, was a Cranwell cadet. A firm of outside caterers laid on the buffet supper, a mobile discothèque was engaged in preference to a live band, spotlights were sited round the house. David's birthday was in the particularly unseasonable month of February so that not many people would want to walk in the garden, but Jocelyn didn't care. He wanted Mereford to look at its best and he had engaged a photographer, an important part of whose job it was to photograph the house from the outside as well as to take lots of photographs of the rooms. Jocelyn had decided to make a picture album of Mereford.

David's birthday was on a Wednesday, and the dance was to be held on the following Friday so that all his friends could get there and make a joyful weekend of it. David himself was on a short leave from his squadron. Robert and Sally were coming on Wednesday morning, and the five of them would celebrate the actual birthday privately and quietly. Roger was driving over from Cranwell on Friday. That only left Vivvy, and luckily that weekend was college half term, so David had volunteered to go and collect her on Friday morning.

Vivvy was now in what was called U.C. 3, in Cheltenham's peculiar parlance, which meant that she was a lower sixth former. She was sixteen and a half and David hadn't seen her for more than a year. On Friday he set off in his M.G. and drove into Cheltenham, a distance of roughly seventy miles. The Cheltenham girls lived in a number of big private houses belonging to the College and scattered around the town, some quite a distance from the main buildings. Vivvy was in a house called Roderic which stood in a quiet square not very far from the college, and David drove in through the gates and pulled up in front of the worn stone steps. She had been watching and waiting for him, and came out almost at once.

"Hullo," she said gaily, coming down the steps.

"Hullo, Vivvy." How grown-up she was, he thought. She didn't look like a schoolgirl at all. He glanced up and could see other girls staring at them curiously from the windows of the house. He felt embarrassed. He had never visited a girls' school before.

Vivvy saw a friend and waved negligently before getting into the front seat of the little sports car. David revved up the engine and drove off.

"How's school?" he asked awkwardly. This was not going to be as easy as he thought. She was no longer a kid.

"All right. I shan't be sorry to leave."

"How long now?"

"Another year after this."

"Then what?" he asked.

"I don't know. I don't want to go to university. My people think I should, but I'd rather not. Anyway there's no hurry to decide. How does it feel to be twenty-one? Very grown-up?"

"Not specially."

"Do you like the Air Force?"

"Oh, yes." He came to life suddenly and turned and grinned at her. "You bet I do."

"I'm glad. It must be nice to do what you want most."

"It is, rather. Don't you have anything special you want to do?"

"Mmm," she agreed.

"What?"

"That's a secret."

"Now you're being a tease," he complained.

"No, honestly I'm not, David."

"All right. You keep your secret then. Will you dance with me tonight?"

"Only if I'm asked," she replied solemnly.

"I'm asking you, aren't I?"

"I hope so. Probably I won't know anyone except Roger, and who wants to dance with her own brother?"

They stopped in Oxford and had lunch together at a hotel there. It was midafternoon when they got back to Mereford. David didn't see very much of Vivvy before evening, for she had to unpack and then she had to tell her mother all about college and answer all sorts of questions about clothes, when she was coming out next, and if she was bringing anyone home during the Easter holidays. David found his father in the library after tea. Men were already setting up trestle tables in the dining room for the buffet, and furniture was being moved about to clear the hall and the dining room for dancing.

"Hullo, David. Care for a drink?"

"I'd better not. It's going to be a long night."

"Very sensible of you. It's absolute chaos out there. Sit down and relax."

"Thanks."

"I haven't had a chance to tell you yet, but something's come up. A big group are making a take-over bid for the company."

"Really?"

"Yes. I don't think I'll oppose it. It's a fair enough offer and they can develop it much better than I can."

"Does that mean you'll be out of a job?" David asked.

"Not exactly. What it means is that I get a very large slab of cash and a block of shares in the group that's taking over, and they've offered to keep me on as chairman of Vernon's. They aren't changing the name—not yet anyway. It's a sinecure, of course, but it would keep me in touch with the firm for a little longer. I'll probably accept the chairmanship. It will give me something to do, once or twice a month."

"I see. So it's all over?"

"Not quite, but it will be soon—before the year is out. You don't mind, do you?"

"No, not if it's all right with you," David answered. "It seems a pity to lose the company, but I suppose it had to happen."

"We were getting too big too quickly. A take-over was bound to be attempted sometime. The only way to avoid it was not to expand at all. If I hadn't opened the Newbury store in 1960, I might have hung on to the Reading one till retirement. At least this won't be a sudden break. I'll be appointed chairman for about five years. After that, they'll almost certainly drop me."

"What are you going to do with all that spare time?" David demanded.

"You'll laugh when I tell you."

"No, I shan't. I promise."

"You know the garden center just outside town?"

"Yes, of course. Sonning Nurseries and Garden Center."

"That's it. They're desperately short of money. I'm going in. Harry Torr, who runs it, needs capital, and we were talking about it the other week. I called him yesterday and we had a meeting. I'm going in half shares with him. We're going to open a little tearoom and improve the place a bit. It will be something to do. I'll work there every day, just like anyone else."

"Good lord."

"I've got to do something, and think of all the free flowers I'll get for Mereford!"

"What shall I put on those forms where they ask you to write down father's occupation? Nurseryman?"

"Why not just put gardener? That will fool them," Jocelyn laughed.

David was already standing in the hall when Vivvy came downstairs with Roger. Like himself Roger was wearing a dinner jacket. When he saw Vivvy, David gaped. Her hair was coiled up on her head in a way he had never seen her wear it before. She was wearing a pale green evening dress—Sea Jade the makers called it—beautifully embroidered in silver. She wore a little lipstick and eye makeup, and had on a very attractive necklace of sparkling stones with matching earrings. He stared at her. She was full figured, exciting, and she walked downstairs like a queen. David nervously went to meet them.

"Hu . . . hullo," he stammered. "Vivvy, you look gorgeous."

"I hope so. It took me hours to get ready. This is as bad as a wedding."

"Doesn't she look lovely, Roger?"

Roger stared at his cousin. "You think so? She's all right I suppose."

Vivvy laughed.

"You shouldn't ask me about her," Roger apologized. "She's my brat sister."

The guests had just begun to arrive so David didn't see her for a time. When he did catch a glimpse of her, she was dancing with one of his friends and David scowled. He had to do his duty by the door till all the guests had arrived, then he went off and got himself a drink, a weak whiskey and soda, and looked for Vivvy. She was dancing again, and he followed her impatiently wth his eyes till the dance was finished. He pushed his way toward her.

"The next dance is mine," he said abruptly.

She turned and then smiled when she saw who it was. "Hullo, David. Isn't it a lovely party? Have you seen the buffet?"

"Yes. I'm taking you in at the interval, aren't I?"

"If you say so."

"I do say so. You don't mind, do you?"

"No," she laughed. "Why should I?"

He danced with her once, twice, three times.

"Hadn't you better dance with someone else?" she asked. "Your guests will be upset."

"Yes, all right, but I'll be back, and don't forget I'm taking you in."

He went off and danced with his mother and his aunt, then with two other girls, and felt like a martyr. He did manage one more dance with Vivvy before the interval. Anne turned to Jocelyn as she saw David bending over Vivvy while they walked into the dining room together.

"Have you seen David and Vivvy?"

"Yes, I have," he grinned. "He's showing a surprising interest in his cousin. She's only a schoolgirl."

"If you were twenty-one and you saw a girl like that," Anne replied, "you might not think of her as a schoolgirl. Anyway, she's in the sixth form."

"You're quite right, she is a charmer. How amusing."

"I don't think he should monopolize her like that. He'll turn her head."

"Don't worry," Jocelyn said pleasantly. "She isn't the sort whose head will get turned. Come along, my dear, let's collect Sally and Robert and go in and get some food. I think the dance is a great success."

After supper David dutifully danced with several other girls and then he returned to Vivvy, smiling broadly.

"There, I've done my duty. Now I can please myself."

"You do deserve a rest," she agreed.

"That's not what I meant. I meant I'm going to have the next dance and the next and the next . . . with you."

"You're very possessive."

"I know. Shall we go and have a drink?"

"All right." She followed him through the crowd and

into the library which was empty now. He closed the door behind him.

"This isn't the bar, is it?" Vivvy asked, regarding him with new interest.

"No, but there's whiskey and soda here. Would you like one?"

"Sir, I'm only a schoolgirl," she protested in a high falsetto.

"Can I fetch you something else?"

"I won't have anything, honestly." She sat down near the fireplace and examined the embroidered fire screen.

"Vivvy, I'm very fond of you," he said hesitantly.

"Yes, I thought you were." She was completely calm.

"You're only a third cousin, you know."

She smiled at that. "Well?" she encouraged him.

"Probably you think it's stupid of me, but when you're older . . . I'd like to marry you." He watched her closely.

This time she hid her smile. Poor man-child, she was thinking, he's only just twenty-one and unsure of himself.

"We're both very young, David."

"I know. I didn't mean soon. In a year or two."

"I tell you what," she said pleasantly. "You come to my twenty-first birthday party and if you still feel the same way, you can propose to me then."

"And if *you* still feel the same way, what will your answer be?" he asked.

"Why, yes, of course."

They were quite still, looking into each other's eyes.

"You don't think I'm a fool, talking to you like this when we're both so young?"

"No. One can look ahead. Do you remember asking me this morning if there was anything special I want to do, and I said it was a secret?"

"Yes."

"For the past two or three years I've wanted to marry you—even though I haven't seen you for nearly a year."

"Do you think," he said very slowly and distinctly, "that I could kiss you?"

After all, he was thinking, she might still think kissing was soppy.

"I rather think you'd better before we both burst," she laughed, and a second later she was on her feet and in his arms.

It was Sally who discovered them; fortunately, because she had no preconceived ideas about when a young woman was "too young." She stood in the doorway for a second and saw what was going on. With a smile and a shrug she closed the door, not quietly. As she had intended, it put a temporary stop to the kissing. At least they ought to be more discreet.

Chapter 29

V IVVY returned to the comparatively chaste atmosphere of Cheltenham Ladies' College, and David returned to his other love, his fighter squadron. No one else knew that they exchanged letters every week.

Jocelyn became busy in connection with the take-over, and early in the spring the matter was settled. He left his office in the building where a Vernon had presided over the daily doings for so long. It wasn't the original office used by Captain Henry, but it had been used for a long time just the same. It was a wrench going away, and the staff gave him a send-off and the local paper—no longer the *Berkshire Herald*, which had gone out of publication during the war—wrote up the occasion and spoke glowingly of the service the Vernons had given to both county and country. If they weren't the most publicized family in Reading, they were certainly the best loved. As people said, they had not only provided a lot of jobs for a long time, and given Reading some of its best shopping, but every time there was a war they went off and won medals, and then came home and got on with the job again.

When the news got out that Jocelyn had gone into partnership with Harry Torr, people talked, and business picked up very quickly at the garden center. Jocelyn had to admit that it was all gratifying, but this goodwill was a diminishing asset. The family business had passed out of his control now, wars he sincerely hoped were a thing of the past, and although it would be no hardship just to be anonymous private citizens, going about their affairs quietly and without fuss, it was another end to another era. There were too many endings these days.

In 1970 Vivvy came home from college for the last time, and Roger joined his first squadron. He was not in fighters, as he had hoped, but on Nimrods, belonging to a maritime reconnaissance squadron. His twenty-first birthday was on May 28, and Robert and Sally arranged a dance similar to David's, not in their house which was too small, but at the Connaught Rooms in London. The invitations went out at the beginning of the month and Roger applied for and was granted leave. David did the same but was refused for a surprising reason. His group captain sent for him.

"Vernon, you applied to be a test pilot, didn't you?"

"Yes, sir."

"Well, you've been extremely lucky. Farnborough want someone in a hurry and you have an outstanding assessment as a pilot, and somebody has picked on you. I'm sorry I can't give you leave. You have to pack up and get over to Farnborough by the day after tomorrow. I don't know what all the fuss is about. Your squadron commander knows you're going, by the way."

"I see, sir, thank you."

"I sent for you because I wanted to tell you you've done very well. You've got a future in the R.A.F., though I'm sorry we're losing you, and your squadron will be sorry too. If you carry on the way you've started off, I think you'll have a good career."

He was a kindly man who liked to encourage youngsters when he could do so legitimately. David flushed with pleasure. It was nice to be praised, even nicer to have been posted to Farnborough. He hadn't expected that. It was difficult to get a test pilot's job at all, and certainly not normal after such a short time in the service. He was only twenty-three and a fairly newly promoted flying officer.

He sat down and wrote letters, characteristically first to Vivvy, and then to his parents, and finally to Roger whose birthday party he was going to miss. He left two days later, and discovered to his delight that he was to be the new member of a highly experienced team testing an experimental aircraft which had certain revolutionary features about it. His would be the most routine and humdrum work of all, but he didn't mind that. It was a beginning.

Roger received the news somewhat wryly. Somehow in the beginning it had never occurred to him that if he went to Cranwell his career would be any different from his cousin's. He was interested in single-seat fighters, and not very much in anything else. It had been a blow to him when he had been posted to maritime reconnaissance. He wasn't even captain of an aircraft. Yet David had not only served on fighters but he was now a sort of apprentice test pilot. Somehow Roger had not associated service life with the sort of unfairness one came across in school and elsewhere. He had done well at Cranwell, passed out high on the list for his year, and he had always flown easily. All his assessments were above average.

He sat in his room in the mess, rather an austere and monkish room, for he was not the sort of person to decorate his quarters, and apart from a small pile of books on the chest of drawers, the room might easily have been mistaken for an unoccupied one. Outside he could see some plane trees and a stretch of grass beyond which were the married quarters. For just a few moments he felt miserable. Then common sense slowly began to assert itself. In the long run it would not make much difference. The

R.A.F. was his career. If he did well in his present posting, there was no reason why in seven or eight years, or less, he should not command a squadron, and then one day perhaps an R.A.F. station. When you reached the rank of group captain, it did not much matter what you had flown. Indeed there might be a slight advantage in *not* being a fighter boy.

He got up and sat on the window ledge. He'd got his wings and his commission, and that was the big thing, the thing that counted. There was now a great deal to learn. Much more than he had ever imagined.

It's not what you do, it's the way that you do it, he reflected with amusement. He walked over to the mirror and viewed himself in it. How would he look with four rings on his cuff and gold oak leaves on his cap brim? He began to chuckle. He decided to go along to the crew room. He was officially on stand-down this morning, but it would be nice to see what was going on, to talk to the boys. He put David's letter neatly in a small drawer and dismissed the matter from his mind.

On Friday, May 22, just a few days before Roger's birthday, and the day before he was going home on leave, a Nimrod aircraft exploded in midair. Since it happened a few miles out to sea, the cause of the explosion was never discovered. Several people saw it, but they contributed little to the accident investigation, and nothing was recovered from the seabed.

Sally had been getting Roger's room ready when the telegram arrived. Robert was out and Vivvy was in her room. Sally opened the telegram unsuspectingly, and then staggered. She told the messenger there was no reply, managed to shut the door . . . and then fainted. Vivvy found her on the floor, the telegram by her side. She had heard a noise and had come downstairs thinking that it was Robert home for tea. She read the telegram and turned very pale. Then she helped Sally to her feet, put her in a chair, and poured her a stiff brandy.

When Robert came home they were sitting together numbly. Sally at once began to weep.

"What's wrong?" Robert asked, astonished. "Is someone ill?"

Vivvy got up with the telegram in her hand.

"It's bad news, Daddy."

"Roger?" he asked suddenly.

"Yes. He's dead."

"He can't be," Robert cried. "It's impossible."

She handed him the telegram and he read it. Then he sat down facing Sally and they stared at each other blankly. Vivvy went into the kitchen and began to make strong tea in their largest teapot.

Afterward Robert took Sally upstairs. She lay down on the bed, looking very white. He sat beside her, miserable and heartbroken, not knowing what to say. After a few moments she stretched out her hand and slid it into his. He squeezed it gently.

"I suppose it's always the same," he said quietly. "Everybody must ask the same unanswerable question. *Why?* It always seems so senseless, so cruel."

He saw tears in her eyes and her hand gripped his like a vice.

"Can I get you anything?" he asked anxiously.

"Yes," she gasped. "Some water, please."

He left her and brought a glass of water from the bathroom. When he returned, she was propped against the pillows, looking quite ghastly. Before she drank, her left hand went up to her mouth. He noticed and frowned.

"What's that?" he asked.

She did not reply at once. When she did it was with a shaky laugh.

"Tranquilizers."

"Where and when did you get those?" he demanded.

"From the doctor, recently. I've been waking up feeling tired and he prescribed them."

"You didn't say anything."

"Well, it's nothing." She managed a smile. "I'll feel better soon. You ought to get yourself a drink, darling. I'm sure you need one."

"A drink won't help. It never has helped me, as you know. I'll have more tea soon. Are you sure you're all right?"

She gave another shaky little laugh. "Of course. It's just shock."

He looked doubtful. She had never been to the doctor that he knew of, except when she was pregnant. This was the first he had heard of tranquilizers.

"How long have you been on these pills?" he demanded.

"Oh, Robert darling, stop fussing." She was looking better already. "Just a few days, not long. I'll soon have finished them."

"Why do you need tranquilizing? Sally, is there something wrong you're not telling me?"

"We don't know. The doctor thought something must be bothering me subconsciously which is why I wasn't sleeping so well. So he gave me a few pills, and that's all."

"Do they help?"

"As a matter of fact they do. Quite a lot. I've been feeling ever so much better."

"Oh, well, that's all right. I wish you'd told me."

"It was nothing." Her voice was strong again. He felt reassured and leaned over to kiss her.

"I'm going to get tea. I'll bring up some," he said.

"Thank you."

When he had gone, she took another pill and washed it down with the rest of the water. She must remember to keep them hidden in case he ever saw the label. It might mean nothing to him, of course, but one could never tell. She did not want him to know the truth. She lay staring at the ceiling, miserably, waiting for the last of the pain to subside. When he returned she had fallen asleep.

Roger's tragic and unexplained death threw a pall of gloom not only over the house at Hampstead but at Mereford too. After all David, too, was an R.A.F. pilot. Jocelyn and Anne gave up their gliding for several weeks, and when David finally came home on a short leave, he found his mother inclined to be tearful and his father wearing a long face.

"How dangerous is it?" Jocelyn asked him frankly.

"Flying? Safer than driving a car—infinitely safer. I should have thought that was obvious."

"What about Roger?"

"The chances of an aircraft exploding are about the same as a gas main exploding—less, probably. Sometimes you read about houses being blown up by exploding mains, don't you? Well, how often do you read about an airplane being blown up? Not so often."

"All right." Jocelyn and Anne exchanged slightly reassured glances. "But what about this test piloting you're doing? That's dangerous, isn't it?"

"Everything's dangerous," David protested. "Crossing the road in London is dangerous. We live with danger. There hasn't been a test pilot killed at Farnborough for years, if that's what you want to know."

"That's something, I suppose."

"Look, there are three of us here and we each have our own car. Mathematically our chances of being killed in a car are far more than mine of being killed in an aircraft incident."

He wasn't sure if that was literally true, but it was the sort of statistical statement it was difficult to contradict, and he spoke with all the authority and confidence of youth.

"I'm sorry," Jocelyn apologized. "We've all been very upset since Roger died. You can imagine what it's been like. Are you going to Hampstead?"

"Yes, I planned to go to see them the day after tomorrow. Vivvy's expecting me."

He was able to give some small comfort to Robert and Sally, and to make them realize that what had happened to Roger was a million-to-one-chance, not a normal occupational hazard. It had been a fine day, a good aircraft, and an experienced crew. Vivvy, surprisingly, was more difficult to reassure.

Vivvy would soon be nineteen. She knew her mind about David now, although she intended to wait till her twenty-first birthday before agreeing to an engagement. They were deeply in love. Even the families realized that nothing short of a miracle would stop those two getting married one day. Vivvy began to understand that marrying a test pilot was not going to be the most placid of existences, yet nothing could change David. Flying was his thing.

"You're a glum one," David remarked when they were alone in the television lounge, which used to be the dining room.

"I know. I keep thinking of Roger and wondering if one day there will be a telegram about you."

"Oh, Vivvy, I thought you at least understood better than that."

"It's all very well being logical, rational, and statistical. Unfortunately I'm a mere woman, which means I'm emotional."

"Darling, do you think I don't worry about you?" he demanded. "When I'm living in the peace and quiet of Farnborough I think of you driving in London among all those lunatic drivers, and I worry."

"That's no longer funny, David."

"It's not funny," he protested. "I mean it. I hate London."

"There's nothing wrong with London. I'd rather live in the country myself, but Mummy and Daddy chose Hampstead, so there you are. There's nothing wrong with Hampstead."

"No, of course not, but you mustn't let everything get out of proportion."

"I'll try not to," she promised.

When David had gone Sally spoke to Vivvy about him.

"Darling," she said, "*are* you in love with David?"

Vivvy colored. "Yes, I am."

"Then promise me something."

"What?" Vivvy asked, intrigued.

"Marry him."

"What a strange thing to say. Do you want to get rid of me?" she asked lightly.

"No, darling, I don't ever want to get rid of you."

Something in her voice struck Vivvy. "Sorry, Mummy." She was contrite.

"I want you to have your happiness. We can't keep you forever. We have to learn to give you away. One day you'll have children and you'll find out. I want you to have what you want. Only, there's one thing."

"Yes?"

"Well, if ever anything happened to me, you'd keep an eye on your father, wouldn't you? He's not terribly good at managing by himself. You and David, I mean. You wouldn't just leave him to flounder on his own, would you?"

"Of course we wouldn't, but what could happen to you?"

"I'm just feeling low. I might get knocked down by a bus next time I go out shopping. You know how dangerous daily life is. I want you to be happy, darling, but I also want to be sure your father won't ever be abandoned."

"Well he won't. Silly."

Sally gave a lighthearted laugh. "I'm sorry if I sounded terribly solemn. It's difficult to talk about serious things, isn't it? I'm really far more concerned about you and David. I wouldn't want you to turn your back on your own happiness just because he's in the R.A.F., for instance."

"I wouldn't do that."

"Good. It's always seemed to me that happiness is rationed in some mysterious way, and I believe we should take our share where we find it."

Vivvy grew suspicious. "You're not trying to tell me that you had some handsome man you were madly in love with and whom you gave up for Daddy, are you?" she asked.

"Good heavens, no!" Sally's peal of laughter was convincing. "What a hilarious idea. That's what happens when one tries to be serious for a few moments. No, I never loved anyone else, and I never stopped loving him, not even when he was in prison. It was bad for a time when he came out, but that's all history now. I've been terribly happy. I've been a lucky woman. I want you to be happy too. Yet, you know, when I met and married him, your father wasn't exactly what would be regarded as a great prize on the marriage market. He had a little money but not much, no ambition, and he was very shy and withdrawn. If I'd been *sensible* I'd have crossed the road and looked for someone else. Thank God I wasn't sensible."

"I agree. There would have been no me," Vivvy said.

"Well, that's all right then. I'm glad about you and David. Marry him as soon as you're ready. Don't make yourself wait longer than you need."

"I won't, Mummy."

Vivvy quickly forgot the conversation, and it did not

come back to her till quite a long time afterward, when it took on a new and terrible significance.

Fate had not finished with the family at Hampstead, however. Vivvy had a job working for a Member of Parliament. She had learned shorthand and typing after leaving college and was now secretary to an up-and-coming man. Occasionally this meant working on weekends at his home in Surrey, where he lived with his wife and three young children.

One November week in 1971 she told Sally and Robert she would not be home on Friday evening. She was going to Surrey and would return sometime during Sunday. By now they were quite accustomed to this. On Friday at about six, Robert came home. He opened the door, closed it behind him, took off his coat and gloves, hung up the coat, and went into the sitting room. It was empty. He looked into the television lounge, but to his surprise Sally wasn't there either. She must be upstairs.

"Sally," he called, starting to walk up. "Are you up there, darling?"

There was no answer, and he wondered if she was out in the garden. Surely not, on such a raw, bitter evening. He opened the bedroom door and glanced inside. She was lying on top of the bed, fully dressed. He smiled and shook his head. He walked over and nudged her. There was something about the limpness of her body which alarmed him suddenly. He stared at her in disbelief. He put his fingers on her wrist, and then when that produced no result, he ran to her dressing table drawer and got a hand mirror and held it to her mouth.

She's dead, he thought incredulously. Sally's dead.

He telephoned their doctor who hurried round from his house nearby and examined the body. He turned to Robert, puzzled.

"I haven't seen Mrs. Vernon for some time now, over a

year I think. She had a bad cold then. Has she been complaining of anything?"

"No."

"Depressed? Is anything wrong?"

"No, of course not. Oh, our son was killed a few months ago, but we'd got over it—as much as one does get over it."

"Ah."

"What's wrong?"

"She's died of an overdose of some sort of drug. I'm afraid there will have to be a postmortem examination before a death certificate can be issued."

"You mean she committed suicide?" Robert asked in an awed voice.

"I can't say about that. Had she any reason to?"

"No."

"The police will have to be told, of course. That's the law. I'm sorry about this, Mr. Vernon."

Robert telephoned to Vivvy and she came hurrying back that night. She found him distraught. He was pacing about the house, drinking rather a lot. She made him sit down, gave him hot coffee, and began to cook a meal. He had had nothing to eat since lunch.

The result of the postmortem came as an even bigger shock. Sally had cancer, in a very advanced stage. She had died of an overdose of pain-killers given to her on a prescription. The police traced the doctor who issued the prescription, and he confirmed that he had been treating Mrs. Vernon for some months.

Robert's own doctor explained it to him gently, while Vivvy sat listening.

"She knew, but she told the doctor she wouldn't tell either of you till it became essential for her to go into hospital. She was dying, and dying quite quickly. Cancer is a funny thing; it affects people differently. She wouldn't have had long to live in hospital. In fact, if she hadn't killed herself, it is quite possible she might have died here at home in a week or two. She must have been in great pain and realized that it was almost time to go into hospital, and that once in she would *never come out*."

"I see."

"Rather than face that, she took an overdose of drugs. It was no accident. She had asked for a three weeks' supply of drugs, to save repeated visits to the doctor. She didn't want to give the game away to you. He warned her about the dosage. Didn't you know she was going to a doctor?"

"No, I had no idea at all. Vivvy?"

Vivvy shook her head. "She kept the secret to herself."

"That's the story, Mr. Vernon. There will be an inquest, purely a formality. She definitely died of a self-administered overdose, knowing that she was dying anyway. The verdict is a foregone conclusion."

"Thank you," Robert said heavily.

When the doctor had gone he turned to Vivvy, his face ravaged by grief.

"Why, Vivvy? Why did she choose to suffer alone? That's what upsets me so much, thinking of her all alone that last day, deciding to end it all, neither of us here to give her comfort or love."

"I think I understand," Vivvy said slowly. "I might want to do the same. What could we do to help? Death sentence had been passed on her. It would have been pretty bad for us, once she went into hospital. She was trying to spare us, because she loved us so much. We couldn't help her, Daddy. You must remember that. There was nothing we could do."

"We could love her, couldn't we?"

"We did and she knew it. She preferred to face it alone."

Chapter 30

Sᴀʟʟʏ's death changed life at Hampstead. Vivvy gave up her job to stay at home and look after her father. Robert had lost interest in his work, and went to the office in the mornings only. The months passed uneventfully until one Saturday afternoon late in May 1972 when Jocelyn and Anne went to Hampstead. Robert and Vivvy were sitting in their small garden, reading, when the car arrived. Vivvy went to greet them while Robert stood by his seat and waited.

When they had all sat down, Jocelyn came to the point.

"We've been talking about you two, and I had a long talk with David on the telephone. It's ridiculous for you to stay on here like this. Vivvy will be twenty-one in a couple of months. We all know what is going to happen then—it's the most unsecret secret in the world. She and David are going to announce their engagement. I don't know if you plan a big party or a small family affair, but why not have it at Mereford?"

"That would be nice," Vivvy murmured, puzzled. Was this what it was all about, the birthday party? Surely not?

"Then you'll want to get married quite soon afterward, won't you?"

Vivvy nodded and glanced at her father who smiled back at her.

"So, what's the fun for you, Robert, living here alone, with or without a housekeeper? Why don't you sell up, and come to live with us now? Mereford was your home for so many years before and during the war, and remember how long Sally lived there too, taking care of everything for all of us. Besides, Vivvy and David will want to come to Mereford for holidays, won't you, Vivvy?"

"Yes," she agreed. "I suppose so."

"And the rest of the time you'd be at Farnborough with David, or wherever he happened to be posted, isn't that right?" Jocelyn pressed her.

"That's true. I'd live with David, naturally."

"Then come to us, Robert."

"It's nice of you to offer. I had never thought of it. Are you sure you'd want a sort of permanent lodger?"

"You're family, Robert, and now that Sally's gone, you belong with us."

"It's kind of you, but I don't know. I don't like giving up my independence."

"I have a suggestion," Anne said. "Don't sell this house. Keep it. House prices are still going up and Hampstead houses are gold mines. Let it, furnished. It will always be there for you to go back to if you get tired of us, and it will give you an income too."

"That ought to please the chancellor of the exchequer," Robert laughed. "He seems to think I'm made of money and that my favorite pastime is paying taxes."

"It's a good idea, Daddy," Vivvy said after a moment. "I *will* be leaving you quite soon now. It would be nicer for you to live at Mereford than to stay on here with a housekeeper, even if you could get a good one, which is problematical nowadays. I think it's worth a try."

"Let me think about it, then. Please don't imagine I'm ungrateful, Anne. You and Jocelyn are kind to offer to have me back. I have very happy memories of Mereford. It's a big decision, that's all. It needs some thought."

"Of course, we realize that. You think about it."

They stayed to dinner and when they drove home they were pleased. It looked very much as though Robert would give in. The idea of the three of them under one roof, convenient for David and Vivvy to visit, appealed to Anne who liked life to be arranged tidily.

Robert and Vivvy came to Mereford for the birthday celebration. It was a very quiet affair, for none of them really felt like making a splash of it. The deaths of Roger and Sally were fresh in everyone's minds, and it did not help matters that Roger had died just when they were getting ready for *his* twenty-first birthday dance.

Five of them sat down to dinner together on August 15, after a day spent in the garden. David's present to Vivvy had been a platinum and diamond brooch in the form of an R.A.F. pilot's wings, and Jocelyn and Anne had bought her a lovely jade necklace. Robert's gifts included an expensive gold watch and her own first car, a small bright red sedan which had been delivered that morning. There were other things, little things such as perfume, chocolates, and an enormous jar of bath oil. Vivvy wore the watch, the brooch, and the necklace to dinner. The necklace went beautifully with her new green dress, the two greens complementing each other exactly.

In David's pocket, however, nestled another present in its small, velvet-lined box. After the dessert he stood up awkwardly.

"I think you know what this is about," he said nervously. "Vivvy and I are announcing our engagement tonight. I don't want to make a speech. I'll just give Vivvy the ring."

He walked round to her and pulled out the box, opened it, took out the ring, and placed it on her finger. Then he kissed her. Red-faced, he sat down again.

"To Vivvy and David," Robert said, standing with his glass, and they all toasted the young couple. They admired the ruby ring which had been bought several days previously, but the most heartwarming thing of all was to see the happiness in their faces. When they had gone off alone after dinner to walk in the garden at sunset, Robert turned to Jocelyn and Anne.

"It's funny how things work out, isn't it? Your son and my daughter to be married. It's not so many years ago, really, that Captain Henry was kicked out of St. James's Place. My own father hardly ever spoke of this house, and when he did it was nothing complimentary. As a child I was always told that you were a worthless lot, not fit to bear the name Vernon."

"It's better for the split in the family to end," Jocelyn said. "I'm so glad those two have made a match of it. And I know they'll be very happy."

The following morning, while David and Vivvy were still trying to make up their minds exactly when to get married, the telephone rang. Anne answered.

"Is Flying Officer Vernon there please?" a strange voice asked.

"Yes, who's calling please?"

"This is the *Daily Recorder* in London."

"Oh. One moment."

She went into the drawing room and found them huddled together on the window seat.

"It's a call for you, darling," she told David. "A newspaper, the *Daily Recorder*."

"Oh, damn. Thanks, Mother."

Anne and Vivvy watched, filled with curiosity, as David left the room. He was gone for two or three minutes. When he returned they waited.

"What were we saying?" he asked Vivvy.

"Never mind that. What did the newspaper want? Is it about the engagement?"

"No, of course not. It's some blasted reporter."

"What did he want with you, darling?" Anne asked.

"Well, he wants to come to see me. I had to agree—he'd come anyway. They're a persistent lot."

"What's happened?"

"I've got a medal. It's been announced and some reporter has decided it's a story. It's nothing to make a fuss about."

"A medal? What medal? What for?"

"The Air Force Cross. You get it, er, well like . . . um . . . for doing a good job at your work. Sort of like getting an M.B.E. in the New Year's Honours List."

"But this isn't the New Year," Vivvy said suspiciously.

"They must have made a mistake. I expect they meant it to come out in January and got it all mixed up. These things happen."

"Where did you do this good job?" Anne asked.

"I don't know. I'm a test pilot after all."

"Oh, I see," Anne smiled. "All test pilots get it, do they? After a year, or something?"

"Not exactly, but it's something like that," he answered vaguely.

Obviously he didn't want to talk about it. The reporter arrived just before lunch and David took him into the library. The man left before anyone could talk to him. David saw to that. When Jocelyn came home that evening, Anne tackled him at once.

"Darling, what's the Air Force Cross?"

"It's an R.A.F. decoration for officers."

"What do they get it for?"

"Bravery in peacetime. It's purely a flying thing. They get the D.F.C. for heroism against the enemy, and the A.F.C. for other kinds of heroism. Why do you ask?"

"Because David's got it, that's why."

"*What?*"

"David's been given it, and he says it's just for doing a good job, like an M.B.E."

"That's not quite right. How did you find out?"

She told him and he listened carefully.

"I tell you what, let's just check up on that son of ours. I have an idea."

He picked up the telephone, called the offices of the *Recorder* in London and asked to speak to the news editor. When he was connected, he introduced himself and put his query. The news editor was amused and told him all he wanted to know.

The R.A.F. was developing a new fighter, a very sophisticated variation of the Lightning, which was still in its experimental stage. David had taken up one on a purely routine check. As the junior member of the unit, he was lucky to be allowed to fly a prototype at all, but it was the sort of trifling check nobody senior to David really wanted to bother making. Over Reading there had been some sort of engine failure and David had made a distress call. He had been told to bail out, but in the end he had refused because the aircraft was almost bound to land in a built-up area. He said he would bring it back. It was barely under control, but he managed to crash-land it on the airfield, although not on the runway. He was lucky to escape with his life, but because of a very fine piece of airmanship the plane was not seriously damaged and all the electronics equipment in it—which was of great importance—was intact.

A blanket of silence had been thrown over the incident, because the aircraft was very much on the secret list. Even now the announcement of the award was cautious and guarded in its wording and spoke simply of engine failure during a test (unspecified) and how David had chosen to crash-land an aircraft (type unmentioned) rather than risk bailing out with other people probably getting killed.

"Oh, my God," Anne said when she heard the story. "He told us flying is safe."

"I daresay he will still insist that it is," Jocelyn answered, shaking his head. "He'll say he could have bailed out easily, and only stayed with his machine because he wanted to."

"Jocelyn, I'm scared."

"Aren't we all? First Roger and now this. I suppose we'd better go and tackle him. Vivvy doesn't know about it, does she?"

"No more than I did."

They confronted David with the facts. He shrugged.

"It was a simple business. I had to choose between jumping for it and trying to get the thing down, and I thought I'd have a go at landing. If I hadn't thought I could do it, I wouldn't have bothered."

Jocelyn knew this was a lie. It was a miracle David had survived, and the citation had specifically mentioned the great risks of attempting a landing.

"You said it was a routine thing," Vivvy accused him.

"It is, really. Lots of people get the A.F.C."

"For acts of bravery," Jocelyn interjected.

"Sometimes they call it that, but honestly, it was all over in minutes. It was no worse than swerving to avoid a child on an icy road. You stand a chance of wrecking your car, but you still do it. There's no need to make a fuss."

"That's not what the papers think."

"Only one paper, and that's the *Recorder*, which is a sensational rag."

He insisted on making light of it all. When he went back to Farnborough, with a little red and white striped ribbon sewn under his pilot's wings, Vivvy sighed. They were getting married the following month. David had already arranged to get some more leave.

Anne found her wandering in the rose garden after David had gone, and joined her.

"It isn't much fun when they go away, is it?" she said gently.

"No, none," Vivvy smiled.

"I remember during the war how I used to keep my fingers crossed for Jocelyn, and I wasn't married to him at the time. After I was married, it was ten times worse."

"War must have been awful. I'm glad there's no war now."

"Aren't we all? It's going to be difficult for you, Vivvy, because David flies all the time. You're always going to be uneasy, until he gets too old and they ground him or whatever they do."

"You and Jocelyn still go gliding, don't you?"

"Yes, we started again. It's fun."

"It doesn't scare you?"

"It never does when you're doing something yourself," Anne laughed. "Anyway, gliding is as safe as sailing. You should join us."

"Perhaps I shall," Vivvy laughed. "Perhaps I shall."

They didn't go back to Hampstead—not to stay anyway. They went home only to collect their personal belongings, and by the time of the wedding the house was advertised to let. It did not stay advertised for long. Accommodation in London was at a premium. Just before the wedding something else happened—Jocelyn's term of office as chairman of Henry Vernon, Son and Company Limited came to an end. He was offered an ordinary directorship and refused. The connection between family and firm was now formally ended . . . forever.

The marriage took place at Mereford, with some friends of David's from Farnborough as guests. It was a jolly affair and a lot of beer was consumed by hearty young flying men. They went to the cottage in Cornwall for their honeymoon. Jocelyn had given it to them as a wedding present, saying that of course Mereford was their home, but they might want to be on their own away from old fogies, so they should have a second home.

In February 1973 an investiture ceremony was held at Buckingham Palace. Before it was held, however, an enterprising newspaper reporter who was at Farnborough on another matter spoke briefly to David about his A.F.C. He was not looking for anything specific. He knew the story had already been dealt with competently by the *Recorder*, and he was merely making sure the *Recorder* had overlooked nothing.

"When's the investiture?" he asked casually.

"Early next month," David answered.

"Looking forward to it?"

"Naturally. Must keep the family flag flying."

"How?" The reporter's ears pricked up. The *Recorder* man, who had been in a tearing hurry, had not done the obvious and asked David about his family.

"I think I'm the sixth generation to go to the Palace."

The reporter dug further. He heard about Sir George, lord mayor of London, who had been knighted by Queen Victoria; and about Sir Godfrey, and Henry, and Edward and Jocelyn. The story about the young Edward going to see his namesake King Edward VII privately, to be given his father's posthumous V.C., was fantastic the reporter decided.

The result of this chat, which turned into a family probe, was a headline in one of the more conservative dailies. *Sixth Generation Meets Queen. The Remarkable Family Vernon.* David was embarrassed when he saw it in print. He thought it looked awful and wished he had said less. Of course it would not have mattered if he had, because once the reporter realized there was a story, the rest was a matter of public record.

David had to undergo some ribbing at the hands of his fellow pilots. He took it in good part but made a mental note never to speak to a reporter again. Then he went home for a few days before the investiture. It was held on a Thursday and he and Vivvy went up to Town the night before to see a show and stayed at a hotel. Robert, Jocelyn, and Anne traveled up next morning. Jocelyn said he would meet them after the ceremony. He'd shaken hands with the King twice, so he let Anne witness her son's triumph.

Shortly before ten-fifteen the three of them joined a stream of people arriving at Buckingham Palace. There were a hundred and fifty people to be honored, and each was allowed two guests. They walked across the quadrangle to the grand entrance and into the grand entrance hall. Life Guards, in gleaming breastplates, wearing plumed helmets and enormous black boots, stood guard at the foot of the grand staircase.

David glanced up as they entered, seeing the gold-edged red carpet leading up to double glass-paneled doors at the top. Ushers stood on the first landing, wearing their official armbands. The guests were directed into the East Gallery and thence into the Ballroom. The recipients were led in a different direction.

Anne and Vivvy were given seats in the Ballroom. In front of them was the red-carpeted dais, edged with gold, and at the rear of it were two beautiful chairs like thrones under an enormous red and gold canopy richly embroidered with the royal arms and the royal crown. Behind them, at the other end of the Ballroom and facing the dais, was the huge organ and the minstrels' gallery, where the band of the Grenadier Guards was playing a selection of light music, as usually happened on these very happy occasions.

Shortly before eleven the yeomen of the guard entered, four of them walking in pairs, carrying glittering halberds and led by a fifth. They took up their position at the back of the dais. At eleven o'clock precisely the Queen entered. She wore a simple pale blue dress and carried a handbag over her left arm. She was accompanied by the lord chamberlain, the home secretary, the secretary of the Central Chancery of the Orders of Knighthood, and the master of the household.

Everyone had stood up, of course, when the Queen entered. She took her place on the dais, facing them, while Queen Victoria, Prince Albert, and their family looked down on the richly colored scene from a gold-framed painting.

"Please be seated," she said.

The recipients entered from the long corridor on the Queen's right, came forward to the corner of the dais, waited beside the usher there, and then moved on in turn to face the Queen. First the Orders of Knighthood were conferred and then David's name was called. He was in uniform of course. Vivvy felt her eyes mist over as he walked forward to face Her Majesty, turn and bow to her. The secretary of the Central Chancery had placed the little silver cross on the cushion, and the master of the household proffered it to the Queen. She took it and clipped it onto the hook which had been fastened to the left breast of David's uniform in readiness.

Then she stood talking to him. She had exchanged a few words with the others, not all of them, but most. She kept talking to David. People began to realize that this was going on longer than usual, and still it went on. After what seemed an incredibly long time—and which was perhaps two minutes, a long time under the circumstances—the Queen shook his hand, David stepped back, bowed again, turned right, and marched out. He followed the corridor round and came in again from the back of the ballroom to sit down and wait till it was all over.

At last the Queen walked to the door, followed by her entourage, and people started to leave the State Ballroom. When they were in the courtyard walking toward the gate,

Vivvy said, "What on earth did the Queen say to you, darling? You talked to her for ages."

He nodded. "Yes. She must have been told about that awful guff in the newspaper. Anyway, she knew all about Father and Grandfather, but she talked mostly about Sir Godfrey and Queen Victoria. There's a portrait of Sir Godfrey at Windsor Castle."

"What?"

"Cross my heart. I'd no idea he was such a favorite with Queen Victoria."

"Did the Queen say anything to you about your A.F.C.?"

"She said it was a good show."

"I bet she didn't say that."

"Not exactly, but it was the same thing. She did ask if my father was here, though. You must tell him that, Mother."

"That's happened before."

"What has?" David asked.

"King Edward asked your grandfather if Sir Godfrey was at an investiture. I remember hearing the story. You can ask your father, but I'm sure I'm right."

"Maybe we ought to send Christmas cards to the Palace," David laughed.

Because of the unfortunate newspaper story the photographers and television cameras were waiting for them, and it took some time to get a taxi to the Savoy where Jocelyn and Robert were waiting. When they were settled with drinks and copies of the menu, David told his father what the Queen had said. Jocelyn laughed.

"I hope next time somebody goes it will be because he's been elected lord mayor of London," he remarked. "It's a more peaceful pursuit."

"Does the Queen make them lord mayor?" Vivvy asked doubtfully.

"No, but they get baronetcies with the job nowadays. Well, here are the drinks."

After the waiter had left Jocelyn raised his glass.

"Here's to the sixth generation," he toasted. "May you both be very happy and successful."

"Hear, hear," Robert agreed, and they drank.

The final triumph came at Mereford however, a few days after the investiture. It was just before David and Vivvy returned to Farnborough. She had gone out in her car, shopping so far as the others knew. When she returned, they were sitting in the drawing room drinking coffee. She accepted a cup.

"Get what you wanted, darling?" David asked her.

"Yes, I did."

There was something about her voice which caught his attention. He started and she smiled back serenely.

"What was it?" he asked.

Jocelyn, who had been talking to Robert, stopped suddenly. He turned and looked at David inquiringly. Vivvy laughed.

"What do you think? We've been married long enough."

"You've been to the doctor," David exclaimed as the truth dawned on him.

"That's right, darling." She picked up her coffee cup and gestured briefly. "Here's to the seventh generation."

Jocelyn let out a bark of delighted laughter as he too understood. As he moved his head, his eye was caught by a gold-framed portrait on the wall facing him. It was one of Alice, commissioned by Henry many years ago to celebrate their tenth wedding anniversary. She was smiling gently at them. As Jocelyn let his gaze linger on it briefly, it seemed to him that the smile was just a little broader than usual.

Bless you, Alice, he thought . . . and smiled back at her.

*This book was
designed by Jerry Tillett
composed in linotype Electra
by Maryland Linotype Composition Company, Inc.
of Baltimore, Maryland
with display lines in Bodoni types
printed and bound by The Book Press
of Brattleboro, Vermont*